Mrs. Bennet rang the bell, and Miss Elizabeth was summoned to the library.

"Come here, child," said her father as she appeared. "I have sent for you on important business. I understand that Mr. Collins has made you an offer of marriage. Is it true?" Elizabeth replied that it was. "Very well. And you have refused this offer?"

"I have, sir."

"Very well. We now come to the point. Your mother insists that you accept him. Is that not so, Mrs. Bennet?"

"Yes, or I will never see her again."

"An unhappy choice is before you, Elizabeth," said Mr. Bennet. "From this day you must be a stranger to one of your parents. Your mother will never see you again if you do not marry Mr. Collins, and I will never see you again if you do."

A Background Note about *Pride and Prejudice*

Here are a few notes that will help a modern reader fully enjoy *Pride and Prejudice,* which was written in (and about) England in the early 1800s.

Social class plays a large role in the novel. It is helpful to understand that there were basically four classes of people in England of this era. First came the nobility—people who had titles such as earl and duchess, lord and lady. Lady Catherine de Bourgh belongs to this class. Then there were the landowners, whose money came from the farmers who used their land. Mr. Darcy and Mr. Bennet are both landowners, but Mr. Darcy's estate is much larger than Mr. Bennet's. The third class included the professional people, such as doctors, lawyers, clergymen, and teachers. These people might be well educated, but they work for a living and are not considered as high-class as landowners. Finally there was everybody else: servants, shopkeepers, and so on.

Another important aspect of *Pride and Prejudice* is that Mr. Bennet's small estate is "entailed." "Entailment" was an old legal method of keeping property in one family, rather than having it pass, for instance, into a son-in-law's hands. According to the entailment of the Bennet estate, the property could only be inherited by a son. As the Bennets had no son, by law the estate had to be passed on to the next male relative.

A third point that is helpful to understand is what is going on when Mr. Collins and another character, Mr. Wickham, talk about being "given a living" as clergymen. The answer goes back to the idea of British landowners being powerful people. Large landowners owned so much property that their holdings often included entire villages. Those villages included churches, and those churches needed ministers. It was traditionally the privilege of the landowner to give the "living," or job, of minister to a person of his or her choosing.

PRIDE ~AND~ PREJUDICE

JANE AUSTEN

Edited, and with an Afterword,
by Beth Johnson

 THE TOWNSEND LIBRARY

PRIDE AND PREJUDICE

TP **THE TOWNSEND LIBRARY**

For more titles in the Townsend Library,
visit our website: **www.townsendpress.com**

ISBN 13: 978-1-59194-067-8
ISBN 10: 1-59194-067-2

Library of Congress Control Number:
2006926040

CONTENTS

CHAPTER
1

Everyone knows that a rich single man needs a wife. When such a man moves to a new neighborhood, no matter how little is known about his thoughts or feelings, local families are so convinced of this truth that he is considered the rightful property of one or another of their daughters.

"My dear Mr. Bennet," said Mrs. Bennet to her husband one day, "have you heard that Netherfield Park has finally been leased?"

Mr. Bennet replied that he had not.

"But it has," she answered. "Mrs. Long has just been here, and she told me all about it."

Mr. Bennet said nothing.

"Don't you want to know who has taken it?" asked his wife impatiently.

"You want to tell me, and I don't object to hearing it," he answered.

This was enough of an invitation for Mrs. Bennet.

"Why, my dear, Mrs. Long says that Netherfield has been taken by a young man from the north of England who has a large fortune. He came down on Monday to see the place, and was so delighted with it that he agreed to take it immediately. He will move in quite soon, and some of his servants will be in the house by the end of next week."

"What is his name?"

"Bingley."

"Is he married or single?"

"Oh! Single, my dear, to be sure! A bachelor, very rich. What a fine thing for our girls!"

"How so? How can it affect them?"

"My dear Mr. Bennet," replied his wife, "how can you be so tiresome! You know that I am thinking about him marrying one of them."

"Ah, I see. Is that why he is moving here?"

"You are making fun of me," his wife responded. "But still, it is very likely that he will fall in love with one of them, and so you must visit him as soon as he comes."

"I don't know why I must go. You and the girls may go, or you may send them by themselves. That might be best, actually. You are as good-looking as any of them, and Mr. Bingley might like you the best of all."

"My dear, you flatter me!" cried his wife. "I certainly had my share of beauty once, but I do not pretend to be anything special now. When a woman has five grown daughters, she has to stop thinking of her own beauty."

"In such cases, a woman generally didn't have much beauty to think of," said her husband.

"But, my dear, you really must go and see Mr. Bingley when he moves into the neighborhood," Mrs. Bennet said insistently.

"That sounds like a great deal of bother to me."

"But think of your daughters! Imagine what a great match it would be for one of them. Sir William and Lady Lucas are already planning to visit Mr. Bingley, just for that reason. In general, you know, they do not visit newcomers. You really must go! For if you don't, you know he won't be able to visit us."

"You are too concerned about etiquette, surely. I imagine Mr. Bingley will be very glad to see you. I will send a note along, giving him my permission to marry whichever of the girls he chooses, although I must throw in a good word for my little Lizzy."

"You shall do no such thing. Lizzy is not a bit better than the others. She is not half as pretty as Jane, or half as good-humored as Lydia. But she has always been your favorite."

"None of them have much to recommend them," he answered. "They are all silly and ignorant like most girls, but Lizzy is better than the others."

"Mr. Bennet, how can you speak about your own children in such a way? You enjoy tormenting me. You have no compassion on my poor nerves."

"You are mistaken, my dear. I have the highest respect for your nerves. They are my old friends. I have listened to you talk about them for at least twenty years."

"Ah! You do not know how I suffer."

"But I hope you will get over it, and live to see many rich young men come into the neighborhood."

"It will be no use to us if twenty should move here, since you will not visit them," said his wife bitterly.

"Believe me, my dear, when there are twenty I will visit them all."

Mr. Bennet was such an odd mixture of witty talk, sarcastic humor, shyness, and impulsiveness, that even after twenty-three years of marriage his wife did not understand him. She had a less complicated character. She was an ignorant woman without interests or finer feelings. When she was bored and restless, she complained of her nerves. The business of her life was to get her daughters married; her comfort was visiting neighbors and gossiping.

CHAPTER
2

Mr. Bennet was one of the first neighbors to visit Mr. Bingley. He had always intended to visit him, although he continued to tell his wife that he would not do so. She did not learn of the visit until the evening after it occurred. This is how it happened. Noticing his second daughter decorating a hat, Mr. Bennet said, "I hope Mr. Bingley will like it, Lizzy."

"We are not likely to learn what Mr. Bingley likes," said her mother angrily, "since we are not going to visit him."

"But you forget, Mama," said Elizabeth, "that we will see him at the neighborhood parties, and that Mrs. Long has promised to introduce us to him."

"I do not believe Mrs. Long will do any such thing," her mother retorted. "She has two unmarried nieces of her own. She is a selfish, hypocritical woman, and I dislike her greatly."

"So do I," said Mr. Bennet, "and I am glad to find that you do not trust her to do you any favors."

Mrs. Bennet was too busy pouting to answer him, but to express her irritation she began scolding one of her daughters.

"Don't keep coughing so, Kitty, for heaven's sake! Have a little compassion on my nerves. You tear them to pieces."

"Kitty is so inconsiderate in her coughs," said her father. "She times them badly."

"I do not cough for my own amusement," replied Kitty fretfully.

"When is the next ball, Lizzy?" asked her father.

"In two weeks,' she replied.

"You see, there it is," cried her mother. "Mrs. Long will not come back from her trip until the day before that, so it will be impossible for her to introduce him. She will not have met him herself."

"Then, my dear," said her husband, "you will have the upper hand, and can introduce Mr. Bingley to her."

"Impossible, Mr. Bennet, impossible, when I do not know him myself. Why do you tease me so?" responded his exasperated wife.

"That is a very good point. Two weeks' acquaintance is certainly very little. One cannot truly know a man by the end of only two weeks. But if we do not introduce them, somebody else will. Yes, now that I think of it, I do believe Mrs. Long and her nieces must take their chances. In fact, if you refuse to introduce them, I will do it myself."

The girls stared at their father. Mrs. Bennet said only, "Nonsense, nonsense!"

"Why do you say 'Nonsense'?" he cried. "Do

you think the forms of introduction, and the importance that we put on them, are nonsense? I cannot quite agree with you there." He turned to another daughter. "What do you say, Mary? For I know that you are a young lady who thinks deeply and reads great books."

Mary wanted to say something very sensible, but she could not think of anything.

"While Mary is considering my question," he continued, "let us return to Mr. Bingley."

"I am sick of Mr. Bingley," cried his wife.

"I am sorry to hear that, but why didn't you tell me before?" Mr. Bennet replied. "If I had known this morning, I would not have called on him. It is very unlucky, but now that I have actually met him, we cannot help but be acquainted."

The astonishment of the ladies was just what he wanted. Mrs. Bennet was most surprised of all, but when the first tumult of joy was over, she began to insist that she had expected Mr. Bennet to call on their neighbor all along.

"How good it was of you, my dear Mr. Bennet!" she exclaimed. "But I knew I would persuade you at last. I was sure you loved our girls too much to ignore Mr. Bingley. Well, how pleased I am! And what a good joke, too, that you went this morning and never said a word about it until now."

"Now, Kitty, you may cough as much as you like," said Mr. Bennet. As he spoke, he left the room, tired out by the emotions of his wife.

"What an excellent father you have, girls," she said, when the door was shut. "I do not know how you will ever repay him for his kindness, or me either, for that matter. At our age it is not so pleasant, I can tell you, to be making new acquaintances every day. But for your sakes, we would do anything. Lydia, my love, although you are the youngest, I imagine Mr. Bingley will dance with you at the next ball."

"Oh!" said Lydia confidently, "I am not worried about that. For though I am the youngest, I'm the tallest."

The rest of the evening was spent in discussing how soon Mr. Bingley would return Mr. Bennet's visit, and planning when they should ask him to dinner.

CHAPTER 3

Nothing that Mrs. Bennet and her five daughters did could make Mr. Bennet give any satisfactory description of Mr. Bingley. They attacked him in various ways—with barefaced questions, ingenious guesses, and theories—but he resisted them all. It was finally necessary to accept the second-hand report of their neighbor, Lady Lucas. Her report was highly favorable. Her husband, Sir William, had been delighted with their new neighbor. He was quite young, wonderfully handsome, extremely agreeable, and, best of all, he planned to be at the next neighborhood ball and to bring a large group of friends. Nothing could be more delightful! Dancing was a certain step toward falling in love, and Mrs. Bennet's fondest wish seemed closer to coming true.

"If I can only see one of my daughters happily settled at Netherfield," she said to her husband, "and all the others equally well married, I will have nothing more to wish for."

In a few days, Mr. Bingley returned Mr. Bennet's visit, and talked with him for about ten minutes in his library. He had hoped to glimpse the young ladies, of whose beauty he had heard much, but he saw only the father. The ladies were somewhat more fortunate. From an upstairs window they were able to determine that he wore a blue coat and rode a black horse.

The Bennets promptly sent Mr. Bingley an invitation to dinner, and Mrs. Bennet was already planning a menu to impress the guest, when a note arrived which spoiled it all. Mr. Bingley wrote that he was obliged to be in London the following day, and as such could not accept their kind invitation.

Mrs. Bennet was quite disturbed. She could not imagine what business he could have in town so soon after his arrival in Hertfordshire. She began to worry that he might always be flying about from one place to another and never settle at Netherfield as he should. Lady Lucas calmed her a little by suggesting that he had gone to London in order to collect his friends for the ball. Sure enough, a report soon followed that Mr. Bingley was bringing twelve ladies and seven gentlemen with him to the party. The girls grieved over such a large number of ladies, but they were comforted the day before the ball when they heard that, instead of twelve, he had brought only six with him from London, and that they included his five sisters and a cousin. And in fact, when the group entered the ballroom, it included a total of only five: Mr. Bingley, his two sisters (Miss Bingley and Mrs. Hurst), his brother-in-law Mr. Hurst, and another young man.

Mr. Bingley was good-looking and gentleman-like, with a pleasant face, and easy, relaxed manners. His brother-in-law, Mr. Hurst, did not draw much attention. It was Mr. Bingley's friend, Mr. Darcy, whom everyone noticed. They were impressed by his fine, tall figure, handsome face, and the news (which had made the rounds of the room within five minutes) that he was even richer than Mr. Bingley. The gentlemen all said he was a fine figure of a man, the ladies declared he was much handsomer than Mr. Bingley, and he was looked at with great admiration for about half the evening.

But then the tide of his popularity shifted, for his manners did not please. He appeared to be proud and to hold himself above the other people at the ball. The opinion soon flew through the room that Mr. Darcy's wealth, and his large estate in Derbyshire, was not enough to make up for his disagreeable attitude.

Mr. Bingley, on the other hand, had soon become acquainted with everyone in the room. He was lively and talkative, danced every dance, was angry that the ball ended so early, and mentioned giving one himself at Netherfield. What a contrast between him and his friend! Mr. Darcy danced only once, with Miss Bingley. He did not wish to be introduced to any other lady, and spent the rest of the evening walking about the room, speaking occasionally to one of his friends. Everyone agreed that he was the proudest, most disagreeable man in the world, and they hoped that he would never come to Hertfordshire again.

The person who criticized him most was Mrs. Bennet. Her dislike of his general behavior was sharpened into personal resentment by his insult to one of her daughters.

Because there was a shortage of gentlemen, Elizabeth Bennet had been obliged to sit down for two dances. During part of that time, Mr. Darcy had been standing near her—near enough for her to overhear a conversation between him and Mr. Bingley, who came over to encourage his friend to participate.

"Come, Darcy," Mr. Bingley said. "You really must dance. I hate to see you standing about by yourself in this stupid manner."

"I certainly shall not," Mr. Darcy replied. "You know how I detest dancing, unless I know my partner well. At a ball like this, dancing would be unbearable to me. Your sisters are already taken, and it would be a punishment to me to dance with any other woman in this room."

"You are amazingly picky!" cried Bingley. "On my honor, I have never met so many pleasant girls in my life as I have this evening. And there are several of them who are uncommonly pretty."

"You are dancing with the only handsome girl in the room," said Mr. Darcy, looking at Jane Bennet, the oldest of the sisters.

"Isn't she the most beautiful creature you ever

beheld? But one of her sisters is sitting just behind you. She is very pretty, and I'm sure she is pleasant. Let me ask my partner to introduce you."

"Who do you mean?" Mr. Darcy said. Turning around, he glanced at Elizabeth, then said coldly, "She is bearable, but not pretty enough to tempt me. I am not in the mood to notice young ladies whom no one else wants to dance with. You had better return to your partner and enjoy her smiles, for you are wasting your time with me."

Mr. Bingley followed his advice. Mr. Darcy walked off, and Elizabeth was left without very friendly feelings for him. But she later told the story to her friends with great amusement, for she had a lively, playful disposition, and she was delighted by anything ridiculous.

All in all, the evening passed off pleasantly for the whole family. Mrs. Bennet had seen her oldest daughter, Jane, much admired by the Netherfield party. Mr. Bingley had danced with her twice, and his sisters had been friendly to her. Jane was just as pleased by all this as her mother, though in a quieter way. Mary had heard someone call her the cleverest girl in the neighborhood, and the younger girls, Kitty and Lydia, had danced every dance. And so they returned in good spirits to their home at Longbourn.

At home they found Mr. Bennet still awake and curious to hear the details of an evening which had raised such splendid expectations. He had rather hoped that his wife would be disappointed in Mr. Bingley, but he soon found otherwise.

"Oh, my dear Mr. Bennet," she said as soon as she entered the room. "We have had a most delightful evening, a most excellent ball. I wish you had been there. Jane was so admired! Everybody said how handsome she looked, and Mr. Bingley thought her quite beautiful and danced with her twice. Only think of that, my dear—he actually danced with her twice, and she was the only girl in the room that he asked a second time. First of all, he danced with Miss Lucas. I was so irritated to see him with her, but it was clear he did not admire her at all—indeed, nobody can, you know—and he seemed quite struck with Jane as soon as he saw her. So, he asked who she was, and got introduced, and asked her for the next dance! Then, he danced with Miss King, and then the younger Lucas girl, and then with Jane again, and then with Lizzy, and the Boulanger girl—"

"If he had had any pity for me," cried her husband impatiently, "he would not have danced half so much! For God's sake, do not tell me any more of his partners. I wish he had sprained his ankle in the first dance!"

"O, my dear," continued Mrs. Bennet, "I am quite delighted with him. He is so excessively handsome! And his sisters are charming women. I never in my life saw anything more elegant than their dresses. Why, the lace alone on Mrs. Hurst's gown—"

Here she was interrupted again. Mr. Bennet flatly refused to listen to a description of anyone's dress. She was therefore forced to find another topic of discussion, so she described, with much bitterness and some exaggeration, the shocking rudeness of Mr. Darcy.

"But I assure you," she added, "that Lizzy loses nothing by not suiting his tastes. He is a disagreeable, horrid man, not at all worth pleasing. So haughty and conceited, he was quite unbearable. He walked here, and he walked there, as if he were so very great! Lizzy not pretty enough to dance with! I wish you had been there, my dear, to give him one of your put downs. I absolutely detest the man."

When Jane and Elizabeth were alone, Jane (who had been careful not to praise Mr. Bingley too much in front of their mother) made it clear to her sister how very much she admired him.

"He is just what a young man ought to be," she said, "sensitive, good-humored, lively, and I've never seen nicer manners. And yet there's nothing at all stuffy about him."

"He is also handsome," replied Elizabeth, "which a young man ought to be, if he possibly can. His character is thereby complete."

"I was very much flattered by his asking me to dance a second time. I did not expect such a compliment."

"Didn't you?" Elizabeth said. "I expected it for you. But that is one great difference between us. Compliments always take you by surprise, and me never. What could be more natural than his asking you again? He could not help seeing that you were about five times as pretty as any other woman in the room. He doesn't deserve any great credit for that. Well, he certainly is very agreeable, and you have my permission to like him. You have liked many a stupider person."

"Lizzy!"

"Well, it's true, you know! You are in general too ready to like people. You never see a fault in anybody. All the world is good and agreeable in your eyes. I've never heard you speak ill of a human being in my life."

"I don't want to be hasty in criticizing anyone, but I always say what I think."

"I know you do, and that is what is so amazing. With your good sense, you are still blind to the foolishness and nonsense of others. Many people pretend to be kindly and generous. But you notice the good in everybody's character, and never mention the bad. That is truly unusual. And so, do you like this man's sisters too? Their manners are not as good as his."

"Certainly not at first. But they are very pleasant when you talk with them. Miss Bingley—the younger, unmarried sister, you know—will live with her brother and keep house for him. I am sure she'll be a charming neighbor."

Elizabeth listened in silence but was not convinced. The Bingley ladies had not impressed her. She was quicker to judge than Jane, and her opinion was not affected by any attention from Mr. Bingley. It seemed to her that while these were fine, well-bred young ladies who could be agreeable and good-humored when they chose, that they were also proud and conceited. They were good-looking, educated in the finest private schools in London, had plenty of money which they spent freely, and associated with people of high rank. All in all, they seemed to think highly of themselves and not so well of others. They seemed to forget that their wealth had come from the hard work of their parents and grandparents, and had not been handed down from some ancient noble family.

The Bingleys' father had inherited a considerable fortune from his father, and had intended to purchase an estate, but he died before doing so. Now young Mr. Bingley likewise intended to buy an estate, and occasionally he talked of where in England he might settle. But as he had now leased a fine house, many of his friends (knowing his easygoing nature) doubted that he would ever go to the bother of purchasing. They suspected he would spend the remainder of his days at Netherfield, and let the next generation worry about buying.

His sisters were very anxious for him to have an estate of his own. But even though he was now established only as a tenant, Miss Bingley was very ready to act as her brother's hostess. His married sister, Mrs. Hurst, whose husband was more fashionable than rich, was also planning to spend a good deal of time at her brother's home. Mr. Bingley had heard just by chance of Netherfield House. He looked at it for half an hour, was pleased with everything, and took it immediately.

Between him and Darcy there was a very steady friendship, in spite of having almost completely opposite personalities. Darcy loved Bingley for his friend's easiness, openness, and sweetness of temper. Bingley relied greatly on Darcy's opinions. While he was an intelligent man, he knew that Darcy had the superior intellect. At the same time, Darcy was haughty, reserved, and particular about everything. While his manners were perfect, his personality was not warm and inviting. In that respect, Bingley had the great advantage. Bingley was sure of being liked wherever he went, while Darcy was constantly offending people.

Their conversation at the ball was a perfect example of their contrasting characters. Bingley had never met with pleasanter people or prettier girls in his life. Everybody had been most kind and attentive to him; there had been no formality, no stiffness; he had soon felt comfortable with everyone there; and he could not imagine an angel more beautiful than Jane Bennet. Darcy, on the contrary, had seen a collection of people who possessed little beauty and no fashion. He had not felt the slightest spark of interest in any of them. He admitted that Jane was pretty, but thought she smiled too much.

Mrs. Hurst and Miss Bingley agreed with Darcy, but still they admired and liked Jane. They called her a sweet girl whom they would not mind knowing better. Their brother, therefore, felt he had his sisters' permission to think of her as he liked.

Only a short walk from Longbourn lived a family with whom the Bennets were on close terms. Sir William Lucas had been a merchant in Meryton, where he had made a small fortune and been honored with a knighthood after making a speech before the King. He had, perhaps, taken this honor too seriously. It had made him feel disgusted with both his business and his home in a small market town and so, leaving them both, he had moved with his family to a house about a mile from Meryton. At "Lucas Lodge," as he named it, he could think with pleasure about his own importance, and spend his time being pleasant to all the world. For his knighthood had not made him haughty; on the contrary, he was kind and attentive to everybody. His wife, Lady Lucas, was a good woman, and not too clever to be friends with Mrs. Bennet. They had several children. The oldest of them, Charlotte, was a sensible, intelligent young woman of twenty-seven. She was Elizabeth's intimate friend.

It was absolutely necessary for the Lucases and the Bennets to talk over the ball, so the next morning the Lucases arrived for this discussion.

"You began the evening well, Charlotte," said Mrs. Bennet with polite self-control. "You were Mr. Bingley's first choice."

"Yes—but he seemed to like his second better."

"Oh! You mean Jane, I suppose, because he danced with her twice. To be sure he did seem to admire her. Indeed, I heard something about it, but I hardly know what. Something about Mr. Robinson."

"Perhaps you mean what I overheard between him and Mr. Robinson. Didn't I mention it to you? Mr. Robinson asked him how he liked our Meryton parties, and whether he did not think there were a great many pretty women in the room. When he asked which he thought was the prettiest, Mr. Bingley answered immediately, "Oh! Miss Jane Bennet beyond a doubt, there cannot be two opinions on that point."

"Upon my word!" exclaimed Mrs. Bennet. "Well, that was very definite indeed! That does seem as if—but, however, it may all mean nothing, you know."

"My overhearings were more pleasant than yours, Eliza," said Charlotte. "Mr. Darcy is not as worth listening to as his friend, is he? Poor Eliza! To be only 'bearable.'"

"Please, do not encourage Lizzy to mind that. He is such a disagreeable man, no one would want to be liked by him. Mrs. Long told me that he sat close to her for half an hour without once opening his lips."

"Are you quite sure, ma'am" said Jane. "I certainly saw Mr. Darcy speaking to her."

"Well, yes, but only when she asked him at last how he liked Netherfield, and he could not help answering her. But she said he seemed angry at being spoke to."

"Miss Bingley told me," said Jane, "that he never speaks much unless among his close friends. With them he is remarkably pleasant."

"I do not believe a word of it, my dear. If he had been so very pleasant, he would have talked to Mrs. Long. But everybody says that he is eaten up with pride."

"I do not mind his not talking to Mrs. Long," said Charlotte, "but I wish he had danced with Eliza."

"Another time, Lizzy," said her mother, "I would not dance with him, if I were you."

"I believe I may safely promise you that I never will dance with him," answered Elizabeth.

"His pride does not offend me as much as pride often does, because there is an excuse for it," said Charlotte. "It is no wonder that such a fine young man, with family, fortune, everything in his favor, should think highly of himself. He has a right to be proud."

"That is very true," replied Elizabeth, "and I could easily forgive his pride, if he had not hurt mine."

"Pride," observed Mary Bennet, who took

pleasure in her deep thoughts, "is a very common failing, I believe. From all that I have ever read, I am convinced that it is very common indeed, and that there are very few of us who do not cherish a feeling of self-satisfaction about some quality or other, real or imaginary. Vanity and pride are different things, though the words are often used interchangeably. A person may be proud without being vain. Pride relates more to our opinion of ourselves, vanity to what we want others to think of us."

"If I were as rich as Mr. Darcy," said one of the young Lucas boys, who came with his sisters, "I would not care how proud I was. I would keep a pack of foxhounds, and drink a bottle of wine every day."

"Then you would drink a great deal more than you should," said Mrs. Bennet, "and if I saw you doing it, I would take away your bottle directly."

The boy protested that she would not, she continued to declare that she would, and the argument ended only with the visit.

The ladies of Longbourn soon visited those of Netherfield. That visit was returned promptly. Jane's pretty manners continued to please Mrs. Hurst and Miss Bingley. They found Mrs. Bennet unbearable and the younger sisters not worth speaking to, but they expressed a wish to become better acquainted with the two oldest girls. Jane received this attention with the greatest pleasure, but Elizabeth still suspected that they thought themselves superior to everyone, even to Jane. It was clear whenever they met that Mr. Bingley did admire Jane, and to Elizabeth it was equally obvious that Jane was well on her way to being in love with him. Elizabeth was glad to know that the world in general was not likely to notice this fact, as Jane had a calm, composed, cheerful manner that hid her deepest feelings from all but her closest friends. Eliza mentioned this to her friend Miss Lucas.

"It is perhaps a good thing to be able to hide one's feelings from the public," replied Charlotte, "but it may not be entirely a good thing to be so private. If a woman conceals her affection from the man she loves, she may lose the chance to win him. Most people need a bit of encouragement to really be in love. Bingley obviously likes your sister, but he may never do more than like her, if she does not help him along."

"But she does help him, as much as her nature will allow," Elizabeth said. "If I can notice her feelings for him, he would have to be an idiot not to see them too."

"Remember, Eliza, that he does not know Jane as well as you do."

"But if a woman likes a man, and does not try to conceal it, he must notice it."

"Perhaps, if he sees enough of her. But though Bingley and Jane meet fairly often, it is never for very long at one time. And as they always see each other in mixed parties, they cannot spend every moment conversing together. Jane should therefore make the most of every minute in which she has his attention. When she is sure she has won him, then she will have leisure to fall in love as much as she chooses."

"Your plan is a good one," replied Elizabeth, "where nothing exists but the desire of being well married. If I were determined to get a rich husband, I dare say I would adopt it. But this is not Jane's way. She is not acting with that goal in mind. As yet, she cannot know for sure the depth of her feelings. She has known him only two weeks. She has danced four dances with him, she saw him one morning at his own house, and she has been at four dinner parties with him. This is not quite enough to make her understand his character."

"Not the way you explain it," agreed Charlotte. "If she had merely dined with him, she might only have discovered whether he had a good appetite. But those dinners involved spending four evenings together—and four evenings may do a great deal."

"Yes, these four evenings have allowed them to discover that they both like playing blackjack better than bridge. But I don't imagine they have learned much more of importance."

"Well," said Charlotte, "I wish Jane success with all my heart, and if she married him tomorrow, I would think she had as good a chance of happiness as anyone. Happiness in marriage is entirely a matter of chance. If the partners know each other perfectly beforehand, it does not guarantee their happiness. They manage to both change enough as to have their share of irritations. It is better to know as little as possible about the faults of the person with whom you are to pass your life."

"You make me laugh, Charlotte, but it is not true. You know it is not true, and that you would never act in this way yourself."

Because she was so busy observing Mr. Bingley's attentions to her sister, Elizabeth did not notice that she herself was being watched by his friend. Mr. Darcy had at first scarcely admitted that she was even pretty. He had barely glanced at her at the ball, and when they next met, he looked at her only to criticize. But no sooner had he made it clear that she had barely one good feature in her face than he began to notice it was a wonderfully intelligent face, with a beautiful expression in its dark eyes. To this discovery he added others that were equally surprising. He was forced to admit that she had a light and pleasing figure. In spite of his declaration that her manners were not fashionable, he was attracted by their easy playfulness. Of all this Elizabeth was unaware. To her, Darcy was only the man who never made himself agreeable, and who had not thought her pretty enough to dance with.

He began to want to know her better, and as a step toward talking with her himself, he eavesdropped on her conversation with others. She noticed him doing so. It was at Sir William Lucas's, where a large party was going on.

"What does Mr. Darcy mean," she said to Charlotte, "by listening to my conversation with Colonel Forster?"

"That is a question which only Mr. Darcy can answer."

"But if he does it any more, I shall certainly let him know that I notice it. He seems to find everything he hears ridiculous, and if I do not begin being bold, I shall soon grow afraid of him."

When he approached them soon afterward, although without seeming to have any intention of speaking, Elizabeth turned to him and said, "Didn't you think, Mr. Darcy, that I expressed myself uncommonly well just now, when I was teasing Colonel Forster about hosting a ball?"

"With great energy—but it is a subject which always makes a lady energetic."

"You are hard on us."

"It will be her turn soon to be teased," said Miss Lucas. "I am going to open the piano, Eliza, and you know what that means."

"You are a very strange sort of friend!" Elizabeth responded. "Always wanting me to play and sing before everybody! If I were proud of my music, I would appreciate your efforts, but as it is, I would really rather not perform for people who are in the habit of hearing much better performers." On Miss Lucas's insistence, however, she added, "Very well; if it must be so, it must." And gravely glancing at Mr. Darcy, she added, "There is a fine old saying: 'Keep your breath to cool your porridge.' And I shall keep mine to swell my song."

Her performance was pleasing, though by no means excellent. After a song or two, and before she could reply to the requests that she would sing again, her place was eagerly taken by her sister Mary. Mary, as a result of being the only plain-looking one in the family, worked hard for knowledge and accomplishments, and was always impatient to show off.

Unfortunately, Mary had neither talent nor taste. Although her hard work had given her some ability, it had also given her a schoolmarmish air and conceited manner, which would have been unpleasant even if she had played better. Elizabeth, easy and unaffected, had been listened to with much more pleasure, although she had not played half so well. Mary performed a long concerto. She then, however, gained some genuine gratitude by playing a few lively Scotch and Irish tunes at the request of her younger sisters, who, with some of the Lucases and two or three officers, joined eagerly in dancing at one end of the room.

Mr. Darcy stood near them in silent indignation at such a foolish way of passing the evening. He was too occupied by his own thoughts to notice that Sir William Lucas was standing by him until Sir William began to speak.

"What a charming amusement for young people this is, Mr. Darcy! There is nothing like dancing. I consider it one of the finest ways of passing the time in polished societies."

"Certainly, sir," answered Darcy. "And it has the advantage of being popular amongst the less polished societies of the world. Every savage can dance."

Sir William only smiled. "Your friend dances delightfully," he continued after a pause, noticing that Bingley had joined in the entertainment, "and I do not doubt that you are an expert dancer yourself, Mr. Darcy."

"You saw me dance at Meryton, I believe, sir."

"Yes, indeed, and received no inconsiderable

pleasure from the sight. Do you often dance at the King's court at St. James's?"

"Never, sir."

"Do you not think it would be a proper compliment to the place?"

"It is a compliment which I never pay to anyplace, if I can avoid it."

"But you have a house in London, I believe?"

Mr. Darcy nodded.

"I have thought of moving to London myself, for I am fond of superior society," Sir William went on. "But I did not feel quite certain that the London weather would agree with Lady Lucas."

He paused, hoping for an answer, but Mr. Darcy said nothing. As Elizabeth was walking near them, Sir William was struck with an idea that seemed to him very gallant. He called out to her, "My dear Miss Eliza, why are you not dancing? Mr. Darcy, you must allow me to present this young lady to you as a very desirable partner. You cannot refuse to dance, I am sure, when so much beauty is before you." And taking her hand, Sir William tried to give it to Mr. Darcy.

That gentleman, although extremely surprised, was not unwilling to receive it, but Elizabeth instantly drew back. She said with some discomfort, "Indeed, sir, I have not the least intention of dancing. Please do not think that I came this way in order to beg for a partner."

Mr. Darcy, with grave politeness, requested the honor of a dance with her, but in vain. Elizabeth was determined, and Sir Williams's persuasion did nothing to shake her.

"You dance so beautifully, Miss Eliza, that it is cruel to deny me the happiness of seeing you," Sir William said. "And although this gentleman dislikes the amusement in general, he can have no objection, I am sure, to obliging us for one half hour."

"Mr. Darcy is very kind," said Elizabeth, smiling.

"He is indeed, but considering the circumstances, my dear Miss Eliza, we cannot wonder. For who would object to such a partner?"

Elizabeth turned away with a mischievous look. Her refusal had made her even more attractive in Mr. Darcy's mind, and he was thinking of her with some pleasure, when Miss Bingley spoke to him.

"I can guess your thoughts."

"I doubt that."

"You are thinking how unbearable it would be to pass many evenings in this manner, in such society, and indeed I agree. I was never more annoyed! The silliness and the noise, the nothingness and yet the self-importance of all these people!"

"Your guess is totally wrong, I assure you. My mind was more happily engaged. I have been thinking about the great pleasure provided by a pair of fine eyes in the face of a pretty woman."

Miss Bingley looked hard at him, and asked which lady had inspired such thoughts. Mr. Darcy replied calmly, "Miss Elizabeth Bennet."

"Miss Elizabeth Bennet!" repeated Miss Bingley. "I am astonished. How long has she been such a favorite? And when am I to wish you joy at your wedding?"

"That is exactly the question which I expected you to ask. A lady's imagination is very rapid. It jumps from admiration to love, from love to matrimony, in a moment. I knew you would be wishing me joy."

"No, if you are so serious about it, I shall consider the matter absolutely settled. You will certainly have a charming mother-in-law, and of course she will always be at your home at Pemberley with you."

He listened to her calmly while she entertained herself in this manner. As his composure convinced her that all was safe, her amusement continued for a very long time.

CHAPTER
7

Mr. Bennet's property consisted almost entirely of an estate and the yearly income it provided. Unfortunately for his daughters, that estate was entailed, or promised by law to a male heir. As Mr. Bennet had no sons, upon his death it would be inherited by a distant male relative. Mrs. Bennet's own money, although plenty for her situation in life, would not go far toward making up for the loss of the estate. Her father had been an attorney in Meryton and had left her a fair inheritance. She had one sister who was married to a Mr. Philips, who had been their father's clerk and taken over his business, and a brother settled in London in a respectable line of trade.

The village of Longbourn was only one mile from Meryton. This was a very convenient situation for the young ladies, who were usually tempted there three or four times a week to visit their aunt, as well as a hatmaker's shop along the way. The two youngest girls, Kitty and Lydia, were particularly frequent visitors. Their minds were emptier than their sisters', and when they had nothing else to do, a walk to Meryton was necessary to amuse their morning hours and furnish conversation for the rest of the day. They also managed to learn some gossip from their aunt. At present they were well supplied both with news and happiness by the recent arrival of an army regiment in the neighborhood. It was to remain the whole winter, and Meryton was the headquarters.

Their visits to Mrs. Philips now produced the most interesting news imaginable. Every day they learned something more about the officers' names and connections. Eventually, they began to meet the officers themselves. Mr. Philips visited them all, and this gave his nieces a source of happiness they had never before known. They could talk of nothing but officers. Mr. Bingley's large fortune, the mention of which threw their mother into raptures of joy, was worthless in their eyes when compared to an officer's handsome scarlet uniform.

After listening one morning to their excitement on this subject, Mr. Bennet coolly observed, "From all that I can tell, you must be two of the silliest girls in the country. I have suspected it for some time, but I am now convinced."

Kitty was embarrassed and made no answer, but Lydia ignored him. She continued to express her admiration of Captain Carter, and her hope of seeing him that day, as he was going the next morning to London.

"I am astonished, my dear, that you should be so ready to think your own children silly," said Mrs.

Bennet. "If I want to think badly of anybody's children, it should not be of my own."

"If my children are silly, I hope that I am aware of it."

"Yes—but as it happens, they are all of them very clever."

"This is the only point, I believe, on which we do not agree. I had hoped that our opinions were identical on all things, but I must say that I think our two youngest daughters are uncommonly foolish."

"My dear Mr. Bennet, you must not expect such girls to have the sense of adults. When they get to be our age, I dare say they will not think about officers any more than we do. But I remember the time when I liked a red coat myself very well. Indeed, I still do, and if a smart young officer with a good income should want one of my girls, I shall not refuse him. I thought Colonel Forster looked very handsome in his uniform the other night at Sir William's."

"Mama," cried Lydia, "my aunt says that Colonel Forster and Captain Carter do not go visit Miss Watson as often as they did when they first came. She sees them now very often at the Clarke's instead."

Mrs. Bennet was prevented from replying by the entrance of the footman with a note for Jane. It came from Netherfield, and the servant waited for an answer. Mrs. Bennet's eyes sparkled with pleasure while her daughter read.

"Well, Jane, who is it from? What is it about? What does he say? Well, Jane, make haste and tell us; make haste, my love."

"It is from Miss Bingley," said Jane, and then read it aloud.

My dear friend,

If you are not kind enough to dine today with Louisa and me, we shall be in danger of hating each other for the rest of our lives, for a whole day's solitude between two women can never end without a quarrel. Come as soon as you can. My brother and the gentlemen are dining out with the officers.

Yours ever,

Caroline Bingley

"With the officers!" cried Lydia. "I wonder why my aunt did not tell us of that."

"Dining out," said Mrs. Bennet, "that is very unlucky."

"May I use the carriage?" said Jane.

"No, my dear, you had better go on horseback, because it seems likely to rain, and then you must stay all night."

"That would be a good plan," said Elizabeth, "if you were sure that they would not offer to send her home in their carriage."

"But the gentlemen will have used Mr. Bingley's carriage to go to Meryton," her mother reminded her.

"I would much rather go in the coach," Jane protested.

"But, my dear, your father cannot spare the horses, I am sure. They are needed on the farm, Mr. Bennet, are they not?"

In fact the horses were being used. Jane was therefore forced to go on horseback, and her mother saw her to the door with many cheerful predictions of bad weather. Her hopes were answered; Jane had not been gone long before it rained hard. Her sisters were uneasy for her, but her mother was delighted. The rain continued the whole evening without a break; Jane certainly could not come back.

"This was a lucky idea of mine, indeed!" said Mrs. Bennet, more than once, as if she had herself created the rain. Until the next morning, however, she was not aware of all the happy results of her idea. Breakfast was scarcely over when a servant from Netherfield brought the following note for Elizabeth:

My dearest Lizzy,

I am not at all well this morning, which, I suppose, is because I got soaking wet yesterday. My kind friends will not hear of my returning home until I am better. They insist also on my seeing Dr. Jones. Therefore, do not be alarmed if you should hear of him coming here to see me. Except for a sore throat and headache, there is not much the matter with me.

Your loving sister,

Jane

"Well, my dear," said Mr. Bennet, when Elizabeth had read the note aloud, "if your daughter should be dangerously ill and die, it will be a comfort to know that it was all in pursuit of Mr. Bingley, and under your orders."

"Oh! I am not at all afraid of her dying," his wife retorted carelessly. "People do not die of little trifling colds. She will be taken good care of. As long is she stays there, it is all very well. I would go and see her, if I could have the carriage."

Elizabeth, feeling really anxious, was determined to go to her, although the carriage was not available. As she was no horsewoman, walking was her only alternative. She declared her intention to go.

"How can you be so silly as to think of such a thing, in all this mud!" cried her mother. "You will not be fit to be seen when you get there."

"I shall be very fit to see Jane, which is all I want."

"Is this a hint to me, Lizzy," said her father, "to send for the horses?"

"No, indeed. I do not mind walking. The distance is nothing, only three miles. I shall be back by dinner."

"We will go as far as Meryton with you," said Kitty and Lydia. Elizabeth accepted their company, and the three young ladies set off together.

"If we hurry," said Lydia, as they walked along, "perhaps we may see Captain Carter before he goes."

In Meryton they parted. The two youngest headed for the home of one of the officers' wives, and Elizabeth continued her walk alone. She crossed field after field at a quick pace, jumping over stiles and springing over puddles. She found herself at last near the house, with weary ankles, dirty stockings, and a face glowing with the warmth of exercise.

She was shown into the breakfast room, where everyone but Jane was sitting, and where her appearance created a great deal of surprise. That she should have walked three miles so early in the day, in such dirty weather, and by herself, was almost unbelievable to Mrs. Hurst and Miss Bingley. Elizabeth was convinced that they held her in contempt for it. They were coolly polite. Mr. Bingley was more than polite; he was full of good humor and kindness. Mr. Darcy said very little, and Mr. Hurst nothing at all. Darcy was divided between admiration for the color which exercise had given to her complexion, and doubt that Jane's illness really justified her coming so far alone. Mr. Hurst was thinking only of his breakfast.

Her questions about her sister were answered disturbingly. Jane had slept poorly. Although she was awake, she was very feverish and not well enough to leave her room. Elizabeth was glad to be taken to her immediately. Jane, who had been longing for Elizabeth's visit, but reluctant to inconvenience anyone, was delighted to see her. She was not well enough to talk much, however, and when Miss Bingley left them together, she said little except to express her gratitude at everyone's kindness.

When breakfast was over, they were joined by the sisters, and Elizabeth began to like them herself when she saw how much affection and care they showed for Jane. The doctor came, and having examined his patient, confirmed that she had caught a severe cold. He advised her to return to bed and promised her some medicine. She was glad to follow his advice, for her fever was rising and her head ached acutely. Elizabeth did not leave her room for a moment, nor were the other ladies often absent. The gentlemen were out, so the ladies had in fact nothing to do elsewhere.

When the clock struck three, Elizabeth felt that she must go, and very unwillingly said so. Miss Bingley offered her the carriage. But Jane expressed such unwillingness to part with her sister that Miss Bingley invited Elizabeth to remain at Netherfield for the present. Elizabeth thankfully consented, and a servant was sent to Longbourn to let the family know of her change of plan, and to bring back a supply of clothes.

At five o'clock the two ladies retired to dress, and at half past six Elizabeth was called to dinner. To the polite questions of her hosts (she had the pleasure of noting real concern from Mr. Bingley) she could not offer a very cheerful answer. Jane was not at all better. The sisters, on hearing this, repeated three or four times how sorry they were, how horrid it was to have a bad cold, and how much they disliked being ill themselves. They then forgot all about the matter. Their indifference toward Jane, when she was not right in front of them, reminded Elizabeth of why she had originally disliked them.

Their brother, indeed, was the only one of the group whose company she much enjoyed. He was clearly worried for Jane, and his attentions to Elizabeth were very pleasant. His kindness prevented her feeling herself as much an intruder as she believed she was considered by the others. No one else paid her much attention. Miss Bingley had eyes only for Mr. Darcy, her sister scarcely less so. And as for Mr. Hurst, who Elizabeth sat beside, he was a lazy man who lived only to eat, drink, and play cards.

When dinner was over, she returned directly to Jane. Miss Bingley began criticizing her as soon as she was out of the room. Her manners were pronounced to be very bad indeed, a mixture of pride and boldness. She had no conversation, no style, no taste, no beauty. Mrs. Hurst thought the same, and added, "She has nothing, in short, to recommend her, except for being an excellent walker. I shall never forget her appearance this morning. She really looked almost wild."

"She did indeed, Louisa," added her sister. "I could hardly keep from laughing. It was nonsense for her to come at all! Why must she be scampering about the country because her sister had a cold? Her hair so untidy, so blowsy!"

"Yes, and her petticoat! I hope you saw her petticoat, six inches deep in mud, I am absolutely certain. The gown which had been let down to hide it was not doing its job."

"Your picture may be very exact, Louisa," said Bingley, "but this was all lost upon me. I thought Miss Elizabeth Bennet looked remarkably well when she came into the room this morning. Her dirty petticoat quite escaped my notice."

"You noticed it, Mr. Darcy, I am sure," said Miss Bingley, "and I am sure that you would not wish to see your sister make such a display of herself."

"Certainly not."

"To walk three miles, or four miles, or five miles, or whatever it is, above her ankles in dirt, and alone, quite alone! What could she mean by it? It shows an abominable sort of conceited independence, a most countrified indifference to manners."

"It shows an affection for her sister that is very pleasing," said Bingley.

"I am afraid, Mr. Darcy," observed Miss Bingley in a half-whisper, "that this adventure has rather affected your admiration of her fine eyes."

"Not at all," he replied. "They were brightened by the exercise."

A short pause followed this speech, and Mrs. Hurst began again. "I have a great regard for Jane Bennet. She is really a very sweet girl, and I wish with all my heart she were well settled. But with such a father and mother, and such low connections, I am afraid there is no chance of it."

"I think I have heard you say that their uncle is an attorney in Meryton," Bingley remarked.

"Yes, and they have another, who lives somewhere near Cheapside."

"That is perfect!" added her sister, and they both laughed heartily.

"If they had uncles enough to fill all Cheapside," cried Bingley, "it would not make them one bit less agreeable."

"But it certainly does lessen their chance of marrying men of any standing in the world," replied Darcy.

To this speech Bingley made no answer. But his sisters agreed with it heartily, and they laughed for some time at the expense of their dear friend's vulgar relations.

They acted more tenderly, however, when they returned to Jane's room, and sat with her until they were summoned to coffee. She was still very unwell, and Elizabeth would not leave her at all until late in the evening when Jane finally fell asleep. Then it seemed to her more right than pleasant that she should go downstairs herself. On entering the drawing room, she found the whole party playing cards, and was immediately invited to join them. But as she suspected them to be playing for high stakes she declined, and making her sister the excuse, said she could remain downstairs for only a short time and would amuse herself with a book. Mr. Hurst looked at her with astonishment.

"Do you prefer reading to cards?" he said. "That is rather unusual."

"Miss Eliza Bennet," said Miss Bingley, "despises cards. She is a great reader and takes no pleasure in anything else."

"I deserve neither such praise nor such criticism," said Elizabeth. "I am not a great reader, and I have pleasure in many things."

"You clearly take pleasure in nursing your sister," said Bingley, "and I hope it will soon be increased by seeing her quite well."

Elizabeth thanked him from her heart, and then walked toward a table where a few books were lying. He immediately offered to fetch her others, anything that his library contained.

"And I wish my collection were larger for your benefit, but I am an idle fellow. Although I have not many books, I have more than I ever look at."

Elizabeth assured him that she could suit herself perfectly with those in the room.

"I am astonished," said Miss Bingley, "that my father should have left so small a collection of books. What a delightful library you have at Pemberley, Mr. Darcy!"

"It ought to be good," he replied, "it has been the work of many generations."

"And then you have added so much to it yourself. You are always buying books."

"I cannot understand the neglect of a family library in such days as these," he agreed.

"Neglect! I am sure you neglect nothing that can add to the beauties of that noble place. Charles, when you build your house, I hope it will be half as delightful as Pemberley."

"I hope it will."

"But I would really advise you to make your purchase in Derbyshire and to model your house after Pemberley. There is not a finer county in England than Derbyshire or a finer house then Pemberley."

"I will buy Pemberley itself if Darcy will sell it."

Elizabeth was more interested in this conversation than her book. Soon laying it aside, she drew near the card table, and stationed herself between

Mr. Bingley and his oldest sister to observe the game.

"Has Miss Darcy grown much since the spring?" asked Miss Bingley. "Will she be as tall as I am?"

"I think she will," answered Darcy. "She is now about Miss Elizabeth Bennet's height, or a bit taller."

"How I long to see her again! I never met with anybody who delighted me so much. Such a pretty face, such manners, and so extremely accomplished for her age! Her performance on the piano is exquisite."

"It is amazing to me," said Bingley, "how young ladies can have patience to be so very accomplished as they all are."

"All young ladies accomplished! My dear Charles, what do you mean?"

"Yes, all of them, I think. They all paint tables, cover screens, and crochet purses. I know almost no one who cannot do all this, and I am sure I never heard a young lady spoken of for the first time without being informed that she was very accomplished."

"You are accurate in your list of what is generally called accomplishments," said Darcy, "The word is applied to many a woman who can do no more than crochet a purse or cover a screen. But I do not agree with your opinion of ladies in general. I have not known more than half a dozen ladies who I would call truly accomplished."

"Then," observed Elizabeth, "you must mean a great deal when you call a woman accomplished."

"Yes, I do mean a great deal," Darcy agreed.

"Oh! certainly," cried Miss Bingley, his faithful assistant. "No one really can be called accomplished who does not possess far more than what is usually met with. A woman must have a thorough knowledge of music, singing, drawing, dancing, and the modern languages, to deserve the word. Besides all this, she must possess a certain something in her air and manner of walking, the tone of her voice, her address and expressions, or the word will be but half-deserved."

"Yes, all this she must possess," agreed Darcy. "And to this she must add something more substantial: the improvement of her mind by extensive reading."

"I am no longer surprised at your knowing only six accomplished women," Elizabeth remarked. "Indeed, I am surprised that you know any."

"Are you so hard on your own sex as to doubt the possibility of all this?" asked Darcy.

"I never saw such a woman," Elizabeth replied. "I never saw such talent, and taste, and elegance as you describe, united in one person."

Mrs. Hurst and Miss Bingley both cried out against such injustice. Both were protesting that they knew many women who fulfilled this description, when Mr. Hurst called them to order, complaining bitterly of their neglect of the card game. As all conversation was thereby at an end, Elizabeth soon left the room.

"Eliza Bennet," said Miss Bingley, once the door was closed, "is one of those young ladies who try to improve themselves in men's eyes by criticizing other women. With many men, I dare say, it succeeds. But, in my opinion, it is a cheap device, a very mean trick."

"Undoubtedly," replied Darcy, to whom this remark was chiefly addressed. "There is meanness in all the tricks which ladies sometimes use in hopes of captivating a man. Whatever borders on dishonesty is despicable."

Miss Bingley was not entirely satisfied with this reply, and so she dropped the subject.

Elizabeth joined them again only to say that her sister was worse, and that she could not leave her. Bingley urged that Dr. Jones be sent for immediately. His sisters, convinced that no country doctor could be of any service, recommended that a London physician be summoned at once. This Elizabeth would not hear of, but she was willing to agree with their brother's proposal. It was settled that Dr. Jones should be sent for early in the morning if Miss Bennet were not decidedly better. Bingley was quite uncomfortable; his sisters declared that they were miserable. They comforted themselves, however, by singing duets after supper, while he relieved his feelings by giving his housekeeper orders to pay every possible attention to the sick lady and her sister.

CHAPTER
9

Elizabeth passed most of the night in her sister's room. In the morning she was happy to report that Jane seemed a little better. In spite of this positive change, however, she asked to have a note sent to Longbourn, requesting that her mother visit Jane and give her own opinion of her situation. The note was immediately sent, and its contents quickly acted upon. Mrs. Bennet, accompanied by her two youngest girls, reached Netherfield soon after the family breakfast.

If she had found Jane in any real danger, Mrs. Bennet would have been very miserable. But once she saw that her daughter's illness was not serious, she did not want Jane to get well immediately, because if she were fully well she would have no reason to remain at Netherfield. She, therefore, would not listen to her daughter's proposal of being taken home. The doctor, who arrived at about the same time, agreed that it would not be wise to move her. After visiting a little while with Jane, Mrs. Bennet and her three daughters accepted Miss Bingley's invitation to join them in the breakfast parlor. Bingley joined them, expressing his hopes that Mrs. Bennet had not found Jane worse than she expected.

"Indeed I have, sir," was her answer. "She is a great deal too ill to take home. Dr. Jones says we must not think of moving her. We must trespass a little longer on your kindness."

"Moved!" cried Bingley. "It must not be thought of. My sister, I am sure, will not hear of her leaving."

"You may depend upon it, madam," said Miss Bingley, with cold politeness. "Miss Bennet shall receive every possible attention while she remains with us."

Mrs. Bennet gushed her thanks.

"I am sure," she added, "if it was not for such good friends, I do not know what would become of her. For she is very ill indeed, and suffers a great deal, though with the greatest patience in the world—which is always the way with her, for she has the sweetest temper I ever met with. I often tell my other girls they are nothing compared to her. You have a sweet room here, Mr. Bingley, and a charming view over that gravel walk. I do not know a place in the country that is equal to Netherfield. You will not think of leaving it in a hurry, I hope, even though you have but a short lease."

"Whatever I do is done in a hurry," he replied. "Therefore, if I should decide to leave Netherfield, I should probably be off in five minutes. At present, however, I consider myself quite at home here."

"That is exactly what I should have expected of you," said Elizabeth.

"You begin to comprehend me, do you?" he cried, turning toward her.

"Oh! Yes—I understand you perfectly."

"I wish I might take that for a compliment, but to be so easily seen through is quite pitiful, I am afraid."

Elizabeth smiled. "It is not necessarily true that a deep, intricate character is more or less worthwhile than a character such as yours."

"Lizzy," cried her mother, "remember where you are, and do not speak so freely as you do at home."

"I did not know that you were such a student of character!" Bingley said. "It must be an amusing study."

"Yes, but it is true that complicated characters are the most amusing."

"The country must not provide many subjects for such a study," said Darcy. "In a country neighborhood, there is not much variety."

"But people themselves change so much that there is something new to be observed in them forever," answered Elizabeth.

"Yes, indeed," cried Mrs. Bennet, offended by Darcy's manner of speaking of a country neighborhood. "I assure you there is quite as much of that going on in the country as in town."

Everybody was surprised, and Darcy, after looking at her for a moment, turned silently away. Mrs. Bennet, who imagined she had gained a complete victory over him, continued her triumph.

"I cannot see that London has any advantage over the country, except for the shops and public places," she said. "The country is a great deal pleasanter, is it not, Mr. Bingley?"

"When I am in the country," he replied, "I never wish to leave it, and when I am in town it is pretty much the same. They each have their advantages, and I can be equally happy in either."

"Yes, that is because you have the right disposition. But that gentleman," she said, looking at Darcy, "seems to think the country is nothing at all."

"Indeed, Mama, you are mistaken," said Elizabeth, blushing for her mother. "You misunderstood Mr. Darcy. He only meant that there is not such a variety of people in the country as in town, which you must admit to be true."

"Certainly, my dear, nobody said there were. But as to not meeting with many people in this neighborhood, I believe there are few neighborhoods that are larger than ours. I know there are twenty-four families that we dine with on occasion."

Nothing but concern for Elizabeth could keep Bingley from laughing aloud. His sister was less polite, and looked toward Mr. Darcy with a very expressive smile. Elizabeth, for the sake of changing the subject, now asked her if Charlotte Lucas had been at Longbourn since she had been gone.

"Yes, she called yesterday with her father. What an agreeable man Sir William is, Mr. Bingley, don't you agree? So much the man of fashion! So mannerly and yet so easy! He has always something to say to everybody. That is my idea of a fine gentleman, rather than those persons who fancy themselves very important and never open their mouths."

"Did Charlotte dine with you?"

"No, she needed to go home. I believe she was needed to help make the mince pies. For my part, Mr. Bingley, I always keep servants that can do their own work; my daughters are brought up differently. But everybody is to judge for themselves, and the Lucases are a very good sort of girls, I assure you. It is a pity they are not handsome! Not that I think Charlotte so very plain—but then she is our particular friend."

"She seems a very pleasant young woman," said Bingley.

"Oh dear, yes; but you must admit she is very plain. Lady Lucas herself has often said so, and envied me Jane's beauty. I do not like to boast of my own child, but one does not often see anybody better looking. It is what everybody says. When she was only fifteen, there was a gentleman at my brother Gardiner's in town, so much in love with her, that my sister-in-law was sure he would propose to her before we left. But, however, he did not. Perhaps he thought her too young. However, he wrote some verses about her, and very pretty they were."

"And so ended his affection," said Elizabeth

impatiently. "There have been many affections, I believe, overcome in the same way. I wonder who first discovered the usefulness of poetry in driving away love!"

"I have always heard that poetry was the food of love," said Darcy.

"Of a fine, stout, healthy love it may," Elizabeth answered. "Everything nourishes what is strong already. But if it is only a slight, thin sort of liking, I am convinced that one good sonnet will starve it entirely away."

Darcy only smiled, and the silence which followed made Elizabeth tremble in case her mother should embarrass herself again. She wanted to speak, but could think of nothing to say. After a short silence, Mrs. Bennet began repeating her thanks to Mr. Bingley for his kindness to Jane, adding an apology for troubling him also with Lizzy. Mr. Bingley was sincerely polite in his answer and forced his younger sister to be polite also. She performed her part without much graciousness, but Mrs. Bennet was satisfied, and soon ordered her carriage. Upon this signal, the youngest of her daughters put herself forward. The two girls had been whispering to each other during the whole visit, and they had agreed that the youngest should remind Mr. Bingley of his promise to give a ball at Netherfield.

Lydia was a tall, well-grown girl of fifteen, with a fine complexion and good-humored face. She was her mother's favorite, and she had been spoiled and allowed to participate in adult activities from an early age. She had high animal spirits, and a sort of natural self-confidence which the attentions of the officers had greatly increased. She was quite up to the task, therefore, of speaking to Mr. Bingley on the subject of the ball, and abruptly reminded him of his promise. She added that it would be the most shameful thing in the world if he did not keep his word. His answer to this sudden attack was delightful to their mother's ear.

"I am perfectly ready, I assure you, to keep my word, and when your sister is recovered, you shall name the very day of the ball. But you would not wish to be dancing while she is ill."

Lydia was well satisfied. "Oh yes, it will be much better to wait until Jane is well. And by that time most likely Captain Carter will be at Meryton again. And when you have given your ball," she added, "I shall insist on the officers giving one also. I shall tell Colonel Forster it will be quite a shame if he does not."

Mrs. Bennet and her daughters then departed. Elizabeth returned instantly to Jane, leaving her own and her relatives' behavior to be discussed by the two ladies and Mr. Darcy. Darcy, however, could not be persuaded to join in their criticism, in spite of all Miss Bingley's jokes about Elizabeth's fine eyes.

The day passed much as the day before had done. Mrs. Hurst and Miss Bingley had spent some hours of the morning with the invalid, who continued to improve, although slowly. In the evening Elizabeth joined their party in the drawing room. Mr. Darcy was writing. Miss Bingley, seated near him, was watching the progress of his letter, and was repeatedly interrupting him by sending messages to his sister. Mr. Hurst and Mr. Bingley were playing cards, and Mrs. Hurst was observing their game.

Elizabeth took up some needlework, and amused herself by listening to what passed between Darcy and his companion. The constant compliments of the lady either on his handwriting, or on the evenness of his lines, or on the length of his letter, along with his complete lack of interest in her praises, formed a strange sort of dialogue.

"How delighted Miss Darcy will be to receive such a letter!"

He made no answer.

"You write uncommonly fast."

"You are mistaken. I write rather slowly."

"How many letters you must have to write in the course of the year! Letters of business, too! How I would hate to have to write those!"

"It is fortunate, then, that they are my duty and not yours."

"Please tell your sister that I cannot wait to see her."

"I have already told her so once, at your request."

"I am afraid you do not like your pen. Let me mend it for you. I mend pens remarkably well."

"Thank you, but I always mend my own."

"How can you manage to write so evenly?"

He was silent.

"Tell your sister I am delighted to hear of her improvement on the harp. And please let her know that I am in raptures over her beautiful little design for a table, and I think it much better than Miss Grantley's."

"May I postpone your raptures until I write again? I really do not have room to do them justice here."

"Oh, it does not matter. I shall see her in January. But do you always write such charming long letters to her, Mr. Darcy?"

"They are generally long, but whether they are always charming is not for me to say."

"I always say that a person who can write a long letter with ease cannot write it badly."

"That will not do for a compliment to Darcy,

Caroline," said her brother, "because he does not write with ease. He tries too hard to use four-syllable words. Don't you, Darcy?"

"My style of writing is very different from yours."

"Oh!" cried Miss Bingley, "Charles writes in the most careless way imaginable. He leaves out half his words and blots the rest."

"My ideas flow so rapidly that I do not have time to express them," Bingley said. "As a result, my letters sometimes convey no ideas at all."

"Your humility excuses you, Mr. Bingley," said Elizabeth.

"You excuse him too easily," said Darcy. "Nothing is less honest than the appearance of humility. It is often only carelessness, and sometimes an indirect boast."

"And which of the two do you call my little recent piece of modesty?" asked Bingley.

"The indirect boast," Darcy declared. "You are actually proud of your defects in writing. You are bragging about your rapid thoughts and careless execution which you think is highly interesting. The power of doing anything quickly is always prized by the possessor, even though the speed often damages the performance. For example, when you told Mrs. Bennet this morning that if you ever decided to leave Netherfield you should be gone in five minutes, you meant it as a sort of compliment to yourself. And yet what is so praiseworthy about haste, which always leaves necessary business undone?"

"No," cried Bingley, "this is too much, to remember at night all the foolish things that were said in the morning. And yet, I believed what I said about myself to be true, and I believe it at this moment. I was not merely showing off."

"I dare say you did believe it, but I am not convinced that you would leave so promptly. You make all your decisions based on chance. If you were mounting your horse and a friend said, 'Bingley, you had better stay till next week' you would probably do it. You would probably not go—and, at another word, you might stay a month."

"You are only demonstrating Mr. Bingley's good disposition, far more than he did himself," said Elizabeth.

"I appreciate you turning Darcy's remarks into a compliment," Bingley said. "But I am afraid he did not intend it so. He would think more of me if, under such circumstances, I flatly refused and rode off as fast as I could."

"Would Mr. Darcy think that the impulsiveness of your original decision meant that you should stubbornly stick to it?" asked Elizabeth.

"Upon my word, I cannot say. Darcy must speak for himself."

"All right, then," said Mr. Darcy. "You must remember, Miss Bennet, that the friend who wants him to change his mind and stay at the house has asked this without offering a single reason why."

"So," said Elizabeth, "to you, the willingness to give in easily to a friend is not a good point?"

"To give without understanding the reason? No, that does not do credit to either of them."

"It seems to me, Mr. Darcy, that you give no credit to the influence of friendship and affection. One's affection for a friend can make one ready to agree without waiting to be argued into it. In general, between two friends, if one of them wants the other to change a decision that is of no great importance, would you think badly of that person for agreeing to do so, without waiting to be argued into it?"

"Before we go on," said Darcy, "shall we decide how intimate these two friends are, as well as the importance of the decision?"

"By all means," cried Bingley. "Let us hear all the details, especially their comparative height and size. That has more importance in the argument, Miss Bennet, than you may be aware of. If Darcy were not such a great tall fellow, I would not be half so respectful to him."

Mr. Darcy smiled, but Elizabeth thought that he was rather offended, and, therefore, she silenced her laughter. Miss Bingley warmly resented any criticism of Mr. Darcy, and scolded her brother for talking such nonsense.

"I see your plan, Bingley," said Darcy. "You dislike an argument and want to silence this."

"Perhaps I do. Arguments are too much like quarrels. If you and Miss Bennet will postpone yours till I am out of the room, I will be very thankful. And then you may say whatever you like of me."

"What you ask is no sacrifice for me," said Elizabeth, "and Mr. Darcy had better finish his letter."

Mr. Darcy took her advice, and did finish his letter.

When that work was over, he asked Miss Bingley and Elizabeth if they would provide some music. Miss Bingley moved promptly to the piano and seated herself.

Mrs. Hurst sang with her sister. As they sang, Elizabeth could not help noticing how frequently Mr. Darcy was watching her. It seemed strange that such a great man might admire her; yet the idea he should look at her because he disliked her was even more strange. She decided at last that he looked at her because there was something more wrong with her (according to his ideas of right) than in any other person in the room. The idea did not bother her. She disliked him too much to care for his approval.

After playing some Italian songs, Miss Bingley performed a lively Scotch tune. Mr. Darcy said to Elizabeth, "Doesn't that music make you want to dance a reel?"

She smiled, but did not answer. He repeated the question, with some surprise at her silence.

"Oh!" she said. "I heard you before, but I was not sure what to say in reply. You wanted me, I know, to say 'Yes,' so that you might enjoy despising my taste. But I always like spoiling such plans. I have therefore made up my mind to tell you that I do not want to dance a reel at all—and now despise me if you dare."

"Indeed, I do not dare."

Elizabeth, who had rather expected to offend him, was surprised at his politeness. But there was a mixture of sweetness and mischief in her manner which made it difficult for her to offend anybody. In fact, Darcy had never been so bewitched by any woman as he was by her. He really believed that if it were not for her low-class family, he should be in some danger.

Miss Bingley saw, or suspected, enough to be jealous. Her great anxiety for the recovery of her dear friend Jane was now increased by her desire to get rid of Elizabeth.

She often tried to provoke Darcy into disliking Elizabeth by sarcastically speaking of their supposed marriage.

"I hope that after this happy event takes place," she said, as they were walking together the next day, "you will give your mother-in-law a few hints about holding her tongue. And if you can manage it, do cure the younger girls of running after the officers. And, if I may mention so delicate a subject, try to discourage your fiancee's tendency toward rudeness."

"Have you anything else to suggest for my married happiness?"

"Oh, yes! Do have portraits of Elizabeth's uncle and aunt Philips hung in the gallery at Pemberley. Put them next to your great uncle, the judge. As for your Elizabeth's picture, you must not attempt to have it painted, for what artist could do justice to those beautiful eyes?"

"It would not be easy, indeed, to catch their expression. But their color and shape, and the remarkably pretty eyelashes, might be copied."

At that moment, they were met by Mrs. Hurst and Elizabeth herself, coming from another direction.

"I did not know that you were planning to take a walk," said Miss Bingley in some confusion, fearing that they had been overheard.

"How awful of you to run away without telling us that you were going out!" replied Mrs. Hurst. Then taking Mr. Darcy's free arm, she left Elizabeth to walk behind them by herself. The path was only wide enough for three.

Embarrassed by their rudeness, Mr. Darcy immediately said, "This walk is not wide enough for our group. Let's move into the avenue."

But Elizabeth, who did not want to stay with them in the least, laughingly answered, "No, no; stay where you are. You look absolutely charming together. The whole picture would be spoiled by adding a fourth. Goodbye!"

She then ran cheerfully off, rejoicing at the thought of being at home again in a day or two.

Jane was already so much better that she intended to leave her room for a couple of hours that evening.

CHAPTER
11

After dinner, Elizabeth ran up to Jane's room, and, after making sure she was well wrapped up against the cold, accompanied her to the drawing room. There she was welcomed by Miss Bingley and Mrs. Hurst with cries of pleasure, and Elizabeth had never seen them so pleasant as they were during the next hour before the gentlemen joined them.

But when the gentlemen entered, Jane was no longer the main attraction. Miss Bingley's eyes instantly turned toward Darcy, and she had something to say to him as soon as he came near. He spoke to Jane, politely congratulating her on her recovery. Mr. Hurst also made her a slight bow, and said he was "very glad" to see her. But Bingley was overflowing with joyful attention. He spent the first half hour piling up the fire, so that she might be warm enough; then he insisted that she move to the other side of the room, so that she might not feel a draft from the door. Finally he sat down by her, and said barely a word to anyone else. Elizabeth, doing her needlework in the opposite corner, saw this all with great delight.

When tea was over, Mr. Hurst reminded his sister-in-law of the card table—but in vain. She had learned that Mr. Darcy did not wish to play, so she rejected Mr. Hurst's request. Mr. Hurst had therefore nothing to do but to stretch himself on one of the sofas and go to sleep. Darcy picked up a book; Miss Bingley did the same. Mrs. Hurst, mostly occupied in playing with her bracelets and rings, joined now and then in her brother's conversation with Jane.

Miss Bingley's attention was focused more on watching Mr. Darcy than on reading her book. She was constantly either asking him questions or looking over his shoulder at his page. She could not succeed, however, in engaging him in conversation; he merely answered her question and read on. Finally, quite exhausted by the attempt to be amused with her own book (which she had chosen only because it was the sequel to his), she gave a great yawn and said, "How pleasant it is to spend an evening in this way! I declare, there is no enjoyment like reading! How soon any other activity bores one! When I have a house of my own, I shall be miserable if I do not have an excellent library."

No one made any reply. She then yawned again, threw aside her book, and looked around the room in quest of some amusement. When she heard her brother mentioning a ball to Jane, she turned suddenly toward him and said, "By the way, Charles, are you really serious in thinking about a dance at Netherfield? Please, first consult the wishes of your friends here. If I am not mistaken, there are some among us to whom a ball would be a punishment rather than a pleasure."

"If you mean Darcy," replied her brother, "he may go to bed, if he chooses, before it begins. But as for the ball, it is quite a settled thing. As soon as all can be made ready, I will send out my invitations."

"I would like balls infinitely better," Miss Bingley replied, "if they were carried on in a different manner. There is something so boring in the usual process of such a meeting. It would be much more rational if conversation instead of dancing were the main event."

"Much more rational, I dare say, but it would not be nearly so much like a ball."

Miss Bingley made no answer, and soon afterward she got up and walked about the room. Her figure was elegant, and she walked gracefully—but Darcy, at whom it was all aimed, was still absorbed in his book. Desperate to distract him, she decided on one further effort, and turning to Elizabeth she said, "Miss Bennet, let me persuade you to follow my example, and take a turn around the room. I assure you it is very refreshing after sitting still for so long."

Elizabeth was surprised, but agreed. Miss Bingley succeeded in the real purpose of her invitation: Mr. Darcy looked up. Without thinking about it, he closed his book. Miss Bingley immediately invited him to join them. He refused, however, adding that he could imagine only two reasons why they were walking up and down the room, and that his joining them would ruin either purpose.

"What do you mean? I am dying to know."

"It is very simple," Darcy answered. "You have chosen this activity either because you have secret affairs to discuss, or because you are conscious that your figures appear to the greatest advantage as you walk. If the first is true, I would be completely in your way. If it is the second, I can admire you much better as I sit by the fire."

"Oh, shocking!" cried Miss Bingley. "I never heard anything so outrageous. How shall we punish him for such a speech?"

"Nothing is easier!" said Elizabeth. "We can all plague and punish one another. Tease him; laugh at him. As well as you know each other, you must know how to do that."

"But upon my honor I do not. How can one tease someone who is so eternally calm and collected? And as to laughter, it is quite useless with him."

"So Mr. Darcy is not to be laughed at!" cried Elizabeth. "That is very unfortunate. I dearly love to laugh at my friends."

"Miss Bingley gives me too much credit," said Darcy. "The wisest and best of men can be made to look ridiculous by a person whose first goal in life is a joke."

"Certainly, there are such people," replied Elizabeth, "but I hope I am not one of them. I hope I never ridicule what is wise or good.

Foolishness and nonsense do amuse me, I admit, and I laugh at them whenever I can. But these, I suppose, are precisely what you are lacking."

"Perhaps that is not possible for anyone. But it has been a goal of my life to avoid those weaknesses."

"Such as vanity and pride."

"Yes, vanity is a weakness indeed. But pride—where there is a real superiority of mind, pride will always be kept under control."

Elizabeth turned away to hide a smile.

"Your examination of Mr. Darcy is over, I see," said Miss Bingley. "What is the result?"

"I am convinced by it that Mr. Darcy has no faults. He admits it himself."

"No," said Darcy, "I said no such thing. I have faults enough. My temper is far from perfect. It is too rigid. I cannot forget the foolishness and vices of others as soon as I should. My feelings are not affected by every attempt to move them. My temper is overly resentful. My good opinion, once lost, is lost forever."

"That is a failing indeed!" cried Elizabeth. "Unshakable resentment is a dark mark against a character. But you have chosen your fault well: I really cannot laugh at it. You are safe from me."

"I believe that every personality has some natural defect which not even the best education can overcome," said Darcy.

"And your defect is a tendency to hate everybody."

"And yours," he replied with a smile, "is to willfully misunderstand them."

"Let's have a little music," cried Miss Bingley, tired of a conversation in which she had no part. "Louisa, you will not mind my waking Mr. Hurst?"

Her sister did not object, and the piano was opened. Darcy, after a few moments of thought, was not sorry for it. He had begun to feel the danger of paying too much attention to Elizabeth.

CHAPTER
12

As the two sisters had agreed, Elizabeth sent a note to her mother the next morning, requesting that the carriage be sent for them during the day. But Mrs. Bennet had calculated on her daughters remaining at Netherfield till the following Tuesday (which would make Jane's stay last exactly a week), and she was not willing to receive them earlier. Her answer, therefore, did not please Elizabeth, for she was impatient to get home. Mrs. Bennet sent word that they could not possibly have the carriage before Tuesday. In her postscript she added that if Mr. Bingley and his sister wished them to stay longer, she could spare them very well.

Elizabeth did not want to stay longer, nor did she expect them to be invited to do so. On the contrary, she worried that they had already intruded too long at Netherfield. She urged Jane to ask to borrow Mr. Bingley's carriage immediately.

Their announcement brought forth many concerned comments, enough to persuade Jane to delay their departure by one day. Miss Bingley was then sorry that she had suggested the change, for her jealousy and dislike of one sister was much greater than her affection for the other.

The master of the house heard with real sorrow that they were to go so soon. He repeatedly tried to persuade Jane that it would not be safe for her, but Jane was firm.

To Mr. Darcy their departure was welcome news; Elizabeth had been at Netherfield long enough. She attracted him more than he liked, and Miss Bingley was rude to her, and more teasing than usual to himself. He wisely decided to be particularly careful not to show any sign of admiration for her, nothing that could give her any hope of engaging his affection. Indeed, if such an idea had occurred to her, his behavior during the last day must have crushed it. He scarcely spoke ten words to her through all of Saturday. Although at one time they were left by themselves for half an hour, he kept his attention solely on his book, and would not even look at her.

On Sunday, after morning services, the separation (so welcome to almost everyone) took place. Miss Bingley's politeness to Elizabeth increased very rapidly, as well as her affection for Jane. When they parted, after assuring Jane of the pleasure it would always give her to see her either at Longbourn or Netherfield, and embracing her most tenderly, she even shook hands with Elizabeth. Elizabeth headed for home in the liveliest spirits.

They were not welcomed very warmly by their mother. Mrs. Bennet could not understand why they had come, and thought them very wrong to have troubled Bingley for his carriage. But their father, though he said little, was really glad to see them. The family's evening conversation had lost much of its liveliness, and almost all its sense, by the absence of Jane and Elizabeth.

They found Mary, as usual, deep in the study of human nature, and they had to admire her latest moral lessons. Kitty and Lydia had information of a different sort for them. There was much gossip involving the officers, and it was even rumored that Colonel Forster was going to be married.

CHAPTER
13

"I hope, my dear," said Mr. Bennet to his wife at breakfast the next morning, "that you have ordered a good dinner today, because I expect a guest."

"Who do you mean, my dear? I know of nobody that is coming, I am sure, unless Charlotte Lucas should happen to drop in. I hope my dinners are good enough for her. I do not believe she often sees as good at home."

"The person of whom I speak is a gentleman and a stranger."

Mrs. Bennet's eyes sparkled. "A gentleman and a stranger! It is Mr. Bingley, I am sure. Why Jane, you never dropped a word of this, you sly thing! Well, I am sure I shall be extremely glad to see Mr. Bingley. But, good Lord! How unlucky! There is not a bit of fish to be had today. Lydia, my love, ring the bell. I must speak to cook this moment."

"It is not Mr. Bingley," said her husband. "It is a person whom I have never seen in my life."

This was greeted with general astonishment, and he had the pleasure of being eagerly questioned by his wife and five daughters at once.

After amusing himself for a while at their expense, he explained. "About a month ago I received this letter, and about two weeks ago I answered it. It is from my cousin, Mr. Collins. When I am dead, it is he who may turn you all out of this house as soon as he pleases."

"Oh, my dear," cried his wife, "I cannot bear to hear that mentioned. Please do not talk of that hateful man. I think it is the worst thing in the world that your estate should be entailed away from your own children. If I had been you, I would have tried to do something or other about it long ago."

Jane and Elizabeth attempted to explain to her that entailment was a legal matter over which Mr. Bennet had no control. They had often tried it before, but it was a subject on which Mrs. Bennet was beyond the reach of reason. She continued to complain bitterly against the cruelty of settling an estate away from a family of five daughters in favor of a man whom nobody cared anything about.

"It certainly is a most wicked affair," said Mr. Bennet, "and nothing can clear Mr. Collins from the guilt of inheriting Longbourn. But if you will listen to his letter, you may perhaps be a little softened by his manner of expressing himself."

"No, I am sure I shall not, and I think it was very impolite of him to write to you at all, and very hypocritical," his wife said emphatically. "Why couldn't he keep on quarrelling with you, as his father did before him?"

"Why, indeed, he does seem to have had some ethical concerns on that matter, as you will hear."

Mr. Bennet unfolded the letter and began to read:

Dear sir,

The argument that existed between yourself and my late honored father always gave me much uneasiness. Since I have had the misfortune to lose him, I have frequently wished to heal the injury between us. But for some time I was kept back by my own doubts, fearing that it might seem disrespectful to his memory for me to be on good terms with anyone with whom it had always pleased him to disagree.

"There, Mrs. Bennet," Mr. Bennet commented, then resumed reading.

My mind however is now made up on the subject, for I have now been ordained a minister of the church. In addition, I have been so fortunate as to be honored by the patronage of the Right Honorable Lady Catherine de Bourgh, widow of Sir Lewis de Bourgh. Through Lady Catherine's bounty and goodness, she has seen fit to offer me the position of rector of this parish. From this point on it shall be my earnest endeavor to demonstrate my grateful respect toward her ladyship, and be ever ready to perform those rites and ceremonies which are instituted by the Church of England.

As a clergyman, I feel it my duty to promote the blessing of peace in all families within the reach of my influence. On these grounds I flatter myself that my overtures of goodwill are highly welcome, and that the unfortunate fact of my being heir to the Longbourn estate will be kindly overlooked on your side, and not lead you to reject the offered olive branch. I cannot help but be concerned about being the means of injuring your amiable daughters, and I beg leave to apologize for it, as well as to assure you of my readiness to do all in my power to make this up to them—but more of this later.

If you should have no objection to receiving me into your house, I propose the pleasure of visiting you and your family on Monday, November 18th, by four o'clock. I shall probably trespass on your hospitality until a week from the following Saturday. I assure you I can do this without any inconvenience, as Lady Catherine is far from objecting to my occasional absence on a Sunday, providing that some other clergyman is engaged to do the duty of the day.

I remain, dear sir, with respectful compliments to your lady and daughters, your well-wisher and friend,

William Collins

"At four o'clock, therefore, we may expect this peacemaking gentleman," said Mr. Bennet, as he folded up the letter. "He seems to be a most conscientious and polite young man, upon my word. I am sure that he will be a valuable acquaintance, especially if Lady Catherine will allow him to visit us again. At any rate, there is some sense in what he says about the girls, and if he is inclined to do something for them, I will certainly not discourage him."

"It is difficult to imagine what he thinks he can do," said Jane. "However, the wish is certainly to his credit."

Elizabeth was struck with his extraordinary respect for Lady Catherine, and his kind intention of christening, marrying, and burying his parishioners whenever required.

"He must be rather odd, I think," she said. "I cannot quite understand him. There is something very pompous in his style. And what can he mean by apologizing for being next in the entail? I do not suppose that he would help it, if he could. Do you think he can be a sensible man, Father?"

"No, my dear; I think not," answered her father. "I have great hopes of finding him quite the reverse. There is a mixture of groveling servility and self-importance in his letter which promises well. I am impatient to see him."

"And yet," said Mary, "his letter was not badly composed. The idea of offering the olive branch perhaps is not wholly new, yet I think it is well expressed."

To Kitty and Lydia, neither the letter nor its writer were in the least bit interesting. It was next to impossible that their cousin should come in an officer's scarlet coat, and it had been many weeks since they had received pleasure from the society of a man wearing any other color. As for their mother, Mr. Collins's letter had done away much of her ill-will. She was calmly prepared to see him.

Mr. Collins was punctual to the minute, and was received with great politeness by the whole family. Mr. Bennet said little, but the ladies were ready enough to talk, and Mr. Collins was chatty. He was a tall, heavy young man of twenty-five. His air was grave and stately, and his manners very formal. As soon as he arrived, he complimented Mrs. Bennet on having such a fine family of daughters. He said he had heard much of their beauty, but that the reality was better still. He added that he was sure she would soon see them disposed of in marriage. This flattery did not please all of his hearers, but Mrs. Bennet always welcomed any compliment. She answered, "You are very kind, sir. I hope with all my heart you are right, for else they will be penniless enough. Things are settled so oddly."

"You refer, perhaps, to the entail of this estate."

"Ah, sir, I do indeed. It is a sad affair for my poor girls, you must admit. Not that I am blaming you; for such things, I know, are all by chance in this world."

"I am very aware, madam, of the hardship to my fair cousins. I could say more on the subject, but I am cautious of appearing too forward and hasty. But I can assure the young ladies that I come prepared to admire them. At present I will not say more, but perhaps when we are better acquainted . . ."

He was interrupted by a call to dinner, and the girls smiled at each other behind his back. They were not the only objects of Mr. Collins's admiration. The hall, the dining room, and all its furniture were examined and praised. His compliments would have touched Mrs. Bennet's heart, except for her suspicion that he was viewing it all as his own future property. The dinner too, in its turn, was highly admired, and he begged to know which of his fair cousins was the excellent cook. But here he was corrected by Mrs. Bennet, who indignantly assured him that they were very well able to afford a good cook, and that her daughters had nothing to do in the kitchen. He begged pardon for having displeased her. She declared herself not at all offended, but he continued to apologize for a quarter of an hour.

CHAPTER
14

During dinner, Mr. Bennet hardly spoke at all. But once the servants had left, he thought it time to have some conversation with his guest. Therefore, he introduced a subject in which he expected him to shine, by observing that Mr. Collins seemed very fortunate in having Lady Catherine de Bourgh as his patroness.

Mr. Bennet could not have chosen better. Mr. Collins was flowery in his praise of her. The subject inspired him to be even more solemn than usual, and in the most pompous way imaginable he declared that he had never in his life witnessed such gracious behavior as he had himself experienced from Lady Catherine. She had (he reported) been good enough to approve of both the sermons which he had already had the honor of preaching before her. She had also invited him to dine twice at Rosings, her lovely estate, and had sent for him only the Saturday before, to make up her card table for the evening. She had even been so good as to advise him to marry as soon as possible, providing that he chose his wife wisely. Indeed, she had once even visited his humble parsonage, where she had approved all the changes he had been making, and had even honored him by suggesting an alteration herself—some shelves in the closets upstairs.

"That is all very proper and polite, I am sure," said Mrs. Bennet, "and she sounds like an excellent woman. It is a pity that great ladies in general are not more like her. Does she live near you, sir?"

"My humble home is separated by only a lane from Rosings Park, her ladyship's residence."

"I think you said she was a widow, sir? Has she any family?"

"She has one only daughter. She is the heiress of Rosings, and of a great fortune."

"Ah!" cried Mrs. Bennet, shaking her head, "then she is better off than many girls. And what sort of young lady is she? Is she handsome?"

"She is a most charming young lady indeed. Lady Catherine herself says that when it comes to true beauty, Miss de Bourgh is far superior to the handsomest lady, because she is clearly a young woman of noble birth. Unfortunately, she has always been rather sickly, and her health has prevented her making progress in many accomplishments. I have no doubt that if it were not for her ill health, she would excel in all she did. But she is a delightful young woman, and often drives by my humble abode in her little carriage and ponies."

"Has she been presented at court? I do not remember hearing her name mentioned."

"Her state of health unhappily prevents her from going to London. As a result, as I told Lady Catherine myself one day, the British court has been deprived of its brightest jewel. Her ladyship seemed pleased with the idea. As you may imagine, I am happy to frequently offer those little delicate compliments which are always acceptable to ladies. I have more than once told Lady Catherine that her charming daughter seems born to be a duchess. These are the kind of little things which please her ladyship, and it is a sort of attention which I consider it my duty to pay."

"Very proper," said Mr. Bennet, "and it is fortunate for you that you have the talent of flattering so delicately. May I ask whether you think up these pleasing compliments on the spot, or do you plan them in advance?"

"They usually arise from what is happening at the time. But I sometimes amuse myself with thinking up elegant little compliments that I may adapt to different occasions. When I deliver them, of course, I always try to give them as unplanned an air as possible."

Mr. Bennet's expectations were fulfilled. His cousin was as ridiculous as he had hoped, and he listened to him with the greatest enjoyment, maintaining at the same time the most serious attitude. Except for an occasional glance at Elizabeth, he required no partner in his pleasure.

When teatime was over, however, he had had

enough, and Mr. Bennet was glad to take his guest into the drawing room again and to invite him to read aloud to the ladies. Mr. Collins readily agreed, and a book was produced. But when he examined it, he was quite startled, protesting that he never read novels. Kitty stared at him, and Lydia exclaimed in loud disbelief. Other books were produced, and after some deliberation, he chose Fordyce's *Book of Sermons.* Lydia stared openmouthed as he opened the volume, and before he had read three pages, she interrupted him like this:

"Do you know, Mama, that my uncle Philips is thinking of letting his servant Richard go, and if he does, Colonel Forster will hire him. My aunt told me so herself on Saturday. I shall walk to Meryton tomorrow to hear more about it and to ask when Mr. Denny comes back from town."

Lydia was scolded by her two oldest sisters and told to hold her tongue. But Mr. Collins, much offended, laid aside his book, saying, "I have often observed how few young ladies are interested in serious books, even those written solely for their benefit. It amazes me, I confess, for certainly there can be nothing so advantageous to them as instruction. But I will no longer inconvenience my young cousin."

Then, turning to Mr. Bennet, he offered to play him a game of backgammon. Mr. Bennet accepted the challenge, commenting that he acted wisely in leaving the girls to their own foolish amusements. Mrs. Bennet and her daughters apologized for

Lydia's interruption, and promised that it would not occur again if he would resume reading. But Mr. Collins, after assuring them that he was not at all offended, seated himself at another table with Mr. Bennet, and prepared to play.

CHAPTER
15

Mr. Collins was not a sensible man, and the faults he was born with had not been corrected by either his education or society. He had spent most of his life under the guidance of his ignorant and miserly father, and although he had enrolled in a university, he had spent little time there and not made any acquaintances who might improve him.

Being brought up under the thumb of his father had originally given him a humble manner. But that humility was now challenged by a silly nature, easy living, and his good fortune in stumbling across early and unexpected prosperity. By a lucky chance, he had become acquainted with Lady Catherine de Bourgh when the post of rector of Hunsford was available. The respect which he felt for her high rank and for her position as his patroness, mingled with his very good opinion of himself and of his authority as a clergyman, created in him an odd mix of pride and servility, self-importance and humility.

Now that he had a good house and a good income, he intended to marry. This was his reason for coming to visit the Longbourn family. He meant to choose one of the daughters, if he found them as handsome and pleasant as they were said to be. By this marriage he planned to make up for inheriting their father's estate, and he thought his plan an excellent one—highly proper, and extremely generous on his part.

His plan was confirmed upon seeing them. Jane's lovely face settled it. To him, it seemed highly appropriate to choose her, the eldest. And so on that first evening, she was his choice. The next morning, however, forced a change in plan. He had a brief, private conversation with Mrs. Bennet before breakfast. The conversation began with his description of the parsonage, and led to the declaration of his hopes that a mistress for it might be found at Longbourn. His conversation produced from her, amid her satisfied smiles and general encouragement, a caution against the very girl he had decided on.

"As to my younger daughters, I cannot say," she informed him. "I cannot positively answer; that is, I do not know for certain of any promises that have been made. But as to Jane, I must just mention that she is very likely to be engaged soon."

That was only a small problem. Mr. Collins had only to change from Jane to Elizabeth, and that was soon done, with the encouragement of Mrs. Bennet. Elizabeth, who was second to Jane in both birth and beauty, was now Mr. Collins's favorite.

Mrs. Bennet treasured this conversation, and trusted that she might soon have two daughters married. The man whom she could not bear to speak of the day before was now high in her good graces.

Lydia's intention of walking to Meryton was not forgotten, and all the sisters except Mary agreed to go with her. Mr. Collins was to accompany them (this at the request of Mr. Bennet, who was most anxious to get rid of him and have his library to himself).

The journey passed, full of pompous nothings on his side, and polite agreements on that of his cousins, until they entered Meryton. At that point, he completely lost the attention of the younger girls. Their eyes immediately wandered up in the street in quest of the officers, and nothing less than a very fashionable hat indeed, or a really new dress in a shop window, could distract them.

But the attention of every lady was soon caught by a young man, whom they had never seen before, walking with an officer on the other side of the street. The officer was their friend Mr. Denny, and he bowed as they passed. All the sisters were impressed with the stranger; all wondered who he could be. Kitty and Lydia, determined to find out, led the way across the street, under the pretense of wanting something in a shop there. They had just reached the pavement, when the two gentlemen, turning back, reached the same spot.

Mr. Denny spoke to them, asking permission to introduce his friend, Mr. Wickham, who had returned with him from London the day before. He added that Mr. Wickham had accepted a position in their officers' corps. This was exactly as it should be, for the young man needed only an officer's uniform to make him completely charming.

He was extremely attractive, with a handsome face, good figure, and very pleasing personality. As soon as he was introduced, he displayed a cheerful readiness to make conversation—a readiness that was perfectly mannerly and proper. The whole group was still standing and talking together very happily when the sound of horses drew their attention. Darcy and Bingley were seen riding down the street. When they noticed the ladies of the group, the two gentlemen came directly toward them and began the usual polite conversation. Bingley was the principal spokesman, and Jane the principal object of his attention. He explained that he had been on his way to Longbourn to ask how she was. Mr. Darcy was attempting not to look at Elizabeth when his eyes fell on the stranger.

Elizabeth happened to see the faces of both men as they looked at each other, and she was astonished by the effect. Both changed color—one turned white, the other red. Mr. Wickham, after a few moments, touched his hat—a greeting which Mr. Darcy only barely returned. What could be the meaning of it? It was impossible to imagine; it was impossible not to want to know.

In another minute, Mr. Bingley, without seeming to have noticed what happened, said goodbye and rode on with his friend. Mr. Denny and Mr. Wickham walked with the young ladies to the door of Mr. Philips's house. There they said goodbye, in spite of Lydia's suggestion that they come in, and even in spite of Mrs. Philips throwing up the parlor window and loudly seconding the invitation.

Mrs. Philips was always glad to see her nieces. Jane and Elizabeth, because of their recent absence from home, were particularly welcome, and she was expressing her surprise at their sudden return home when she was interrupted by Jane's introduction of Mr. Collins. She welcomed him with her very best politeness, which he returned twofold. He apologized for his intrusion, but noted that he could not help flattering himself that she might overlook his breach of etiquette due to his relationship with the young ladies who introduced him.

Mrs. Philips was quite awed by such an excess of good manners, but her attention to this stranger was soon put to end an by the young ladies' questions about Mr. Wickham. She could only tell them what they already knew: that Mr. Denny had brought him from London, and that he was to have a lieutenant's commission in the regiment. She had been watching him for the last hour, she said, as he walked up and down the street. Some officers were to dine with the Philipses the next day, and their aunt promised to make her husband invite Mr. Wickham as well, if the family from Longbourn would come. This was agreed to, and Mrs. Philips promised that they would have some nice comfortable noisy games and a little bit of hot supper afterward. The prospect of such delights was very cheering, and they parted in mutual good spirits. Mr. Collins repeated his apologies as he left the room, and was assured with unwearying politeness that they were perfectly needless.

As they walked home, Elizabeth described to Jane what she had seen pass between Darcy and Mr. Wickham, but Jane could no more explain the behavior than her sister could.

Mr. Collins, on his return, greatly pleased Mrs. Bennet by praising Mrs. Philips's manners and politeness. He insisted that except for Lady Catherine and her daughter, he had never seen a more elegant woman, noting that she had not only welcomed him with the utmost civility, but had even included him in her invitation for the next evening, although he had been utterly unknown to her before. He assumed it was explained by his connection to the Bennets, but he had never met with so much pleasant attention in his life.

CHAPTER 16

Mr. and Mrs. Bennet had no objection to the young people's plan to visit their aunt, and once all of Mr. Collins's apologies for leaving Mr. and Mrs. Bennet alone for the evening were accepted, the coach took him and his five cousins to Meryton. There the girls had the pleasure of hearing that Mr. Wickham had accepted their uncle's invitation, and was then in the house.

When Mr. Wickham entered the room, Elizabeth felt that her earlier admiration of him had been, if anything, too mild. The officers of the regiment were in general a very admirable, attractive group, and the best of them were present tonight. But Mr. Wickham was as far above them all in good looks and personality as they were superior to broad-faced stuffy uncle Philips, smelling of port wine, who followed them into the room.

Mr. Wickham was the lucky man toward whom almost every female eye was turned, and Elizabeth was the happy woman by whom he finally seated himself. The agreeable manner in which he immediately drew her into conversation (although it was only on it being a wet night, and on the probability of a rainy season), made her feel that the dullest topic might be made interesting by the skill of the speaker.

With such rivals for the ladies' attention as Mr. Wickham and the officers, Mr. Collins seemed likely to sink into insignificance. To the young ladies he certainly was nothing, but he had still a kind listener in Mrs. Philips, who abundantly supplied him with coffee and muffins.

When the card tables were placed, he had an opportunity of pleasing her in return, by sitting down to play bridge.

"I know little of the game at present," he said, "but I shall be glad to improve myself, for in my situation of life—" Mrs. Philips was very thankful for his participation, but could not wait for his reason.

Mr. Wickham did not play bridge, and Elizabeth and Lydia were delighted when he sat between them at the other table to play a board game. At first there seemed a danger that Lydia would require all his attention, for she was a most determined talker. But as she was also very fond of games, she soon grew too much interested in making bets and exclaiming over prizes to pay attention to anyone in particular. Therefore, aside from the demands of the game, Mr. Wickham was able to talk to Elizabeth. She was very willing to hear him, although she did not dare ask about what she most wanted to learn—that is, his acquaintance with Mr.

Darcy. Her curiosity was unexpectedly satisfied when Mr. Wickham opened the subject himself. He asked how far Netherfield was from Meryton and, after receiving her answer, asked hesitantly how long Mr. Darcy had been staying there.

"About a month," said Elizabeth. Then, unwilling to let the subject drop, she added, "He has a very large property in Derbyshire, I understand."

"Yes," replied Wickham, "his estate there is a fine one. You could not have met with a person better able to tell you about it than myself—for I have been connected with his family since I was a child."

Elizabeth could only look surprised.

"You may well be surprised to hear this, after seeing the very cold manner of our meeting yesterday. Do you know Mr. Darcy well?"

"As well as I ever wish to," said Elizabeth indignantly. "I have spent four days in the same house with him, and I think he is very disagreeable."

"I have no right to give my opinion as to his being agreeable or otherwise," said Wickham. "I have known him too long and too well to be a fair judge. But I believe your opinion of him would surprise most people. Perhaps you would not express it so strongly anywhere else as you would here, among your own family."

"Upon my word, what I say here is no different from what I might say in any house in the neighborhood, except Netherfield. He is not at all liked here.

Everybody is disgusted with his pride. You will not find anyone here to speak favorably of him."

"I cannot pretend to be sorry that he or any man should not have their virtues exaggerated," said Wickham. "But with him I believe it does not often happen. The world is blinded by his fortune and importance, or frightened by his haughty manners, and sees him only as he chooses to be seen."

"I would judge him, even on my slight acquaintance, to be an ill-tempered man," Elizabeth said.

Wickham only shook his head. "I wonder," he said, at the next break in the game, "whether he is likely to be in this area much longer."

"I do not know, but I heard nothing of his going away when I was at Netherfield. I hope your plans to join the regiment will not be affected by his being in the neighborhood."

"Oh, no! I will not be driven away by Mr. Darcy. If he wishes to avoid seeing me, he must go. We are not on friendly terms, and it always gives me pain to meet him, but I have no reason for avoiding him. I have only a sense of having been badly used, and most painful regrets at his being what he is."

He went on. "His father, Miss Bennet, was one of the best men that ever breathed, and the truest friend I ever had. I can never be in the presence of Mr. Darcy without being grieved to my soul by a thousand tender memories. Darcy's behavior to myself has been shameful, but I believe I could forgive him anything other than the way he disappointed the hopes of his father."

Elizabeth found all this intensely interesting, and listened with all her heart, but the subject seemed too personal to allow her to ask further questions.

Mr. Wickham began to speak on more general topics: Meryton, the neighborhood, the local people. He appeared highly pleased with everything that he had seen, and he spoke of the people he had met with special warmth.

"The prospect of constant company, and good company, was the chief reason I joined the regiment," he said. "I knew it was a most respectable corps, and my friend Denny tempted me further by describing the excellent society available in Meryton. Society is necessary to me. I have been a disappointed man, and my spirits will not bear solitude. I must be busy and surrounded by people. A military life is not what I was intended for, but circumstances have made it necessary. The church should have been my profession. I was brought up to be a clergyman, and I would now have a most valuable living, if it were not for the gentleman we were speaking of just now."

"Indeed!"

"Yes. It was in the power of the late Mr. Darcy to grant that living, and before his death he promised it to me. He was my godfather, and greatly attached to me. I cannot do justice to his kindness. He meant to provide for me generously, and thought he had done it. But when it came time to grant the living, it was given elsewhere."

"Good heavens!" cried Elizabeth. "But how could that be? How could his will be ignored? Why did you you take legal action?"

"His will was so informal in its terms that the law could not help me. A man of honor could not have doubted my godfather's intention, but Mr. Darcy chose to doubt it—or to treat it as a mere recommendation, and to claim that I had given the position up due to extravagance, imprudence—in short, anything or nothing. What is certain is that the living became vacant two years ago, exactly as I came of age to hold it, and that it was given to another man. Just as certain is that I cannot blame myself for having done anything to deserve to lose it. I have a warm, unguarded temper, and I may have sometimes spoken my opinion of Darcy, and to him, too freely. I can recall nothing worse. But the fact is that we are very different sort of men, and that he hates me."

"This is quite shocking! He deserves to be publicly disgraced."

"Some time or other he will be—but it will not be by me. Until I can forget his father, I can never expose him."

Elizabeth thought these feelings very honorable, and he seemed handsomer than ever as he expressed them.

"But," she said after a pause, "what can have

been his motive? Why would he have behaved so cruelly?"

"A thorough dislike of me—a dislike which I cannot help but think is rooted in jealousy. If the late Mr. Darcy had liked me less, his son might have tolerated me more willingly, but his father's attachment to me irritated him. He was not the sort to tolerate any sort of competition."

"I had not thought Mr. Darcy was this bad," Elizabeth said. "I had suspected that he despised people in general, but I did not think he could descend to such malicious revenge, such injustice, such inhumanity as this!"

After a few minutes thought, however, she continued. "I do remember his boasting one day, at Netherfield, of his unforgiving temper. His disposition must be dreadful."

"I cannot trust myself to speak on the subject," replied Wickham.

After thinking further, Elizabeth exclaimed, "To treat his father's godson in such a way!" To herself, she added, "A young man like you, whose very face shows how pleasant you are," but she satisfied herself by saying, "And someone, too, who had probably been his own companion from childhood!"

"We were born in the same parish; the greatest part of our youth was passed together. We lived in the same house, shared the same amusements. My father was an attorney, like your uncle, but he gave up all his other employment to be of use to the late

Mr. Darcy, and devoted his time to the care of the Pemberley property. He was most highly esteemed by Mr. Darcy, and was an intimate, confidential friend. Mr. Darcy often said that he owed the greatest debt to my father for his overseeing of the estate. Then, immediately before my father's death, Mr. Darcy gave him a voluntary promise that he would provide for me. I am convinced that he felt it to be as much a debt of gratitude to my father as a gesture of affection to myself."

"How strange!" cried Elizabeth. "How dreadful! One would think that Mr. Darcy's pride would require him to be just to you! Isn't he too proud to be dishonest? For I must call this dishonesty."

"It is remarkable how almost all his actions are tied to his pride. Pride, indeed, has often been his best friend."

"Can such dreadful pride as his ever done him good?"

"Yes. It has often led him to be liberal and generous—to give his money freely, to display hospitality, to assist his tenants, and to help the poor. Family pride has done this. It is a powerful motive to him to never appear to disgrace his family or to lose the influence of Pemberley House. He also has brotherly pride, which with some brotherly affection, makes him a very kind and careful guardian of his sister. You will hear him generally described as the most attentive and best of brothers."

"What sort of a girl is Miss Darcy?"

He shook his head. "I wish I could praise her. It gives me pain to speak ill of a Darcy. But she is too much like her brother—very, very proud. As a child, she was affectionate and pleasant, and extremely fond of me. I have spent hours and hours amusing her. But she is nothing to me now. She is a handsome girl, about fifteen or sixteen, and, I understand, highly accomplished. Since her father's death, her home has been London. A lady lives with her there, and supervises her education."

"I am astonished at his friendship with Mr. Bingley! How can Mr. Bingley, who seems good humor itself, be connected with such a man? How can they suit each other? Do you know Mr. Bingley?"

"Not at all."

"He is a sweet tempered, amiable, charming man. He cannot know what Mr. Darcy is."

"Probably not. But Mr. Darcy can please when he chooses. He has plenty of abilities. He can be a pleasant companion if he thinks it worth his while. Among those who are his social equals, he is a very different man from what he is to the less prosperous. His pride never deserts him, but with the rich, he is liberal-minded, just, sincere, honorable, and perhaps even agreeable."

The bridge game was breaking up; the players gathered round the other table, and Mr. Collins took his place between his cousin Elizabeth and Mrs. Philips. Their hostess began to inquire what luck he had had. He replied that he had not done very well; he had lost every point. But when Mrs. Philips expressed her concern, he assured her very solemnly that it was not of the least importance, that he considered the money as a mere trifle, and begged her not to worry.

"I know very well, madam," he said, "that when persons sit down to a card table, they must take their chances. And, happily, I am not in such circumstances that I need to worry about my losses tonight. There are undoubtedly many who could not say the same, but thanks to Lady Catherine de Bourgh, I am relieved from the necessity of worrying about such little matters."

Mr. Wickham's attention was caught. After observing Mr. Collins for a few moments, he asked Elizabeth quietly whether her cousin was very intimately acquainted with the de Bourgh family.

"Lady Catherine de Bourgh," she replied, "has very lately given him the position of rector. I do not know how Mr. Collins was first introduced to her, but he certainly has not known her long."

"I suppose you know that Lady Catherine de Bourgh and Lady Anne Darcy were sisters. Consequently, she is aunt to the present Mr. Darcy."

"No, indeed, I did not. In fact, I never heard of Lady Catherine's existence until the day before yesterday."

"Her daughter, Miss de Bourgh, will have a very large fortune. It is believed that she and Mr.

Darcy will marry and unite the two estates."

This information made Elizabeth smile, as she thought of poor Miss Bingley. All her attentions to Mr. Darcy, all her affection for his sister—all were in vain, if Darcy were already planning to marry another.

"Mr. Collins speaks highly both of Lady Catherine and her daughter," said Elizabeth. "But from some stories that he has told of her ladyship, I suspect his gratitude blinds him, and that in spite of her being his patroness, she is an arrogant, conceited woman."

"I believe her to be both," replied Wickham. "I have not seen her for many years, but I very well remember that I never liked her, and that she was both bossy and rude. She has the reputation of being remarkably sensible and clever, but I believe she derives most of her reputation from her rank and fortune."

Elizabeth thought that his explanation seemed very probable, and they continued talking together until called to supper. There it was too noisy for any personal conversation, but Wickham's manners pleased everybody. Whatever he said was said well; whatever he did, he did gracefully.

Elizabeth went away with her head full of him. She could think of nothing but Mr. Wickham, and of what he had told her, all the way home. But there was not time for her even to mention his name as they traveled, for neither Lydia nor Mr. Collins were silent for a moment. Lydia talked incessantly of the games, of the prizes she had lost and the prizes she had won. Mr. Collins, in praising the civility of Mr. and Mrs. Philips, kept protesting that he did not care in the least about his losses at bridge, fondly remembering all the dishes at supper, and repeatedly worrying aloud that he crowded his cousins. He had more to say than he could manage before the carriage stopped at Longbourn House.

CHAPTER
17

The next day, Elizabeth told Jane everything that Mr. Wickham had said. Jane listened with astonishment and concern. She could scarcely believe that Mr. Darcy could be so undeserving of Mr. Bingley's good opinion. Yet it was unlike her to question the truthfulness of a nice young man like Wickham. The possibility that he had endured such unkindness touched her heart. For a person like Jane, then, all that was possible was to think well of them both, to defend the conduct of each, and assume that some dreadful mistake had been made.

"They must both have been deceived in some way or another," she concluded. "Other people with something to gain must have lied about each one to the other. It is impossible for us to know what has happened."

"Very true, indeed," answered Elizabeth, with a touch of sarcasm. "And now, my dear Jane, what do you say to defend the 'other people with something to gain' who have probably been concerned in the business? Do excuse them too, or we shall be forced to think badly of somebody."

"Laugh as much as you choose, but I will not change my opinion. My dearest Lizzy, consider what a disgrace it would be for Mr. Darcy if he had indeed treated his father's favorite in such a manner. It is impossible. No man of common humanity could be capable of it. Can his closest friends be so wrong about him? Oh, no."

"I can much more easily believe that Mr. Bingley has been misled than that Mr. Wickham had invented the story he told me last night. He named names, gave facts, all in quite a straightforward manner. If it is not true, let Mr. Darcy contradict it. Anyone could see Mr. Wickham was speaking truthfully."

"It is difficult indeed," sighed Jane. "It is distressing. One does not know what to think."

"I beg your pardon; one knows exactly what to think."

But Jane could think with certainty of only one thing—that Mr. Bingley, if he had been misled, would suffer when the story became public.

The two young ladies were interrupted by the arrival of some of the very people of whom they had been speaking. Mr. Bingley and his sisters came to give their personal invitation for the long-expected ball at Netherfield, which was scheduled for the following Tuesday.

The prospect of the Netherfield ball was extremely agreeable to every female of the family. Mrs. Bennet was certain that it was being given as a compliment to her oldest daughter, and was particularly flattered by receiving the invitation from Mr. Bingley himself. Jane pictured a happy evening in the company of her two friends and their brother. Elizabeth thought with pleasure of dancing a great deal with Mr. Wickham, and of seeing Mr. Darcy's looks and behavior confirm everything that she had been told. The happiness anticipated by Kitty and Lydia did not depend on any single event or particular person. A ball was a ball. And even Mary could assure her family that she had no distaste for it.

"As long as I can have my mornings to myself," she said, "that is enough. I think it is no sacrifice to join occasionally in evening engagements. Society has claims on us all, and I consider intervals of recreation and amusement desirable for everybody."

Elizabeth did not often speak unnecessarily to Mr. Collins. But in this case, her spirits were so high that she asked him whether he intended to accept Mr. Bingley's invitation. She was rather surprised to find that he fully intended not only to attend, but to dance.

"I assure you that I do not believe that a ball of this kind, hosted by a young man of good character, can have any evil tendency," he replied. "I do not object to dancing myself; in fact, I hope to be honored with the hands of all my fair cousins in the course of the evening. I take this opportunity to reserve yours, Miss Elizabeth, for the two first dances. I trust that my cousin Jane will recognize that this preference grows from a very proper cause, and not from any disrespect for her."

Elizabeth was horrified. She had fully expected to dance those very dances with Mr. Wickham—and to have Mr. Collins instead! Her lively spirits had never been worse timed. There was nothing to do about it, however, and she accepted Mr. Collins's invitation as graciously as she could.

She was not happy with his suggestion that his gallant invitation might have a particular cause. It occurred to her for the first time that he had chosen her as the mistress of Hunsford Parsonage. She became more convinced of this idea as she noticed his increasing attentions to herself, and listened to his frequent attempts to compliment her wit and vivacity. She was far more astonished than pleased by this effect of her charms. Worse, it was not long before her mother began hinting that the prospect of this marriage was highly agreeable to her. Elizabeth pretended not to understand, as she realized that her mother would be seriously displeased by any argument. She comforted herself with the idea that Mr. Collins might never actually propose, and that until he did, it was useless to quarrel about him.

If there had not been the ball at Netherfield to prepare for and talk about, the younger Miss Bennets would have been in a bad state. For from the day of the invitation to the day of the ball, it rained so steadily that they could not walk to Meryton once. No aunt, no officers, no news! Even

Elizabeth was impatient that the weather made it impossible for her to meet Mr. Wickham again, and nothing less than the prospect of a dance on Tuesday made Friday, Saturday, Sunday, and Monday bearable to Kitty and Lydia.

CHAPTER 18

Until Elizabeth entered the ballroom at Netherfield and looked for Mr. Wickham among the crowd of red coats, it had never occurred to her that he might not attend. She had dressed with the greatest care, and prepared in the highest spirits to win whatever part of his heart was still to be unwon. When she saw that he was not there, she instantly suspected that he had been omitted from the officers' invitation due to Mr. Darcy's interference. This was not exactly the case, however, as explained by his friend Mr. Denny, whom Lydia eagerly questioned. He told her that Wickham had been obliged to go to London on business the day before, and had not yet returned. He added, with a smile and a wink, "I do not imagine his business would have called him away just now, if he had not wanted to avoid a certain gentleman."

This remark convinced Elizabeth that Darcy was indeed to blame for Wickham's absence. Her feelings of displeasure against Darcy were so sharpened that she could barely be polite when he greeted her. To be attentive and civil to Darcy, she decided, was to injure Wickham. She was determined to avoid any conversation with him, and turned away with a degree of bad temper that she could barely hide even when speaking to Mr. Bingley, whose blindness about his friend irritated her.

But Elizabeth could never be ill-humored for long. After she had told all her troubles to Charlotte Lucas (whom she had not seen for a week), she was able to make the transition to the oddities of her cousin, whom she pointed out to Charlotte. The two first dances, however, brought a return of her distress: they were dances of pain. Mr. Collins, awkward and solemn, constantly apologizing instead of paying attention, and often moving wrong without being aware of it, gave her all the shame and misery which a disagreeable partner can give. The moment of her release from him was ecstacy.

She danced next with an officer, and had the pleasure of talking about Wickham and of hearing that everyone liked him. When those dances were over she returned to her conversation with Charlotte Lucas, when she found herself suddenly addressed by Mr. Darcy. She was so surprised by his invitation for the next dance that, without thinking, she accepted. He walked away again immediately, and she was left to fret over her own thoughtlessness.

Charlotte tried to comfort her. "You probably will find him very agreeable."

"Heaven forbid! That would be the greatest misfortune of all! To find a man agreeable when I am determined to hate him! Do not wish me such an evil."

When the dancing began again, however, and Darcy approached, Charlotte could not help warning Elizabeth in a whisper not to be an idiot. "Do not allow your fondness for Wickham to make you unpleasant to a man of such high standing!"

Elizabeth did not answer, and took her position in the dance, amazed that Mr. Darcy was allowing her to stand opposite him, and reading in her neighbors' looks their equal amazement in beholding it. They danced for some time without speaking a word, and she began to imagine that their silence would last through the two dances. At first she was detemined not to speak first, until it occurred to her that it would be greater punishment to her partner to force him to talk. She made some small observation about the dance. He replied, and was again silent. After several minutes, she spoke a second time.

"It is your turn to say something now, Mr. Darcy. I talked about the dance. Now you ought to make some kind of remark on the size of the room, or the number of couples."

He smiled, and assured her that he would say whatever she wished him to say.

"Very well. That reply will do for the present. Perhaps, eventually, I will remark that private balls are much pleasanter than public ones. But now we may be silent."

"Do you always observe rules about talking when you are dancing?"

"Sometimes. One must speak a little, you

know. It would look odd to be entirely silent for half an hour. And yet for the advantage of some, conversation should be arranged as that they may say as little as possible."

"Do you imagine that such an arrangement would please me, or is it you who desires it?"

"Both," replied Elizabeth mischievously, "for I have noticed that we are very similar in that way. We are each unsociable, grimly quiet people. We are unwilling to speak unless we are able to say something that will amaze the whole room, and be handed down to from generation to generation with all the strength of a proverb."

"This does not sound like your character at all," he said. "How much it is like mine, I cannot say. But I take it you think it is a faithful portrait."

"I cannot judge my own creation."

He did not answer, and there was another long silence until he asked her if she and her sisters often walked to Meryton. She told him that they did, and could not resist adding, "When you met us there the other day, we had just been becoming acquainted with someone new."

The effect was immediate. His face grew colder and prouder than ever, but he said not a word. Although she would have liked to say more, Elizabeth held her tongue. At length, Darcy spoke, saying, "Mr. Wickham is blessed with such a pleasant personality that he is sure of making friends. Whether he is equally capable of keeping them is less certain."

"He has been unlucky enough to lose your friendship," replied Elizabeth, "and in a way which he is likely to suffer from all his life."

Darcy did not answer, and seemed to want to change the subject. At that moment Sir William Lucas passed by them. Noticing Mr. Darcy, he stopped with a bow and began to compliment him on his dancing and his partner.

"What a pleasure this is, my dear sir. Such very superior dancing is not often seen. It is clear that you belong to the highest society. Allow me to say that your fair partner does you credit! I hope to have this pleasure often repeated, especially when a certain desirable event takes place." (Here Sir William glanced significantly at Jane and Bingley, who were dancing nearby.) "What congratulations will then flow in! I assure you, Mr. Darcy—but I must not interrupt you further, sir. You will not thank me for keeping you from the bewitching conversation of this young lady, whose bright eyes are also scolding me."

Darcy barely heard his last words, but Sir William's mention of his friend seemed to strike him with great force. He looked toward Bingley and Jane with a startled expression. Recovering himself, he turned to his partner and said, "Sir William's interruption has made me forget what we were talking of."

"I do not think we were speaking at all. Sir William could not have interrupted any two people in the room who had less to say to one another. We have tried two or three subjects without success, and I cannot imagine what we are to talk of next."

"What do you think of books?" he asked, smiling.

"Books! Oh, no. I am sure we never read the same ones, or if we do, not with the same response."

"I am sorry you think so. But if that is the case, at least it provides us with a subject. We may compare our different opinions."

"No, I cannot talk of books in a ballroom. My head is always full of something else."

"So you are always thinking of the present in such circumstances?" he said, with a look of doubt.

"Yes, always," she replied, without knowing what she said. Her thoughts had wandered far from the subject, and she suddenly said, "I remember once hearing you say, Mr. Darcy, that you hardly ever forgave, and that once your resentment is created, it could not be undone. You are very cautious, I hope, about letting it be created."

"I am," he said firmly.

"And you never allow yourself to be blinded by prejudice?"

"I hope not."

"It is particularly important that a person who never changes his opinion be certain that he judges correctly in the first place."

"May I ask what these questions are about?"

"I am merely trying to understand your character," she said, trying to sound less serious.

"And are you succeeding?"

She shook her head. "I am not. I hear such different opinions of you that it all puzzles me a great deal."

"I can easily believe that opinions about me vary a great deal," he said. "I hope, Miss Bennet, that you will not decide on my character at the present moment, as I fear the performance would not do credit to either of us."

"But if I do not decide now, I may never have another opportunity."

"I would never deny you the pleasure of doing as you like," he coldly replied. She said no more, and they completed the dance and parted in silence. Both were dissatisfied, although not in equal ways. For in Darcy's heart there was a powerful feeling for Elizabeth, which soon made him forget her impoliteness, and directed all his anger against someone else.

Soon afterward Miss Bingley came toward Elizabeth with an expression of polite scorn on her handsome face.

"So, Miss Eliza, I hear you are quite delighted with George Wickham!" she said. "Your sister has been talking to me about him and asking me a thousand questions. I find that the young man forgot to tell you that he is the son of old Wickham, the late Mr. Darcy's steward. Let me warn you, as a friend, not to believe everything he says. As far as his claims that Mr. Darcy has done him wrong, that is perfectly false. On the contrary, he has been always remarkably kind to him, though George Wickham has treated Mr. Darcy in the most dreadful manner. I do not know the details, but I know very well that Mr. Darcy is not in the least to blame. He cannot bear to hear George Wickham's name mentioned, and although my brother thought he could hardly avoid including him in his invitation to the officers, Mr. Darcy was very glad to find that he would not attend. It is really outrageous that he has come to this area at all. I pity you, Miss Eliza, to learn of your favorite's guilt. But really, considering his family connections, one could not expect much better."

"You seem to believe that his guilt and his family connections are the same thing," said Elizabeth angrily. "I have heard you accuse him of nothing worse than of being the son of Mr. Darcy's steward. That, I assure you, he told me himself."

"I beg your pardon," replied Miss Bingley, turning away with a sneer. "Excuse my interference. It was kindly meant."

"Rude, insolent girl!" said Elizabeth to herself. "You are badly mistaken if you think you can influence me like this. I see nothing in it but your own ignorance and the wickedness of Mr. Darcy." She then went to talk to Jane, who had promised to ask Bingley for details about Wickham as well.

Jane's smile of sweet satisfaction, her glow of happiness clearly showed how pleasant she was finding the evening. Elizabeth instantly read her feelings, and at that moment she forgot her concern for Wickham, and her resentment against his enemies, in favor of her hopes for Jane's happiness.

"I want to know what you have learned about Mr. Wickham," she said, smiling warmly at her sister. "But perhaps you have been too pleasantly busy to think of any third person, in which case I pardon you."

"No," replied Jane, "I have not forgotten him, but I have nothing satisfactory to tell you. Mr. Bingley does not know the whole story, and he is quite ignorant of the exact circumstances which have offended Mr. Darcy. But he is certain of the good conduct and honor of his friend, and he is convinced that Mr. Wickham has deserved less generosity from Mr. Darcy than he has received. I am sorry to say that both Mr. Bingley and his sister say that Mr. Wickham is not a respectable young man. I am afraid he has been very foolish, and has deserved to lose Mr. Darcy's good opinion."

"Mr. Bingley does not know Mr. Wickham himself?" asked Elizabeth.

"No, he never saw him until the other morning in Meryton."

"This story, then, is what he has heard from Mr. Darcy. I see. But what does he say about the position that was promised Mr. Wickham?"

"He does not exactly remember the circumstances, though he has heard them from Mr. Darcy more than once, but he believes that the position was left to him only if certain conditions were met."

"I do not doubt Mr. Bingley's sincerity," said Elizabeth, "but you must excuse my not being entirely convinced. Mr. Bingley was right to defend his friend, I am sure, but since he does not know several parts of the story, and has learned the rest from Mr. Darcy himself, I will continue to think of both gentlemen as I did before."

She then changed the subject to one that was more pleasant to both of them. Elizabeth listened with delight to Jane's happy, although modest, account of Bingley's attentions, and said everything she could to heighten Jane's confidence. When Mr. Bingley himself joined them, Elizabeth left them alone and joined Charlotte Lucas. When Charlotte asked how she had enjoyed her dance with Mr. Darcy, Elizabeth had barely begun to respond when Mr. Collins came up to them and reported with great excitement that he had just made a most important discovery.

"I have found out," he said, "quite by accident, that there is a close relative of my patroness in this very room! I happened to overhear Mr. Darcy mention the names of his cousin, Miss de Bourgh, and of her mother, Lady Catherine. What an extraordinary coincidence! Who would have thought of my meeting a nephew of Lady Catherine de Bourgh in this party! I am most thankful that I have made this discovery in time to pay my respects to him, which I am now going to do. I trust he will excuse my not having done it before."

"You are not going to introduce yourself to Mr. Darcy?" asked Elizabeth, with some alarm.

"Indeed I am. I shall beg his pardon for not having done it earlier. It will be in my power to assure him that his aunt was quite well a week ago yesterday."

Elizabeth tried hard to talk him out of this idea. She warned him that Mr. Darcy would think it was very odd and forward of him to speak before being introduced. She argued further that it was not in the least necessary that the two men should talk at all, and that if it ever became necessary, that it was up to Mr. Darcy, being the social superior, to begin the conversation.

Mr. Collins listened to her with the determined air of one who has already made up his mind. When she ceased speaking, he replied, "My dear Miss Elizabeth, I have the highest opinion in the world of your excellent judgment in all matters within the scope of your understanding. But there is a wide difference between the forms of etiquette among laypersons, and those which regulate the clergy. I, for one, consider the clergy as equal with the highest rank in the kingdom—provided that the clergyman maintains his proper humility. You must therefore allow me to obey my conscience on this occasion. Pardon me for disregarding your advice, which on every other subject shall be my constant guide. In this case, however, I consider myself more fit to decide on what is right than a young lady like yourself."

With a low bow he left her to address Mr.

Darcy. She watched his reception of Mr. Collins, and his astonishment at being spoken to in this manner was plain to see. Her cousin began his speech with a solemn bow, and though she could not hear a word of it, she felt as if she was hearing it all. Reading his lips, she saw the words "apology," "Hunsford," and "Lady Catherine de Bourgh." Mr. Darcy was looking at him with unrestrained wonder, and when Mr. Collins finally allowed him time to speak, he replied with an air of chilly politeness. Mr. Collins, however, was not discouraged from speaking again, and Mr. Darcy's contempt clearly grew with the length of this second speech. At the end of it he made only a slight bow, and moved away. Mr. Collins then returned to Elizabeth.

"I have no reason, I assure you," said he, "to be dissatisfied with my reception. Mr. Darcy seemed very pleased with the attention. He answered me with the greatest politeness, and even paid me the compliment of saying that he was certain Lady Catherine could never bestow a position unworthily. It was really a very handsome thought. Upon the whole, I am much pleased with him."

Elizabeth now turned her attention almost entirely on her sister and Mr. Bingley, and her observations of the two made her almost as happy as Jane. She imagined Jane settled in that very house, enjoying the joy of a marriage of true affection. She felt capable, under such circumstances, of even trying to like Bingley's sisters. Her mother's thoughts, she knew, were going in the same direction, and she was determined not to go near her, in case she might overhear too much.

Unluckily, when they sat down to supper, she was within easy reach of her mother. She was greatly annoyed to hear Mrs. Bennet talking to Lady Lucas—talking freely, openly, loudly, and endlessly of her expectation that Jane would soon be married to Mr. Bingley. It was an exciting subject to Mrs. Bennet, and it seemed she would never tire of describing the advantages of the match. He was such a charming young man, and so rich, and lived only three miles from them—these were the first points of self-congratulation. After that (she said), it was such a comfort to think how fond the two sisters were of Jane, and how they must desire the marriage as much as she did. It was, in addition, such a promising thing for her younger daughters, as Jane's marrying so well would throw them in the way of other rich men. And finally, it would be so pleasant, at her age, to be able to hand over her single daughters to the care of their sister, so that she (Mrs. Bennet) would not be obliged to go out in the evening more than she liked. (In fact, no one was less likely than Mrs. Bennet to find comfort in staying at home at any period of her life.) She concluded with many good wishes that Lady Lucas might soon be equally fortunate, though she clearly and triumphantly believed there was no chance of that.

Elizabeth tried unsuccessfully to persuade her to

speak less, or at least more quietly. For, to her enormous embarrassment, she saw that most of her mother's words were being heard by Mr. Darcy, who sat opposite them. Her mother only scolded her for being nonsensical.

"What is Mr. Darcy to me that I should be afraid of him? We owe him nothing. I do not care if I say anything that he may not like to hear."

"For heaven's sake, madam, speak lower. What good can come of your offending Mr. Darcy? You will never please his friend by acting so."

Nothing that she could say, however, made the slightest difference. Her mother continued to talk of her views in the same audible tone. Elizabeth blushed and blushed again with shame and irritation. She could not help frequently glancing at Mr. Darcy, although every glance confirmed what she dreaded. For although he was not always looking at her mother, she was convinced that he was listening to every word.

Finally Mrs. Bennet had no more to say; Lady Lucas, who had been yawning at this long list of delights which she saw no likelihood of sharing, was left to enjoy her supper. Elizabeth began to relax. But her period of tranquility did not last long. When supper was over, singing was suggested, and she had the humiliation of seeing Mary preparing to entertain the company. Elizabeth sent Mary many significant looks and silent pleas, but Mary refused to understand them. The opportunity of showing off was delightful to her, and she began her song.

Elizabeth listened to her sister with an impatience that was very badly rewarded at the song's end, for when Mary received the polite thanks of the guests, she detected the weakest encouragement that she might sing again, and after a pause of thirty seconds she began another.

Mary was not well prepared for such a display; her voice was weak, and her manner was silly and affected. Elizabeth was in agonies. She looked at Jane, to see how she bore it, but Jane was calmly talking to Bingley. She looked at his two sisters, and saw that they were mocking Mary, and at Darcy, who continued as grave as before. She looked at her father to beg his interference, so that Mary would not sing all night. He took the hint, and when Mary had finished her second song, he said aloud, "That will do extremely well, child. You have delighted us long enough. Let the other young ladies have time to exhibit."

Mary was embarrassed, and Elizabeth felt sorry for her. The request went out for someone else to entertain the group.

Mr. Collins spoke up. "If I were so fortunate as to be musically talented, it would give me great pleasure to entertain the party with a song, for I consider music to be a very innocent amusement, and perfectly suitable for a clergyman. I do not mean to say, however, that a clergyman is justified in devoting too much time to music, for there are certainly other things to be attended to. The rector of a parish has much to do. In the first place, he must arrange the finances of the parish in a way that is both beneficial to himself and not offensive to his patron. He must write his own sermons. The time that remains will allow for the care and improvement of his dwelling, which he cannot be excused from making as comfortable as possible. And it is of great importance that he should have attentive and pleasant manners toward everybody, especially toward those to whom he owes his position. He must never forget that duty, and I could never think well of a man who overlooked an opportunity to show his respect toward anyone connected with his patron's family." Making a low bow to Mr. Darcy, he finished his speech, which had been spoken so loudly as to be heard by half the room.

His listeners stared at Mr. Collins in astonishment. Many smiled, but no one looked more amused than Mr. Bennet. Meanwhile, Mrs. Bennet observed in a loud half-whisper to Lady Lucas that Mr. Collins was a remarkably clever, good kind of young man.

To Elizabeth, it seemed as though her family had made a secret agreement to show themselves in the worst possible light all evening. Surely it would have been impossible for them to play their parts with more spirit or better success. Her only relief was to think that Bingley had not been a witness to some of the most embarrassing moments. The fact that his two sisters and Mr. Darcy had such an opportunity to ridicule her relations was bad enough. She could not decide whether the silent contempt of the gentleman, or the insolent smiles of the ladies, were more unbearable.

The rest of the evening got no better. Mr. Collins attached himself to her side, and although he could not persuade her to dance again, he made it impossible for her to dance with anyone else. She begged him to invite someone else to dance, and offered to introduce him to any young lady in the room. He assured her that he did not really care to dance, but that his chief desire was to increase his warm friendship with her, and, therefore, he should remain close to her for the entire evening. There was no arguing with him. Her only relief came from her friend Charlotte Lucas, who often joined them and good-naturedly engaged Mr. Collins in conversation.

She was at least free from any further attention from Mr. Darcy; although he was often standing quite near her, he never came close enough to speak. She felt confident that his silence was the result of her allusion to Mr. Wickham, and she was glad of it.

The Bennet party was the last of all to leave the ball, and by a deliberate trick of Mrs. Bennet's, they had to wait for their carriage for a quarter hour after everybody else was gone. This gave them time to see how heartily some of the family wished they would leave. Mrs. Hurst and her sister scarcely opened their mouths, except to complain of how tired they were, and they were obviously impatient to have the house to themselves. They ignored every attempt of Mrs. Bennet at conversation. The resulting silence was broken by the long speeches of Mr. Collins, who complimented Mr. Bingley and his sisters endlessly on the elegance of their entertainment, and of their hospitality and politeness. Darcy said nothing at all. Mr. Bennet, in equal silence, was enjoying the scene. Mr. Bingley and Jane were standing together, a little apart from the rest, and talked only to each other. Elizabeth was as steadily silent as either Mrs. Hurst or Miss Bingley, and even Lydia was too fatigued to offer more than the occasional exclamation of "Lord, how tired I am!" accompanied by a noisy yawn.

When their carriage finally arrived, Mrs. Bennet was insistent in hoping that she would see the whole family soon at Longbourn. Speaking especially to Mr. Bingley, she assured him how happy he would make her by eating a family dinner with them at any time, without any formal invitation. Bingley indicated his grateful pleasure, and he readily agreed to visit her very soon after his return from London, where he was unfortunately obliged to go the next day.

Mrs. Bennet was perfectly satisfied, and left the house under the delightful impression that, allowing time for the preparations of new carriages and wedding clothes, she would surely see her daughter living at Netherfield within three or four months.

She was equally certain of having another daughter married to Mr. Collins—a thought that gave her considerable, if not equal, pleasure. She liked Elizabeth the least of all her children, and thought the man and the match were quite good enough for her.

CHAPTER
19

The next day opened a new chapter at Longbourn. Mr. Collins made his proposal. He had decided to do it promptly, as his leave of absence extended only until the following Saturday. When he found Mrs. Bennet, Elizabeth, and one of the younger girls together soon after breakfast, he addressed the mother: "May I hope, madam, that you will allow me the honor of a private meeting this morning with your fair daughter Elizabeth?"

Before Elizabeth had time for anything but a blush of surprise, Mrs. Bennet answered, "Oh dear! Yes, certainly! I am sure Lizzy will be very happy. I am sure she can have no objection. Come, Kitty, I want you upstairs." And gathering her work together, she was hurrying away when Elizabeth called out, "Dear Mother, do not go! I beg you not to go. Mr. Collins can have nothing to say to me that you may not hear. I am going out myself."

"No, no, nonsense, Lizzy; I want you to stay where you are." Seeing that Elizabeth seemed truly about to escape, she added sharply, "Lizzy, I insist that you stay and hear Mr. Collins."

Elizabeth would not disobey her mother's direct command, and a moment's thought made her also realize that it would be best to get this over with as soon, and as quietly, as possible. So she sat down again, trying to conceal her feelings, which were divided between irritation and amusement. Mrs. Bennet and Kitty walked off, and as soon as they were gone Mr. Collins began.

"Believe me, my dear Miss Elizabeth, that your modesty only makes you appear more perfect in my eyes. This little maidenly unwillingness is most charming, but allow me to assure you that I have your respected mother's permission to speak to you thus. You must know the reason for my asking for this meeting, even though your natural delicacy may lead you to pretend to misunderstand. My attentions to you have been too obvious to be mistaken. Almost as soon as I entered this house I singled you out as the companion of my future life. But before I allow my feelings to run away with me, perhaps I should state my reasons for marrying— and, more, my reasons for coming here with the plan of selecting a wife, as I certainly did."

The idea of solemn, pompous Mr. Collins being run away with by his feelings made Elizabeth want to laugh so badly that she could not interrupt him, and he continued.

"My reasons for marrying are, first, that I think it is the right thing for every clergyman in easy circumstances (like myself) to set the example of matrimony in his parish. Secondly, I am convinced that marriage will add very greatly to my happiness. And thirdly, I have been particularly advised to marry by the very noble lady whom I have the honor of calling my patroness. She has been so good as to give me her opinion on this matter twice. It was the very Saturday night before I left Hunsford that she said, 'Mr. Collins, you must marry. A clergyman like you must marry. Choose properly! Choose a gentlewoman for my sake, and for your own, let her be an active, useful sort of person, not brought up high, but able to make a small income go a good way. This is my advice. Find such a woman as soon as you can, bring her to Hunsford, and I will visit her.'

"Allow me to observe, my fair cousin, that the notice and kindness of Lady Catherine de Bourgh are not the least among the advantages I can offer you. You will find her manners beyond anything I can describe, and your wit and liveliness, I think, will be acceptable to her, especially when restrained by the silence and humility which you will no doubt show her. Thus, you understand my general intention to marry. I will now explain why I have looked to Longbourn for a wife instead of my own neighborhood, where I assure you there are many amiable young women. As the fact is that I will inherit this estate after the death of your honored father, I think it only right that I choose a wife from among his daughters, so that his loss will be felt as little as possible. This is my motive, my fair cousin, and I flatter myself that you will not think less of me for it. And now nothing remains for me but to assure you of the depth of my affection. I care nothing for your fortune, and I shall make no financial demand on your father. On that point, therefore, I shall be absolutely silent. You may be assured that I will never reproach you for your poverty when we are married."

It was absolutely necessary to interrupt him now.

"You are too hasty, sir!" she exclaimed. "You forget that I have not answered you. Let me do it without further delay. Thank you sincerely for the compliment you are paying me. I am very aware of the honor of your proposal, but it is absolutely necessary for me to decline."

"I have long been aware," replied Mr. Collins, with a wave of his hand, "that young ladies frequently reject the proposal of the man who they secretly mean to accept when he first asks for their hand. Sometimes this refusal is repeated a second or even a third time. I am therefore not at all discouraged by what you have just said, and I shall hope to lead you to the altar before long."

"Upon my word, sir," cried Elizabeth, "your hope is a strange one after what I have just said. I promise you that I am not one of those young ladies (if they truly exist) who are so reckless as to risk their happiness on the chance of being asked a second time. I am perfectly serious in my refusal.

You could not make me happy, and I am convinced that I am the last woman in the world who would make you happy. Indeed, I am sure that if your friend Lady Catherine knew me, she would find me unsuitable in every way."

"Oh, I cannot imagine that her ladyship would at all disapprove of you," Mr. Collins said reassuringly. "And you may be certain that when I have the honor of seeing her again, I shall speak in the highest terms of your modesty, economy, and other qualifications."

"Indeed, Mr. Collins, it will not be necessary to praise me at all. You must allow me to judge for myself, and honor me by believing what I say. I hope that you will be very happy and very rich, and by refusing your hand, I am doing all that I can to prevent you from being otherwise. In making me this offer, you have honored your concerns about my family, and you may take possession of the estate without any self-blame. This matter is quite settled." She rose from her chair and would have left the room if Mr. Collins had not spoken again.

"When I do myself the honor of speaking to you next on this subject, I will hope to receive a more favorable answer. I am not accusing you of cruelty at present, because I know it is the custom of your sex to reject a man at his first proposal. Your words have, indeed, only encouraged me to regard you as a truly delicate female character."

"Really, Mr. Collins," cried Elizabeth with

some anger, "you puzzle me greatly! If you inter-
pret what I have said as encouragement, I really do
not know how to express my refusal in such a way
that you will believe."

"I flatter myself, my dear cousin, that your
refusal is merely a convention of form. My reasons
for thinking thus are these: It does not seem to me
that my hand is unworthy of your acceptance. The
establishment that I can offer you is highly desirable. My situation in life, my connections with the
de Bourgh family, and my relationship to your own
family, are circumstances highly in its favor. You
should take into consideration, too, that in spite of
your many attractions, it is by no means certain that
anyone else will want to marry you. Your fortune is
unhappily so small that it will, in all likelihood,
undo the effects of your loveliness and fine qualities. Therefore, I must conclude that you are not
serious in your rejection of me. I choose to believe
it is due to your wish to increase my love by suspense, as is common practice among elegant
females."

"I do assure you, sir, that I do not admire the
kind of elegance which involves tormenting a
respectable man," Elizabeth answered indignantly.
"I would rather you compliment me by believing
that I am sincere. I thank you again and again for
the honor you have done me in your proposal, but
to accept it is absolutely impossible. My feelings
completely forbid it. Can I speak plainer? Do not

consider me now an elegant female intending to tease you, but a rational creature speaking the truth from her heart."

"You are entirely charming!" he cried, with an air of awkward gallantry. "And I am sure that when my proposal is backed by the authority of both your excellent parents, it will not fail to be acceptable."

To such stubborn self-deception, Elizabeth could make no reply, and she silently left the room. If Mr. Collins persisted, she decided to beg her father's assistance. His refusal to Mr. Collins, at least, could not be mistaken for the pretense of an elegant female.

CHAPTER 20

Mr. Collins was not left for long to silently think about the success of his proposal, for Mrs. Bennet had been lurking nearby to watch for the end of the conference. As soon as she saw Elizabeth leave the room, she herself darted in and began to congratulate both Mr. Collins and herself on the prospect of the coming wedding. Mr. Collins received and returned these good wishes with equal pleasure, but then proceeded to tell the details of his interview with Elizabeth. He assured Mrs. Bennet that he was not at all discouraged, since he understood that Elizabeth's refusal had flowed naturally from her bashful modesty and maidenly reserve.

This information, however, startled Mrs. Bennet. She would have loved to believe that her daughter had refused Mr. Collins only as a means of encouraging him, but she knew Elizabeth too well. She could not help saying so.

"But believe me, Mr. Collins"; she added, "Lizzy shall be brought to reason. I will speak to her about it immediately. She is a headstrong, foolish girl, and does not know what is good for her, but I will make her know it."

"Pardon me for interrupting you, madam," cried Mr. Collins, "but if she is really headstrong and foolish, I do not know if she would be a desirable wife for a man like me. If she actually insists on rejecting my proposal, perhaps it is better not to force her to accept it."

"Sir, you quite misunderstand me," said Mrs. Bennet in alarm. "Lizzy is only headstrong in matters such as these. In everything else she is as good-natured a girl as ever lived. I will go directly to Mr. Bennet, and we shall very soon settle this matter, I am sure."

Without giving him time to reply she hurried instantly to her husband, calling out as she entered the library, "Oh! Mr. Bennet, you are needed immediately; we are all in an uproar. You must come and make Lizzy marry Mr. Collins, for she vows she will not have him, and if you do not hurry, he will change his mind and not have her."

Mr. Bennet raised his eyes from his book as she entered, and looked at her calmly.

"I do not understand you," he said, when she had finished her speech. "What are you talking about?"

"Of Mr. Collins and Lizzy! Lizzy declares she will not have Mr. Collins, and Mr. Collins begins to say that he will not have Lizzy."

"Well, it seems a hopeless business, then. What am I to do?"

"Speak to Lizzy about it yourself! Tell her that you insist upon her marrying him."

"Call her down. She shall hear my opinion."

Mrs. Bennet rang the bell, and Miss Elizabeth was summoned to the library.

"Come here, child," said her father as she appeared. "I have sent for you on important business. I understand that Mr. Collins has made you an offer of marriage. Is it true?" Elizabeth replied that it was. "Very well. And you have refused this offer?"

"I have, sir."

"Very well. We now come to the point. Your mother insists that you accept him. Is that not so, Mrs. Bennet?"

"Yes, or I will never see her again."

"An unhappy choice is before you, Elizabeth," said Mr. Bennet. "From this day you must be a stranger to one of your parents. Your mother will never see you again if you do not marry Mr. Collins, and I will never see you again if you do."

Elizabeth could not help but smile at this unexpected statement, but Mrs. Bennet (who had convinced herself that her husband felt as she did) was excessively disappointed.

"What do you mean, Mr. Bennet, by talking in this way? You promised me you would make her marry him."

"My dear," replied her husband, "I have two small favors to ask. First, that you allow me to use my best judgment in this situation, and secondly, that you let me have my library to myself again."

In spite of her disappointment in her husband, Mrs. Bennet was not ready to give up the fight. She talked to Elizabeth again and again, coaxing and threatening her by turns. She tried to involve Jane, but Jane politely refused to interfere. Meanwhile, Elizabeth replied to her mother's attacks, sometimes earnestly and sometimes playfully, but always with the same steadfast determination.

Mr. Collins, meanwhile, was thinking in solitude about what had happened. He thought too highly of himself to understand why his cousin had refused him. Although his pride was hurt, he did not suffer in any other way. His affection for Elizabeth was quite imaginary, and the possibility that she was indeed headstrong prevented him from feeling any regret.

While the family was in this confusion, Charlotte Lucas came by to spend the day with them. She was met in the entryway by Lydia, who ran to her, whispering, "I am glad you have come, for something so funny is going on! What do you think has happened this morning? Mr. Collins has proposed to Lizzy, and Lizzy will not have him."

Charlotte hardly had time to answer before Kitty rushed in to tell the same news. As soon as they had entered the breakfast room, where Mrs. Bennet was alone, she began on the subject as well. She begged Charlotte to persuade her friend Lizzy to go along with the wishes of all her family. "Please do, my dear Miss Lucas," she added in a melancholy tone, "for nobody is on my side, nobody helps me. I am very badly used, and nobody feels for my poor nerves."

Before Charlotte could reply, Jane and Elizabeth entered.

"Oh yes, there she is," cried Mrs. Bennet, "looking as unconcerned as can be, and caring no more for us than if we were in London, provided that she can have her own way. But I tell you what, Miss Lizzy, if you go on refusing every offer of marriage in this way, you will never get a husband at all, and I am sure I do not know who will support you when your father is dead. I won't be able to keep you, so I warn you, I will be done with you from this very day. I told you in the library, you know, that I would never speak to you again, and I mean it. Speaking with ungrateful, undutiful children gives me no pleasure. But indeed, I do not have much pleasure in talking to anybody. People who suffer from nerves as I do are never inclined to talk much. Nobody can tell what I suffer! But it is always so. People who suffer silently like me are never pitied."

Her daughters listened in silence to this torrent of words, knowing that any attempt to reason with her or soothe her would only irritate her further. She, therefore, talked on and on without interruption from any of them until they were joined by Mr. Collins. He entered looking more pompous than usual, and when she saw him she said to the girls, "Now, I insist, all of you, hold your tongues, and let

Mr. Collins and me have a little conversation together."

Elizabeth left the room quietly, and Jane and Kitty followed. But Lydia stood her ground, determined to hear all she could. Charlotte was delayed first by Mr. Collins, who asked in great detail about herself and her family, and then by curiosity—she strolled to look out the window and pretended not to be listening. In a tragic voice Mrs. Bennet began: "Oh! Mr. Collins—"

"My dear madam," he interrupted, "let us be forever silent on this matter. Far be it from me," he continued, in a voice dripping with displeasure, "to resent the behavior of your daughter. We all must learn to gracefully accept the evils of life, and I am ready to accept this one. It is easier to accept since I have come to question my happiness if my fair cousin had honored me with her hand. For I have often observed that it is easier to resign oneself to loss when the object lost begins to lose something of its value. You will not, I hope, believe me to be disrespectful to your family if I now withdraw my offer to your daughter without having asked you and Mr. Bennet to use your authority on my behalf. I have certainly meant well through the whole affair. My desire was to secure an amiable companion for myself, with due consideration for the advantage of all your family. If my manner has been in any way objectionable, I beg leave to apologize."

The discussion of Mr. Collins's proposal was now nearly over, and Elizabeth had only to put up with her own discomfort and the occasional resentful remark from her mother. As for Mr. Collins himself, he expressed his feelings, not by seeming embarrassed or depressed, but by being stiff and resentfully silent. He scarcely spoke to Elizabeth, and he spent the rest of the day showering his attention on Miss Lucas, whose willingness to good-naturedly listen to him was a great relief to everyone, especially Elizabeth.

The next day Mrs. Bennet was still in a very bad mood, and Mr. Collins stalked about in the same state of injured pride. Elizabeth had hoped that his anger might make him shorten his visit, but this did not seem to be the case. He had planned to stay until Saturday, and until Saturday he would stay.

After breakfast, the girls walked to Meryton to see if Mr. Wickham had returned and to complain about his absence from the Netherfield ball. He met them as they entered the town and accompanied them to their aunt's, where he spoke of his regret over having missed the dance. To Elizabeth, however, he privately admitted that it had been his own choice not to attend.

"As the time for the ball drew near," he explained, "I realized that it was better that I not meet Mr. Darcy. To be in the same room with him for the whole evening might be more than I could bear. I was concerned that a scene might develop which would be unpleasant to everyone."

She greatly approved his self-discipline, and they enjoyed a long talk during the walk back to Longbourn, as Wickham and another officer offered to accompany them. She was delighted by his company for two reasons: first, she recognized it as a compliment to herself; and second, it offered an excellent opportunity to introduce him to her father and mother.

Soon after their return, a letter arrived from Netherfield for Jane. Elizabeth noticed that it was written in a lady's elegant hand, and she saw her sister's face fall as she read it. Jane put the letter away and tried to join the conversation with her usual cheerfulness, but Elizabeth detected an anxiety which distracted her even from Wickham. As soon as he and his companion had left, the two girls went upstairs. Once in their own room, Jane took out the letter and said, "This is from Caroline Bingley. What she says has surprised me a good deal. The whole group has left Netherfield and are on their way to London, and they do not have any intention of coming back again. I will read you what she says."

She read the first few lines, which informed her that the group had decided to follow Mr. Bingley to London. Next Caroline wrote,

> I will not pretend that I will miss anything in Hertfordshire except for your companionship, my dearest friend. But we will hope to be able to meet again in the future, and until then I shall depend on having frequent letters from you.

To these warm declarations of friendship, Elizabeth listened with a growing sense of distrust. She comforted herself with the thought that while their departure from Netherfield was sudden, there was nothing about it that would prevent Mr. Bingley from soon returning there.

"It is unlucky that you were not able to see your friends before they left," Elizabeth said. "But certainly your reunion will occur earlier than Miss Bingley knows, and that you may soon know her as a sister-in-law. For surely Mr. Bingley will not stay in London simply because they are there."

Jane shook her head. "Caroline says that none of the party will return to Hertfordshire this winter. I will read it to you."

> When my brother left us yesterday, he imagined that the business which took him to London might be finished in three or four days. But we are certain it will take much longer, and we are also convinced that when Charles gets to town he will be in no hurry to leave it again. So we have

determined on following him there, that we may enjoy one another's company. Many of my acquaintances are already there for the winter. I wish that you, my dearest friend, would be there as well, but I know that is not to be. I sincerely hope your Christmas in Hertfordshire may be very joyful, and that your admirers will be so numerous that you will not feel the loss of the three that we are taking away."

"It is clear from this that he will not be back this winter," added Jane.

"It is only clear that Miss Bingley does not want him to return," retorted Elizabeth.

"Why do you say that? It must be his own decision; he is his own master. But you do not know everything. I will read you the part which particularly hurts me. I will not have any secrets from you."

She opened the letter again and read:

Mr. Darcy is impatient to see his sister, and to tell the truth, so are we. I really do not think that Georgiana Darcy has any equal for her beauty, elegance, and accomplishments. The affection that Louisa and I feel for her is heightened by our hope that she will soon be our sister-in-law. I do not remember whether I ever mentioned this subject to you before. My brother already admires her greatly, and now he will have the opportunity of seeing her almost every day. Her relatives all want the match as much as we do, and (granted that I am a fond sister), I do believe that Charles is capable of capturing any woman's heart. With all these advantages and no disadvantages to the match, am I wrong, my dearest Jane, to hope for an event which will make so many people happy?

"What do you think of this, my dear Lizzy?" asked Jane as she finished. "Isn't it clear enough? It tells me that Caroline neither expects nor wishes me to be her sister, that her brother is indifferent to me, and that if she suspects the nature of my feelings for him, she means—very kindly!—to put me on my guard. Can there be any other opinion on the subject?"

"Yes, there can, for mine is totally different. May I tell it to you?"

"Of course."

"It is simple enough. Miss Bingley sees that her brother is in love with you, and she wants him to marry Miss Darcy. She has followed him to town in the hopes of keeping him there, and is trying to persuade you that he does not care about you."

Jane shook her head, but Elizabeth went on impatiently.

"Indeed, Jane, you ought to believe me. No one who has ever seen you together can doubt his affection. Miss Bingley sees it; she is not such an idiot. If she had seen half as much affection from Mr. Darcy for herself, she would have ordered her wedding clothes. But the problem is this: We are not rich enough or grand enough for them. She is anxious to get Miss Darcy for her brother, thinking that if there is one marriage between the families, she may be able to bring a second one about. Her idea is ingenious, and I dare say she might succeed, if Miss de Bourgh were out of the way. But, my dearest Jane, you cannot seriously imagine, simply because Miss Bingley tells you her brother admires Miss Darcy, that he is a particle less in love with you than he was last Tuesday. And you cannot believe that it is within Miss Bingley's powers to persuade him that, instead of being in love with you, he is in love with her friend."

"I cannot believe that of Miss Bingley," replied Jane. "I know her too well. Caroline could not deliberately lie to anyone. All that I can hope is that she is mistaken."

"That is right. Believe that idea, if you will not believe mine. Believe her to be deceived. You have now done your duty, and you must fret no longer."

"But, my dear Lizzy . . . Even supposing the best, can I be happy in accepting a man whose sisters and friends all want him to marry elsewhere?"

"You must decide for yourself," said Elizabeth. "After you've thought about it carefully, if your misery at displeasing his sisters outweighs the happiness of being his wife, I most definitely advise you to refuse him."

"You are laughing on me," said Jane, smiling faintly. "You must know that while I would be very sorry to disappoint them, I could not hesitate. But if he does not return this winter, I will never have to make that choice. A thousand things could happen in six months!"

Elizabeth treated the idea of his not returning with the utmost contempt. She believed it to be merely Caroline's wish, and she could not believe for a moment that those wishes could so strongly influence an independent young man.

She explained her views to her sister, and soon had the pleasure of seeing Jane's hopes rising again. The sisters agreed that they would tell Mrs. Bennet only that the family had left, without adding any of the more alarming portions of the letter. Even this information concerned her greatly, and she wailed that it was very unlucky that the ladies should happen to go away just as they were all getting to be such good friends. After mourning, she comforted herself by thinking that Mr. Bingley would soon be down again and would dine at Longbourn. She concluded by declaring that, although he had been invited only to a family dinner, she would take care to make it a magnificent one.

CHAPTER
22

The Bennets were invited to dine with the Lucases, and again Miss Lucas was kind enough to listen to Mr. Collins. Elizabeth thanked her privately. "It keeps him in a good mood," she said, "and I am more grateful to you than I can say." Charlotte assured her friend that it was very little bother. This was very pleasant of her, but Charlotte's kindness had a motive that Elizabeth never dreamed of: she had determined to obtain Mr. Collins's affections for herself. Such was her scheme, and all was going so well that when they parted that night, she would have felt almost sure of success if he had not been scheduled to leave Hertfordshire so very soon. But here, she did too little credit to the fire and independence of his character. For he left Longbourn House the next morning, with admirable slyness, and hurried to Lucas Lodge to throw himself at her feet.

He was anxious to avoid his cousins' attention, for he knew that if they saw him depart, they would almost surely guess his purpose. He was not willing to have his plan known until he was sure of success. And while Charlotte had been encouraging, he felt a certain lack of confidence since his adventure on Wednesday.

His reception, however, was of the most flattering kind. From an upstairs window, Miss Lucas spied him walking toward the house. She instantly set out to meet him accidentally in the lane. She had never dared to hope that so much love and wordiness awaited her there.

In as short a time as Mr. Collins's long speeches would allow, everything was settled between them. As they entered the house, he earnestly begged her to name the day that she would make him the happiest of men. The lady was pleased to do so. Mr. Collins's stupidity drained his courtship of any charms that could make a woman wish for it to last long, and Miss Lucas, who accepted him only from the pure desire of gaining her own house and home, was glad to claim those benefits soon.

Sir William and Lady Lucas were asked for their consent, which they granted with joyful eagerness. Mr. Collins's circumstances made him an excellent match for their daughter (to whom they could give little money), and his prospects of future wealth were very good. Lady Lucas immediately began to calculate how many more years Mr. Bennet was likely to live. The whole family, in short, was overjoyed. The younger girls began to hope that they might be allowed to formally come out and attend balls in a year or two sooner than they might have otherwise, and the boys were relieved of their fears that Charlotte might die an old maid.

Charlotte herself was calm and collected; she had attained her goal. Mr. Collins, it is true, was not a sensible or likeable man. He was irritating company, and his affection for her was clearly imaginary. But still, he would be her husband.

Although Charlotte did not think highly either of men or of matrimony, she had always intended to get married. Marriage was the only respectable course of action for well-educated young women who were not wealthy. Although their marriages might give them little happiness, they were at least their safest insurance against poverty. Charlotte now had this insurance, and as a woman of twenty-seven who had never been pretty, she felt fortunate. Her only regret in the whole business was that she knew how it would surprise Elizabeth, whose friendship she valued more than that of anyone else. Elizabeth would be shocked and probably would think badly of her. Although Charlotte was determined to go through with the marriage, the thought of Elizabeth's disapproval was painful to her. She decided she needed to tell Elizabeth herself, and, therefore, asked Mr. Collins to say nothing when he returned to Longbourn. He dutifully promised, but it was a promise difficult to keep, for the family was curious about his long absence and asked many questions, while he, of course, was bursting to announce his success.

As he was going to depart for home too early on Saturday morning to see any of the family, he said his farewells late Friday evening. Mrs. Bennet politely told him how happy they would be to see him at Longbourn again, whenever he could find the time to visit them.

"My dear madam," he replied, "this invitation is particularly welcome, because it is exactly what I had been hoping to receive. You may be very certain that I shall return as soon as possible."

They were all astonished, and Mr. Bennet (who most certainly did not want him to return) immediately said, "But is there no danger that Lady Catherine might disapprove, my good sir? You had better neglect your relations than run the risk of offending your patroness."

"My dear sir," replied Mr. Collins, "I am exceedingly grateful to you for this friendly warning, and you may depend that I will not take such a step without her ladyship's approval."

"You cannot be too careful," Mr. Bennet warned. "Risk anything other than her displeasure. If you think there is the smallest chance she will resent your leaving to come here again (and I believe that is extremely probable), why, you should stay quietly at home. Please believe that we shall not be offended."

"Believe me, my dear sir, I cannot fully express the gratitude I feel for your affectionate attention. You may trust that you will speedily receive a letter of thanks from me for this, as well as for every other kindness you have shown during my stay in Hertfordshire. And now, my fair cousins, though my absence may not be long enough to make it necessary, I take the liberty of wishing you all health and happiness, even my cousin Elizabeth."

The ladies were all greatly surprised to learn that he planned a quick return. Mrs. Bennet decided that it meant he was going to court one of her younger girls, and she thought that Mary might accept him. She thought more highly of him than any of the other sisters did; she believed that if he were encouraged to read and improve himself by following her example, he might become an agreeable companion. But on the following morning, every hope of this kind vanished. Miss Lucas came by soon after breakfast, and privately told Elizabeth all that had happened the day before.

It had occurred to Elizabeth within the last day or two that Mr. Collins might imagine himself in love with her friend. But the idea that Charlotte would encourage him seemed utterly absurd. Her astonishment was so great at the news that she could not help crying out, "Engaged to Mr. Collins! My dear Charlotte—impossible!"

Miss Lucas's calm attitude deserted her for a moment, to be replaced by discomfort at Elizabeth's words. But after a moment she replied, "Why should you be surprised, my dear Eliza? Do you think it is impossible that Mr. Collins could deserve any woman's good opinion, because he was not so fortunate as to succeed with you?"

Ashamed of her outburst, Elizabeth assured Charlotte that she was very pleased for her, and that she wished her all imaginable happiness.

"I know what you are feeling," replied Charlotte. "You must be surprised, very much surprised, since Mr. Collins so recently wanted to marry you. But when you have had time to think it over, I think you will understand. I am not a romantic, you know. I never was. I ask only a comfortable home. Considering Mr. Collins's character and his situation in life, I believe that my chance of happiness with him is as good as most people entering into marriage."

Elizabeth quietly answered "Undoubtedly." After an awkward pause, they returned to join the family. Charlotte did not stay much longer, and Elizabeth was then left to think about what she had heard.

It was a long time before she became used to the idea of such an unsuitable match. The strangeness of Mr. Collins's making two offers of marriage within three days was nothing compared to the strangeness of Charlotte accepting him. Elizabeth had always known that Charlotte thought about marriage differently than she did, but she never would have imagined that her friend would marry only for the sake of material comfort. Charlotte the wife of Mr. Collins! What an awful thought. Elizabeth felt pain for two reasons: First, she thought that Charlotte had disgraced herself, and secondly, she could not believe that her friend would be at all happy with the fate she had chosen.

CHAPTER
23

Elizabeth was sitting with her mother and sisters, thinking about what she had heard and wondering if she was expected to tell her family, when Sir William Lucas himself appeared. He had been sent by his daughter to announce her engagement. After paying many polite compliments to them he announced his news to an audience that was not merely surprised, but unbelieving.

Mrs. Bennet protested that he had to be mistaken, and Lydia (who always talked too much, often rudely) loudly exclaimed, "Good Lord! Sir William, how can you tell such a lie? Don't you know that Mr. Collins wants to marry Lizzy?"

Only someone with Sir William's excellent manners could have responded without anger, but he politely assured them he was telling the truth and listened to their arguments with the greatest courtesy.

Elizabeth felt obligated to support Sir William, so she told about her conversation with Charlotte. She tried to silence her mother and sisters by warmly congratulating Sir William and by pointing out all the good points of the marriage.

Mrs. Bennet was too stunned to say a great deal

while Sir William was there, but as soon as he left she found her tongue. In the first place, she insisted, the whole matter was not true; secondly, she was very sure that Mr. Collins had been trapped in some most dishonest way; third, she knew that they would never be happy together; and fourth, the engagement might be broken off. She was utterly certain of two things: one, that Elizabeth was the real cause of all the mischief; and two, that she herself had been very badly used by all of them. She talked of these two points endlessly for the rest of the day. Nothing could comfort her, and one day was not enough to wear out her resentment. A week passed before she could see Elizabeth without scolding her. It was a full month before she could speak to Sir William or Lady Lucas without being rude. Many months were gone before she could begin to forgive Charlotte.

Mr. Bennet's emotions were far calmer than those of his wife; in fact he claimed to be pleased. It was satisfying, he said, to discover that Charlotte Lucas, whom he used to think quite sensible, was as foolish as his wife, and more foolish than his daughter.

Jane admitted that she was surprised at the match, but she warmly expressed her sincere desire for their happiness. Elizabeth tried and failed to persuade her that Charlotte could never be happy in such a marriage. Kitty and Lydia did not envy Charlotte, for Mr. Collins was only a clergyman. To them, this was only a piece of gossip to spread at Meryton.

Lady Lucas, of course, felt quite triumphant about having a well-married daughter when Mrs. Bennet, after all her talk, had not a single wedding on the horizon. She visited Longbourn more often than usual to say how happy she was, although Mrs. Bennet's sour looks and ill-natured remarks might have been enough to drive anyone's happiness away.

The discomfort that now existed between Elizabeth and Charlotte kept them from talking of the coming wedding, and Elizabeth could not believe that they would ever be such close friends again. As a result she turned more than ever to her sister, whose happiness she worried about more every day. Bingley had now been gone for a week, and nothing was heard about his return.

Jane had answered Caroline's letter promptly, and was counting the days until she might reasonably expect to hear from her again. The letter of thanks that Mr. Collins had promised arrived on Tuesday. It was written with all the solemn gratitude that he might have felt if he had lived with the Bennets for a full year. After expressing his thanks, he proceeded to inform them (with many flowery expressions) of his happiness in having obtained the affection of Miss Lucas. He explained that it was in order to see her again that he had accepted their kind invitation to return to Longbourn. He announced that he would be returning in two weeks, for Lady Catherine so heartily approved of his marriage plans that she wished it to take place as soon as possible.

The idea of Mr. Collins coming back to Hertfordshire no longer pleased Mrs. Bennet. On the contrary, she was as unhappy about it as was her husband. She complained loudly that it was very odd that Mr. Collins should come to Longbourn instead of to Lucas Lodge; it was also very inconvenient and troublesome. She added that she hated having visitors in the house while her health was so poor, and that lovers (of all people) made the most disagreeable guests. These were the kinds of gentle murmurs heard from Mrs. Bennet, and she interrupted them only to complain about Bingley's continued absence.

Neither Jane nor Elizabeth were comfortable with this subject. Day after day passed without bringing any news about him. The rumor in Meryton was that he would not return to Netherfield all winter. This report enraged Mrs. Bennet, and whenever she heard it she contradicted it as the most outrageous falsehood.

Elizabeth was beginning to really worry. She could not believe that Bingley didn't care for Jane, but she was afraid that his sisters would succeed in keeping him away. She hated to admit this fear, as it was destructive to Jane's happiness, and it reflected badly on Bingley, but she could not help feeling it. The united efforts of his two sisters and of his powerful friend, assisted by the attractions of Miss Darcy and the amusements of London, might overwhelm the attachment he felt to Jane.

Jane was even more anxious than Elizabeth, but

she hid her feelings and never spoke of the subject. Naturally, her mother felt no such restraint. Hardly an hour passed in which Mrs. Bennet did not mention Bingley, express her impatience for his return, and insist that Jane should feel she had been very badly used if he did not come back. It took all of Jane's steady mildness to listen calmly to her mother.

Mr. Collins returned to Longbourn punctually two weeks later. His welcome was not quite as warm as the first had been. He was too happy, however, to need much attention. Luckily for the Bennets, the business of courting Charlotte took up most of his time. He spent the better part of every day at Lucas Lodge, and he sometimes returned to Longbourn only in time to apologize for his absence before the family went to bed.

Mrs. Bennet was really in a pitiful state. The very mention of the marriage threw her into an agony of ill humor, and wherever she went she heard the marriage talked about. She hated the very sight of Miss Lucas. Whenever Charlotte entered the house, Mrs. Bennet regarded her with jealous horror. Whenever Charlotte spoke in a low voice to Mr. Collins, Mrs. Bennet was convinced that they were talking about the Longbourn estate, and planning how they would throw her and her daughters out of the house as soon as Mr. Bennet died. She complained bitterly of all this to her husband.

"Indeed, Mr. Bennet," she said, "it is very hard to think that Charlotte Lucas will be mistress of this house, and that I will live to see her take my place in it!"

"My dear, do not give way to such gloomy thoughts. Let us hope for better things. Perhaps you will die before I do."

This was not very comforting to Mrs. Bennet, so without answering, she went on as before. "I cannot bear to think that they should have this estate. The fault is all in this wicked entail. How anyone could entail away an estate from one's own daughters I will never understand, and all for the sake of Mr. Collins, too! Why does he deserve it more than anybody else?"

"I leave it to you to figure that out," said Mr. Bennet.

CHAPTER 24

Caroline Bingley's letter arrived and put an end to Jane's doubts. The very first sentence confirmed that the party was staying in London for the winter. It ended by passing on her brother's apologies for not having had time to say goodbye to his friends in Hertfordshire before he left.

Hope was over, entirely over. When Jane recovered enough to read the rest of the letter, she found little (except for Caroline's flowery expressions of affection) that could give her any comfort. Most of the letter was in praise of Miss Darcy. The young lady's many attractions were again described, and Caroline boasted joyfully of how close they were all becoming, and again predicted that she would some day become Bingley's wife. She mentioned also with great pleasure that her brother was staying in Mr. Darcy's house, and enthusiastically mentioned some plans of Mr. Darcy to purchase new furniture.

When Jane shared this information with her sister, Elizabeth listened with silent indignation. She was not sure which she felt more strongly: concern for her sister, or resentment against all the others.

She still did not take seriously Caroline's hints that her brother cared for Miss Darcy. She believed as much as ever that he was really fond of Jane, but she could not think of him now without anger and even contempt. Apparently, his easy-going nature had now made him the slave of his friends, and led him to sacrifice his own happiness for their sake. If it was only his own happiness that was at risk, Elizabeth could forgive him squandering it, but her sister's happiness was at stake as well—a fact she was sure that Bingley was aware of.

A day or two passed before Jane had the heart to speak of her feelings to Elizabeth. Mrs. Bennet had left them together, after a long series of irritated remarks about Netherfield and its master, and Jane said, "Oh, how I wish that our dear mother had more self-control. She can have no idea how she hurts me when she constantly speaks of him. But this cannot last long. He will be forgotten, and we will all be as we were before."

Elizabeth looked at her sister with love and disbelief but said nothing.

"You are doubting me," said Jane, blushing. "You should not. He may live in my memory as the most agreeable man I have known, but that is all. I have nothing either to hope or fear, and nothing to blame him for. So, in a little while . . . I shall certainly try to get better."

In a stronger voice she added, "It comforts me to think that this has only been a mistake on my side, and that it has done no harm to anyone but myself."

"My dear Jane!" exclaimed Elizabeth, "you are too good. You are truly sweet as an angel. I don't know what to say to you."

Jane insisted that she was not at all good, but Elizabeth went on.

"It is true," she said. "You want to think well of everybody, and you are hurt if I criticize anybody. I see that you are perfect, and you object to that as well. You know, there are only a few people whom I really love, and even fewer whom I admire. Every day makes me more convinced that human beings are inconsistent, and that you cannot depend on people to act with honor or good sense. I have seen two such examples lately. One I will not mention; the other is Charlotte's marriage. It is unbelievable!"

"My dear Lizzy, do not let such feelings run away with you. They will ruin your happiness. You do not allow for the great differences in people's tastes and situations. Mr. Collins is a respectable man, and Charlotte is a sensible, steady young woman. Remember that she is one of a large family, without much money. The marriage will assure that she is taken care of financially. And please try to believe, for everybody's sake, that she feels something like admiration and respect for our cousin."

"To make you happy, I would try to believe almost anything, but not that. If I believed that Charlotte admired him, I would only think worse of her than I do. My dear Jane, Mr. Collins is a conceited, pompous, narrow-minded, silly man. You know that as well as I do. You surely must agree that the woman who marries him cannot be thinking properly. You must not defend her, even though it is Charlotte Lucas."

"I think you are too critical of both of them," replied Jane, "and I hope eventually you will see them happy together, and change your mind. But enough of this. You mentioned something else— you said you had seen *two* examples. I know what you are referring to. But I beg you, dear Lizzy, do not pain me by thinking Mr. Bingley is to blame and saying your opinion of him is lowered. We must not be so ready to think that others have hurt us on purpose. We cannot expect a lively young man to always be careful and on guard. It is very often nothing but our own vanity that misleads us. Women like to think admiration means more than it does."

"And men encourage them to do so."

"If that is done deliberately, such men deserve blame. But I do not believe there is much such wickedness in the world."

"I do not for a minute think that Mr. Bingley deliberately acted wickedly," said Elizabeth. "But there are ways to make others unhappy that are not deliberate. Thoughtlessness, lack of attention to other people's feelings, and lack of determination are enough to do the business."

"And do you put the blame on one of those?"

"Yes, to lack of determination. But if I go on, I will offend you by saying what I think of persons you admire. Stop me while you can."

"You still believe, then, that his sisters influence him."

"Yes, along with his friend."

"I cannot believe it. Why should they try to influence him? They can only want him to be happy. And if he was truly attached to me, no other woman could gain his affection."

"Your first belief is false. His sisters may want many things other than his happiness. They may want to increase his wealth and importance. They may want him to marry a girl who has money, great connections, and pride."

"Undoubtedly, they do want him to choose Miss Darcy," replied Jane. "But this may be from better feelings than you are supposing. They have known her much longer than they have known me; it is no wonder if they love her better. Do not distress me by encouraging me to think badly of him or his sisters. Let me see this situation in the best light that I can."

Elizabeth could not oppose Jane's wish, and from that time Mr. Bingley's name was hardly ever mentioned between them.

Mrs. Bennet still continued to fuss and worry about Bingley's failure to return, and there seemed little chance she would ever give the subject up. Elizabeth tried hard to convince her of what she did not believe herself—that his attention to Jane had been only the effect of a common, passing liking, which ceased when he left her company. But while Mrs. Bennet would admit the possibility of the statement, she re-opened the topic every day, and Elizabeth had to try again.

Mr. Bennet treated the matter differently. "So, Lizzy," he said one day, "I hear that your sister has been crossed in love. I congratulate her. Next to being married, a girl likes to be crossed in love a little now and then. It is something to think about, and gives her a bit of status among her friends. When will it be your turn? There are officers enough in Meryton to disappoint all the young ladies in the neighborhood. Why not let Wickham be your man? He is a pleasant fellow, and would let you down with great style."

"Thank you, sir, but a less agreeable man would satisfy me. We must not all expect Jane's good fortune."

"True," said Mr. Bennet, "but it is a comfort to think that, whatever romantic troubles may befall you, you have an affectionate mother who will always make the most of it."

Mr. Wickham's company greatly helped lighten the gloomy mood which had descended on the family. They saw him often, and he spoke freely to all of them. The whole story that Elizabeth had already heard—all about Mr. Darcy, and all that Wickham had suffered from him—was now openly discussed. Everybody was pleased to think how much they had always disliked Mr. Darcy even before knowing anything of the matter.

Jane was the only person who thought there might be another way of looking at the story. She quietly pleaded for the family to consider the possibility of some mistake. But everyone else condemned Mr. Darcy as the worst of men.

CHAPTER 25

After a week spent happily courting his fiancee, Mr. Collins was forced to separate from his love and return home. The pain of leaving, however, was lessened by the fact that Charlotte would be joining him soon. He left his relations at Longbourn as solemnly as before, wished his fair cousins health and happiness again, and promised their father yet another letter of thanks.

On the following Monday, Mrs. Bennet was happy to greet her brother and his wife, who came as usual to spend Christmas at Longbourn. Her brother, Mr. Gardiner, was a kind, gentleman-like man, far more intelligent and sensible than his sister. Mrs. Gardiner, who was several years younger than Mrs. Bennet and Mrs. Philips, was a pleasant, intelligent, elegant woman who was popular with all her nieces. She, Jane, and Elizabeth were particularly close, and the two girls had often visited her in London.

Mrs. Gardiner's first task upon arrival was to hand out her presents and to describe the latest London fashions. When this was done, it was her turn to listen. Mrs. Bennet had a great deal to complain about. They had all been very badly used since she last saw her sister-in-law, she explained. Two of her girls had been on the point of marriage, but nothing had come of it.

"I do not blame Jane," she continued, "for Jane would have gotten Mr. Bingley if she could. But Lizzy! Oh, sister! It is very hard to think that she could have been Mr. Collins's wife by this time if it weren't for her own foolishness. He made her an offer of marriage in this very room, and she refused him. The result is that Lady Lucas will have a daughter married before I have, and that our estate is just as much entailed as ever. The Lucases are very tricky people indeed, sister. They are all about what they can get. I am sorry to say it about them, but so it is. My nerves and health have been very badly damaged by such ill-treatment by my own daughter, and by neighbors who think only of themselves. However, your visit is a great comfort to me, and I am very glad to hear what you tell us about long sleeves."

Mrs. Gardiner had already learned most of this news from Jane and Elizabeth's letters, so she answered Mrs. Bennet only briefly. Then, out of consideration for her nieces, she changed the subject.

When she was alone with Elizabeth afterward, she spoke more frankly. "It sounds as though it would have been a good match for Jane," she said. "I am sorry it didn't work out. But these things happen so often! A young man like Mr. Bingley so easily falls in love with a pretty girl for a few weeks. Then when some accident of fate separates them, he easily forgets her."

"But that's not quite what has happened here," said Elizabeth. "Jane is not suffering because of an 'accident.' It does not often happen that the interference of friends will convince a young man to forget a girl with whom he was madly in love only a few days before."

"But that expression of 'madly in love' is so over-used that it gives me very little idea how strong his feelings were. People sometimes use it to describe feelings produced by only a half-hour's meeting. Just how madly was Mr. Bingley in love?"

"I never saw anything more clear. He was paying less and less attention to other people and was completely wrapped up by her. Every time they met, it was more obvious. At his own ball, he offended two or three young ladies by not asking them to dance, and I spoke to him twice myself without receiving any answer. Could there be better symptoms? Isn't general rudeness a clear sign of love?"

Mrs. Gardiner sighed sympathetically. "Poor Jane! I am sorry for her. With her personality, it will be hard for her to get over this. It would be better if it had happened to you, Lizzy. You would have laughed yourself out of it sooner. Do you think I could persuade Jane to go back to London with us? A change of scene might do her good."

Elizabeth was very pleased with this idea and felt certain that Jane would agree.

"I hope that her thoughts of Mr. Bingley will not influence her," added Mrs. Gardiner. "We live in a completely different part of town and do not know the same people at all. It is very unlikely that they should meet, unless he comes to see her."

"Oh, that is quite impossible, for Mr. Bingley is now in Mr. Darcy's custody. Mr. Darcy would never allow his friend to even enter your part of London, and the idea of calling on Jane there—my dear aunt, how could you think of it? Mr. Darcy would rather die than set foot in such a place as Gracechurch Street, and believe me, Mr. Bingley never makes a move without him."

"Good. I hope they will not meet at all. But Jane corresponds with Mr. Bingley's sister, doesn't she? The sister will have to visit."

"She will completely drop her friendship with Jane," Elizabeth predicted.

But in spite of the certainty with which Elizabeth spoke, she did feel a glimmer of hope as she thought of Jane being in London near Bingley.

Jane accepted her aunt's invitation with pleasure. Her only thought about the Bingleys was that she might be able to occasionally spend a morning with Caroline, as she was not living in the same house with her brother.

The Gardiners stayed at Longbourn for a week. What with visits with the Philipses, the Lucases, and the officers, there was not a single day without a social engagement. When the officers were on hand, Mr. Wickham was always among them. On these occasions, Mrs. Gardiner (made suspicious by Elizabeth's warm praise of him) closely watched them both. She did not believe them to be seriously in love, but their liking for each other was obvious enough to make her a little uneasy. She decided to speak to Elizabeth on the subject before she left Hertfordshire, and remind her how unwise it would be to fall in love with a man with so little money.

Mrs. Gardiner herself enjoyed Wickham's company for a particular reason. About ten years earlier, before her marriage, she had spent a fairly long period in the same part of Derbyshire that was his home. As a result, they knew many people in common, and although Wickham had not been there much since the death of Darcy's father, he was able to give her fresher news of her old friends than she had known previously.

Mrs. Gardiner had seen Pemberley (Darcy's estate), and had heard much about the late Mr. Darcy. She took delight in hearing Wickham describe the place and praise its late owner. When she heard the story of the present Mr. Darcy's treatment of Wickham, she tried to remember anything she had ever heard of the younger man. Finally, she was nearly certain that she had heard people refer to Fitzwilliam Darcy as a very proud, ill-natured boy.

Mrs. Gardiner spoke kindly to Elizabeth the first time they were alone together. After honestly telling her what she thought, she added, "You are too sensible a girl, Lizzy, to fall in love merely because I have warned you against it. Therefore, I am not afraid of speaking frankly. I hope you will be careful. Do not become too involved with Mr. Wickham, or encourage his affection. I am not saying a word against him. He is a most interesting young man, and if he had the fortune he ought to have, I don't think you could do better. But as it is, you must not let your feelings run away with you. I am sure that your father depends on your sensible conduct. I hope you will not disappoint him."

"My dear aunt, you are being very serious."

"Yes, and I want you to be serious as well."

"Well, then, you do not need to be alarmed. I will be careful of myself, and of Mr. Wickham, too. He will not be in love with me if I can prevent it."

"Elizabeth, *you* are not being serious."

"I beg your pardon. I will try again. At present, I am not in love with Mr. Wickham. He is, I will admit, the most agreeable man I ever saw. If he fell in love with me . . . But no, I see that it is better that he does not. Oh, that hateful Mr. Darcy!"

"Perhaps it would be best if you discouraged his coming here so often," Mrs. Gardiner said. "At least, you should not remind your mother to invite him."

"As I did the other day," said Elizabeth, with a self-conscious smile. "You are right; I should not do that. But don't imagine that he is always here so often. It is on your account that he has been so frequently invited this week. You know my mother likes to have constant company for her friends. But really, upon my honor, I will try to act wisely. Now, I hope you are satisfied."

Her aunt promised her that she was, and Elizabeth thanked her for her kind concern. It was a wonderful example of advice being given on a delicate topic and not being resented.

Soon after the Gardiners and Jane departed for London, Mr. Collins returned to Hertfordshire. But as he was staying with the Lucases, his arrival did not inconvenience Mrs. Bennet. She was accustomed enough to the idea of the marriage that she managed to say several times, in an ill-natured tone, that she hoped they might be happy.

The wedding was to be on Thursday. On Wednesday, Charlotte paid her farewell visit. As she rose to leave, Elizabeth, who was ashamed of her mother's ungracious behavior and sincerely moved to see her friend, accompanied her out of the room. As they went downstairs together, Charlotte said, "I will count on hearing from you very often, Eliza."

"That you certainly shall."

"And I have another favor to ask. Will you come and see me?"

"We shall often meet, I hope, when you visit your parents."

"I am not likely to do that for some time. Please promise to come see me in Hunsford."

Elizabeth could not refuse, though she did not expect to enjoy such a visit.

"My father and Maria are coming to see me in March," added Charlotte. "I hope you will come with them. Truly, Eliza, I would be as glad to see you as either of them."

The wedding took place, and the bride and bridegroom set off for Hunsford. Elizabeth soon heard from Charlotte, and the two wrote to each other frequently, although Elizabeth could not expect their friendship to ever be as intimate again. She read Charlotte's first letters with a good deal of curiosity. She wondered how her friend would like her new home; what she would think of Lady Catherine; and how happy she would claim to be. The tone of the letters were exactly what Elizabeth had expected from her. She wrote cheerfully, seemed surrounded with comforts, and praised everything that she mentioned. She had only positive things to say about the house, furniture, and neighborhood, and she described Lady Catherine as kind and helpful. Elizabeth knew she would have to form her own opinions when she visited.

Jane had already written a brief note to her sister to let her know that they had arrived safely in London. When she wrote again, Elizabeth hoped there would be some news of the Bingleys.

But when Jane wrote her second letter, she had been in London for a week. She had neither seen nor heard from Caroline. She excused this, however, by thinking that the letter she had sent Caroline from Longbourn, telling of her visit to London, must have been lost.

"My aunt," she wrote, "is going to that part of town tomorrow, so I shall take the opportunity of visiting Caroline in Grosvenor Street."

She wrote again later, saying that she had seen Miss Bingley.

"Caroline did not seem quite like herself," she said, "but she was very glad to see me, and she scolded me for not letting her know I was coming to London. I was right, therefore; my last letter had never reached her. I asked how their brother was, of course. She said he was well, but so busy with Mr. Darcy that they hardly ever see him. I learned that Miss Darcy was coming to dinner. I wish I could see her. My visit was not long, as Caroline and Mrs. Hurst were going out. I'm sure they will visit me here soon."

Elizabeth shook her head over this letter. It

convinced her that Mr. Bingley's sisters would not inform him that Jane was in town.

Four weeks passed, and Jane did not see him. She tried to persuade herself that she did not care, but she could no longer be blind to the fact that Caroline was ignoring her. After waiting at home every morning for two weeks, and inventing every evening a fresh excuse for her, Jane finally did receive a visit. But the shortness of her stay and the coldness of her manner finally forced Jane to see the truth. She wrote:

My dearest Lizzy,

I am sure you are too kind to say "I told you so" when I confess that I was entirely wrong about Miss Bingley. But, my dear sister, even though you were right, I still say that her behavior made my confidence as natural as your suspicion. I do not at all understand why she pretended to be so fond of me, but if the same situation were to happen again, I would again be deceived.

Caroline did not return my visit until yesterday, and I did not receive a single note from her in the meantime. When she did come, it was very obvious that she did not want to be there. She made a slight, chilly, apology for not coming earlier, and did not say a word about wanting to see me again. By the time she left, I was convinced that the friendship was entirely over.

I pity her, even though I cannot help blaming her. She was very wrong to pretend such affection for me. But she must feel that she has acted wrong, and because I am sure that anxiety about her brother is the reason. I do not have to explain to you what I mean. But I have to wonder why she feels any such fears now, because if he had cared for me at all, we would have met by now. He knows I am in town, I am certain, from something she said herself. Yet as I listen to her, it seems to me that she is trying to convince herself that he cares for Miss Darcy. I cannot understand it. If I were not afraid of judging harshly, I would be tempted to say that there is some deception going on.

But I will try to banish every painful thought, and think only about happy things. Let me hear from you very soon. Miss Bingley suggested that her brother may give up Netherfield entirely and never return there again, but she was not certain of that. It is probably better not to mention it. I am extremely glad that you have such pleasant news from our friends Charlotte and Mr. Collins. Please do go to see them with Sir William and Maria. I am sure you will be very comfortable there.

This letter caused Elizabeth some pain, but she was relieved to think that Jane would no longer be fooled by Caroline Bingley. Any hopes Elizabeth had about Mr. Bingley were now entirely over. The more she thought of him, the more her opinion of him sank. She began to seriously hope that he might really marry Mr. Darcy's sister. If what

Wickham had said of her was true, she would make him abundantly sorry.

About this time, Mrs. Gardiner reminded Elizabeth of her promise concerning Wickham and asked for an update. Elizabeth had to give a report that pleased Mrs. Gardiner more than herself. Wickham's attentions had shifted; he was now the admirer of some other young lady. Elizabeth could see it and write about it without any great pain. Her heart had been only slightly touched, and she had the satisfaction of believing that she would have been his choice, if fortune had permitted it. A sudden inheritance was the greatest charm of the young lady to whom he was now paying attention. Elizabeth (less critical in his case, perhaps, than in Charlotte's), did not blame him for wanting material comfort. She hoped that it had caused him a few pangs to give her up, but she could sincerely wish him to be happy.

She wrote all this to Mrs. Gardiner and then added, "I am now convinced, my dear aunt, that I was never much in love. I think if I had been, I would now detest his very name, and wish him all manner of evil. But I not only do not hate him, I do not even hate Miss King. Kitty and Lydia are much more upset about his defection than I am. They are too young to realize that handsome young men, as well as plain ones, must have something to live on."

With little of interest going on in the Bennet family, January and February passed slowly. In March, Elizabeth would visit Charlotte in Hunsford. She had not really expected to go, but she realized that Charlotte was depending on the visit, and she began to look forward to it to some extent. Absence had made her miss Charlotte, and time had weakened her disgust of Mr. Collins. Besides, being at home with her mother and younger sisters was not especially pleasant. She would accompany Sir William and his second daughter, Maria, stopping to spend one night with Jane in London. The only pain was in leaving her father, who would certainly miss her. He so disliked her going that he told her to write to him, and almost promised to answer her letter.

She and Mr. Wickham said their goodbyes on perfectly friendly terms. His pursuit of Miss King could not make him forget that he had liked Elizabeth first, and the sincere regard with which he said farewell convinced her that, married or single, he would always be her model of an pleasant, attractive man.

Her fellow travelers the next day were not likely to make her forget him. Sir William Lucas and his daughter Maria (a good-humored girl, but as empty-headed as himself), had nothing to say that was worth hearing. Their conversation had as much charm and interest as the rattling of the carriage. Elizabeth loved all things ridiculous, but she had known Sir William too long. He could tell her no new stories about the wonder of being presented to the King and receiving his knighthood.

It was a journey of only twenty-four miles, and they began early enough to reach Gracechurch Street by noon. As they drove to Mr. Gardiner's door, Jane was watching for them at a window and ran to welcome them. Elizabeth, looking earnestly in her face, was happy to see it healthful and lovely as ever. On the stairs was a troop of little boys and girls, the Gardiner children, waiting to greet their cousin. All was joy and kindness. The day passed very pleasantly—the morning in bustle and shopping, and the evening at the theater.

In a private chat with her aunt, Elizabeth was sorry, but not surprised, to hear that although Jane always kept a cheerful face, she was sometimes depressed. Mrs. Gardiner then spoke with her niece about Wickham's desertion, and complimented her on bearing it so well.

"But, my dear Elizabeth," she added, "what sort of girl is Miss King? I would be sorry to think our friend was only interested in money."

"But my dear aunt, what is the difference between being practical and only interested in money? Last Christmas you were afraid I would marry him because it would be impractical. But now because he is trying to get a girl with a small fortune, you suspect he is interested only in money."

"If you will tell me what sort of girl Miss King is, I shall know better what to think."

"She is a very good kind of girl, I believe. I know nothing bad about her."

"But he did not pay her the slightest attention until her grandfather's death left her this money," her aunt pointed out.

"No, but why should he? If he was not allowed to fall in love with me because I had no money, why would he pay attention to a girl who he didn't care about, and who was equally poor?"

"But it seems unbecoming that he should pursue her so immediately after her grandfather's death."

"A man who needs money badly does not have time for matters of etiquette. If she does not object, why should we?"

"Her not objecting does not justify him. It only shows that she is lacking in sense herself."

"Well, then," cried Elizabeth, "have it your way. He is money-hungry, and she is foolish."

"I don't want to believe that. I would be sorry to think badly of a young man who has lived so long in Derbyshire."

"Oh mercy, I have a very poor opinion of young men who live in Derbyshire. Their close friends who live in Hertfordshire are not much better. I am sick of them all. Thank heavens, tomorrow I am going to visit a man who does not have a single agreeable quality—neither manners nor sense. Stupid men are the only ones worth knowing, after all."

"Take care, Lizzy. That sounds a great deal like the speech of a disappointed woman."

Before the evening ended, her aunt and uncle pleasantly surprised her by inviting her to go on vacation with them the following summer.

"We have not quite decided how far to travel," said Mrs. Gardiner, "but perhaps to the Lakes."

Nothing could have been more agreeable to Elizabeth, and she accepted the invitation with the greatest delight.

CHAPTER
28

During the next day's journey, everything was new and interesting to Elizabeth. Her spirits were high, for she had seen her beloved sister looking well, and the prospect of the coming trip with her aunt and uncle filled her with excitement.

When they left the main road and started along the lane to Hunsford, she searched eagerly for her first glimpse of the parsonage. As Rosings Park came into view, Elizabeth smiled to remember all that she had heard about the people who lived there.

Finally, they reached their destination. At the sound of the carriage wheels Mr. Collins and Charlotte appeared at the door, smiling and waving. Charlotte welcomed her friend with the greatest pleasure, and Elizabeth was happy she had come when she saw Charlotte's joy. She noticed that her cousin's manners were not changed at all; he was as polite as ever, and he kept her standing at the gate for several minutes as he asked about each member of her family. Once they arrived in the parlor, he welcomed them a second time with great formality, repeating Charlotte's offers of food and drink.

As Mr. Collins gave them a tour of the house,

demonstrating all its good points, its views, and its furniture, Elizabeth could not help thinking that he was speaking especially to her, as if to make her realize what she had lost by refusing to marry him. But although everything was neat and comfortable, she did not feel any regret. Instead, she wondered how Charlotte could seem so cheerful with such a husband. When Mr. Collins said anything especially foolish or embarrassing, she automatically glanced at Charlotte. Once or twice she noticed a faint blush, but in general Charlotte wisely seemed not to hear.

After resting long enough to describe their journey and all that had happened in London, Mr. Collins invited them to take a stroll in the large garden. He led the way over every inch, explaining every detail. With special pride he pointed through a gap in the trees to Lady Catherine's home. Rosings was a handsome modern building, well situated on a nearby hill.

After the tour of his garden, Mr. Collins wanted to lead the group around his two meadows, but as the ladies' shoes were not up to that, only Sir William accompanied him. Charlotte took her sister and friend back to the house, probably very pleased to have the chance to show it without her husband's help. It was rather small, but well built and convenient. When Mr. Collins could be forgotten, it was really a very comfortable home, and judging from Charlotte's enjoyment of it, Elizabeth supposed that he must be often forgotten. She learned from Charlotte that Lady Catherine was currently away from home. Mr. Collins brought her ladyship up again at dinner, saying, "Yes, Miss Elizabeth, you will have the honor of seeing Lady Catherine de Bourgh next Sunday at church, and it goes without saying that you will be delighted with her. She is a very gracious lady, and I do not doubt that she will honor you with her attention when services are over. I am almost certain that she will include you and our sister Maria in every invitation with which she honors us during your stay here. Her behavior to my dear Charlotte is charming. We dine at Rosings twice every week and are never allowed to walk home. Her ladyship's carriage is provided for us. I should say, *one* of her ladyship's carriages, for she has several."

"Lady Catherine is a very respectable, sensible woman indeed," added Charlotte, "and a most kind neighbor."

"Very true, my dear, that is exactly what I say," chimed in Mr. Collins. "She is the sort of woman to whom one cannot show too much respect."

About the middle of the next day, as Elizabeth was in her room getting ready for a walk, a sudden noise below indicated that the whole house was in confusion. Next, she heard someone running up the stairs in a violent hurry, and calling loudly for her. She opened the door and met Maria, quite out of breath. She cried out, "Oh, my dear Eliza! Please, hurry and come into the dining room, for there is such a sight to be seen! I won't tell you what it is. Rush down this minute!"

Elizabeth did as she was asked, greatly curious. But in looking out the window she saw only two ladies stopping their low carriage at the garden gate.

"Is this all?" asked Elizabeth. "I thought that the pigs had gotten into the garden at least, but it is nothing but Lady Catherine and her daughter!"

"Oh, my dear!" said Maria quite shocked at her mistake. "That is not Lady Catherine. The old lady is Mrs. Jenkinson, who lives with them. The other is Miss de Bourgh. Look at her—she is quite a little creature. Who would have thought she would be so thin and small?"

"She is certainly rude to keep Charlotte standing outdoors in all this wind. Why doesn't she come in?"

"Oh, Charlotte says she hardly ever does. It is the greatest of favors when Miss de Bourgh comes in."

"I like the way she looks," said Elizabeth, struck with another idea. "She seems sickly and cross. Yes, she will make a perfect wife for Mr. Darcy."

Mr. Collins and Charlotte were both standing at the gate in conversation with the ladies. Sir William, to Elizabeth's amusement, was stationed in the doorway reverently gazing at the greatness before him, and bowing whenever Miss de Bourgh looked his way.

At last there was nothing more to be said. The ladies drove on, and the others returned into the house. As soon as Mr. Collins saw the two girls he began to congratulate them on their good fortune, and Charlotte explained that the whole party was invited to dine at Rosings the next day.

CHAPTER 29

Mr. Collins was almost too delighted by the dinner invitation to express himself. It gave him exactly what he had hoped: the opportunity to show off the grandeur of his patroness to his visitors, as well as the chance to let them see the attention she paid to himself and his wife.

"I confess that I would not have been at all surprised if her ladyship had asked us on Sunday to drink tea and spend the evening at Rosings," he said. "I even expected, from my knowledge of her great kindness, that it would happen. But who could have imagined such an honor as this? Who could have imagined that we should receive an invitation to dine there so immediately after your arrival!"

Hardly anything was talked of the whole day, or the next morning, other than their visit to Rosings. Mr. Collins carefully instructed all of them in what to expect, so that they might not be completely overwhelmed by the sight of such rooms, so many servants, and such a splendid dinner.

As the ladies went to dress for the occasion, he

said to Elizabeth, "Do not worry, my dear cousin, about your clothing. Lady Catherine does not require that others dress as elegantly as she and her daughter. I would advise you merely to wear whatever of your clothes is superior to the rest. Trust me when I say that Lady Catherine will not think the worse of you for being simply dressed. She prefers that people of lesser rank show that they know their place."

While they were dressing, he came two or three times to their doors to recommend that they hurry, as Lady Catherine hated to be kept waiting for her dinner. Such remarks absolutely terrified Maria, and she was as worried about the evening as her father had been about his presentation at the King's court.

As the weather was fine, they had a pleasant half-mile walk across the park. Every park has its beauties, and Elizabeth saw much she was pleased with, but she could not manage to be quite as awestruck as Mr. Collins apparently wished. She was not especially impressed, for example, when he explained how many windows there were in front of the house, or what they had originally cost Sir Lewis de Bourgh.

When they climbed the steps to the house, Maria's alarm increased every moment, and even Sir William did not look perfectly calm. But Elizabeth's courage did not fail her. She had heard nothing about Lady Catherine that made her expect the lady to have any extraordinary talents or miraculous virtue. The mere facts that she was rich and high-ranking did not terrify Elizabeth.

From the entrance hall, they followed the servants through a series of rooms until they reached the area where Lady Catherine, her daughter, and Mrs. Jenkinson were sitting.

Introductions were made. In spite of having been at St. James Court, Sir William was so completely awed by all the grandeur that he had only enough courage to make a very low bow and sit down without saying a word. Maria, frightened almost out of her senses, sat on the edge of her chair, not knowing which way to look. Elizabeth was perfectly calm and observed the three ladies before her with interest. Lady Catherine was a tall, large woman, with strong features which might have been handsome in her younger years. She bore a slight resemblance to her nephew, Mr. Darcy. Her manner was very grand and stately and designed to intimidate visitors of lesser rank. Elizabeth remembered Mr. Wickham's description of her and decided that he had been quite accurate.

When she turned her gaze on the daughter, she could understand Maria's astonishment at her being so thin and small. She did not resemble her impressive mother in the least. Miss de Bourgh was pale and sickly; her face was unremarkable, and she spoke very little, except in a low voice to Mrs. Jenkinson. That lady's entire purpose seemed to be to listen to Miss de Bourgh and to place the screen between her and the fire.

After sitting a few minutes, they were all sent to one of the windows to admire the view. Mr. Collins went with them to point out its beauties, and Lady Catherine kindly informed them that it was much more beautiful in the summer.

The dinner was very grand. There were all the servants, all the magnificent dinnerware and silver which Mr. Collins had promised. He sat at the foot of the table and looked as if life could furnish no greater honor. He praised every dish, and Sir William (who was now partially recovered) echoed every word his son-in-law said, in an exaggerated, gushing style which Elizabeth wondered how Lady Catherine could bear. But Lady Catherine seemed greatly pleased by their admiration, especially when they expressed astonishment at dishes that they had never seen before. There was not much other conversation. Elizabeth was ready to talk, but she was seated between Charlotte and Miss de Bourgh. Charlotte was busy listening to Lady Catherine, and Miss de Bourgh did not say a single word to her. Mrs. Jenkinson spent her time watching how little Miss de Bourgh ate, encouraging her to try some other dish, and wondering aloud if she felt ill. Maria was much too awestruck to speak, and the gentlemen did nothing but eat and admire.

When dinner was ended, the ladies returned to the drawing room. At that point, there was nothing to do but to listen to Lady Catherine talk, which she did steadily until coffee was served. She delivered her opinion on every subject so firmly that it was clear she was not used to hearing those opinions questioned. She asked about Charlotte's housekeeping, giving her a great deal of advice about how to manage everything. She lectured her about how to budget for groceries and instructed her on the care of her cows and her poultry. Nothing was too small for this great lady's attention, as long as it gave her the chance to tell others what to do.

Along with advising Mrs. Collins, she directed a number of questions to Elizabeth. She asked her how many sisters she had, whether they were older or younger than herself, whether any of them were soon to be married, whether they were handsome, where they had been educated, what sort of carriage her father kept, and what had been her mother's maiden name? Elizabeth considered this questioning to be quite rude, but she answered Lady Catherine calmly. Lady Catherine then commented, "Your father's estate is entailed on Mr. Collins, I think. For your sake," she said, turning to Charlotte, "I am glad of that. But in general I see no excuse for entailing estates away from the female line. It was not thought necessary in Sir Lewis de Bourgh's family. Do you play and sing, Miss Bennet?"

"A little."

"Well, then, some time or other we shall be

happy to hear you. Our piano is an excellent one, probably better than you are accustomed to. You shall try it some day. Do your sisters play and sing as well?"

"One of them does."

"Why did they not all learn? They should all have learned. Our neighbors, the Miss Webbs, all play, and their father has less money than yours. Do you draw?"

"No, not at all."

"What, none of you?"

"Not one."

"That is very strange. But I suppose you had no opportunity to learn. Your mother should have taken you to London every spring to study with drawing masters there."

"My mother would have had no objection to that, but my father hates London."

"As your sisters are growing up, I suppose your governess has left you?"

"We never had any governess."

"No governess! How is that possible? Five daughters brought up at home without a governess! I never heard of such a thing. Your mother must have been quite a slave to your education."

Elizabeth could hardly help smiling at the thought. She assured Lady Catherine that had not been the case.

"Then, who taught you? Without a governess you must have been neglected."

"Compared with some families, I suppose we were. But those of us who wished to learn never lacked the opportunity. We were always encouraged to read, and had all the tutors that were necessary. Those who chose to be idle, though, could be idle."

"Yes, and that is what a governess will prevent. If I had known your mother, I should have strongly advised her to engage a governess. I always say that nothing can be accomplished in education without regular instruction, and nobody but a governess can give it. It is wonderful how many families I have assisted in that way. I am always glad to get a young person employment in that manner. I have assisted four nieces of Mrs. Jenkinson in finding delightful situations. Only the other day I recommended another young person, and the family is quite delighted with her. Mrs. Collins, did I tell you that Lady Metcalfe visited yesterday to thank me? She says that Miss Pope is a treasure. 'Lady Catherine,' she said, 'you have given me a treasure.' Are any of your younger sisters yet out in society, Miss Bennet?"

"Yes, ma'am, all of them."

"All! What, all five out at once? How very odd! The younger ones out before the oldest are married! Your younger sisters must be very young?"

"Yes, my youngest is not yet sixteen. Perhaps she is young to be in public much. But really, ma'am, I think it would be very hard on them to deny them their share of society and amusement only because the older sisters did not marry early. The last-born has as much right to the pleasures of youth as the first. And to be kept out of society because the oldest had not married—I do not think that would be likely to promote sisterly affection."

"Upon my word," said her ladyship, "you state your opinion very firmly for so young a person. How old are you?"

"With three younger sisters grown up," replied Elizabeth, smiling, "your ladyship can hardly expect me to admit my age."

Lady Catherine seemed quite astonished that she had not received a direct answer. Elizabeth suspected that she was the first creature to ever attempt to tease her ladyship.

"You cannot be more than twenty, I am sure," protested Lady Catherine. "Therefore, you need not conceal your age."

"I am not quite twenty-one," Elizabeth admitted.

When the gentlemen had joined them, card playing began. Lady Catherine, Sir William, and Mr. and Mrs. Collins sat down to one game, and Miss de Bourgh, Elizabeth, Maria, and Mrs. Jenkinson to another. Their table was extremely stupid. The players said nothing that did not relate to the game, except when Mrs. Jenkinson expressed her fears that Miss de Bourgh was too hot or too cold. A great deal more happened at the other table. Lady Catherine talked more or less constantly, stating the mistakes the others had made, or telling some story about herself. Mr. Collins was kept busy agreeing with everything her ladyship said, thanking her for every point he won, and apologizing if he thought he won too many. Sir William did not say much. He was concentrating on memorizing Lady Catherine's anecdotes and the noble names she dropped.

When Lady Catherine and her daughter were tired of playing, the evening was over. Lady Catherine offered to send everyone home in her carriage, which was immediately ordered. The party then gathered round the fire to hear Lady Catherine proclaim what kind of weather they were to have the next day. The coach arrived, and with many speeches of thankfulness on Mr. Collins's side, and as many bows on Sir William's, they departed.

As soon as they had driven from the door, Mr. Collins insisted that Elizabeth give her opinion of everything that she had seen at Rosings. For Charlotte's sake, she made her report more favorable than it really was. But her approval did not satisfy Mr. Collins, and he was soon forced to take over the job of praising her ladyship.

CHAPTER
30

Sir William stayed at Hunsford only a week, but his visit was long enough to convince him that his daughter was comfortably settled, and that she possessed a husband and a neighbor of very high quality indeed. While Sir William was with them, Mr. Collins spent his mornings driving him around the countryside, but when he went away, the family returned to their usual activities. Elizabeth was thankful to find that the change did not mean they would see more of Mr. Collins, for he spent most of his day either working in the garden, or in reading and writing and looking out the window of his own library, which faced the road. From there he could observe what carriages came along, and how often Miss de Bourgh drove by—a fact that he never failed to inform them of, although it happened almost every day. She frequently stopped at the parsonage and had a few minutes' conversation with Charlotte, although she hardly ever left her carriage.

Mr. Collins walked to Rosings almost every day, and, Charlotte often accompanied him. Now and then they were honored with a call from her ladyship, and nothing escaped her observation during these visits. She examined everything, looked at their work, and advised them to do it differently. She criticized the arrangement of the furniture, and blamed the housemaid for laziness.

The group dined at Rosings about twice a week. Except for the loss of Sir William, every such entertainment was a copy of the first. There were few other social engagements. Elizabeth did not mind this, and she spent her time comfortably enough. There were pleasant conversations with Charlotte, and the weather was so fine for the time of year that she was often able to enjoy long walks. Her favorite walk, and where she frequently went while the others were calling on Lady Catherine, was along the open grove which edged one side of the park. There she had found a nice sheltered path, which no one but herself ever seemed to visit.

In this quiet way, the first two weeks of her visit passed away. Easter was coming, and a visitor was expected at Rosings: Mr. Darcy. Elizabeth would have preferred to see almost anyone else, but at least it might be amusing to see how hopeless Miss Bingley's plans to marry him were, if he was indeed intended for his cousin Miss de Bourgh.

The news of Mr. Darcy's arrival soon reached her, because Mr. Collins spent the whole morning strolling along the lane leading to Rosings so that he would be the first to know. After bowing to the carriage as it turned into the park, he rushed home to share his news. The next morning he hurried to Rosings to pay his respects. There he found not one but two nephews of Lady Catherine, for Mr. Darcy had brought with him his cousin, Colonel Fitzwilliam, the younger son of his uncle, who was an earl of even greater magnificence than Lady Catherine. To Elizabeth's great surprise, when Mr. Collins returned from his visit, the two gentlemen came with him. Charlotte saw them coming, and said to her friend, "I must thank you, Eliza, for this honor. Mr. Darcy would never have come so soon to visit me."

Elizabeth hardly had time to reject this idea before the three gentlemen entered the room. Colonel Fitzwilliam, who led the way, was about thirty. He was not a handsome man, but he had pleasant, gentlemanly manners. Mr. Darcy looked just as he always had in Hertfordshire. He made his usual reserved greetings to Mrs. Collins, and spoke calmly to Elizabeth. She merely curtseyed to him, without saying a word.

Colonel Fitzwilliam immediately began a conversation with the readiness and ease of a well-bred man. But his cousin, after having made a brief comment about the house and garden to Mrs. Collins, sat for sometime without speaking to anybody. Finally, however, he asked Elizabeth if her family was well. She answered him in the usual way, and after a moment's pause, added, "My older sister has been in London for the past three months. Have you happened to see her there?"

She knew perfectly well that he had not, but she wanted to see his reaction. She thought he looked a little confused as he answered that he had never been so fortunate as to meet Miss Bennet. The subject was dropped, and the gentlemen went away soon afterward.

CHAPTER 31

Everyone at the parsonage liked Colonel Fitzwilliam, and the ladies all felt sure he would make the gatherings at Rosings more pleasant. But the next invitation to Lady Catherine's was slow in arriving. While there were visitors there, the Collins household was not necessary, and it was not till Easter Sunday, almost a week after the gentlemen's arrival, that they were honored by any attention. Even then, they were only asked as they left church to come there in the evening.

The invitation was accepted, of course, and at the proper hour they arrived in Lady Catherine's drawing room. Her ladyship received them politely, but it was plain that she did not value them as much as she did when she could get nobody else. For the most part, she ignored them and spoke primarily to her nephews, especially to Darcy.

Colonel Fitzwilliam seemed really glad to see them. Anything was a relief to him after the boredom of Rosings, and Mrs. Collins's pretty friend pleased him very much. He now sat down by Elizabeth, and talked so amusingly of Kent and

Hertfordshire, of traveling and staying at home, of books and of music, that Elizabeth had never been half so well entertained in that room before. They laughed and talked with so much spirit as to draw the attention of Lady Catherine herself as well as of Mr. Darcy. He watched them with growing curiosity, and her ladyship apparently shared his feeling. She did not bother to disguise hers, and soon she called out, "What is that you are saying there, Fitzwilliam? What is it you are telling Miss Bennet? Let me hear what it is."

"We are speaking of music, madam," he said.

"Of music! Then please speak aloud. No subject delights me more. I must join the conversation, if you are speaking of music. There are few people in England, I suppose, who enjoy music more than I, or have better natural taste. If I had ever learned, I would have been a wonderful performer. And so would Anne, if her health had allowed her to study. I am confident that she would have performed delightfully. How does Georgiana get on with her musical studies, Darcy?"

Mr. Darcy affectionately praised his sister's musical talent.

"I am very glad to hear it," said Lady Catherine. "Please tell her for me that she cannot expect to excel if she does not practice a great deal."

"I promise you, madam, that she does not need any advice," he replied. "She practices constantly."

"Excellent. It cannot be done too much, and

when I write to her next, I will tell her not to neglect it on any account. I often tell young ladies that they will never be really excellent performers unless they practice. I have told Miss Bennet several times that she will never be a superior player unless she practices more, and although Mrs. Collins has no piano, she is very welcome (as I have often told her) to come to Rosings every day and play the piano in Mrs. Jenkinson's room. She would not be in the way in that part of the house."

Mr. Darcy looked a little ashamed of his aunt's rudeness and said nothing.

When coffee was over, Colonel Fitzwilliam reminded Elizabeth that she had promised to play for him. She sat down at the piano as he drew a chair near her. Lady Catherine listened to half a song, and then began talking to her other nephew until Darcy walked away from her and stood where he could watch Elizabeth's face. Elizabeth saw what he was doing. When she paused between songs, she turned to him with a smile and said, "Do you mean to frighten me, Mr. Darcy, by listening so closely? But I will not be alarmed, even though your sister does play so well. I am too stubborn to be frightened. In fact, I become braver when anyone tries to intimidate me."

"I will not bother saying you are mistaken," he answered, "because you could not honestly believe that I am trying to alarm you. I have known you long enough to be aware that you sometimes enjoy stating opinions that you do not, in fact, believe."

Elizabeth laughed heartily at this picture of herself. She said to Colonel Fitzwilliam, "I'm afraid your cousin will give you a very poor opinion of me, and teach you not to believe a word I say. It is certainly unlucky for me to meet a person who knows my bad character, when I had hoped to behave so well here! Mr. Darcy, it is very unkind of you to mention all of my faults that you observed in Hertfordshire. I might say that it is unwise, too, for you to tempt me to pay you back. I may be forced to say things that your relatives will be shocked to hear."

"I am not afraid of you," Darcy said, smiling.

"Oh, please let me hear!" cried Colonel Fitzwilliam. "I would like to know how he behaves among strangers."

"You shall hear then—but prepare yourself for something very dreadful. The first time I ever saw him in Hertfordshire was at a ball—and what do you think he did? He danced only four dances! I am sorry to hurt you, but it is the truth. He danced only four dances, although there were not enough gentlemen to go around, and more than one young lady was sitting down for want of a partner. Mr. Darcy, you cannot deny the fact."

"At the time, I did not have the honor of knowing any lady at the ball except those in my own party."

"True, and certainly nobody can ever be introduced in a ballroom. Well, Colonel Fitzwilliam, what shall I play next? I await your orders."

"Perhaps I should have asked to be introduced," admitted Darcy, "but I am not inclined to approach strangers."

"Shall we ask your cousin why this is?" said Elizabeth, still speaking to Colonel Fitzwilliam. "Shall we ask him why a man of sense and education, and who has traveled and been in society so much, does not dare to approach strangers?"

"I can answer that question," said Fitzwilliam. "It is because he will not trouble himself to do so."

"I certainly do not have the talent of talking easily with strangers," Darcy said. "I cannot quickly connect with them, or appear interested in their concerns, as some people can."

"My fingers," said Elizabeth, "do not move over the piano as quickly and skillfully as some women's do. But I have always supposed that was my own fault, because I do not take the trouble of practicing. It is not that I think my fingers are less capable of playing than another woman's."

Darcy smiled, and said, "You are perfectly right. You have used your time much better. No one who has the privilege of hearing you can think anything is missing. Neither you nor I perform for strangers."

Here they were interrupted by Lady Catherine, who wanted to know what they were talking about. Elizabeth immediately began playing again. Lady

Catherine approached and, after listening for a few minutes, said to Darcy, "Miss Bennet would not play at all badly if she practiced more and could have the advantage of a London teacher. She has a very good notion of fingering, although her taste is not as good as Anne's. Anne would have been a delightful performer, if her health had allowed her to learn."

Elizabeth looked at Darcy to see how he reacted to hearing Miss de Bourgh praised. But Darcy did not show any sign of love for, or even interest in, his cousin. If Miss Bingley were his relation, Elizabeth thought, he would be just as likely to marry her.

Lady Catherine continued her comments about Elizabeth's performance, mixing in much advice on fingering and taste. Elizabeth accepted it all politely. She continued to play, at the gentlemen's request, until her ladyship's carriage was ready to take them home.

Elizabeth was sitting by herself the next morning, writing to Jane. Mrs. Collins and Maria had gone into the village. A ring at the door startled her. She thought it might be Lady Catherine, so she hurriedly put away her half-finished letter in order to avoid any personal questions. When she opened the door, she was astonished to find Mr. Darcy there.

He seemed surprised as well to find her alone. He apologized, telling her that he had thought all the ladies were home.

They sat down, and seemed in danger of sinking into total silence. She felt she had to say something, so she remarked, "How very suddenly you all left Netherfield last November, Mr. Darcy! It must have been a nice surprise for Mr. Bingley to have you all join him in London so soon. I hope he and his sisters were all well when you last saw them?"

"Perfectly well, thank you."

He was silent again, so she went on. "I think I have heard that Mr. Bingley may never return to Netherfield again?"

"I have never heard him say so, but he is unlikely to spend much time there. He has so many friends in London and is constantly busy there."

"If he does not intend to be there much, it would be better for the neighborhood if he gave up the place entirely," Elizabeth answered. "Then a pleasant family might settle there."

"I would not be surprised if he gave it up, if anyone made him a suitable offer," Darcy said.

Elizabeth did not answer. She was hesitant to say anything more about Mr. Bingley, and decided to let Mr. Darcy have the trouble of finding a subject of conversation.

He took the hint, saying, "This seems a very comfortable house. I believe that Lady Catherine did a great deal to it when Mr. Collins first came to Hunsford."

"I believe she did. And I am sure she could not have shown her kindness to anyone who would have been more grateful."

Darcy continued. "Mr. Collins appears very fortunate in his choice of a wife."

"Yes, indeed," Elizabeth said. "His friends should be happy that he met a sensible woman who would accept him, not to mention make him happy. My friend Charlotte is very sensible, although I am not certain that marrying Mr. Collins was the wisest thing she ever did. She seems perfectly happy, however, and in practical terms it is certainly a very good match for her."

"It must be agreeable to her to be settled so near to her own family and friends."

"Near, you call it?" asked Elizabeth. "It is nearly

fifty miles."

"And what is fifty miles of good road? Little more than half a day's journey. Yes, I call it a very easy distance."

"It does not seem near to me," said Elizabeth. "I would never have said Mrs. Collins was settled near her family."

"That is a proof of your own attachment to Hertfordshire," Darcy responded. "Anything beyond the very neighborhood of Longbourn, I suppose, would appear far."

He spoke with a sort of smile. Elizabeth imagined that he was thinking of Jane and Netherfield. She blushed as she answered, "I do not mean to say that a woman must live very near her family. Distance is relative, and depends on the circumstances. If the expense of traveling is no object, then distance is not a problem. But that is not the case here. Mr. and Mrs. Collins have a comfortable income, but not one that will allow frequent journeys."

Mr. Darcy drew his chair a little toward her, and said, "I cannot understand your very strong local attachment. You cannot have always lived at Longbourn."

Elizabeth looked surprised. Darcy seemed to catch himself. He drew back his chair and took a newspaper from the table. Glancing at it, he said, in a colder voice, "Are you enjoying the local scenery?"

They spoke briefly about the countryside, and

were soon interrupted by Charlotte and her sister, who returned from their walk. Mr. Darcy repeated his apologies for the unexpected visit. After sitting a few minutes longer without saying much to anybody, he went away.

"What can be the meaning of this!" said Charlotte, as soon as he was gone. "My dear Eliza, he must be in love with you, or he would never have called on us so unexpectedly."

But when Elizabeth described his almost silent visit, that did not seem very likely, even in Charlotte's imagination. The young women eventually decided that his visit was explained only by the fact that he could not find anything else to do. Granted, the parsonage was very near Lady Catherine's home, and the walk was pleasant. Darcy and Colonel Fitzwilliam often called, sometimes separately, sometimes together, and now and then accompanied by their aunt. It was plain to them all that Colonel Fitzwilliam came because he genuinely enjoyed their company.

But why Mr. Darcy came so often to the parsonage—that was more difficult to understand. It could not be for the company, as he frequently sat there for a full ten minutes without opening his mouth. When he did speak, it seemed to be because he knew he should, not because he wanted to. Mrs. Collins did not know what to make of him. Colonel Fitzwilliam often laughed at his behavior, proving that he was generally different. She watched him whenever they were at Rosings, and whenever he came to the parsonage, but she did not learn much. He certainly looked at Eliza a great deal, but the expression was hard to read. It was an earnest, steadfast gaze, but she could not tell if there was admiration in it. Sometimes it seemed to be nothing but absent-mindedness.

Once or twice she had mentioned to Elizabeth the possibility that Darcy was in love with her, but Elizabeth always laughed at the idea. Charlotte dropped the subject, rather than raise expectations which might only end in disappointment. For in her opinion, all of Eliza's dislike would vanish in a moment if she thought Darcy cared for her.

In her loving schemes for Elizabeth, Charlotte sometimes planned for her to marry Colonel Fitzwilliam. He was far more pleasant than his cousin, and he certainly admired her.

CHAPTER 33

More than once, in her daily walk in the Park, Elizabeth unexpectedly met Mr. Darcy. She was annoyed at this, and to prevent it happening again, she made sure to explain that this was a favorite walking place of hers. And yet it happened a second time, and even a third! Very odd! It seemed willfully rude on his part, or perhaps a means of self-punishment. For not only did he exchange a few remarks with her, he actually reversed his direction and walked with her.

He never said a great deal, and she did not bother talking or listening much. But she noticed in the course of their third meeting that he was asking some odd, unconnected questions. He asked about how well she liked Hunsford, about her love of solitary walks, and her opinion of Mr. and Mrs. Collins's happiness.

One day as she walked along, reading Jane's last letter, she encountered not Mr. Darcy but Colonel Fitzwilliam. Putting away the letter, and forcing a smile, she said, "I did not know that you ever walked this way."

"I have been walking the length of the Park," he replied, "I do it every year, and intend to finish with a visit to the parsonage. Are you going much farther?"

"No, I should have headed back that way a moment ago." She turned, and they walked toward the parsonage together.

"Are you still planning to leave Kent on Saturday?" Elizabeth asked.

"Yes, if Darcy does not put it off again," answered Fitzwilliam. "But we will do as he likes. He arranges the business just as he pleases."

"I do not know anybody who enjoys the power of doing what he pleases more than Mr. Darcy," said Elizabeth.

"He likes to have his own way very well," agreed Colonel Fitzwilliam. "But so do we all. It is only that he is better able to have it, because he is rich, and many others are poor. I speak from experience. A younger son like me, you know, must get accustomed to self-denial and dependence."

Elizabeth laughed. "In my opinion, the younger son of an earl can know very little of either. Now, seriously, what do you know about self-denial and dependence? When have you been prevented by lack of money from going where you chose, or buying what you wanted?"

"It is true; perhaps I have not experienced many hardships of that nature. But in matters of greater importance, I may suffer from the lack of money. For instance, younger sons cannot marry as they like."

"Unless they like rich women, which I think they very often do," Elizabeth answered.

"Our expensive living habits make us too dependent," Fitzwilliam said. "There are not many men in my position who can afford to marry without some attention to money."

"Is he talking about me?" thought Elizabeth, and she blushed at the idea. But she answered without embarrassment, asking in a lively tone, "And tell me—what is the usual price of an earl's younger son? Unless the older brother is very sickly, I suppose you would not ask more than fifty thousand pounds?" He answered her in a similar joking style, and the subject was dropped.

To break the silence, which might make him think she was troubled by their conversation, she said, "I imagine your cousin Mr. Darcy brought you here with him so that he could always have a companion available. I wonder why he does not marry, so he would have a lasting convenience of that kind. But, perhaps his sister does as well for now. If she is under his care, he may do what he likes with her."

"No," said Colonel Fitzwilliam, "that is an advantage which he must share with me. He and I are both guardians of Miss Darcy."

"Are you really? I wonder what sort of guardians you make? Does she give you much trouble? Young ladies of her age are sometimes difficult to manage, and if she has the true Darcy spirit, she may like to have her own way."

As she spoke, she observed him looking at her hard. He asked why she thought Miss Darcy was likely to give them any uneasiness. His manner convinced her that she had somehow struck a nerve.

She replied, "Oh, do not worry. I have never heard any harm of her, and I imagine she is a sweet and gentle girl. She is a great favorite of some ladies I know, Mrs. Hurst and Miss Bingley. I think you are acquainted."

"I know them a little. Their brother is a pleasant man, and a great friend of Darcy's."

"Oh yes," said Elizabeth dryly. "Mr. Darcy is uncommonly kind to Mr. Bingley, and takes a great deal of care of him."

"Care of him! Yes, I really believe Darcy does take care of him in the most important ways," answered Fitzwilliam. "From something that he told me during our trip here, I think Bingley owes him a great deal. But I am speaking out of turn, for I do not really know that Bingley was the person meant. I was just putting two and two together."

"What is it that you mean?" asked Elizabeth.

"It is a story which Darcy would not want to have repeated, because if it were to reach the lady's family, it would be an unpleasant thing."

"You may depend upon my not mentioning it," Elizabeth said.

"And remember that I am not sure the story is about Bingley at all. What Darcy told me was merely this; that he had recently saved a friend from making a very foolish marriage. He did it without mentioning names or any other details, and I only suspected it was Bingley because he seems the kind of young man to get into a scrape like that, and from knowing that they were together all last summer."

"Did Mr. Darcy explain why he felt he should interfere?"

"I understood that there were some very strong objections against the lady."

"And what arts did he use to separate them?"

"He did not talk to me of his own arts," said Fitzwilliam, smiling. "He only told me what I have now told you."

Elizabeth did not answer, but walked on, her heart swelling with anger. After watching her a little, Fitzwilliam asked her why she was so thoughtful.

"I am thinking of what you have told me," she said. "I do not agree with your cousin's behavior. What right did he have to judge?"

"You think he was wrong to become involved?" Fitzwilliam asked.

"I do not see what right Mr. Darcy had to decide whether his friend's attachment was suitable," Elizabeth said. "But," she continued, "as we do not know the details, it is not fair to condemn him. There must not have been much strong affection in the case."

"That is a reasonable guess," said Fitzwilliam, "but makes my cousin's triumph much less impressive."

He said this as a joke, but his words painted so accurate a picture of Mr. Darcy that she could not trust herself to answer politely. She changed the subject and they talked of other matters until they reached the parsonage. There she shut herself into her own room, where she could think without interruption of what she had heard.

She could not believe that the story was about anyone but Bingley. There could not be two men over whom Mr. Darcy could have so much influence. She had always assumed that Darcy had been involved in the effort to separate Mr. Bingley and Jane, but she had believed that Miss Bingley had had the leading role. But unless Darcy exaggerated his own role in the affair, he was the cause of all that Jane had suffered. He had ruined every hope of happiness for the most affectionate, generous heart in the world.

"There were some very strong objections against the lady," were Colonel Fitzwilliam's words. And what would these strong objections be? Probably her having one uncle who was only a country attorney, and another who was in business in London.

"To Jane herself," Eliza told herself, "there could be no possible objection. She is everything lovely and good. She is intelligent, well read, and wonderfully kind and polite. And no one could object to my father. While he has his peculiarities, he is an able and respected man." When she thought of her mother, her confidence weakened a little. But she convinced herself that Mr. Darcy's pride would not allow his friend to marry into a family without important connections. She decided at last that he had been influenced by the worst kind of pride.

She was so upset that she cried, and crying brought on a headache. It grew so much worse through the afternoon that she decided not to go with her hosts to Rosings, where they were invited for the evening. Mrs. Collins, seeing that she was really unwell, did not encourage her to go. She tried to prevent her husband from pressing Eliza as well, but Mr. Collins could not conceal his worry that Lady Catherine might be displeased by her staying at home.

CHAPTER 34

When they were gone, Elizabeth, as though she wanted to make herself as angry as possible, re-read all the letters Jane had written to her since she was in Kent. In them, Jane did not complain of anything. She did not mention Bingley's name, or say that she was sad. But they were not happy letters. There was none of the cheerfulness which had always been her style; none of that relaxed, easy tone which flowed from a happy heart. It made Eliza furious to think of Darcy's boast that he had caused this misery. It was some comfort to think that his visit to Rosings was to end the day after tomorrow.

While thinking about these things, she was startled by the sound of the doorbell. She wondered if it might be Colonel Fitzwilliam. He had once called this late in the evening, and might be dropping in to inquire about her health.

But this idea quickly vanished when, to her utter amazement, Mr. Darcy walked into the room. He hurriedly asked how she was feeling. She answered him with cold politeness. He sat down briefly, then got up and began walking about the room. Elizabeth was surprised, but she did not say a word.

After a silence lasting several minutes, he came toward her, his face upset and excited, and burst out with these words. "I have struggled in vain. It is useless. My feelings will not be ignored. You must allow me to tell you how deeply I admire and love you."

Elizabeth's astonishment was boundless. She stared at him in stunned silence, blushing, unable to believe what she had heard. He took this for encouragement, and began to pour out all that he had long felt for her.

He spoke well, but he spoke not only about his love for her. In addition, he talked about her social inferiority, stressing the fact that in the eyes of the world, she was a poor choice for him. He spoke of the inequalities existing between their families. He talked of these things with a passion that was impressive, but was not likely to please his listener.

In spite of Eliza's deeply-rooted dislike for Darcy, she was aware that he was paying her a great compliment. Although she never for a moment thought of accepting him, she felt sorry at first for the pain that she was going to cause him. But as he continued to talk, all her compassion was swallowed up by her anger.

Darcy finally stopped after assuring her again of the strength of his love, which, as hard as he had tried, he had found impossible to conquer. He added that he hoped he would now be rewarded with her hand in marriage.

As he said this, Eliza could see that he was certain she would accept his proposal. His confidence angered her further, and when he was silent, the color rose in her cheeks as she began to speak.

"In situations such as this, I believe a lady is expected to voice her gratitude for the feelings that have been expressed, no matter how one-sided they might be," Eliza began. "If I could feel gratitude, I would now thank you. But I cannot. I have never wanted your good opinion, and you have certainly given it most unwillingly. I am sorry to have caused pain to anyone. It has been done without my intention, however, and I hope it will not last long."

Mr. Darcy was leaning against the mantlepiece with his eyes fixed on her face. He seemed to hear her words with equal surprise and resentment. His face became pale with anger, and he was visibly struggling to control himself. Finally, in a voice of forced calmness, he said, "And this is all the reply which I can expect? I might, perhaps, ask why you reject me so rudely. But it hardly matters."

Eliza responded, "And I might ask why you chose to tell me you liked me in such a deliberately offensive way! You tell me that you cared for me against your will, against your good sense, and even against your character! If I was rude, isn't that an excuse? But I have other reasons. You know I have. Even if my own feelings toward you had been different, do you think I would consider accepting the man who has ruined the happiness of my most beloved sister?"

As she said these words, angry color flooded Mr. Darcy's face, but he listened without attempting to interrupt her as she continued.

"I have every reason in the world to think badly of you," Eliza went on. "Nothing can excuse the cruel and unjust way you acted. You cannot deny that you deliberately divided them from each other. You have made Mr. Bingley look foolish, flighty, and unstable, and you have exposed Jane to being mocked and pitied for her disappointed hopes. You have caused them both misery of the most painful kind."

She paused, and saw with indignation that he was listening, not with a look of guilt or remorse, but with a forced smile of amusement. "Can you deny that you have done it?" she repeated.

Darcy calmly replied, "I will not deny that I did everything in my power to separate my friend from your sister, or that I am glad that I succeeded. I have been kinder to him than to myself."

Eliza pretended not to hear this final remark. "But it is not only this affair which makes me dislike you," she continued. "Long before it took place, I had formed my opinion of you. I learned the truth about your character many months ago from Mr. Wickham. What do you have to say on that subject? What imaginary act of friendship were you performing then?"

"You are very interested in that gentleman's affairs," said Darcy less calmly.

"Anyone would take an interest when they hear the misfortunes that have befallen him!" she replied.

"His misfortunes!" repeated Darcy mockingly.

"Yes, his misfortunes have been great indeed."

"And you caused them!" cried Elizabeth with energy. "You have reduced him to his present state of poverty. You have denied him the position that was meant for him. You have taken away the independence that he deserved during the best years of his life. You have done all this! And yet you ridicule the mention of his misfortunes."

"So this is your opinion of me!" cried Darcy, as he walked quickly across the room, "I thank you for explaining it so fully. According to you, my faults are heavy indeed! But perhaps you might have overlooked them if I had not hurt your pride by speaking honestly. You might not have made these bitter accusations if I had flattered you blindly. But I hate deception of every sort. And I am not ashamed of the feelings I described. They were natural and just. Could you expect me to be happy about the inferiority of your connections? Should I be pleased to marry into a family whose condition in life is so decidedly beneath my own?"

Elizabeth felt herself growing more angry every moment. Yet she tried with all her might to speak calmly as she said, "You are mistaken, Mr. Darcy, if you think that the way you declared yourself affected me in any way other than this: It spared me the pity which I would have felt in refusing you if you behaved like a gentleman." She saw he was startled at this, but he said nothing, and she continued. "You could not have offered me your hand in any way that would have tempted me to accept it." Again, his astonishment was obvious. He looked at her with an expression of mixed disbelief and embarrassment.

She went on. "From the first moment I met you, it was clear that you were full of hateful arrogance and pride and selfish disregard for the feelings of others. Getting to know you better has only made me dislike you more. By the time I had known you a month, I felt that you were the last man in the world whom I would ever agree to marry."

Darcy broke in. "You have said quite enough, madam. I understand your feelings, and I am only ashamed of what my own have been. Forgive me for having taken up so much of your time, and accept my best wishes for your health and happiness." With these words he hastily left the room, and Elizabeth heard him open the front door and leave the house.

Her mind was a whirlwind of emotion. Weak and shaking, she sat down and cried for half an hour. Her astonishment only grew as she considered what had just happened. Mr. Darcy had asked her to marry him! He had been in love with her for months! So much in love that he wanted to marry her in spite of all the objections he had had to Bingley marrying Jane! It was flattering to have caused such a strong affection. But his pride, his shameless admission of what he had done to Jane, his cruelty toward Mr. Wickham—all these things overcame any feeling of pity that she might have for him. She sat in confusion until she heard the sound of Lady Catherine's carriage. Not wanting Charlotte to see her in this condition, she hurried to her room.

When Eliza woke the next morning, her thoughts were still a confused blur. She was unable to think of anything except what had happened the night before. After breakfast, she decided to go out for some air and exercise, in hopes that activity might clear her mind. She avoided her favorite walk in the Park, remembering that Mr. Darcy sometimes walked there himself, and instead headed out on a path that ran along the Park's outer border.

Passing the gates of the Park itself, she caught sight of a man standing in a small grove of trees. He was moving her way, so she turned and headed back in the direction from which she had come. But the person was now close enough to see her, and she heard Mr. Darcy calling her name. He was walking quickly toward her, holding out a letter.

"I have been walking in the grove for some time, hoping to meet you," he said. "Will you do me the honor of reading this letter?" Putting the letter into her hand, he gave a slight bow. He turned away and was soon out of sight.

Not expecting anything pleasant, but very

curious, Eliza opened the envelope to see two sheets of paper closely covered with writing. As she continued her walk, she began to read:

Do not be alarmed at receiving this letter. It does not contain any mention of those feelings which were so disgusting to you last night. I am writing without any wish to cause either you or me pain. But there are things that I must say. You must, therefore, pardon me for demanding your attention. I know that you give that attention unwillingly, but I ask it out of your sense of justice.

Last night, you accused me of two offenses. The first was that, ignoring the feelings of either, I had separated Mr. Bingley from your sister. The other was that I had cruelly and inhumanely ruined the future of Mr. Wickham.

If I had deliberately betrayed the companion of my youth, my father's favorite, a young man who had been brought up to depend upon my family's generosity—that would be a far greater evil than separating two young persons who had known one another only a few weeks. I hope that my explanation will excuse me from some of the blame which you so generously heaped upon me last night. If, as I explain, I have to say things which are offensive to you, I can only say that I am sorry.

Very soon after I arrived in Hertfordshire, I saw that Bingley liked your oldest sister better than any other young woman there. But it was not until the ball at Netherfield that I began to suspect he was becoming seriously involved. I had often seen him in love before. At that ball, while I had the honor of dancing with you, I realized from Sir William Lucas's comments that the neighbors expected them to marry. Sir William spoke of the marriage as a certain event, as if it were only a matter of setting the date.

From that moment I watched my friend's behavior carefully. I realized that his affection for Miss Bennet was beyond anything I had ever witnessed in him. I also watched your sister. She seemed as cheerful and charming as ever, but I saw no sign of particular feeling for Bingley. I became convinced that while she enjoyed his attentions, she did not attach any great meaning to them. If you are correct here, I was mistaken. You know your sister much better than I. If I *was* mistaken and caused her pain, I understand your resentment. But I still say that your sister's calm, serene manner make it seem that her heart had not been deeply touched.

My objections to the marriage were not only the lack of family connections which I mentioned last night. There were other causes for concern. They are causes which I have tried to forget, because they were not immediately in front of me. But I must state those causes.

It is true that the status of your mother's family is not desirable. But that is nothing compared to the wildly improper behavior so frequently shown by her, by your three younger sisters, and occasionally even by your father. Pardon me. It pains me to offend you. I hope it will comfort you to know how completely you and your older sister escape any similar criticism. That is greatly to the credit of you both.

In short, the evening of the ball convinced me that I should try to save my friend from what I felt sure would be a very unhappy situation. As you know, he left Netherfield for London the following day, expecting to return soon. I will now explain my actions. Bingley's sisters were equally worried about his attachment to your sister. When we discovered our mutual concern, we decided to join him in London. Once we arrived, I wasted no time in pointing out to Bingley the disadvantages of such a marriage. I do not think that would have been enough to prevent his return, but I also told him my opinion that your sister did not greatly care for him. He had believed that she returned his affection, if not as strongly as he gave it. But Bingley is a very modest man, and he depends upon my judgment. It was not difficult to convince him that he had been mistaken. After that, convincing him to stay in London was simple indeed.

There is only one thing that I did that disturbs me. That is hiding the fact that your sister was in London. I knew she was there; so did Miss Bingley, but Bingley does not know to this day. Probably, if they had met, nothing would have happened, but I was not certain enough that his feelings for her had died, and there might have been some danger. Perhaps keeping this secret was beneath me. It is done, however, and it was done for the best. On this subject I have nothing more to say and no other apology to offer. If I have hurt your sister, I did it unknowingly. Although my reasons probably seem inadequate to you, I still believe they were sound.

Now, about the other accusation of having injured Mr. Wickham. I can only explain matters by telling you how he is connected with my family. I do not know exactly what he has accused me of, but I can easily prove the truth of all I am about to say.

Mr. Wickham is the son of a very good, respectable man who managed the Pemberley estates for many years. As a result, my father took a special interest in his son, George Wickham, who was his godson. My father supported Wickham at school, and afterward at university. This assistance was very important, as his own father would not have been able to give him a gentleman's education.

Wickham was always a charming young man, and my father not only enjoyed his company but thought very highly of him. He hoped that Wickham would become a clergyman, and he intended to help him along in that career.

But I had begun to think of Wickham differently many years ago. He had developed wicked tendencies and a completely immoral nature. These he carefully hid from my father. But I was a young man of his own age and was able to observe him when he had his guard down. Here, again, I am afraid I will cause you pain. But whatever affection you may have for Mr. Wickham gives me another motive for revealing his real character.

My dear father died about five years ago. His friendship to Mr. Wickham was steady to the end. In his will, he recommended that I help Wickham's career in the church in any way possible. If he became a pastor, my father wanted him to be given a valuable family living when it became available. There was also a legacy of one thousand pounds.

Old Mr. Wickham did not live long after my father's death. Perhaps six months later, Mr. Wickham wrote to tell me that he had decided against entering the church. Since he could not benefit from the living, he asked for me to give him some immediate financial settlement. He added that he intended to study the law. I hoped that he was sincere, although I did not believe it. But, at any rate, I was perfectly ready to agree. I knew that Mr. Wickham should not be a clergyman. The business was therefore soon settled. He gave up all claim to my family's assistance in the church in exchange for three thousand pounds.

I believed that all connection between us was now ended. I thought too badly of him to invite him to Pemberley. He went on living in London, but his studying the law was a mere pretense. Now being free to do as he liked, he lived a life of idleness and vice. For about three years I heard little about him. But when the person holding the living which had once been intended for him died, he wrote me again. He told me that his circumstances were very bad, which I could easily believe, and that he had not liked the study of law. He claimed that he was now determined to become a clergyman, and asked me to give him the vacant position. He added that he was sure I would go along with his wishes, as they had been the desire of my respected father.

I am sure you will not blame me for refusing his request. He was most angry and resentful, and I am sure he spoke very badly of me to others. After this incident, we had no further contact. I have no idea how he was living.

But last summer I was most painfully forced to notice Mr. Wickham again. I must now tell you something which I wish I could forget myself, and which nothing less than the present situation could make me tell another human being. I know that I can trust in your secrecy.

My sister is more than ten years younger than I. Being an orphan, she is the ward of Colonel Fitzwilliam and myself. About a year ago, she left school and I settled her in London, in the care of Mrs. Younge, a woman we had every reason to believe was trustworthy and respectable. Last summer, Georgiana and Mrs. Younge went on holiday to a seaside village. Mr. Wickham went there as well. He had made secret arrangements with Mrs. Younge, whom he had known for many years. This lady aided Mr. Wickham in wooing Georgiana, who had affectionate memories of his kindness to her as a child. Wickham convinced her that she was in love, and she agreed to elope with him. She was only fifteen.

I am happy to add that I learned of this situation from Georgiana herself. I visited her unexpectedly a day or two before the intended elopement. Georgiana was unable to bear the idea of wounding me, whom she looked on almost as a father. She told me the whole story.

You may imagine what I felt. Concern for my sister's reputation and feelings prevented me from publicly exposing Mr. Wickham, but I wrote to him, and he left the place immediately. Mrs. Younge, of course, I immediately fired.

Mr. Wickham's reason for targeting my sister was undoubtedly her fortune, which is thirty thousand pounds. But I cannot help thinking that his actions were also designed as a revenge against me.

This, madam, is a truthful account of both events. If you do not believe me to be an outright liar, I hope you will withdraw your accusation that I have been cruel to Mr. Wickham. I do not know what lies he has told you, but his success is not surprising. He can be very charming. You knew none of our history, and you are not by nature a suspicious person.

You may wonder why I did not tell you all this last night. I was not in a calm enough state of mind to decide what I should or should not reveal. You may check the truth of everything I have said by speaking with Colonel Fitzwilliam. As one of the executors of my father's will, he was involved in the details of this sorry tale. In the meantime, I shall hope to find some opportunity to put this letter in your hand. I will only add, God bless you.

Fitzwilliam Darcy

CHAPTER 36

Elizabeth had no idea what Mr. Darcy's letter would contain. It is easy to imagine how eagerly she read it and what confusion his words created in her. She began it with a firm belief that nothing he could say would excuse his conduct. She read his account of what had happened at Netherfield with the strongest prejudice against everything that he might say. She read so hastily that she could hardly understand the words, out of impatience to know what the next sentence would bring.

She instantly rejected as false his belief that Jane had not been in love. His comments about her family made her too angry to consider them. He did not apologize in any way that satisfied her. His style was not apologetic, but haughty. It was all pride and insolence.

But when she read his story about Mr. Wickham, her feelings were more difficult to define. She was filled with wonder, worry, and even horror. She wanted to disbelieve it all, and she repeatedly said out loud, "This must be false! This cannot be! This must all be lies!" When she had read through the whole letter she hastily put it away, swearing that she would never look at it again. In this disturbed state of mind she walked on. But within thirty seconds she had unfolded the letter again. Calming herself the best she could, she began re-reading the section about Wickham, forcing herself to pay attention to every sentence.

Mr. Darcy's description of Mr. Wickham's connection with his family was exactly as Mr. Wickham himself had explained it. If anything, the late Mr. Darcy's kindness to him had been greater than he had said. So far, the two men's stories were the same. But when it came to the will, the differences were great. What Wickham had said about being promised the position in the church was fresh in her memory. As she remembered his words, it was clear that one of the two stories was grossly false.

For a few moments, she told herself that it was Wickham who was being truthful. But when she read and re-read the details about Wickham giving up all claims to the position in the church in exchange for the very generous sum of three thousand pounds, she was forced to hesitate.

Every line showed more clearly that the affair, which she had believed showed so clearly that Mr. Darcy had acted wickedly, was open to a different interpretation. She was shocked by Mr. Darcy's claims of Mr. Wickham's extravagance and loose living. She was even more disturbed when she realized she had no evidence that those claims were untrue.

She had never heard of him before his entrance into the militia. No one in Hertfordshire knew anything about his former life except what he had chosen to tell them. She knew nothing of his true character.

His good looks, graceful manners, and easy speech had convinced her instantly that he was a nearly perfect man. She tried to remember any incident that had shown him to be good, honorable, or generous—anything that might rescue him from Mr. Darcy's attacks. But no such memory came to her. She could see him easily in her mind, completely charming in appearance and personality, but she could not remember anything about him that was more substantial than that. And then the story about him and Miss Darcy—she realized that might have been confirmed by the conversation between her and Colonel Fitzwilliam only the day before.

She remembered perfectly every word that had passed between Wickham and herself during their first evening at Mr. Philips's. Thinking of that evening, she was now struck by how strange it was that he would tell such a story to a person he had only just met. She wondered why she had not thought of this before. His behavior, too, had been inconsistent. She remembered how he had boasted that he had no fear of seeing Mr. Darcy, and yet he had avoided the Netherfield ball the very next week. She remembered also, that until the Bingleys and Darcy had left Netherfield, he had told his story to no one but herself. But after they were gone, he had told it everywhere.

How differently everything regarding Wickham now looked! His courtship of Miss King now seemed like nothing but the lowest form of money-hunger. His attentions to herself could have only one of two motives, neither of them good: Either he had believed her to have more money than she did, or else he had been feeding his vanity by playing with her affections.

Her struggle to think well of him grew weaker. She remembered then when Jane had asked Mr. Bingley about the affair, Mr. Bingley had assured her that Darcy had acted correctly. As disgustingly proud as Darcy was, Eliza had never seen anything that suggested he could be petty or dishonorable. His friends and family thought very highly of him.

She grew absolutely ashamed of herself. She could not think of either Darcy or Wickham without feeling that she had been blind, prejudiced, and absurd.

"What a fool I have been!" she cried. "I, who have been so proud of my ability to see clearly! I have allowed vanity to blind me. I was pleased with the attention from Wickham, and offended by Darcy's neglect. From the very beginning of our acquaintance, I have shut my eyes to the reality of both. Until this moment, I never knew myself."

Her thought ran in a line from herself to Jane, and then from Jane to Bingley. Recalling her rejection of the first part of Mr. Darcy's letter, she read it again. Her response to this reading was quite different. How could she refuse to give credit to what he said? When he claimed he had been unaware of Jane's attachment to Bingley, she was forced to remember that Charlotte had warned Jane of exactly that. Although Jane felt deeply, her feelings were seldom displayed.

When she came to that part of the letter concerning her family, she was overwhelmed with shame. Her memories of their humiliating behavior the night of the Netherfield ball struck her with full force; those memories would not be denied. She appreciated Darcy's compliment to herself and to Jane, but it could not make up for the contempt which the rest of her family had invited. Realizing that her nearest relations had been the cause of Jane's heartbreak depressed her greatly.

She wandered the lanes for another two hours, turning everything over in her mind. Finally, she returned home, entering the house with every effort at appearing as cheerful as usual. She was immediately told that the two gentlemen from Rosings had come separately to see her during her absence. Mr. Darcy had stayed for only a few minutes, but Colonel Fitzwilliam had waited at least an hour, hoping to see her before he left. Elizabeth could only pretend regret at having missed him. She could think only of her letter.

The two gentlemen left Rosings the next morning. Mr. Collins had waited along the road to make his final bows to them, so he was able to bring home the news that they appeared to be in very good health, and in as good spirits as could be expected, after the sad experience of leaving Lady Catherine.

Next, he hurried to Rosings to comfort Lady Catherine and her daughter. When he returned home he announced, with great satisfaction, that her ladyship was feeling so dull that she wanted them all to dine with her.

When the guests were shown in, Elizabeth could not help thinking that, if she had chosen it, she might by now have been presented to Lady Catherine as her future niece. She also imagined how indignant her ladyship would have been. "What would she have said? How would she have behaved?" she asked herself with some secret amusement.

The first subject of conversation was the departure of the two young men. "I assure you, I feel it exceedingly," said Lady Catherine. "I do not believe anyone feels the loss of friends as much as I do. But I am particularly attached to these young men, and they are equally attached to me. They were extremely sorry to go! But they always are. The dear colonel kept his spirits up until the very end, but Darcy seemed greatly distressed to leave, more than last year. He becomes more attached to Rosings all the time."

After dinner, Lady Catherine observed that Miss Bennet did not seem as cheerful as usual. Immediately explaining it herself, she said that Eliza must be dreading going home again so soon. She added, "But if that is the case, you must write to your mother to ask if you may stay a little longer. Mrs. Collins will be very glad of your company, I am sure."

"Thank you for your kind invitation," replied Elizabeth, "but I am unable to accept it. I must be in London next Saturday."

"Why, at that rate, you will have been here only six weeks!" exclaimed Lady Catherine. "I expected you to stay two months. I told Mrs. Collins so before you came. There can be no reason for you to go so soon. Mrs. Bennet can surely spare you for another two weeks."

"But my father cannot," explained Eliza. "He wrote last week to say that I must come home soon."

"Oh! Your father can do without you, if your mother can," answered her ladyship. "Daughters never matter as much to a father. And if you will stay for another full month, I will be able to take you as far as London, for I am going there early in June."

"You are very kind, madam, but I believe we

must stay with our original plan."

Lady Catherine seemed to give up. But then she changed the direction of her attack. "Mrs. Collins, you must send a servant with Miss Bennet and Miss Lucas. You know I always speak my mind, and I cannot bear the idea of two young women traveling by themselves. It is highly improper. I have the greatest dislike in the world for that sort of thing. Young women should always be properly guarded, according to their situation in life. When my niece Georgiana went to the seaside last summer, I made certain that two manservants went with her. The daughter of Mr. Darcy of Pemberley and Lady Anne could not travel with anything less. You must send John with the young ladies, Mrs. Collins. I am glad it occurred to me to mention it, for it would really be disgraceful to let them go alone."

Eliza broke in. "My uncle is sending a servant for us."

"Oh! Your uncle! He keeps a manservant, does he? I am very glad you have somebody who thinks of those things. Where shall you change horses? Oh! Bromley, of course. Mention my name at the Bell, and you will be properly taken care of."

Lady Catherine asked many other questions regarding their journey, and as she did not answer all of them herself, Eliza was forced to pay some attention. This was fortunate, for her mind was so occupied that otherwise she might have forgotten where she was. She allowed herself to think only when she was alone, and not a day passed during which she did not go on a solitary walk, in which she allowed herself to reflect on unhappy memories.

She soon knew Mr. Darcy's letter almost by heart. She studied every sentence, and her feelings toward its writer changed almost hourly. When she remembered the haughty way he had spoken to her, she was still full of indignation. But when she considered how unjustly she had condemned him, her anger was turned against herself. At those moments, she was sorry for his disappointed feelings. She felt grateful for, and complimented by, his love for her; and she respected his general character. But she could not approve of him, or regret her refusal, or feel the slightest desire to ever see him again.

She was ashamed and sorry of her own past behavior, and the faults of her family were an even unhappier subject to think of. They were hopeless to repair. Her father was content with laughing at them all. He would never bother himself to restrain the wild behavior of his youngest daughters. And her mother, whose own manners were so far from correct, took no notice of their misbehavior. Eliza and Jane had frequently tried to correct the foolishness of Kitty and Lydia, but while their mother indulged and spoiled them, what chance of improvement could there be? Kitty was weak-spirited, irritable, and completely under Lydia's control, and she had always been offended by their advice. Lydia, strong-willed and careless, did not listen to them at all. They were ignorant, idle, and vain. If there was an officer in Meryton, they would flirt with him, and as long as Meryton was within walking distance of Longbourn, they would go there.

Eliza was also worried about Jane. Mr. Darcy's explanation had restored her former good opinion of Bingley, and heightened her sense of what Jane had lost. He had loved Jane after all. And he had done nothing wrong, unless one could blame him for putting too much confidence in a trusted friend. How tragic to think that the prospect of a marriage that was so desirable in every way, so promising of happiness, had been taken away from Jane by the foolish behavior of her own family! When these thoughts were added to what Eliza now knew of Wickham's character, her usually happy spirits became so downtrodden as to make it almost impossible for her to appear cheerful.

Their invitations to Rosings were as frequent during the last week of her stay as they had been at first. They spent her very last evening there, and her ladyship asked detailed questions about their journey, instructed them in the best method of packing, and was so insistent about her method of placing gowns that when they returned home, Maria believed she had to undo all her packing of the morning and do it over again.

When they parted, Lady Catherine wished them a good journey, and invited them to come to Hunsford again next year. Miss de Bourgh troubled herself enough to curtsey and shake hands with both of them.

CHAPTER 38

On Saturday morning, Eliza and Mr. Collins met at the breakfast table a few minutes before the others appeared. He took the opportunity of expressing that which he felt necessary.

"I know not, Miss Elizabeth," he said, "whether Mrs. Collins has yet expressed her sense of your kindness in coming to see us, but I am very certain you will not leave the house without receiving her thanks for it. The favor of your company has been much felt, I assure you. We know how little there is to tempt anyone to our humble abode. Our plain manner of living, our small rooms, and few servants, must make Hunsford extremely dull to a young lady like yourself. But I hope you will believe us grateful for your visit, and that we have done everything in our power to make your time pass pleasantly."

Elizabeth thanked Mr. Collins with all sincerity. She had enjoyed her six week visit, and seeing Charlotte, and all the kind attention she had received. Mr. Collins was pleased. With more smiling solemnity he replied, "It gives me the greatest happiness to hear that you have passed your time not disagreeably. We have certainly done our best. Most fortunately, we have it in our power to introduce you to very superior society through our connection with Rosings. Our situation with regard to Lady Catherine's family is, indeed, the sort of blessing which few can boast."

Words were not enough to express his feelings, and he was forced to get up and walk about the room, while Elizabeth tried to think of a reply that would be both polite and true. But Mr. Collins went on:

"You may, my dear cousin, carry a very happy report of us back to Hertfordshire. You have witnessed Lady Catherine's great attentions to Mrs. Collins. Altogether, I believe you can see that your friend has not been unfortunate—but on this point, it is well to be silent. Only let me assure you, my dear Miss Elizabeth, that I wish you equal happiness in marriage. My dear Charlotte and I share one mind and one way of thinking. We are identical in our characters and ideas. We seem to have been designed for each other."

Elizabeth could safely say that it was wonderful when this happened, and with equal truthfulness, that she could see he was very happy and comfortable. She was not sorry, however, to have the conversation interrupted by Charlotte's entrance. Poor Charlotte! It was sad to leave her with such a man! But she had chosen him with her eyes open. And while she seemed sorry that Eliza and Maria were leaving, she did not ask for their pity. Her home and her housekeeping, as her work in her husband's parish, all still interested her.

At last the carriage arrived, the trunks were tied on top, the parcels placed inside, and it all was ready. After an affectionate parting between the friends, Elizabeth was shown to the carriage by Mr. Collins. As they walked down the garden, he was reminding her to deliver his best respects to all her family. She and Maria settled in their seats and the door was on the point of being closed when he suddenly reminded them, with some excitement, that they had forgotten to leave any message for the ladies at Rosings.

"But," he added, "you will, of course, wish to have your humble respects delivered to them, with your grateful thanks for their kindness to you while you have been here." Elizabeth did not object. He then allowed the door to be shut, and the carriage drove off.

"Good gracious!" cried Maria, after a few minutes silence, "It seems like only a few days since we first came! And yet how many things have happened!"

"A great many indeed," said her companion with a sigh.

"We have dined at Rosings nine times, besides having tea there twice! added Maria. "How much I shall have to tell!"

Elizabeth silently added, "And how much I shall have to hide."

Their journey continued without much conversation. Within four hours they reached Mr. Gardiner's house, where they were to stay for a few days. Jane looked well, but their aunt had kindly arranged so many amusements for them that she did not have much opportunity to determine how her sister was really feeling. But Jane was to go home with her, and at Longbourn there would be plenty of time for observation.

It was difficult to wait even for Longbourn before she told her sister of Mr. Darcy's proposal. To know that she possessed information which would so astonish Jane made it very tempting to speak, but she was still undecided exactly how open to be. She was afraid that, once she began talking, she might repeat things about Bingley which might only hurt her sister more.

CHAPTER
39

It was the second week in May when the three young ladies set out together for their homes in Hertfordshire. As they drew near the inn where Mr. Bennet's carriage was to meet them, they saw both Kitty and Lydia looking out of a dining room upstairs. These two girls had been waiting for more than an hour, happily employed in visiting the local hatmaker, watching the officers on guard, and tossing a cucumber salad.

After welcoming their sisters, they proudly displayed a table set with lunch, exclaiming, "Isn't this nice? Isn't this a pleasant surprise?"

"And we meant to treat you all," added Lydia, "but you must lend us the money, for we have just spent ours at the hat shop." Showing her purchases, she explained, "Look at the bonnet I bought. I do not think it is very pretty, but I thought I might as well buy it. I'll pull it to pieces as soon as I get home, and see if I can make it up any better." When her sisters criticized it as ugly, she added cheerfully, "Oh, but there were two or three in the shop that were much uglier. When I have bought some prettier satin to trim it with, I think it will be all right. Besides, it will hardly matter what anyone wears this summer, because the militia is leaving Meryton. They will go in two weeks."

"Are they really going?" cried Elizabeth, with mixed happiness and relief.

"Yes, they are going to be encamped near Brighton, and I do so want Papa to take us all there for the summer! It would be such fun, and I think it would hardly cost anything at all. Mama wants to go, too. Only think what a miserable summer we will have otherwise!"

"Yes," thought Elizabeth, "that would be great fun, indeed, and completely wreck our family's reputation. Good heavens! What would happen if we were in Brighton, near a whole camp full of soldiers? One little regiment and the balls of Meryton were bad enough for us."

"Now I have got some news for you," said Lydia, as they sat down to eat. "What do you think? It is excellent news, about a certain person that we all like."

Jane and Elizabeth looked at each other, and Eliza signaled Lydia to be silent until the waiter was gone. Lydia laughed, and said, "Oh, why are you so formal and stuffy? You thought the waiter must not hear, as if he cared! I'm sure he often hears worse things said than what I am going to say. What an ugly fellow! I am glad he is gone. I never saw such a long chin in my life. Well, but now for my news.

It is about dear Wickham. It turns out there is no danger of him marrying Miss King. She has moved away to live with her uncle in Liverpool. So Wickham is safe."

"And Mary King is safe!" added Elizabeth. "Safe from a marrying unwisely."

"She is a great fool for going away, if she liked him," retorted Lydia.

"But I hope there is no strong attachment on either side," said Jane.

"I am sure there is not on his," Lydia said. "Who could care about such a nasty little freckled thing?"

As soon as the girls had eaten, and the older ones paid, the whole group and their luggage (with the unwelcome addition of Kitty's and Lydia's purchases) were loaded into the carriage. "How nicely we are crammed in!" cried Lydia. " Well, now let us be quite comfortable and snug, and talk and laugh all the way home. To begin, let us hear what has happened to you all, since you went away. Have you seen any pleasant men? Have you been flirting? I had high hopes that one of you would get a husband before you came back. Jane will be quite an old maid soon, I declare. She is almost twenty-three! Lord, how ashamed I would be if I were single at twenty-three! My aunt Philips wants you all to get husbands. She says that Lizzy should have taken Mr. Collins, but I do not think that would have been any fun at all. Lord! How I would like to be married before any of you, and then I would chaperone you to all the balls. Dear me! We had such fun the other day at Colonel Forster's. Kitty and I were spending the day there, and Mrs. Forster promised to have a little dance in the evening, and what do you think we did? We dressed up Mr. Chamberlayne in woman's clothes! No one knew of it but Colonel and Mrs. Forster, and Kitty and me, except for my aunt, because we had to borrow one of her gowns, and you cannot imagine how beautiful Chamberlayne looked! When Denny, and Wickham, and Pratt, and two or three more of the men came in, they did not recognize him at all. Lord! How I laughed! And so did Mrs. Forster. I thought I would die. And that made the men suspect something, and then they soon found out what was the matter."

With more chatter and jokes, Lydia attempted to amuse her companions all the way home. Elizabeth listened as little as she could, but she could not ignore the frequent mention of Wickham's name.

At home they received a warm reception. Mrs. Bennet rejoiced to see that Jane was as beautiful as ever. More than once during dinner Mr. Bennet said to Elizabeth, "I am glad you are back, Lizzy." There was a crowd at the dinner table, for almost all the Lucases came to meet Maria and hear the news. Lady Lucas was asking Maria, across the table, about Charlotte's health and well-being. Mrs.

Bennet was very busy, collecting information on the current London fashions from Jane (who sat to her left) and then passing on those details to the younger Lucas girls, on her right. Lydia, speaking more loudly than anyone else at the table, was describing her morning's pleasures to anyone within earshot. "Oh! Mary," she said, "I wish you had gone with us, for we had such fun! As we went along, Kitty and me pulled down all the blinds, and pretended there was nobody in the coach. I would have gone on that way if Kitty had not gotten sick. When we got to the inn, we behaved very well, for we treated the other three to the nicest lunch in the world. If you had gone, we would have treated you too. And then when we left it was such fun! I thought we should never all get into the coach. I was ready to die from laughing. And then we were so merry all the way home! We talked and laughed so loud that people could hear us from ten miles off." To this, Mary replied very seriously, "I am sure most females would enjoy such pleasures, Lydia. But I confess they hold no charms for me. I would much prefer a book." But Lydia did not hear a word of this. She rarely listened to anybody for more than thirty seconds at a time, and never listened to Mary at all.

In the afternoon, Lydia tried to persuade the rest of the girls to walk to Meryton, but Elizabeth refused. She did not want it said that the Bennet girls were not home half a day before they began chasing after officers. There was another reason for her resistance. She dreaded seeing Wickham again and was determined to avoid it as long as possible. Her relief at knowing that the regiment was leaving town was beyond words. In two weeks they would be gone, and after that she hoped she would never hear his name again.

That same day she realized that the plan of visiting Brighton was under discussion between her parents. Elizabeth saw that her father had no intention of agreeing. But his answers were so vague and non-committal that her mother still hoped of succeeding.

By the next morning, Eliza could not wait any longer to tell Jane what had happened. Leaving out the conversation about Jane and Bingley, she described what had passed between herself and Darcy. Jane was at first astonished, but her sisterly loyalty soon convinced her that it was perfectly natural that anyone should be in love with Elizabeth. She was sorry that Darcy had expressed himself in such a haughty manner, but she was even sorrier to think how unhappy he must have been when Elizabeth refused him.

"He was wrong to be so sure of himself," she said, "but think how disappointed he must have been!"

"I am sorry for him," Eliza agreed. "But you don't blame me for refusing him, do you?"

"Blame you! Oh, no," Jane assured her.

"But you will blame me for one thing," Eliza said. "I should not have criticized him about Wickham as I did. You will understand why when I tell you what happened the next day."

She then told Jane about the letter—at least the

part of it that concerned George Wickham. The story distressed poor Jane very badly. She would have liked to go through life believing that no one could be as wicked as Wickham apparently was.

"I do not know when I have been so shocked," Jane said. "Wickham so very bad! It is almost unbelievable. And poor Mr. Darcy! Lizzy, think how it must have hurt him to hear you speak so badly of him. It is really too upsetting. You must feel the same way."

"Oh, no," Eliza said teasingly. "You are regretful enough for both of us. I know you will be so concerned for him that I feel less worried every moment. If you fret over him much longer, my heart will be as light as a feather."

Jane ignored her. "Poor Wickham! He has such a pleasant, honest face! His manner seems so open and so gentle."

"It is certainly odd," Eliza agreed. "Of those two young men, it seems one has gotten all the goodness, and the other has gotten all the appearance of it."

"I never thought that Mr. Darcy seemed as bad as you did," Jane reminded her.

"And I thought I was so clever in disliking him!" Eliza said, still poking fun at herself. "It is so inspiring to dislike someone that much, you know. I could make fun of him constantly, without ever saying anything fair. When you laugh continually at a man, you eventually do say some witty things."

Jane shook her head. "Lizzy when you first

read that letter, I am sure you could not treat the matter as lightly as you do now."

"Indeed, I could not," Eliza agreed. "I was very uncomfortable, very unhappy. And I had no one to talk to, no Jane to comfort me and say that I had not been as weak and vain and silly as I knew I had! How I needed you!"

"It is too bad that you spoke so strongly about Wickham to Mr. Darcy, because now it does seem your criticism of him was undeserved."

"That is very true. And now, I need your advice. I want to know whether to tell our friends here what I have learned about Wickham's character."

"Why would you expose him?" Jane asked. "I cannot see the reason for it. What do you think?"

"I agree, I will not tell," Eliza said. "Mr. Darcy told me the story in confidence. Clearly he would not want the part about his sister to be made public. And goodness—who will believe me? The general dislike against Mr. Darcy is so strong that it would be the death of half the good people in Meryton to try to change their opinions. I am not up to the job. Wickham will soon be gone, and after that it won't matter to anybody here what he is really like. Sometime he will be all found out, and then you and I may laugh at their stupidity at not knowing it earlier."

"You are quite right," agreed Jane. "To have his story made public might ruin him forever. Perhaps he is now sorry for what he has done, and is trying to change. We must not interfere with that."

This conversation made Elizabeth feel better. She had gotten rid of two of the secrets that had weighed her down, and she knew that Jane would be a willing listener when she needed to talk of them again. But her heart was still heavy. She did not dare tell Jane the other half of Darcy's letter, or explain to Jane how sincerely Bingley had cared for her. Under the circumstances, this was knowledge that could only cause Jane further sorrow.

Now that Eliza was settled at home, she was able to observe her sister closely. She saw that Jane was not happy, and that she still felt deeply for Bingley. Jane had never even imagined herself to be in love before, so her feelings for him had all the fire of first love, plus the warmth and depth which maturity brought. She remembered him so fondly, and preferred him so much over any other man, that it took all her good sense not to spend every day steeped in regret.

"Well, Lizzy," said Mrs. Bennet one day, "what do you think of this sad business of Jane's? As far as I'm concerned, I am determined never to speak of it again. I told my sister Philips so the other day. But I cannot find out if Jane saw him at all in London. Well, he is a very undeserving young man—and I do not suppose there is the least chance of her ever getting him now. No one has heard of him coming to Netherfield again in the summer, and I have asked everybody who is likely to know."

"I do not believe that he will ever live at

Netherfield again," Eliza answered.

"Oh, well! Fine, then. Nobody wants him to come. Though I will always say that he treated my daughter very badly, and if I was her, I would not have put up with it. Well, my comfort is that I am sure Jane will die of a broken heart, and then he will be sorry for what he has done."

But Elizabeth was not comforted by this thought, so she remained silent.

"Well, Lizzy," continued her mother soon afterward, "so the Collinses live very comfortable, do they? Well, I only hope it will last. I imagine that Charlotte is an excellent manager, if she is half as sharp as her mother. I am sure there is nothing wasteful in her housekeeping."

"No, nothing at all."

"She will manage well, depend upon it. They will not live above their income. They will never be distressed for money. Well, much good may it do them! I suppose that they often talk about having Longbourn, once your father dies. I'm sure they look upon it as their own, whenever that happens."

"Naturally, they did not speak of that before me," Eliza answered.

"No, it would have been strange if they had," her mother continued. "But I am certain that they often talk of it between themselves. Well, if they can rest easy with an estate that is not lawfully their own, they can have it. I would be ashamed of having one that I got through an entailment."

CHAPTER
41

It was the last week of the regiment's stay in Meryton, and the young ladies in the neighborhood were growing very depressed. Only Jane and Elizabeth Bennet were still able to eat, drink, and sleep, and go about their usual activities. Kitty and Lydia constantly scolded them for their hardheartedness in the face of the younger girls' misery.

"Good heavens, what will become of us! What will we do?" they often exclaimed, with great bitterness. "How can you be smiling, Lizzy?"

Their affectionate mother shared their grief. She remembered what she had endured on a similar occasion, twenty-five years earlier. "I am sure that I cried for two days when Colonel Millar's regiment went away," she said. "I thought my heart would break."

"I am sure I will break mine," said Lydia.

"If only we could go to Brighton!" observed Mrs. Bennet.

"Oh, yes! If only! But Papa is so disagreeable," said Lydia. "A little time by the sea would be wonderful."

"And my aunt Philips is sure it would do me a great deal of good," added Kitty.

These were the sort of complaints echoing constantly through the Bennet household. Elizabeth tried to be amused by them, but her pleasure was lost in shame. She heard her mother and sisters as Mr. Darcy would have—ridiculous, vain, and foolish—and she had to admit that he was justified in wanting to protect his friend from marrying into such a family.

But then Lydia's gloom turned to joy. She received an invitation from Mrs. Forster, the wife of the colonel of the regiment, to accompany her to Brighton. Mrs. Forster was a very young woman, and only recently married. She very much resembled Lydia in good humor and high spirits, and the two had quickly become intimate friends.

The happiness of Lydia on this occasion, her adoration of Mrs. Forster, the delight of Mrs. Bennet, and the anger and jealousy of Kitty can scarcely be described. Completely ignoring her sister's feelings, Lydia flew about the house in ecstasy, demanding everyone's congratulations, and laughing and talking more than ever. Poor Kitty complained loudly of her fate. "I cannot see why Mrs. Forster did not invite me as well as Lydia," she said. "Even if we are not as close friends, I have just as much right to be asked as she has, and more too, for I am two years older."

Elizabeth was deeply concerned about this invitation. In her opinion, if Lydia went to Brighton under such conditions it would completely destroy the girl's common sense. As much as Lydia would hate her for it, Eliza secretly advised her father not to let Lydia go. She reminded him of Lydia's foolish, reckless behavior. She told him that no good could come of Lydia's friendship with a woman such as Mrs. Forster. She assured him that Lydia would be more, rather than less, wild on her own in Brighton, where the temptations would be greater than at home.

Mr. Bennet listened to her, then said, "Lydia will never be satisfied until she has made a great fool of herself in public, and we may never have another chance for her to do it at so little cost or inconvenience to her family."

"If you realized the problems that Lydia's behavior has already created for us, I am sure you would act differently," said Elizabeth.

"Already created?" repeated Mr. Bennet. "What, has she frightened away some of your lovers? Poor little Lizzy! But do not be discouraged. A young man who cannot bear a little foolishness is not worth regretting. Come, let me see the list of the fellows who have been kept away by Lydia's idiocy."

"That is not what I mean," Elizabeth answered. "I am talking of more general harm. Our whole family's reputation has been injured by Lydia's wild behavior. Excuse me, but I must speak plainly. If you, my dear father, will not bother to rein her in, it will soon be too late. She will, at sixteen, be the biggest flirt that ever made herself and her family ridiculous. She has no attractions besides youth and good looks. Her ignorance and the emptiness of her mind makes her unable to deal with the contempt that society will feel for her. Kitty is also in danger. She will follow wherever Lydia leads. They are both vain, ignorant, idle, and absolutely uncontrolled! Oh, my dear father, don't you realize how they will be despised wherever they are known? Don't you see that their sisters will be affected by their disgrace?"

Mr. Bennet saw how serious she was. Affectionately taking her hand, he replied, "Do not make yourself uneasy, my love. Everyone who knows you and Jane will respect and value you. You will not be blamed for having a couple of—or I may say, three—very silly sisters. We will have no peace if Lydia does not go to Brighton. Let her go then. Colonel Forster is a sensible man, and will keep her out of any real mischief. Luckily, she is too poor to be a real target for anyone. At Brighton, she will be just one of hundreds of common flirts. The officers will find women that are better worth their notice. Let us hope that being there may teach her how unimportant she is."

Elizabeth had to be satisfied with this answer, and she left him feeling let down and sorry. But she was not someone who wallowed in disappointment. She believed that she had done her duty, and she refused to worry about possible future developments.

If Lydia and her mother had known about her talk with her father, they would have been angry beyond belief. In Lydia's imagination, a visit to Brighton involved every type of earthly happiness. She imagined the streets of that seaside town packed with officers. She pictured herself seated beneath a tent, tenderly flirting with at least six of them at once. But she was ignorant of Elizabeth's efforts, and her happiness grew until the day she was to leave home.

Elizabeth was now to see Mr. Wickham for the last time. She had been at several parties with him since her return, and she was calm about the idea of their final meeting. She had begun to see, behind his gentle manner, a sort of artificial quality that wearied and disgusted her. In addition, he had begun to pay the same kind of special attention to her that he had when they first met. Given the circumstances, this irritated rather than pleased her. It annoyed her that he apparently believed that she would be happy to have his affection.

On the very last day of the regiment's stay in Meryton, Wickham and a number of the other officers dined at Longbourn. In the past, she might have protected him from the knowledge that she had seen Mr. Darcy. But now she cared little about his peace of mind. When he asked about her visit to Hunsford, she mentioned that Colonel Fitzwilliam and Mr. Darcy had spent three weeks at Rosings. She asked if he was acquainted with the colonel.

Wickham looked surprised and alarmed at her question. But then, with a charming smile, he replied that when he was younger he had seen the colonel often. He asked how she had liked him. She answered that she had liked him a great deal.

A little later, acting very casual, Wickham asked, "How long did you say that Colonel Fitzwilliam was at Rosings?"

"Nearly three weeks," Elizabeth answered.

"And you saw him frequently?"

"Yes, almost every day."

"His personality is very different from his cousin's," Wickham remarked.

"Yes, very different. But I think Mr. Darcy improves when one knows him better."

"Indeed!" cried Wickham, giving Elizabeth a sharp look. "And exactly how—?" But then he stopped himself and added in a lighter tone, "Has he become more polite? For I dare not hope that his actual character has changed."

"Oh, no," said Elizabeth. "I believe that his character is just the same as it ever was."

Wickham looked as if he didn't know whether to be happy or alarmed at her words. She added, "When I said that he improves on acquaintance, I did not mean that he is easier to get along with. I meant that when one knows him better, one can understand him better."

Wickham now looked unmistakeably alarmed. He was silent for some time, before saying to Elizabeth in the gentlest, most confiding tone of voice, "You know my feelings toward Mr. Darcy, so you will understand how glad I am to hear that he can assume even the appearance of what is right. I worry, though, that this improvement is only pretended during visits to his aunt. He has always been in awe of her. I imagine much of his attitude concerns his desire to marry Miss de Bourgh, a desire I am sure is uppermost in his mind."

Elizabeth could not help smiling at this, but she said nothing. She saw that he wanted to talk about the old subject of how Darcy had done him wrong, and she was in no mood to hear him. The rest of the evening passed without much conversation between the two. They parted politely, perhaps with a mutual desire of never meeting again.

When the party broke up, Lydia went home with Mrs. Forster, as they were to leave for Brighton early the next morning. The separation between her and her family was noisy rather than touching. Kitty was the only one who cried, but her tears were those of anger and envy. Mrs. Bennet loudly advised her daughter to have as much fun as possible. In the noisy happiness of Lydia's departure, her older sisters' more gentle farewells were not even heard.

If all Elizabeth's opinions had been based on her own family, she could not have formed a very pretty picture of married happiness. Her father had been swept away by a girl's youth and beauty, and by the appearance of good humor which youth and beauty generally give. As a result, he had married a woman whose foolishness and ignorance soon put an end to all real affection for her.

Although his expectations about happy married life were destroyed, Mr. Bennet was not the sort of man to seek comfort in drinking or gambling or other vices which often console men who have made foolish choices. He was fond of the country and of books, and these things provided most of his enjoyments. He had very little to do with his wife, aside from being amused by her foolish behavior. This is not the sort of enjoyment which a man in general wants from his wife, but when nothing else is available, a reasonable man will make do.

Elizabeth had never been blind to her father's failures as a husband. His behavior caused her pain, but she respected his abilities and was grateful for his affectionate treatment of herself. So she tried to forget what she could not overlook, and to ignore the lack of husbandly loyalty which made him invite people to treat his wife with contempt. But never before had she felt so strongly the disadvantages of her parents' marriage. Her father was an intelligent and talented man. He could have used those talents to protect his daughters' reputations, even if he could not have improved his wife's mind.

Although Elizabeth was relieved that Wickham was gone, the loss of the regiment did not make her happy otherwise. There were few parties to go to, and at home she had a mother and sister who were constantly complaining about being bored. Elizabeth hoped that Kitty might eventually regain some good sense, but she felt sure that Lydia's bad qualities would only grow stronger while she was in Brighton. All in all, Elizabeth badly needed something to look forward to. Her upcoming visit to the Lakes with her aunt and uncle was now the focus of her happiest thoughts.

When Lydia left, she had promised to write often to her mother and Kitty. But her letters were few and always very short. The letters to Mrs. Bennet rarely said anything more than that they had just returned from the library, where such and such officers had taken them, and where she had seen such beautiful jewels as made her quite wild; or that she had bought a new gown, or a new parasol, which she would have described more fully, but she had to leave that moment, as Mrs. Forster called her and they were going to the camp.

The family learned even less from her letters to Kitty, for a great deal of what she wrote there was to be kept secret.

After the first two or three weeks of her absence, life at Longbourn began to return to normal. The families who had been in London for the winter came back again, and summer fashions and summer parties followed. Mrs. Bennet returned to her usual self-pitying cheeriness, and by the middle of June, Kitty was so much better that she could mention Meryton without bursting into tears. Their tour of the Lakes was only two weeks away, when a letter arrived from Mrs. Gardiner, which both delayed the beginning of the trip and shortened it. She explained that Mr. Gardiner's business would not allow him to depart for another two weeks, and that he must return to London in only a month. That did not allow the group to travel as far as they had planned, so they were forced to give up the Lakes and substitute a shorter tour. The new plan, then, was to go no farther northward than Derbyshire. There was plenty to see there to occupy them for three weeks, and the idea was particularly attractive to Mrs. Gardiner. They would be able to visit the beautiful area where she had lived for several years.

Elizabeth was extremely disappointed. She had set her heart on seeing the Lakes, and still thought there might have been time enough. But she was an even-tempered, easily satisfied young woman, and it was soon all right again.

Derbyshire was the home of Mr. Darcy, and it was impossible to think of that county without thinking of Pemberley and its owner. "But surely I am allowed to enter his county," she told herself, "and even to take away a few fossils without him ever knowing."

Her waiting period was now doubled. Four weeks were to pass before her uncle and aunt's arrival. But finally they did pass by, and Mr. and Mrs. Gardiner and their four children arrived at Longbourn. The children, two girls of six and eight years old, and two younger boys, were to be left in the care of their cousin Jane, who was a great favorite with them.

The Gardiners stayed only one night at Longbourn and set off the next morning with Elizabeth. They headed for the little town of Lambton, where Mrs. Gardiner had formerly lived, and where she still had friends. While visiting Lambton, Elizabeth learned from her aunt that Pemberley was located only five miles away.

In talking over their route the evening before, Mrs. Gardiner expressed a desire to see Pemberley again, and asked Elizabeth if she wouldn't enjoy going. "My love, wouldn't you like to see a place that you have heard so much about?" said her aunt. "A place which so many of your acquaintances are connected. Wickham lived there for years, you know." Elizabeth did not know what to say. She felt that she had no business at Pemberley, and so she pretended to have no interest in seeing it. She claimed that she was tired of great houses; that she really took no pleasure in fine carpets or satin curtains.

Mrs. Gardiner laughed at her stupidity. "If it were merely a fine, richly furnished house," she said, "I would not care about it myself. But the grounds are magnificent. They have some of the finest woods in England."

Elizabeth did not reply, but her mind was racing. She thought of the dreadful possibility of meeting Mr. Darcy while viewing the place. She blushed at the very idea, and thought it might be better to speak openly to her aunt than to run such a risk. But there were many reasons not to do so. She finally decided that telling her aunt would be her last resource, if she learned that Darcy might be at home. Therefore, when she went to her room that night, she asked the hotel chambermaid a few innocent questions: whether Pemberley was a very fine place, what was the name of its owner, and (with some alarm) whether the owner was there for the summer. To her great relief, the maid answered that the Darcy family was not at home.

Now that her nervousness was relieved, she began to feel a great deal of curiosity about the house herself. So when the subject was brought up again the next morning, she readily agreed to the plan. To Pemberley, therefore, they would go.

CHAPTER 43

As they drove along, Elizabeth watched nervously for the first appearance of Pemberley Woods. When they finally turned in at the lodge, her excitement was great. The park was very large, and contained a great variety of beautiful views. Elizabeth's mind was too full for conversation. Then her eye was caught by Pemberley House, sitting on the opposite side of a valley. It was a large, handsome, stone building, standing well on rising ground, and backed by a ridge of high woody hills. In front, a stream swelled into twists and turns of great natural beauty. Elizabeth was delighted. She had never seen a place for which nature had done more, or where nature had been better helped along by good taste. She and the Gardiners were all warm in their admiration, and at that moment she felt that to be mistress of Pemberley might be something!

They approached the house and were greeted by the housekeeper, a respectable-looking, elderly woman. Mrs. Reynolds was much less proud and more friendly than Elizabeth would have expected. She showed them through the first rooms of the house, and Elizabeth admired the beauty and quiet good taste that was evident everywhere. The views from the windows, too, were beyond compare.

"And I might have been mistress of this place!" she wondered to herself. "By now, I might have felt at home in these very rooms! Instead of viewing them as a stranger, I might have been enjoying them as my own, and welcoming my uncle and aunt as visitors to them.

"But no," she thought, as she remembered her conversation with Darcy. "That could never be. My uncle and aunt would have been lost to me. I would not have been allowed to invite them here." This was a lucky thought, as it kept her from feeling any regret.

She wanted to ask the housekeeper whether her master was really absent, but she did not dare. Eventually, however, her uncle asked the same question. Elizabeth rejoiced to hear Mrs. Reynolds answer that he was away, adding, "but we expect him tomorrow with a large party of friends."

Her aunt called her over to look at a picture. She approached and saw a small portrait of Mr. Wickham hanging, with several other miniatures, over the mantlepiece. Her aunt asked her how she liked it. Mrs. Reynolds came forward and told them it was the picture of a young gentleman, the son of her late master's steward, who had been brought up by the late Mr. Darcy. "He has gone into the army," she added, "but I am afraid he has turned out very wild." Mrs. Gardiner looked at her niece with a smile, but Elizabeth could not return it.

"And that," said Mrs. Reynolds, pointing to another of the miniatures, "is my master. It is very like him. It was drawn at the same time as the other—about eight years ago."

"I have heard so much about your master," said Mrs. Gardiner, looking at the picture. "It is a handsome face. Lizzy, is it a good likeness of Mr. Darcy?"

Mrs. Reynolds looked with respect at Elizabeth. "Does this young lady know Mr. Darcy?" she asked.

Elizabeth blushed as she answered, "A little."

"And do not you think he is a very handsome gentleman, ma'am?"

"Yes, very handsome," Elizabeth admitted.

"I don't know anyone who is handsomer. But in the gallery upstairs you will see a finer, larger picture of him than this. This room was my late master's favorite room, and these miniatures are just as he placed them. He was very fond of them." This explained why Mr. Wickham's was still among them.

Mrs. Reynolds then drew their attention to a portrait of Miss Darcy, drawn when she was only eight years old. "And is Miss Darcy as handsome as her brother?" asked Mr. Gardiner.

"Oh, yes," answered Mrs. Reynolds fondly, "the handsomest young lady that you've ever seen, and so talented! She plays and sings all day long. In the next room you'll see a new piano for her, a present from my master. She will come here tomorrow with him."

Mr. Gardiner, whose manners were easy and

pleasant, encouraged the housekeeper to go on with his questions and remarks. It was clear that Mrs. Reynolds enjoyed talking of her master and his sister.

"Does your master spend much of his time at Pemberley?"

"Not as much as I'd like, sir, but I would say he spends half his time here. Miss Darcy is always here for the summer months."

"Except," thought Elizabeth, "when she goes to the seaside."

"If your master would marry, you might see more of him," Mr. Gardiner commented.

"Yes, sir, but I do not know when that will be. I do not know who is good enough for him."

Mr. and Mrs. Gardiner smiled. Elizabeth could not help saying, "It is very much to his credit that you should think so."

"I am saying no more than the truth, and everybody who knows him will say the same," replied the housekeeper. Elizabeth thought this was going pretty far, and she listened with increasing astonishment as Mrs. Reynolds added, "I have never heard a cross word from him in my life, and I have known him ever since he was four years old."

Of all things that Mrs. Reynolds could have said, this surprised Elizabeth most. She had been firmly convinced that Mr. Darcy was not a good-tempered man. She wanted to hear more, so was grateful to her uncle for saying, "There aren't many people who deserve such praise. You are lucky in having such a master."

"Yes, sir, I know I am," replied the housekeeper. "If I went through the world, I could not meet with a better man. But I have always noticed that people who are good-natured as children are good-natured when they grow up. He was always the sweetest-tempered, most generous-hearted boy in the world."

Elizabeth almost stared at her. "Can she be talking about Mr. Darcy?" she thought.

"His father was a very good man," said Mrs. Gardiner.

"Yes, ma'am, he was indeed, and his son will be just like him—just as kind and generous to the poor."

Elizabeth was impatient to hear more. Although Mrs. Reynolds described the subject of the pictures, the dimensions of the rooms, and the design of the furniture, no other topic could interest Elizabeth.

Mr. Gardiner, who was highly amused by what he took to be Mrs. Reynold's prejudice toward the Darcy family, soon led her back to the subject. She added more enthusiastic thoughts as they climbed the great staircase. "He is the best landlord, as well as the best master that ever lived," she said. "Not like so many wild young men nowadays, who think only of themselves. Every one of his tenants and servants will tell you so. Some people call him proud, but I am sure I've never seen any sign of that. In my opinion, it is only because he does not rattle away like other young men."

Mrs. Gardiner whispered to Elizabeth, "All this praise of him does not quite tie in with his behavior to our poor friend."

"Perhaps we were deceived," Elizabeth answered uneasily.

"That is not very likely," her aunt answered. "We heard it from the source."

They had entered the picture gallery, and Elizabeth saw a striking portrait of Mr. Darcy, with a smile on his face as she remembered having sometimes seen when he looked at her. She stood looking at the picture for several minutes and returned to it again before they left the gallery.

Elizabeth's feelings toward the subject of the portrait were more gentle than she had ever felt before. She had been deeply impressed by Mrs. Reynolds's words about him. What praise is more valuable than the praise of an intelligent servant? As a brother, a landlord, a master, how many people's happiness were in his hands! How much pleasure or pain it was in his power to give! How much good or evil could be done by him!

As she stood before the canvas and looked into the eyes of Mr. Darcy's portrait, she thought of his proposal with more gratitude than she had ever felt.

When they had completed their tour of the house, they were turned over to the gardener who would show them the grounds. As they walked across the lawn toward the river, Elizabeth turned back to look at the house. Her uncle and aunt stopped as well, and while Mr. Gardener was commenting on the date of the building, Mr. Darcy himself walked into view.

They were within twenty yards of each other, and his appearance was so sudden that it was impossible for Elizabeth to hide. Their eyes instantly met, and both blushed deeply. For a moment each seemed paralyzed from surprise. Then, recovering himself, Mr. Darcy came forward and greeted Elizabeth, if not perfectly calmly, at least perfectly politely.

She had instinctively turned away. But she forced herself to stop and respond to his greetings, although her embarrassment was great. Even if the Gardiners had not just seen his portrait, the gardener's exclamation of surprise would have told them who this was. They stood back as he talked to their niece, who, astonished and confused, could barely look him in the face. She stumbled over her answers to his polite questions about her family's health.

Amazed at his polite and gracious manner, she grew more embarrassed with every word. She would always remember this as the most uncomfortable conversation of her life. He did not seem much more at ease. He, too, stumbled over his words, repeated his questions, and seemed greatly distracted. Finally, after standing a few moments without saying a word, he excused himself and left.

Mr. and Mrs. Gardiner joined her then. They expressed their admiration of his fine looks, but

Elizabeth did not hear a word, and followed them across the lawn in silence. She was overpowered by shame. What a fool she had been to come to Pemberley! How strange must it seem to him! It might seem as if she had purposely thrown herself in his way again. Oh, why had she come? And why had he come home a day earlier than he was expected? She blushed again and again over the awful coincidence of their meeting. And his behavior was so different—what could it mean? That he should even speak to her was amazing! But be so polite, to ask after her family? She had never heard him speak so gently. What a contrast to their last meeting in Rosings Park, when he had so coldly put his letter into her hand! She did not know what to think, or how to explain it.

They had now entered a beautiful walk by the side of the stream. Elizabeth could not see any of it; her thoughts were all fixed on that one spot in Pemberley House, whichever it might be, where Mr. Darcy was at that moment. She dearly wanted to know what he was thinking, how he thought of her, and whether—in defiance of everything—she was still dear to him. Perhaps he had been pleasant to her only because he was comfortable—and yet he had not seemed comfortable. Whether he had felt more pain or pleasure in seeing her she could not tell, but he certainly had not been calm.

Finally, her aunt and uncle's remarks on her absent-mindedness forced Elizabeth to pay more attention to her surroundings. Elizabeth would have liked to explore the river's twists and turns. But when they had crossed the bridge and seen how far they were from the house, Mrs. Gardiner (who was not a great walker) could go no farther, and asked to return to the carriage. They headed in that direction, but their progress was slow. Mr. Gardiner was very fond of fishing, and he was enjoying the occasional appearance of trout in the water, and talking to the gardener about them.

As they wandered on in this manner, they were again surprised by the sight of Mr. Darcy approaching them. With a glance she saw that he was still gentle and polite in manner. As she'd had a little time to recover, she imitated his good manners and made some comment about the beauty of the place. Mrs. Gardiner was standing a little behind her, and when she paused, he asked if she would do him the honor of introducing him to her friends. She could hardly keep from smiling at the thought that he was asking to meet some of the same people whom he had considered so beneath him.

"How surprised he will be when he knows who they are!" she thought. "He thinks they are society people." As she introduced them as her aunt and uncle, she stole a sly look at him to see how he reacted, half-expecting him to hurry away from such disgraceful companions. She did see surprise on his face, but he took it well, and began talking with Mr. Gardiner. Elizabeth could not help feeling pleased. It was comforting that he knew she had some relations she did not need to be ashamed of. She listened carefully to their conversation, glorying in every word from her uncle which showed his intelligence, taste, and good manners.

The two men were talking about fishing, and Mr. Darcy invited Mr. Gardiner to fish there as often as he liked while they were in the neighborhood, even offering to lend him fishing tackle, and pointing out those parts of the stream where the trout were most plentiful. Mrs. Gardiner, who was walking arm-in-arm with Elizabeth, looked at her with undisguised wonder.

They walked on like this for some time, the two ladies in front, the two gentlemen behind. But then Mrs. Gardiner, who was really tired from the exercise of the morning, asked to walk with her husband so that she could lean on his arm. Mr. Darcy exchanged places with her, and walked along beside Elizabeth. After a short silence, Elizabeth spoke. She wanted him to know that she had not expected to find him at Pemberley, so she mentioned that his arrival had been unexpected. "For your housekeeper told us that you would certainly not be here until tomorrow. Indeed, before we decided to visit, we were told that you were not in the area at all," she said.

He agreed that this had been his plan, but that some business with the estate's steward had demanded that he arrive before his guests. "They will join me early tomorrow," he continued, "and among them are some who know you—Mr. Bingley and his sisters."

Elizabeth only nodded. Her thoughts instantly went back to the last time that Mr. Bingley had been discussed between them. Judging from Mr. Darcy's blush, he was remembering the same moment.

Then he went on. "There is one other person in the group who would especially like to meet you. Will you allow me to introduce my sister to you during your stay in the area?"

Elizabeth could not have been more surprised. She realized that Mr. Darcy must have spoken well of her to his sister. Without knowing just what it meant, it was good to know that his resentment had not made him think poorly of her. They now walked on in silence; each of them deep in thought.

They had walked much faster than the others, and when they had reached the carriage, Mr. and Mrs. Gardiner were far behind. Darcy invited Elizabeth into the house, but she insisted she was not tired, and they stood silently on the lawn. She wanted to talk, but every subject seemed forbidden. Finally, she began speaking of her trip, and they talked of handsome forests and pretty views with great energy. But time and her aunt moved slowly, and her patience and her ideas had nearly run out before Mr. and Mrs. Gardiner arrived. At that point Mr. Darcy invited them all to go into the house for some refreshment, but they declined, and parted with the greatest politeness on both sides. Mr. Darcy helped the ladies into the carriage, and as it drove off, Elizabeth saw him walking slowly toward the house.

Now her uncle and aunt could begin their discussion of him. Each of them concluded that he was far superior to anything they had expected. "He is perfectly behaved, polite, and modest," said her uncle.

"He is very dignified, to be sure," replied her aunt, "but not in an unbecoming way. I can now agree with the housekeeper that though some people may call him proud, I have seen nothing of it."

"I was never more surprised than by his behavior to us," added Mr. Gardiner. "He was more than polite; he was really attentive, and there was no need for such attention. He barely knows Elizabeth."

"To be sure, Lizzy," said her aunt, "he is not as handsome as Wickham, although he is a very nice-looking man. But why did you tell us that he was so disagreeable?"

Elizabeth excused herself as well as she could. She said that she had liked him better when they met at Rosings than before, and that she had never seen him so pleasant as this morning.

"But perhaps he may be fickle," added her uncle. "Your great men often are. Therefore, I will not take him at his word about the fishing. He might change his mind and chase me off his grounds."

"From what we have seen of him," continued Mrs. Gardiner, "I really would not have thought that he could have behaved so cruelly to poor

Wickham. He does not seem ill-natured. On the contrary, there is something very pleasing about him. But to be sure, the good lady who showed us the house claimed that he was almost angelic! I could hardly help laughing aloud sometimes. But I suppose he pays her well, and that means a great deal to a servant."

Elizabeth felt that she had to say something in defense of Darcy's behavior toward Wickham. Without releasing many details, she told them that reliable sources had convinced her that his actions regarding Wickham could be interpreted very differently. She let them know that his character was not nearly so faulty, nor Wickham's so good, as she had previously believed.

Mrs. Gardiner was surprised and concerned. But as they were now approaching the scene of her former home, she forgot everything in a rush of happy memories, and she was soon pointing out to her husband all the interesting spots. As tired as she had been by the morning's walk, she took off immediately after dinner to look up her former friends, and the evening was pleasantly spent in discussion and catching up.

The earlier part of the day had been too interesting to leave Elizabeth with much attention for these new friends. She could do nothing but think with wonder of Mr. Darcy's pleasant behavior, and above all, of his wish to introduce her to his sister.

CHAPTER 44

The next morning, the Gardiners and Elizabeth had been walking about the place with some of their friends. They had just returned to the inn to dress themselves in preparation for lunching with the same family when the sound of a carriage drew them to a window. There they saw a gentleman and lady driving up the street. Elizabeth, immediately recognizing the coachman's uniform, guessed who it was, and hastily announced the visit to her relatives.

Her uncle and aunt were amazed. As they noticed Elizabeth's embarrassment, they began to put two and two together. There seemed no other way of explaining such attentions except that Mr. Darcy was courting their niece. While these newborn ideas were passing through their minds, Elizabeth's discomfort was increasing with every moment. She was amazed at her own mental disquiet. She worried that Mr. Darcy might have said too much in her favor, and that she could never live up to his sister's expectations.

She retreated from the window, not wanting to be seen. As she walked up and down the room, trying to calm herself, her aunt and uncle's looks of wondering surprise made every thing worse.

Finally, Miss Darcy and her brother appeared, and the terrifying introduction took place. With astonishment, Elizabeth saw that her new acquaintance was at least as anxious as she herself. She had heard that Miss Darcy was exceedingly proud, but a few minutes of observation convinced her that she was only exceedingly shy. It was hard to persuade her to say anything beyond "yes" or "no."

Miss Darcy was tall, and built on a larger scale than Elizabeth. Although she was only a little over sixteen, her figure was well developed, and she had a womanly, graceful appearance. She was not as handsome as her brother, but her face was sensible and good-humored, and her manners modest and gentle. Elizabeth, who had expected to be thoroughly investigated by Miss Darcy, was much relieved by what she actually found.

The visitors had not been there long before Darcy told Elizabeth that Bingley was also coming to visit her. She barely had time to express her pleasure when Bingley's quick step was heard on the stairs, and he entered the room. All Elizabeth's anger against him had melted away long ago, but if any had remained, it hardly could have stood up against his undisguised delight at seeing her. He asked about her family in a friendly, general way, and looked and spoke as easily and good-humoredly as ever.

Mr. and Mrs. Gardiner were almost as interested as Elizabeth to see Mr. Bingley. They had long wanted to meet him. They were fascinated, indeed, by the whole group before them. Their new suspicions led them to closely observe Mr. Darcy and their niece, and they soon concluded that the gentleman, at least, was in love. They were still a little in doubt about the lady's feeling, but it was evident that Mr. Darcy was overflowing with admiration.

Elizabeth, meanwhile, had a great deal to do. She was trying to read the feelings of each of her visitors, she wanted to calm her own heart, and she wanted to be pleasant to everyone. In this last wish, she was most sure of success, for Bingley, Georgiana, and Darcy were all eager to be pleased.

In seeing Bingley, her thoughts naturally flew to her sister, and she wondered if he, too, was thinking of Jane. Sometimes, she imagined that he looked a little sad; once or twice she wondered if, as he was looking at her, he was trying to see a resemblance between the sisters. But while all this might be imaginary, she was sure of one thing: Miss Darcy was not a rival for Bingley's affections. The two did not exchange a single look that spoke of particular affection. Nothing happened that suggested that Caroline Bingley's hopes would come true.

At one moment, when the others were talking together, Bingley expressed his regret that it had been so long since they had met. Before she had a chance to respond, he added, "It has been over eight months. We have not met since the 26th of November, when we were all dancing together at Netherfield." Elizabeth was pleased that he remembered the date so accurately. Later, he asked her in a private moment whether all of her sisters were at Longbourn.

Their visitors stayed for over half an hour, and when they rose to depart, Mr. Darcy and his sister invited Mr. and Mrs. Gardiner and Elizabeth to dinner at Pemberley the day after next. Bingley expressed great pleasure at the idea of seeing Elizabeth again, and reminded her that they still had a great deal to talk about. Elizabeth interpreted this as meaning that he wanted to hear about Jane, and she was greatly pleased.

After they left, Elizabeth was eager to be alone, and fearful of questions from her uncle and aunt. She stayed with them only long enough to hear their positive opinion of Bingley, and then hurried away to dress. But she had no reason to fear Mr. and Mrs. Gardiner's curiosity. They were not people to force information from others. It was clear to them that she was much better acquainted with Mr. Darcy than they had known, and that he was very much in love with her. They saw much to interest them, but nothing to justify being nosy.

This night, Elizabeth's thoughts were at Pemberley even more than they had been before. The evening, although it seemed long, was not long enough to decide how she felt toward the man in that mansion. Later, she lay awake for two hours trying to make them out.

She certainly did not hate him. No; hatred had vanished long ago. For almost as long, she had been ashamed of ever disliking him. The respect she felt for his good qualities had, at first, been given unwillingly. But now that respect was given readily, due to his recent friendly and respectful behavior.

Above all, above respect and esteem, there was a feeling for him that could not be ignored. It was gratitude. Gratitude, not only for having once loved her, but for still loving her well enough to forgive all her petulance and anger, and all the unjust accusations that she had made. He had reason to avoid her as his greatest enemy. Instead, he seemed eager to preserve her friendship. She could only attribute his behavior to love, ardent love.

And she? She respected him, she was grateful to him. She felt a real interest in his welfare. But she was not sure how much she wanted that welfare to depend upon herself. Would it make them both happy if she used her power, which her heart told her she still possessed, and encouraged him to propose again?

She and her aunt had agreed that it would be polite to return Miss Darcy's call. Therefore, they would visit her at Pemberley the following morning.

Mr. Gardiner left them soon after breakfast. Mr. Darcy had repeated his invitation about the fishing, and there were plans for a group of gentlemen to meet at the stream at noon.

CHAPTER
45

Elizabeth was now convinced that Miss Bingley's dislike of her was rooted in jealousy. Therefore, she did not expect her visit to Pemberley to be very welcome by that lady, but she wondered how obvious Miss Bingley's displeasure would be.

Elizabeth and Mrs. Gardiner were shown into a beautiful salon, whose wide-open windows gave a glorious view of the lawns and woods. Here they were received by Miss Darcy, who was sitting with Mrs. Hurst, Miss Bingley, and Mrs. Annesley, the lady with whom she lived in London. Georgiana greeted them politely, but with shy embarrassment. Mrs. Hurst and Miss Bingley only nodded to them, and a silence fell. It was finally broken by Mrs. Annesley, an agreeable-looking woman, whose efforts to make the guests feel welcome showed her to have better manners than either of the Bingley sisters. She and Mrs. Gardiner, with occasional help from Elizabeth, chatted together pleasantly. Miss Darcy looked as if she wished she had the courage to join in, but she only dared speak a few short sentences.

Elizabeth noticed that Miss Bingley was watching her very closely, and that she could not speak a word, especially to Miss Darcy, without Miss Bingley listening. This observation did not bother her much, as her thoughts were elsewhere. She kept expecting some of the gentlemen to enter the room, and she did not know if she wished or dreaded seeing Mr. Darcy.

After sitting for fifteen minutes without hearing Miss Bingley's voice, the lady coldly asked after the Bennet family's health. Elizabeth answered in an equally brief way, and the two said no more. Servants then entered the room, bringing cold meats, cake, and a variety of all the finest fruits in season. This, finally, gave the group something to do; if they could not talk, they could all eat, and the beautiful pyramids of grapes, nectarines, and peaches soon drew them to the table.

While they were eating, Mr. Darcy entered the room. He had been down at the stream with Mr. Gardiner and some other gentlemen, but as soon as he learned that the ladies were visiting Georgiana, he had come to the house. Elizabeth was determined to be easy-going and unembarrassed in his presence—a resolution that was more easily made than kept—when she saw the hostile way that the Bingley ladies looked at her. With her brother present, Miss Darcy relaxed and became more talkative, and Elizabeth saw that he was anxious for his sister and herself to get acquainted. Miss Bingley saw this as well. With the bad judgment born of anger, she joined in the conversation, saying with sneering pretend politeness, "Miss Eliza, I have heard that the regiment has moved from Meryton! That must be a terrible loss to your family." She did not dare mention Wickham's name in Darcy's presence, but Elizabeth knew she was referring to him. She forced herself to answer carelessly. A glance at Darcy showed that he was distressed, and that his sister was overcome with confusion and embarrassment. If Miss Bingley had known what pain she was inflicting on Miss Darcy, she undoubtedly would have remained silent, but she had merely intended to needle Elizabeth. Miss Bingley did not know a word about Miss Darcy's planned elopement.

Elizabeth's calm behavior disappointed Miss Bingley. Georgiana shook off her embarrassment, although she was silent once again. Their visit ended soon after.

While Mr. Darcy was showing them to their carriage, Miss Bingley was venting her criticisms of Elizabeth's looks, behavior, and dress. But Georgiana would not join her. Her brother's high opinion of Elizabeth was enough for her.

When Darcy returned to the salon, Miss Bingley could not help repeating some of the things she had been saying to his sister.

"How dreadful Eliza Bennet looked this morning, Mr. Darcy," she cried. "I never in my life saw any one so much changed. She has grown so brown and common! Louisa and I were agreeing that we would not have recognized her."

Mr. Darcy coolly answered that he saw no change, other than Elizabeth being rather tanned—not a surprising result of traveling in the summer.

"For my own part," Miss Bingley continued, "I must say that I never thought she was at all pretty. Her face is too thin; her complexion is ordinary, and her features are nothing special. Her teeth are not bad, but nothing remarkable. As for her eyes, which some people have called fine, I have never noticed anything extraordinary about them. They have a sharp, shrewish look, which I do not like at all. All together, she appears self-satisfied without being fashionable—a very bad combination."

Miss Bingley was convinced that Darcy admired Elizabeth, so this was not the wisest way of speaking to him, but angry people are not always wise, and she was pleased to see him look somewhat irritated. He said nothing. As she was determined to make him speak, she went on: "I remember, when we first met her in Hertfordshire, how amazed we all were to find that she was thought to be a beauty. I remember you saying one night, after they had dined at Netherfield, 'She a beauty! I would as soon call her mother clever.' But afterward you seemed to change your mind, and I believe you thought her rather pretty at one time."

"Yes," replied Darcy, who could no longer stay silent. "But that was only when I first knew her. For many months since then, I have considered her one of the most beautiful women I know."

He then went away, and Miss Bingley had to satisfy herself with hearing something that had hurt no one but herself.

On their trip home, Mrs. Gardiner and Elizabeth talked of everything that had happened— except for that which interested them most. They discussed the looks and behavior of everyone except the person they were both thinking of. They talked of his sister, his friends, his house, his fruit, of everything but himself. And still Elizabeth was wanting to know what Mrs. Gardiner thought of him, and Mrs. Gardiner would have been very pleased if her niece had mentioned the subject.

Elizabeth had been disappointed not to find a letter from Jane waiting when they first arrived in Lambton, and she continued to be disappointed on the two following days. On the third, however, she received two letters from her at once. The first had been delivered to the wrong address, and not surprisingly, as Jane had addressed it very carelessly. She and the Gardiners had been about to go out for a walk when the letters arrived, and her uncle and aunt set out by themselves, leaving her to enjoy them privately.

The earliest letter had been written five days ago, so Elizabeth opened it first. The letter began with Jane's description of all her little daily activities. But the second half, which she had written a day later and under obvious stress, gave more important information. It said:

Since I wrote the above, dearest Lizzy, something very unexpected and alarming has happened. Everyone is well—it's not that. But it's about Lydia. A message came at twelve last night, just after we were all gone to bed, from Colonel

Forster. It told us that she had run off to Scotland with one of his officers—with Wickham! Imagine our surprise. To Kitty, however, the news does not seem so unexpected. I am very, very sorry. Such a foolish match on both sides! I am hoping for the best, and that his character has been misunderstood. I have to think that he is thoughtless and careless, but perhaps nothing worse than that. At least we know that his purpose cannot be fortune-hunting, for he must know that our father can give her nothing. Our poor mother is terribly upset. Our father is calmer. How thankful am I that we never let them know what has been said against him. We must forget it ourselves.

It seems that they left Saturday night at about twelve, but they were not missed until yesterday morning at eight. My dear Lizzy, they must have passed within ten miles of us. Colonel Forster is on his way here. Lydia left a short note for his wife, telling her of their plan. I must send this off now, for I must return to our poor mother. I am afraid you will not be able to make any sense of this, but I hardly know what I have written.

Without allowing herself time to think, Elizabeth opened the second letter. It had been written a day later than the first. Jane wrote:

By this time, my dearest sister, you have received my hurried letter. I will try to be clear, but my head is so bewildered that I am not sure I will make sense. Dearest Lizzy, I have bad news, and it cannot be delayed. As foolish as a marriage between Mr. Wickham and our poor Lydia would be, we are now hoping that it has taken place. There is too much reason to believe they have not gone to Scotland after all. Colonel Forster came yesterday, although Lydia's note to Mrs. Forster said that they were going to Gretna Green (where, as you know, girls as young as Lydia can legally marry). Wickham's friend Denny dropped a hint that W. never intended to go there, or to marry Lydia at all. When Colonel F. learned this, he instantly began tracing their route. He traced them easily to Clapham, but beyond that, all that is known is that they were seen on the road leading to London.

Our distress, my dear Lizzy, is very great. My father and mother believe the worst, but I cannot think so badly of Wickham. Perhaps they have arranged to be married in London instead of following their first plan. And even if W. intended to seduce Lydia, could she be so lost to everything? I cannot believe it.

Unhappily, I see that Colonel F. is not inclined to depend on their marriage. He shook his head when I expressed my hope, and said he feared W. was not a man to be trusted. My poor mother is really ill and stays in her room. As for our father, I never in my life have seen him so upset. Poor Kitty is angry at herself for hiding their relationship, but as Lydia had told her in confidence, you cannot wonder.

I am truly glad, dearest Lizzy, that you have not had to deal with all of this. But now that the first shock is over, I must admit that I wish you were here. I am not so selfish, however, as to ask you to come, if it is inconvenient. Until later.

But then Jane's writing continued.

Lizzy, I am taking up my pen again to ask what I just said I would not. I am begging you all to come here as soon as possible. Father is going to London with Colonel Forster instantly, to look for Lydia. What he means to do, I do not know, but he is too distressed to think clearly, and Colonel Forster has to return to Brighton tomorrow evening. He desperately needs my uncle's advice and assistance.

"Oh, oh! Where, where is my uncle?" cried Elizabeth, darting from her seat as she finished the letter. She ran to the door, but as she reached it it was opened by a servant and Mr. Darcy appeared. Her pale face and rushed manner startled him, and before he could speak she burst out, "I beg your pardon, but I must leave you. I must find Mr. Gardiner this moment, on business that cannot wait. I do not have a moment to lose."

"Good God! What is the matter?" he cried, with more emotion than politeness. Gathering himself together, he said, "I will not keep you a minute. But let me, or let the servant, go after Mr. and Mrs. Gardiner. You are not well—you cannot go yourself."

Elizabeth hesitated, but her knees shook under her, and she recognized the sense of Mr. Darcy's words. Calling back the servant, she told him (although her voice was shaking so she could barely be understood) to fetch Mr. and Mrs. Gardiner home immediately.

As the servant departed, she sank into a seat, looking miserably ill. In a concerned tone, Darcy said, "Let me call your maid. Is there nothing I can do for you? A glass of wine—shall I get you one? You are not well."

"No, thank you," she replied, trying to pull herself together. "There is nothing the matter with me. I am quite well. I am only distressed by some dreadful news which I have just received from Longbourn." She burst into tears, and for a few minutes could not speak another word. Darcy, in wretched suspense, could only murmur his concern, and wait in silence. Finally, she spoke. "I have just had a letter from Jane, with such dreadful news. My youngest sister has left all her friends and has eloped—with Mr. Wickham. They have run off together from Brighton. You know him too well to doubt the rest. She has no money, no connections, nothing that can tempt him to marry her. She is lost forever."

Darcy sat like a statue.

"And to think that I might have prevented it!" she cried. "I knew what he was! If only I had told some part of it to my own family! If they had known his true character, this could not have happened. But it is all, all too late now."

"I am sorry, indeed," said Darcy, "sorry and shocked. But is it certain, absolutely certain?"

"Yes. They left Brighton together on Sunday night, and were traced almost to London, but not beyond. They have almost certainly not gone to Scotland to marry."

"And what has been done so far?" Darcy asked.

"My father has gone to London, and Jane has written to beg my uncle's immediate help. We will leave here, I hope, in half an hour. But nothing can be done; I know very well that nothing can be done. How will they even be found? It is horrible!"

Darcy did not answer. He seemed scarcely to hear her, and was walking up and down the room deep in thought. Elizabeth saw him and instantly understood. Her power was lost; this final proof of her family weakness could only disgust Darcy. The realization made her finally understand her own wishes—now that it was too late, she honestly felt that she could have loved him.

But there was no time for thoughts of herself now. Thoughts of Lydia—the humiliation, the misery, she was bringing on them all—soon swallowed up every private care. Covering up her face with her handkerchief, Elizabeth was lost to everything else.

After she wept for several minutes, the voice of her companion reminded her that she was not alone. "I am sure that you wish I would go," Darcy said, "and I have no excuse for staying except my concern, as worthless as that may be. I wish to heaven there was something I could do. I'm afraid this unfortunate business will prevent my sister from having the pleasure of seeing you at Pemberley today."

"Oh, yes," Elizabeth responded. "Please, apologize for us to Miss Darcy. Say that urgent business calls us home immediately. And please—conceal the unhappy truth as long as it is possible. I know it cannot be long." He promised his secrecy. Then, again expressing his sorrow for her distress, he went away.

As he left the room, Elizabeth thought sadly how unlikely it was they would ever meet under the same friendly terms as she had enjoyed over the last several days. But her thoughts were interrupted by the entrance of her aunt and uncle, who had hurried back in great alarm, imagining that Elizabeth had become ill.

She read Jane's letters aloud. Although Lydia had never been a favorite with them, Mr. and Mrs. Gardiner were deeply concerned. This affected not only Lydia, but the entire family. After their first expressions of surprise and horror, Mr. Gardiner promised all the help that was in his power. Elizabeth thanked him with tears of gratitude. They agreed that they must be off as soon as possible.

"But what can we do about Pemberley?" asked Mrs. Gardiner.

"Mr. Darcy was here when I sent for you. I told him we would not be able to keep our engagement.

That is all settled."

"That is all settled!" repeated her aunt, as she ran into her room to pack. Within an hour, all preparations were made; Mr. Gardiner had settled their account at the inn, and Elizabeth found herself seated in the carriage and on the road to Longbourn.

CHAPTER 47

"**I** have been thinking it over, Elizabeth," said her uncle as they drove, "and really, I am inclined to think that Jane is right. It seems unlikely that any young man should try such a thing with a girl who has friends and protectors, and who was actually staying with his colonel's family. Could he possibly think that her friends would not step forward? Wouldn't he realize his career in the service would be ruined, after such an insult to Colonel Forster? He would be a fool to take such a risk."

"Do you really think so?" asked Elizabeth, brightening up for a moment.

"Upon my word," said Mrs. Gardiner, "I begin to agree. If he were guilty, it would be not only a violation of decency and honor, but very much against his own interest. I cannot think that badly of Wickham. Can you, Lizzy, think that he is capable of it?"

"Not of ignoring his own welfare, no," Elizabeth replied. "But of everything else, yes. Why didn't they go to Scotland, if he had intended to marry her?"

"In the first place," replied Mr. Gardiner, "there is no absolute proof that they have not gone to Scotland."

"Oh, but the evidence is very strong that they did not," Elizabeth answered.

"Well, then, suppose that they are in London. They may be there, though, simply because it is easy to hide there. Surely they have very little money. Perhaps they decided they could be married more cheaply, although less easily, in London rather than in Scotland."

"But why all this secrecy? Why the fear of detection? No, this is not likely. His closest friend said that he never intended to marry her. Wickham will not marry a woman without some money. He cannot afford it. And what attractions does Lydia have beyond youth, health, and good humor? These are not enough to convince him to give up a chance of ever marrying well. As to what such an action would do to his career, I know nothing of such things. But as to your other objection, I am afraid you are mistaken. Lydia has no brothers to step forward. And Wickham probably imagines, from observing my father's behavior, that he would do as little as any father could do in such a situation."

"But does Lydia have so little decency that she would agree to live with him if they were not married?"

"It is shocking to admit that I doubt my own

sister's sense of virtue. But, really, I do not know what to say. Perhaps I am not doing her justice. But she is very young; she has never been taught to think seriously about anything. And for the last year, she has thought of nothing but amusement and vanity. Since the regiment first arrived in Meryton, nothing but love, flirtation, and officers have been in her head. And we all know that Wickham is fully capable of charming a woman."

"But you see that Jane does not think so badly of Wickham that she believes he would . . ." said Mrs. Gardiner.

"Of whom does Jane ever think badly?" retorted Elizabeth. "But Jane knows, as well as I do, what Wickham really is. We both know that he has been wasteful and reckless in every way. That he has neither integrity nor honor. That he is as false and deceitful as he can be charming."

"And do you really know all this?" cried Mrs. Gardiner, full of curiosity.

"I do, indeed," replied Elizabeth, blushing. "I told you the other day about his wicked behavior to Mr. Darcy. And when you were at Longbourn, you yourself heard how Wickham spoke of the man who had been so generous toward him. And there are other things which I cannot tell you, but his lies about the whole Pemberley family are endless. From what he said about Miss Darcy, I expected to meet a proud, haughty, disagreeable girl. Yet he knew that was not true. He knew that she was sweet and modest as we found her."

"But doesn't Lydia know all of this? Is she ignorant of what you and Jane seem to understand?"

"No—that is the worst of it. Until I visited in Kent, and saw so much of Mr. Darcy and his cousin, Colonel Fitzwilliam, I was ignorant of the truth myself. And when I returned home, the regiment was about to leave Meryton. As that was the case, neither Jane nor I thought we should tell what we had learned, for why expose him then to the scorn of the neighborhood? And even when it was decided that Lydia should go with Mrs. Forster, the need to tell her about his character never occurred to me. It never entered my head that she could be in any danger from him."

"And so when they all left for Brighton, you had no reason to think they were fond of each other?"

"Not the slightest. I remember no sign of affection on either side. When he first joined the regiment she was ready to admire him, but so were we all. Every girl near Meryton was out of her head about him for the first two months. But he never paid her any particular attention. Soon she turned her fancy to other officers who showed her more favor."

Although the Gardiners and Elizabeth could reach no conclusion on this subject, it still occupied them for most of their journey. They traveled as quickly as possible and reached Longbourn by dinner time the next day. The little Gardiners, attracted by the sight of a carriage, were standing on the steps of the house as they approached. When the carriage drove up to the door, the children's joyful surprise lit up their faces. Elizabeth jumped out, and after giving each of them a hasty kiss, hurried into the house. There Jane came running down stairs from her mother's room to meet her.

Elizabeth affectionately hugged her sister, while tears filled the eyes of both girls. She asked if there was any news.

"Not yet," replied Jane. "But now that our dear uncle is here, I hope everything will be well."

"Is Father in London?"

"Yes, he went on Tuesday. He wrote me a few lines on Wednesday, saying that he had arrived safely, and to give me his address. He added that he would not write again until he had something important to tell."

"And Mother? How is she? How are you all?"

"Mother is doing well enough, though her spirits are greatly shaken. She is upstairs, and will be very pleased that you are here. Mary and Kitty are quite well."

Mr. and Mrs. Gardiner had finished greeting their children, and now approached. Jane ran to her uncle and aunt, and welcomed and thanked them both with alternate smiles and tears. After a few moments of conversation the entire group went to see Mrs. Bennet, who greeted them exactly as might be expected. She cried and wailed, raged against Wickham's conduct, complained of being badly used herself, and in general blamed everyone except the one who had spoiled her own daughter with such disastrous results.

"If anyone had listened to me, and let me go to Brighton with my whole family, this would not have happened," she exclaimed. "Poor dear Lydia had nobody to take care of her. Why did the Forsters ever let her go out of their sight? They must have been very careless and neglectful, for she is not the kind of girl to do such a thing. I always thought they were unfit to take care of her, but no one would listen to me, as usual. Poor dear child! And now Mr. Bennet has gone away, and I know he will fight Wickham when they meet, and he will be killed, and what will become of us all? The Collinses will turn us out of the house before he is cold in his grave. If you do not take care of us, brother, I do not know what we shall do."

Everyone burst out in reassurances against such awful thoughts. Mr. Gardiner told her that he would be in London the very next day, and would help Mr. Bennet in every possible way.

"Do not give in to useless alarm," he added. "Although it is good to be prepared for the worst, we know nothing for certain. It is a little less than a week since they left Brighton. In a few days, we probably will have some news of them. Until we know that they are not married, and have no plans of marrying, do not give up hope. As soon as I get to town, I shall find Mr. Bennet and take him to our home, and then we will decide together what to do."

"Oh, my dear brother," replied Mrs. Bennet, "that is exactly what I had hoped. And when you find them, make them get married if they have not already done so. As for the wedding clothes, do not let them wait for that," she added. "Tell Lydia she may have as much money as she wants to buy them, after they are married. And, above all, keep Mr. Bennet from fighting. Tell him what a dreadful state I am in—that I am frightened out of my wits, and have such tremblings, such flutterings all over me, such spasms in my side, and pains in my head, and such beatings in my heart, that I can get no rest by night nor by day. And tell my dear Lydia not to make any decisions about her clothes until she has seen me, for she does not know the best stores. Oh, brother, how kind you are! I know you will fix everything."

Later in the afternoon, Jane and Elizabeth finally were able to talk alone for half an hour. Elizabeth instantly asked Jane for her view of things.

"Tell me everything which I have not already heard. What did Colonel Forster say? Did he have any suspicions before they disappeared?"

"Colonel Forster admitted that he had noticed

some flirtation between them, especially on Lydia's side, but nothing that alarmed him," Jane answered. "I am really sorry for him. He has been so concerned and kind."

"And why was Denny convinced that Wickham would not marry? Did he know of their plan to run off? Had Colonel Forster talked to Denny himself?"

"Yes, but when the colonel questioned him, Denny denied knowing anything about their plan. He did not say anything about them not marrying, and from that, I hope he was misunderstood before."

"And until Colonel Forster came himself, none of you doubted that they were really married?"

"How could we have thought anything else? I felt a little uneasy—fearful of my sister's happiness with him in marriage, because I knew that his conduct had not been always quite right. Father and Mother knew nothing of that; they only worried how poor they would be. Then Kitty told us, feeling triumphant about knowing more than the rest of us, that Lydia's last letter had warned of such a step. Apparently, Lydia had been telling Kitty for many weeks that they were in love."

"And did Colonel Forster seem to think badly of Wickham himself? Does he know his real character?"

"I must admit that he did not speak well of Wickham. He called him reckless and extravagant.

And now I have heard that he left many unpaid bills behind in Meryton."

"Oh, Jane, if only we had told what we knew about him, this would not have happened!"

"Perhaps that would have been better," replied her sister. "But our intentions were good. To expose a person's past faults, when he might have changed for the better, seemed so wrong."

"And the note that Lydia left for Mrs. Forster—did the colonel tell you what it said?"

"He brought it with him for us to see," Jane replied. Taking it from her pocketbook, she handed it to Elizabeth. This is what it said:

> My dear Harriet—You will laugh when you know where I have gone, and I cannot help laughing myself as I think of your surprise tomorrow morning when you read this. I am going to Gretna Green. If you cannot guess who I am with, I will think you are very foolish. For there is only one man in the world I love, and he is an angel. I can never be happy without him, so there is no harm in me going. You do not need to let my family know if you don't want to, for it will make the surprise all the better when I write to them and sign my name Lydia Wickham. What a good joke it will be! I can hardly write I am laughing so hard. Please make my excuses to Pratt for not keeping my engagement to dance with him tonight. Tell him I will dance with him at the next ball, with great pleasure. I will send

for my clothes when I get to Longbourn, but in the meantime please tell Sally to mend the rip in my pink muslin gown. Goodbye, and give my love to Colonel Forster.

Your affectionate friend,

Lydia Bennet

"Oh, foolish, thoughtless Lydia!" cried Elizabeth when she had finished it. "What kind of letter is this, to be written at such a moment. But at least it shows that she expected to marry. Whatever he persuaded her to do later, it was not her original intention. My poor father! How upset he must have been!"

"I never saw anyone so shocked," Jane answered. "He could not speak a word for a full ten minutes. Mother became ill immediately, and the whole house in such confusion!"

"By the end of the day, was there a single servant in the house that did not know the whole story?"

"I do not know. I hope so. But to be quiet and reserved at such a time was impossible. Mother was in hysterics, and although I tried to help her, I was too shocked to be of much assistance."

"This has all been too much for you," Elizabeth replied. "How I wish that I had been here to help you."

"Mary and Kitty have been very kind, and were willing to do more, but I did not want to ask either of them," Jane said. "Kitty is slight and delicate, and Mary studies so much, that she needs her rest.

Aunt Philips came to Longbourn on Tuesday, after Father went away, and she stayed until Thursday with me. And Lady Lucas has been very kind. She walked here on Wednesday morning to comfort us, and offer her help, if she could do anything."

"She should have stayed at home," groaned Elizabeth. "Perhaps she meant well, but in such a situation, one does not want to see the neighbors. And what do you believe Father intends to do in London?"

"I believe he plans to go to Epsom, the place where they last changed horses, and see if anyone there remembers them. His goal is to find out which coach they took from there. I do not know of any other plans that he had made. He was in such a hurry to leave, and he was so greatly upset, that I had difficulty in finding out even that much."

Everyone hoped to see a letter from Mr. Bennet the next morning, but the mail arrived without bringing a single line from him. As soon as he saw there was no news, Mr. Gardiner left. With him gone, the family knew at least that they would receive steady information. Their uncle also promised to persuade Mr. Bennet to return to Longbourn as soon as he could. This greatly comforted Mrs. Bennet, who continued to be convinced her husband would be killed in a duel.

Mrs. Gardiner and the children decided to stay at Longbourn for a few more days, to help her nieces care for their mother. The girls' Aunt Philips also visited regularly. She claimed she came in order to cheer them up, but she never failed to give them some new report of Wickham's extravagance or bad behavior, and she generally left them more depressed than she found them. Everyone in Meryton was now busy criticizing the man who, only three months before, had been almost an angel of light. He was said to be in debt to every merchant; his flirtations and seductions were endless.

Everybody declared that he was the wickedest young man in the world, and everybody insisted that they had always suspected this to be so.

Mr. Gardiner left for London on Sunday. On Tuesday, his wife received a letter from him. It said that he had located Mr. Bennet and taken him to their home; that Mr. Bennet had been to the places where Lydia and Wickham had changed carriages, but had not learned anything new; and that the two of them would be making inquiries at the larger hotels in the city. He added that Mr. Bennet did not yet want to leave London. He wrote:

> I have written to Colonel Forster to ask him to find out from Wickham's friends in the regiment if he has any relatives who would be likely to know his whereabouts. At present we have nothing to guide us. In the meantime, perhaps Lizzy could tell us if he has any living family members.

Elizabeth could not help; she had never heard of him having any relatives besides his parents, who had been dead many years.

Every day at Longbourn was now a day of anxiety, with the most anxious part of each being when the mail arrived. But before they heard again from Mr. Gardiner, a letter arrived for their father from an unexpected source—Mr. Collins. Since Mr. Bennet had instructed Jane to open all letters that arrived for him, she read it, with Elizabeth looking over her shoulder. It said:

> My dear sir,
>
> I feel called upon by our relationship, and by

my position as a spiritual leader, to comment upon the pain you are suffering, of which we learned yesterday. Rest assured that Mrs. Collins and I sincerely sympathize with you and your family. Your distress is of the most bitter kind, because time will never lessen it. I can say nothing to soften the blow. The death of your daughter would have been a blessing in comparison with this.

Your suffering must be especially awful because there is reason to believe (as my dear Charlotte tells me) that your daughter's loose behavior was encouraged by your inadequate supervision. Please comfort yourself with the idea that her character must have been naturally evil from birth. In any case, you are greatly to be pitied. This is not only Mrs. Collins's and my opinion, but also that of Lady Catherine, to whom I told the story. She agrees with me that this false step in one daughter will injure the fortunes of all the others. For, as Lady Catherine herself says, who will be willing to marry into such a family? This thought leads me to remember with satisfaction a certain event of last November, for if things had happened otherwise, I myself would be involved in your sorrow and disgrace. In closing, let me advise you then, my dear sir, to cut your unworthy child out of your heart, and let her suffer the consequences of her own immoral behavior.

Mr. Gardiner did not write again until he

had heard from Colonel Forster. His news was not encouraging. As far as anyone knew, Wickham had no relatives. And there was more news about the wretched state of his finances. Not only had he left merchants with unpaid bills, but the Colonel had learned he had racked up significant gambling debts in Brighton. He owed more than a thousand pounds at the card tables.

Jane heard this news with horror. "A gambler!" she cried. "I thought we knew the worst. But this is too much."

Mr. Gardiner added in his letter that Mr. Bennet would return home the following day. Low-spirited from his lack of success, he had given in to his brother-in-law's pleading to return to his family. When Mrs. Bennet was told this, she did not express as much satisfaction as her children expected.

"What, he is coming home without poor Lydia?!" she cried. "He should not leave London before he has found them. Who will fight Wickham and make him marry her if he leaves?"

Mrs. Gardiner and her children were anxious to return home, so it was agreed they would return to London when Mr. Bennet arrived. As Mrs. Gardiner left, she was filled with curiosity about Elizabeth and Mr. Darcy. Her niece had never mentioned his name. Mrs. Gardiner had half-expected a letter to arrive from him, but nothing had come. Elizabeth was already understandably depressed about the family situation. But in her heart she knew that if she did not have Darcy in her thoughts, she could have borne the pain of Lydia's actions somewhat better.

When Mr. Bennet arrived, he seemed as calm and collected as ever. He said as little as usual, and he did not even mention the business that had taken him away. It was not until that afternoon at tea that Elizabeth made some remark about the pain he must be experiencing. He replied, "Do not say anything about my own pain. Who else should suffer it? This is my fault, and I ought to feel it."

"Don't be so hard on yourself," Elizabeth began.

"No, Lizzy; for once in my life let me feel how much I have been to blame. I am not afraid of being overpowered by guilt—it will pass away soon enough."

"Do you still believe they are in London?" Elizabeth asked.

"Yes; where else could they be so well hidden?"

"And Lydia used to want to go to London," added Kitty.

"She is happy, then," said her father, with grim humor.

He added, "Lizzy, I do not resent you for being right in your advice to me last May. Considering everything, I believe this shows me to be a generous man."

They were interrupted by Jane, who came to fetch her mother's tea. "The sight of this elegant parade does me good," he exclaimed. "Perhaps I will do the same as your mother; I will sit in my library, in my night clothes, and create as much trouble as I can. Or perhaps I will wait to do that until Kitty runs away."

"I am not going to run away, Papa," said Kitty anxiously. "If you send me to Brighton, I will behave better than Lydia."

"Send you to Brighton! I would not send you within ten miles of it, not for fifty pounds. No, Kitty, I have at last learned my lesson, and you will feel the effects. No officer will ever enter my house again, or even pass through the village. Balls will be absolutely forbidden. And you may never step out the door until you can prove that you have spent ten minutes of every day in a sensible manner."

Kitty, who took all these threats seriously, began to cry.

"Well, well," her father said, "do not make yourself unhappy. If you are a good girl for the next ten years, I will review these rules at that time."

Two days later, as Jane and Elizabeth were walking in the yard, they saw Mrs. Hill, the housekeeper, coming toward them.

"I beg your pardon, madam, for interrupting you, but I was hoping you might have gotten some good news from town, so I took the liberty of coming to ask," she said.

"What do you mean, Mrs. Hill? We have heard nothing from town," Jane answered.

"Dear madam," said Mrs. Hill, "don't you know that a special delivery letter has arrived from Mr. Gardiner? The messenger has been here for half an hour, and Mr. Bennet has the letter."

Too eager to speak, the girls ran away to the house. The butler there informed them that their father was walking in a stand of trees, some distance from the house. When they finally caught up with him, Elizabeth gasped out, "Papa, what news? Have you heard from my uncle?"

"Yes, I have had a letter from him."

"And what news does it bring? Good or bad?"

Mr. Bennet handed it to Elizabeth. "Read it aloud," said her father, "for I hardly know myself what it says."

My dear brother-in-law,

At last I am able to send you some news of
my niece. All in all, I hope you will find it satisfactory. Soon after you left me on Saturday, I was
lucky enough to find out where in London they
were. I will tell you the details when I see you. For
now, I will just say that I have seen them both—

"Then they are married!" cried Jane, but
Elizabeth's frown silenced her. She read on:

I have seen them both. They are not married,
and as far as I can tell there was no plan for them
to marry. But if you are willing to agree to the
following terms, I believe they will be soon. All
that you need to do is to guarantee, in writing,
that Lydia will receive her equal share of the five
thousand pounds which will be divided among
your children when you and your wife die. In
addition, you will provide Lydia with the sum of
one hundred pounds per year during your lifetime. All things considered, I had no problem
agreeing with these terms on your behalf. Please
send me your answer as quickly as possible.

You will see from what I have written that
Mr. Wickham's financial condition is not nearly
as bad as we had believed. I am happy to say that
there will be a fair amount of money left over,
even after he settles his debts. If you agree with
the terms I have laid out here, I will instruct my
attorney to prepare the settlement. There is not
the smallest need for you to come to London

again; I will handle everything. We have invited Lydia to stay with us until she is married. I hope you approve of that idea. She will arrive here today. I will write again as soon as there are any new developments.

Edward Gardiner

"Is it possible?" asked Elizabeth, when she had finished. "Can it be possible that he will marry her?"

"Wickham is not so bad, then, as we had thought!" said her sister.

"And have you answered the letter?" said Elizabeth.

"No, but it must be done soon."

"Oh! My dear father," she cried, "come back to the house, and write immediately. There is no time to lose."

"Let me write for you," said Jane, "if you dislike doing it yourself."

"I dislike it very much," he replied, "but it must be done." Saying so, he walked back toward the house.

"And may I ask . . ." said Elizabeth, "the terms —you will agree to them?"

"Agree with them! I am only ashamed that he asks so little. But there are two things that I want very much to know. One, how much money has your uncle given Wickham to make this happen? And two, how will I ever repay him?"

"Our uncle—money to Wickham?!" asked Jane. "What do you mean?"

"I mean that no man in his right mind would marry Lydia for what I will be paying."

"That is very true," said Elizabeth, "although it had not occurred to me before. How will he pay his great debts and still have something left over? It must be my uncle's doings! What a generous, good man. I am afraid to think of it. A small sum could not have done this."

"No," said her father, "Wickham's a fool if he takes her for a penny less than ten thousand pounds. I would be sorry to think so poorly of him in the very beginning of our relationship."

"Ten thousand pounds! Heaven forbid! How could we ever repay half that much?"

Mr. Bennet, in silence, went to the library, while the girls walked into the breakfast room.

"So they really are going to be married!" said Elizabeth, as soon as they were by themselves. "How strange this is! And for this we have to be thankful. As unlikely as it is that they will be happy, we are forced to rejoice. Oh, Lydia!"

"I am trying to tell myself that he would not marry Lydia if he did not have some real affection for her," Jane replied. "Although I'm sure our dear uncle has paid some of his debts, I cannot believe he has spent anything like ten thousand pounds. He has children of his own, and may have more. How could he spare even five thousand?

"But for now, we must try to forget all that has happened, and hope that they will be happy. The fact that he has agreed to marry her proves, I believe, that he is mending his ways. Their mutual affection will steady them. I believe they will settle down so quietly that in time, their past behavior will be forgotten."

"Their behavior is impossible for you, or I, or anybody to ever forget," retorted Elizabeth. "It is useless to talk of it."

It occurred to the girls that their mother was ignorant of what had happened. They went to the library and asked their father whether he would like them to tell her. He was writing, and, without raising his head, coolly replied, "Just as you please."

"May we take Uncle's letter to read to her?" Elizabeth asked.

"Take whatever you like, and go away."

Elizabeth took the letter from his writing table, and they went upstairs together. Mary and Kitty were both with Mrs. Bennet, so they were able to inform the whole family at once.

Mrs. Bennet could hardly contain herself. As soon as Jane had read Mr. Gardiner's assurance that Lydia would be married soon, her joy burst forth. She was now as crazed with delight as she had been with alarm and irritation.

"My darling Lydia!" she cried. "This is delightful! She will be married, and at only sixteen! Oh, my good, kind brother! I knew he would manage everything. How I want to see her, and dear Wickham too! But the clothes, the wedding clothes! I will write to my sister-in-law Mrs.

Gardiner about them immediately. Lizzy, my dear, run down to your father and ask him how much he will give her. No, wait; I will go myself. Ring the bell, Kitty, for Mrs. Hill. My dear, dear Lydia! What fun we shall have over all this!"

Jane and Elizabeth tried to make their mother speak more reasonably, reminding her of the debt that they owed to Mr. Gardiner. "We are convinced," said Jane, "that he has brought this about by paying some of Mr. Wickham's debts."

"Well," cried her mother, "that is all very right. Who should do it but her own uncle? If he did not have a family of his own, I would have had all that money, you know. Well! I am so happy. Soon I will have a married daughter. Mrs. Wickham! How fine that sounds. And she was only sixteen last June. My dear Jane, I am in such a flutter that I cannot write, so I will dictate, and you write for me. I will arrange things with your father about the money later, but some things should be ordered immediately." She then plunged into all the details of the dresses, bonnets, capes, and other items that she thought should be ordered. Jane managed to break in long enough to convince her to wait until Mr. Bennet was free to discuss it.

Other plans quickly replaced the shopping list in Mrs. Bennet's head. "I will go to Meryton as soon as I am dressed to tell this wonderful news to your Aunt Philips," she announced. "And as soon as I come back, I can call on Lady Lucas and Mrs.

Long. Kitty, run down and tell them I want the carriage. Getting out in the fresh air will do me a great deal of good, I am sure. Girls, can I do anything for you in Meryton? Oh! Here comes Mrs. Hill. My dear Mrs. Hill, have you heard the good news? Miss Lydia is going to be married, and you shall all have a bowl of punch to celebrate her wedding."

Elizabeth, sick of this foolishness, went to her own room, where she might think alone. Poor Lydia's situation was bad enough, but she had to be thankful that it was not worse. Looking into the future, she could see neither happiness nor prosperity for her sister. But in looking back to what she had feared only two hours ago, she was forced to be grateful.

CHAPTER 50

In the past, Mr. Bennet had often wished that, instead of spending his whole income, he had saved more so as to provide for his children and wife. He now wished it more than ever. If he had done his duty, Lydia would not have had to rely on her uncle to buy a reputation for her. To have convinced one of the most worthless young men in Great Britain to be her husband would have been Mr. Bennet's task, not his brother-in-law's. Mr. Bennet was determined to find out how much Mr. Gardiner had paid, and to repay him as soon as possible.

When Mr. Bennet was first married, he had not worried about money, for, of course, he expected to have a son. This son would have meant the end of the entailment, and the widow and younger children would have been provided for. But instead, five daughters entered the world. For many years after Lydia's birth, Mrs. Bennet had been certain that a son would yet arrive. At last, it was clear that there would be no son, and by then it was too late to be economical.

Mr. Bennet quickly wrote to Mr. Gardiner, agreeing to everything, and only asking his brother-in-law to inform him how deeply Mr. Bennet was indebted to him. He was too angry to send any message to Lydia.

It had been two weeks since Mrs. Bennet had been downstairs, but on this happy day she took her seat at the head of her dining table in high spirits. No shame dampened her sense of triumph. To see a daughter married had been her greatest wish since Jane turned sixteen, and all her thoughts were now about elegant ceremonies, fine clothes, new carriages, and servants. She was busy mentally searching through the neighborhood for a proper house for her daughter, and, without considering what their income might be, rejected most as not grand or important enough.

"Haye-Park might do," she said, "if only the Gouldings would move out, or the great house at Stoke, if the drawing room were larger. But Ashworth is too far off! I could not bear to have her ten miles away from me. And as for Purvis Lodge, the attics are dreadful."

Her husband allowed her to talk like this while the servants were present. But when they had left, he said to her, "Mrs. Bennet, before you take any house for your daughter and son-in-law, you must understand something. This is one house that they will never enter. I will not encourage their shameless behavior by seeing them here."

A long argument followed, but Mr. Bennet was firm. It was soon followed by another argument, when Mrs. Bennet found, to her amazement and horror, that her husband would not provide a penny to buy clothes for his daughter.

Mrs. Bennet could hardly believe it. To her, the disgrace of Lydia being without new wedding clothes meant more than any sense of shame at the girl eloping and living with Wickham for two weeks before the marriage.

Elizabeth was now deeply sorry that she told Mr. Darcy of her sister's situation. Since Lydia would soon marry, it was possible that he would never had learned of the marriage's unfavorable beginning. She had no fear of him telling the story. There was no one whose secrecy she would trust more. At the same time, there was no one opinion she cared for more. Even if Lydia's marriage had been a completely honorable one, she could not imagine that Mr. Darcy would connect himself with a family which now, on top of every other objection, included the man who he so understandably scorned.

Now that Darcy was lost, Elizabeth began to understand that he was exactly the man who would have best suited her. His heart and his mind, although unlike her own, would have complemented hers perfectly. Her ease and liveliness would have softened him; his judgment and knowledge of the world would have benefited her.

Mr. Gardiner soon wrote again to his brother-in-law. His main news was that Mr. Wickham had decided to quit his regiment, and to enlist in the regular army.

This seems to me by far the best plan. Among Mr. Wickham's former friends, there are still some who are willing to assist him in the army. He has been promised a position in the service of a general whose troops are stationed far in the north of the country. It is an advantage to have him move so far from where he is known. All arrangements will be completed in a week. They will then join the new regiment, unless they are first invited to visit Longbourn. I understand that my niece very much wants to see you all before she leaves.

Yours,

Edward Gardiner

Mr. Bennet and his daughters were all relieved that Wickham and Lydia would be moving far away. But Mrs. Bennet was not pleased. She had expected to take great pride in having a married daughter nearby. Besides, she said, it was a pity that Lydia should be taken away from the local regiment where she knew everybody.

"She is so fond of Mrs. Forster," Mrs. Bennet complained, "it is a great shame to send her away! And there are several of the young men, too, that she likes very much. The officers may not be so pleasant in this new regiment."

At first, Mr. Bennet absolutely refused his daughter's request to see the family. But Jane and

Elizabeth urged him to receive the couple, for the sake of future relations, and he eventually gave in. Mrs. Bennet would then have the satisfaction of showing her married daughter off before she was banished to the North. When Mr. Bennet wrote to Mr. Gardiner again, then, he sent his permission for them to come. It was settled that as soon as they were married, they would travel to Longbourn. Elizabeth was surprised that Wickham had agreed to such a plan. Seeing him was certainly the last thing she desired.

CHAPTER
51

Their sister's wedding day arrived. Jane and Elizabeth felt more concern for their sister than she probably did herself. Both girls dreaded the arrival of the couple, and Jane especially, who continued to try to think the best of Lydia, felt sorry for the shame she believed her sister must be suffering.

They came. The family was waiting in the breakfast room to receive them. Mrs. Bennet was all sunny smiles as the carriage drove up to the door; her husband looked grave as death; their daughters were anxious and uneasy.

Lydia's loud voice echoed through the hallway; the door was thrown open, and she ran into the room. Her mother stepped forward to hug her and welcome her happily. She then gave her hand, with an affectionate smile, to Wickham, and congratulated them both. Their reception from Mr. Bennet was not quite so cheerful. He looked more grim than ever, and he scarcely opened his lips.

The relaxed manners of the young couple, indeed, was enough to irritate anyone. Elizabeth was disgusted, and even Jane was shocked. Lydia was still Lydia: untamed, unashamed, wild, noisy, and fearless. She went from sister to sister, demanding their congratulations. When they finally sat down, she looked eagerly around the room, noticed some minor change in it, and observed with a loud laugh that she had not been there for some time.

Wickham seemed no more troubled than Lydia; his manners were as free and easy as ever. Elizabeth could hardly believe he was so completely without shame. She blushed, and Jane blushed, but there were no blushes on the cheeks of the two who deserved to be embarrassed.

There was plenty of talking. The bride and her mother chattered like magpies, and Wickham began asking after the people he knew in the neighborhood. Meanwhile, Lydia kept bringing the conversation back to subjects that her sisters wished she would avoid. "Only think that it has been three months since I went away!" she exclaimed. "It seems like barely a week, and yet so much has happened. Good gracious, when I left, I had no idea of being married, although I thought it would be very good fun if I was."

Her father looked at her in disbelief. But Lydia, who never heard or saw anything she wanted to avoid, happily continued, "Mama, do the neighbors all know that I am married? I was afraid they might not. We met William Goulding in his carriage on the road, so I let down the window and took off my glove and let my hand just rest where he would see my ring."

Elizabeth could bear it no longer. She got up

and left the room, staying away until she heard them going in for dinner. She joined them just in time to see Lydia take the seat beside her mother's, saying, "Jane, I am taking your place now. You must sit further down, because I am a married woman."

Her good spirits only increased through the meal. She longed to see Mrs. Philips, the Lucases, and all their other neighbors, and to hear them all call her "Mrs. Wickham." In the meantime, she went to the kitchen to show her ring to Mrs. Hill and the two housemaids.

"Well, Mamma," she said, when they had all returned to the breakfast room, "what do you think of my husband? Isn't he a charming man? My sisters must all envy me. I only hope they have half my good luck. They must all go to Brighton—that is the place to get husbands. What a pity it is that we did not all go!"

"Very true," said her mother, "and if I had my way, we would have. But my dear Lydia, I don't like your moving so far away. Must it be so?"

"Oh, yes, and I shall like it very well. You and Papa and my sisters must come to see us. I'm sure there will be some balls, and I will get good partners for them all. And then when you go away, you can leave one or two of my sisters behind, and I will get husbands for them before the winter is over."

"Thank you," said Elizabeth, "but I do not particularly like your way of getting husbands."

The visitors were to stay with them for ten days. No one but Mrs. Bennet wished that they would stay longer. She made the most of their time visiting everywhere with her daughter, and having frequent parties at home. Everyone welcomed these parties; having company was less uncomfortable than being together just as a family.

Wickham's affection for Lydia was just what Elizabeth had expected. It was clearly not equal to Lydia's for him. Lydia was very fond of him. She constantly called him her "dear Wickham," and insisted that he was better than any other man in every way. One morning, soon after their arrival, she said to Elizabeth, "Lizzy, I never told you about my wedding. You were not in the room when I told Mama and the others all about it. Don't you want to hear about it?"

"Not really," replied Elizabeth. "I'd rather not talk about it at all."

"La! You are so strange! But anyway, we were married at St. Clement's Church because Wickham was living in that area. We needed to be there by eleven o'clock. Well, that morning I was in such a state! I was so afraid that something would happen to put it off, and all the time I was dressing my aunt was preaching as if she were reading a sermon.

"We ate breakfast at ten as usual, and I thought it would never be over. You cannot imagine how horrid my aunt and uncle were to me all the time I was with them! If you can believe it, I didn't put my foot out of doors once, even though I was there for two weeks. We didn't have a single party, or go to the theater, or anything.

"Well, so just as the carriage arrived, Uncle was called away upon business. I was so frightened I did not know what to do, for he was supposed to give me away, and if he did not get back in time, I didn't know what would happen. But, luckily, he came back again in ten minutes, so it all worked out. And afterward I realized that if he had not gotten back, the wedding could have happened anyway, for Mr. Darcy could have given me away just as well."

"Mr. Darcy!" repeated Elizabeth, in utter amazement.

"Oh, yes! He was coming with Wickham, you know. But gracious me! I forgot! I was not supposed to say a word about that. I promised! What will Wickham say? It was a great secret!"

"If it was a secret," said Jane, "do not say another word about it."

"Oh, certainly!" said Elizabeth, although she was burning with curiosity. "We will ask you no questions."

"Thank you," said Lydia, "for if you did ask, I know I would tell you everything, and then Wickham would be angry."

With that sort of encouragement, Elizabeth could only resist asking by leaving the room. But she had to try for information, somehow. Mr. Darcy had been at her sister's wedding! She could not bear the suspense. Hastily seizing a sheet of paper, she wrote a short letter to her aunt to beg her to explain.

"You will understand how curious I am to understand why a person outside the family was with you at such a time," she wrote. "Please write immediately and tell me. Of course, if there is a very good reason why it must remain a secret, I will have to be satisfied."

"But I won't be satisfied," she added to herself, as she sealed the letter. "And my dear aunt, if you do not tell me, I will certainly have to find out some other way."

Jane's sense of honor would not let her speak to Elizabeth about what Lydia had blurted out. Elizabeth was glad for that. Until she learned the truth from her aunt, she would rather not have to talk about it to anyone.

CHAPTER 52

Elizabeth received an answer to her letter very promptly. Without opening it, she hurried out to a hidden part of the yard, where she knew she would not be interrupted. There she settled herself comfortably and began to read.

My dear niece,

I have just received your letter, and will spend the morning answering it, as I have a good deal to say. I must confess that I was surprised by your question. I assumed that you knew all about it. Your uncle is as surprised as I am. If he had not believed that you were involved, he would not have acted as he did. But if you really know nothing, I must explain.

On the very day that I left Longbourn, your uncle had an unexpected visitor—Mr. Darcy. He came to tell Mr. Gardiner that he had found out where your sister and Mr. Wickham were, and that he had seen and talked with them both. It seems that he had left Pemberley the day after we went to Longbourn, and came to London to hunt for them himself. In explanation, he said that he blamed himself for what had happened—

that it was his fault for not telling people about Wickham's character, thus protecting any young woman from trusting him. Now, he said, it was his duty to step forward and try to repair the evil that his silence had made possible.

Unlike us, he had an idea where to look in London. There is a woman, a Mrs. Younge, who was once Miss Darcy's governess, but who was fired for some misconduct. She now owns a large house in Edward Street, where she rents rooms. Mr. Darcy knew this Mrs. Younge was a close friend of Wickham's, and he went to her for information. It took him two or three days to get her to talk; I gather he had to bribe her heavily. Eventually, she told him where they were.

He saw Wickham, and afterward insisted on seeing Lydia. He hoped to persuade her to return home, and he offered her any assistance he could give. But Lydia flatly refused to leave Wickham. She was sure they would be married eventually, and it didn't much matter to her when. Since she felt this way, Darcy concluded that all he could do was to arrange the marriage as quickly as possible. It was clear from their conversations that Wickham had never intended to marry her. He confessed that he had left the regiment to escape his gambling debts, and blamed Lydia for her foolish decision to accompany him. Mr. Darcy asked him why he had not married your sister at once. Although Wickham knew that your father was not very rich, he surely would have done something for Lydia, and that would have improved Wickham's situation somewhat. But Wickham openly admitted that he still hoped to make a rich marriage, perhaps in another country.

Darcy and Wickham met several times, for there was much to be discussed. Wickham, of course, wanted more than he could get, but a compromise was eventually reached. That is when Mr. Darcy came to see your uncle.

Mr. Darcy was very stubborn that everything be done as he had arranged. It seems to be, Lizzy, that stubbornness is his one real fault. Your uncle was determined to do more than Mr. Darcy had asked of him, and they argued it out for a long time (which was more than either Wickham or Lydia deserved). But at last your uncle was forced to give in. Instead of being allowed to actually help his niece financially, he was forced to only take credit for that help—this irritated him greatly. I really believe your letter this morning relieved him a good deal, because it forced an explanation that would take the credit away from him and give it to Mr. Darcy, who deserves it.

But, Lizzy, you must not repeat this to anyone, except perhaps Jane. You know pretty well, I believe, what Darcy has done for the young people. He has paid Wickham's debts, which amount to considerably more than a thousand pounds. Darcy has settled another thousand pounds on Lydia, and has paid for Wickham to be offered a position in the general's staff.

When all this was settled, Darcy returned to Pemberley and his friends, but it was agreed that he would be in London for the wedding itself. He would then distribute the money.

I think I have now told you everything. Apparently, this is all a surprise to you; I hope at least it will not displease you. Lydia came to stay with us, and Wickham was a frequent visitor. He acted exactly as he had when I met him before, but I was very displeased with Lydia's behavior. I talked to her several times, very seriously, about the wickedness of what she had done, and all the unhappiness she had brought on her family. If she heard me, it was only by good luck, for she did not listen. It was very irritating, and I could keep my patience only by remembering my dear Elizabeth and Jane. Mr. Darcy came back as promised, and as Lydia informed you, he attended the wedding. He dined with us the next day, and then left London again.

I hope you won't mind, dear Lizzy, if I tell you how much I like him. His behavior has continued to be as pleasant as when we met at Pemberley. His heart and mind are excellent. All he needs is a little more liveliness—and if he marries wisely, his wife can teach him that. I thought he was very sly, for he hardly ever mentioned your name. But slyness seems to be in fashion.

Please forgive me if I have said too much, or at least do not punish me by not inviting me to

Pemberley. I will never be quite happy until I have been all round the park. An open, low carriage with a nice little pair of ponies would be perfect. But I must go now. The children are calling me.

Your affectionate aunt

This letter left Elizabeth reeling with emotion, and it was hard to say whether pleasure or pain had the upper hand. Her most extreme daydreams about what Mr. Darcy had done to promote Lydia's marriage had turned out to be true. He had followed them to London. He had taken on all the trouble and humiliation of this task. He had met with a woman whom he must hate and despise. He had repeatedly met with, reasoned with, persuaded, and finally bribed the man whose very name it was painful for him to pronounce. He had done all this for a girl whom he could not like or respect. Elizabeth's heart whispered that he had done it for her.

But she was not vain enough to depend upon this for an explanation. Could all this have been done for love of her? She, who had already refused him? She, who would make him a brother-in-law of Wickham. Brother-in-law of Wickham! How Darcy's pride must react to that idea!

He had, to be sure, done much. She was ashamed to think how much. But the explanation he had given was reasonable. It might be true only that he felt he had been wrong, and that he had used his money to make amends.

Elizabeth's thoughts were interrupted by the approach of someone. It was Wickham.

"I am afraid I have interrupted your solitude, my dear sister?" he said, as he joined her.

"You have," she replied with a smile, "but that does not mean that the interruption must be unwelcome."

"I would be sorry if that were the case. We were always good friends, and now we are better."

"True. Are the others coming out?"

"I do not know. Mrs. Bennet and Lydia are going to Meryton." He continued, in a somewhat more careful tone, "And so, my dear sister, I hear from our uncle and aunt that you have actually seen Pemberley!" She nodded. "I almost envy you the pleasure," he continued, "and yet it might be too hard for me, or else we could visit it on our way North. Did you see the old housekeeper? Poor Reynolds, she was always very fond of me. But she probably did not mention me to you."

"Yes, in fact she did."

"And what did she say?"

"That you had gone into the army, and she was afraid that you had not turned out well. At such a long distance, you know, people sometimes misunderstand things."

"Yes, certainly," he replied, biting his lip. Elizabeth hoped this would keep him silent, but he went on. "I was surprised to see Darcy in town last month. We passed each other several times. I wonder what he was doing there."

"Perhaps preparing for his wedding to Miss de Bourgh," said Elizabeth, who was beginning to enjoy herself. "It must be something important, to take him there at this time of year."

"Undoubtedly. Did you see him when you were at Pemberley? I thought I understood from the Gardiners that you had."

"Yes, and he introduced us to his sister."

"You met Miss Darcy! And do you like her?"

"Very much."

"I have heard that she has improved in the last year or two. When I last saw her, she was not very promising. I hope she will turn out well."

"Oh, I think she will. She has gotten over the most awkward age."

"Did you go by the village of Kympton?" he asked.

"No, I don't believe so."

"I only ask because it is there that I was supposed to have my position as a clergyman. It is a delightful place with an excellent parsonage. It would have suited me perfectly."

"How would you have liked preaching sermons?"

"I would have liked it very much. It is no use looking back, but ah, that would have been the life for me! A quiet life as a minister in the countryside—that would have been my perfect idea of happiness. Did you ever hear Darcy discuss why he denied me the position?"

"I have heard from sources which seemed very well informed that the position was left to you only on certain conditions, which you did not meet."

"Yes, there was something like that, as I told you when we first met," Wickham said hastily. "Surely you remember."

"I did hear, too, that there was a time when the idea of sermon-making did not appeal to you, and that you actually declared that you would never become a minister, and that other arrangements had been made to satisfy you."

"Did you! And that was not totally untrue. You may remember that I told you something like that, when we first talked about it."

They were now almost at the door of the house, for she had walked fast to get rid of him. For Lydia's sake, she did not want to push him further, so she merely gave him a good-humored smile and said, "Now, Mr. Wickham, we are brother and sister, you know. Let's not quarrel about the past. In the future, I hope we will always be in perfect agreement." She held out her hand and he kissed it politely, although he looked confused and embarrassed, and they entered the house.

Elizabeth had done such a thorough job of making Wickham uncomfortable that he never again raised the subject of his lost career in the church. Everyone but Mrs. Bennet was relieved when the day of his and Lydia's departure arrived.

"Oh, my dear, dear Lydia," she cried, "when will I see you again?" For Mr. Bennet had absolutely refused to consider the family traveling North for a visit.

"Oh, Lord, I don't know," Lydia answered carelessly. "Not for two or three years, probably."

"Write to me very often, my dear," said Mrs. Bennet.

"As often as I can. But, you know, married women never have much time for writing. My sisters may write to me. They will have nothing else to do."

Mr. Wickham's farewells were much more affectionate than his wife's. He smiled, looked handsome, and said many pretty things.

"He is as fine a fellow as I ever saw," said Mr. Bennet, as soon as they were out of sight. "He simpers, and smirks, and flirts with us all. I am ever so proud of him. I defy even Sir William Lucas himself to produce a more worthless son-in-law."

The loss of her daughter made Mrs. Bennet very depressed for several days. But her spirits were then lifted by a piece of news which raced through the neighborhood. The housekeeper at Netherfield had received orders to prepare for the arrival of her master, who was coming down in a day or two, to hunt game there for several weeks.

Mrs. Bennet was beside herself. "Well, well, so Mr. Bingley is coming down, sister," she said to Mrs. Philips, who had first brought her the news. "Well, so much the better. Not that I care about it, though. He is nothing to us, you know, and I never want to see him again. But, however, he is very welcome to come to Netherfield, if he wishes. And who knows what may happen? But that is nothing to us. You know, sister, we agreed long ago never to mention a word about it. And so, is it quite certain he is coming?"

"It is definite," replied the other, "for Mrs. Nicholls was in Meryton last night. I saw her passing by, and went out myself to learn why, and she told me that it was certain true. He comes down on Thursday at the latest, very likely on Wednesday. She was going to the butcher's, she told me, to order in some meat and three pairs of fat ducks."

Poor Jane was blushing furiously in her corner of the room. It was many months since she had mentioned his name to Elizabeth, but now, as soon as they were alone together, she said, "I saw you look at me today, Lizzy, when my aunt told us the news, and

I know I looked distressed. But it wasn't what you think. I was only upset for a moment, because I knew everyone would be looking at me. It doesn't mean anything to me that he is coming. I only dread the silly things that other people might say."

And indeed, Mrs. Bennet lost no time opening the subject again with her husband. "As soon as Mr. Bingley comes, my dear," Mrs. Bennet said to Mr. Bennet, "you must visit him, of course."

"No, no," he responded. "You forced me to visit him last year, and promised, if I went to see him, that he would marry one of my daughters. But it ended in nothing, and I will not be sent on such a foolish errand again."

His wife insisted that it was only good manners for all the neighbor gentlemen to call on him when he returned to Netherfield. "That is etiquette I despise," he said. "If he wants to see us, let him come here. He knows where we live. I will not spend my time running after my neighbors every time they go away and come back again."

"Well, all I know is that it will be terribly rude if you do not go see him. But that won't prevent my asking him to dinner here. We must have Mrs. Long and the Gouldings here soon. I will invite him at the same time." This plan comforted her somewhat, although it was very irritating to know that her neighbors might see Mr. Bingley before she did.

The day of his arrival drew near. "I am beginning to be sorry he is coming at all," Jane told her sister. "It doesn't matter to me; I could see him and feel nothing, but I can hardly bear to hear it talked about constantly. My mother means well, but she can't know how much I suffer over the things she says. I will be happy when his stay at Netherfield is over!"

At last Mr. Bingley arrived. Mrs. Bennet counted the days before their invitation could properly be sent, certain that she would not see him before their dinner party. But on the third morning after his arrival in Hertfordshire, she saw him from her dressing-room window, riding toward the house. She called for her daughters. Jane firmly kept at her place at the table, but Elizabeth, to satisfy her mother, went to the window. Looking out, she saw Mr. Darcy with him, and quickly sat down again by her sister.

"There is another gentleman with him, Mamma," said Kitty. "Who can it be?"

"Some acquaintance or other, my dear. I am sure I do not know."

"La!" replied Kitty, "It looks just like that man that used to be with him before. Mr. what's-his-name. That tall, proud man."

"Good gracious! Mr. Darcy! Well, any friend of Mr. Bingley's will always be welcome here, although I hate the very sight of him."

Jane looked at Elizabeth with surprise and concern. Both sisters were uncomfortable, both for themselves and for the other. As their mother talked on about how she disliked Mr. Darcy and would be polite to him only for Mr. Bingley's sake, they didn't hear her. Elizabeth had sources of uneasiness which not even Jane knew. She had not yet showed her Mrs. Gardiner's letter, or hinted to her about her change of feelings toward him. To Jane, Darcy was only the man whose proposal she had refused.

Elizabeth's astonishment at his coming to see her again was almost equal to her surprise at his changed behavior in Derbyshire. Color flooded her face, and a smile of delight made her eyes shine, as she thought for a moment that perhaps his affection was still strong. But she did not know. "Let me see how he behaves," she thought. "Then I will have some indication." She sat intently at her sewing, trying to be calm and without daring to lift up her eyes, until she glanced anxiously at Jane as the servant approached to announce the gentlemen. Jane looked a little paler than usual, but perfectly composed. When the gentlemen appeared, she blushed, but she greeted them easily, without any show of either resentment or excitement.

Elizabeth said very little and looked down again to her work with an eagerness which she did not often show. She had ventured only one glance at Darcy. He looked serious, as usual, more as he had in the old days than as she had seen him at Pemberley. But perhaps he could not be as relaxed in her mother's presence as he could before her uncle and aunt.

Bingley seemed both pleased and embarrassed. The enthusiastic politeness that Mrs. Bennet showed him embarrassed her daughters, especially when compared to the cold politeness with which she spoke to Mr. Darcy. Elizabeth, who knew how much her mother owed Mr. Darcy on behalf of her favorite daughter, was ashamed of her bad judgment.

After Darcy had asked after the health of Mr. and Mrs. Gardiner, he said almost nothing else. He was not seated near her, so perhaps that was the reason of his silence, but that had not been the case when she had seen him before. There he had talked to her friends, when he could not to herself. But now many minutes went by without him speaking at all. She was disappointed and angry with herself for being disappointed.

"How else could he act?" she asked herself. "Yet, why did he come?" She was in no mood for conversation with any one but him, yet she did not have the courage to speak. She asked after Miss Darcy, and could do no more.

Mrs. Bennet was speaking. "It has been a long time, Mr. Bingley, since you went away. I began to worry you would never come back again. People did say you meant to leave the place entirely, but I hope that is not true. A great many changes have happened in the neighborhood since you went away. Miss Lucas is married and settled. And one of my own daughters is married as well. Did you see the announcement in the papers?"

Bingley replied that he had, and politely congratulated her. Elizabeth did not dare look at Mr. Darcy to see how he was reacting.

"It is a delightful thing to have a daughter well married," continued her mother, "but at the same time, it is very hard to have her move so far away. They have gone quite far north to join my son-in-law's regiment. He has a new position there, you know. Thank heavens he has some loyal friends, not so many as he deserves."

Elizabeth, who knew this was a taunt aimed at Mr. Darcy, was so miserable with shame that she could hardly stay in her seat. She felt that years of happiness could not make up for moments of such painful embarrassment.

When the gentlemen rose to leave, Mrs. Bennet remembered her plan and invited them to dine at Longbourn in a few days. "You have owed me this for some time, Mr. Bingley," she added, "for when you went to town last winter, you promised to share a family dinner with us as soon as you returned. I have not forgotten, you see, for I was very much disappointed that you did not come back and keep your engagement." Bingley looked a little silly at this reminder and said something about having been called away on business. Then they went away.

Mrs. Bennet had been strongly tempted to ask them to stay and dine there that very day. But, although she always served a good dinner, she decided there must be a special meal for a man for whom she had great plans, or for another who was so proud and so rich.

CHAPTER 54

As soon as they were gone, Elizabeth walked outside to think. Mr. Darcy's behavior had confused and irritated her. "If he was only going to be silent and indifferent, why did he come at all?" she asked herself. "If he could still be friendly and pleasant to my uncle and aunt in London, why not to me? If he no longer cares for me, why is he here? Maddening man! I will not think about him any more."

They did not see the gentlemen again until dinner on Tuesday. A large group had gathered, and when they made their way to the dining room, Elizabeth eagerly watched to see whether Bingley would sit by Jane, as he always had in the past. When he entered the room he seemed to hesitate, but when Jane looked around and happened to smile, it was decided. He seated himself at her side. During dinner, his behavior toward her convinced Elizabeth that, if he only followed his own heart, Jane's happiness would soon be complete. This observation lifted her spirits, and they needed lifting. She was not feeling cheerful. Mr. Darcy was almost as far from her as the table could divide them, and he was sitting on one side of her mother.

She knew how little pleasure this would give to either of them. She was not close enough to hear their conversation, but she could see how seldom they spoke to each other, and how formal and cold they were. Her mother's ungraciousness pained Elizabeth to the heart, and she dearly wanted to tell him that she knew and appreciated his kindness. She hoped that during the evening they would have some opportunity for real conversation.

After dinner, as the ladies sat in the drawing room and waited for the gentlemen to join them, she was so anxious as to be almost rude to her companions. "If he does not come to me," she thought, "I will give him up forever."

The gentlemen came in, and she thought he looked as if he wanted to talk with her, but, alas! The ladies had gathered around the table, where Jane was making tea, and Elizabeth was pouring out the coffee, and it was so crowded that there was no room for a chair near her. Darcy walked away to another part of the room. She looked after him, envying everyone to whom he spoke, and barely had patience to help anyone to coffee. All the time, she was scolding herself savagely for being so silly: "You refused him! How could you expect a second chance? Is there a man who would lower himself to propose a second time to the same woman? Who would do such a thing?"

He returned his empty coffee cup, and she took the opportunity to say, "Is your sister still at Pemberley?"

"Yes, she will remain there until Christmas."

"And is she alone? Have all her friends left?"

"Mrs. Annesley is with her. The others have been gone for three weeks."

She could think of nothing more to say. He stood there in silence for a few minutes, until a young lady began a conversation with Elizabeth, and he walked away.

When the tea things were removed, and the card tables placed, Elizabeth's hopes rose again, but he was quickly seized to make up a bridge table nearby. She now lost every expectation of pleasure. They were trapped for the evening at different tables, and she had nothing more to hope for.

As the guests departed into the night, Mrs. Bennet was well pleased with herself. "Well, girls," she said, "What did you think of that? I think everything went extremely well. The dinner was perfect. The venison was roasted to a turn, and the soup was fifty times better than what we had at the Lucases' last week. Even Mr. Darcy said that the partridges were remarkably tasty, and I suppose he has at least two or three French cooks. And, my dear Jane, I never saw you look more beautiful. Mrs. Long said so, too. And what do you think she said besides? 'Ah! Mrs. Bennet, we shall have her at Netherfield at last.' She did indeed. I do think Mrs. Long is as good a creature as ever lived—and her nieces are very nicely behaved girls, and not at all pretty. I like them very much."

In short, Mrs. Bennet was in very great spirits.

She had seen enough of Bingley's behavior to Jane that she was convinced she would get him at last. In fact, she was quite disappointed not to see him there again the next day, to make his proposals.

"It was a very pleasant day," said Jane to Elizabeth. "The guests all seemed to enjoy each other's company. I hope we may all often meet again." Elizabeth only smiled. Embarrassed, Jane added, "Lizzy, you must not smile at me like that. I promise you that I have learned to simply enjoy his conversation as an agreeable and sensible young man, without thinking anything beyond that. I am convinced that he never meant to make me care for him. It is only that he has an unusually sweet nature."

"You are very cruel," said Elizabeth. "You tell me not to smile, but you say things designed to make me laugh."

"You don't believe me!" cried Jane.

"How could I?" answered her sister.

"But why would you want to convince me that I feel more than I say I do?" Jane asked.

"That is a question which only you can answer. Forgive me, but I really cannot help but smile at your amusing fiction."

A few days later, Mr. Bingley called again, and alone. Mr. Darcy had returned to London, but was to come back in ten days. He visited with them for over an hour, and was in remarkably good spirits. Mrs. Bennet invited him to dine with them, but he had already accepted an invitation. "The next time you call, I hope we will be luckier," she said. He assured her that he would be delighted to come on another night soon, and they agreed he would join them the following day.

He came, and so early that none of the ladies had finished dressing. Mrs. Bennet ran into her daughter's room in her nightgown, with her hair half-combed, crying out, "My dear Jane, hurry down! Mr. Bingley is here already. Hurry, hurry! Here, Sarah, help Miss Bennet with her gown. Never mind Miss Lizzy's hair. Come be quick, be quick! Where is your sash, my dear?"

But once her mother was gone, Jane refused to go downstairs without one of her sisters. Later in the evening, Mrs. Bennet showed the same eagerness to leave Jane and Bingley alone. Mr. Bennet had gone to the library, as was his custom, and

Mary went upstairs to the piano. With two obstacles of five out of the way, Mrs. Bennet sat looking and winking at Elizabeth and Kitty for a considerable time, without any effect. Elizabeth pretended not to notice her, and when Kitty did, she innocently said, "What is the matter, Mamma? What do you keep winking at me for? What do you want me to do?"

"Nothing, child, nothing. I did not wink at you." She sat still for five more minutes, but she could not bear to waste such a precious opportunity. She suddenly got up, saying to Kitty, "Come here, my love, I want to speak to you," and took her out of the room. Jane shot a distressed look at Elizabeth. In a few minutes, Mrs. Bennet half-opened the door and called out, "Lizzy, my dear, I want to speak with you." Elizabeth was forced to go. "We may as well leave them by themselves you know," said her mother, as soon as she was in the hall. "Kitty and I are going upstairs to sit in my room." Elizabeth made no attempt to reason with her mother, but remained quietly in the hall until she and Kitty were out of sight. She then returned into the drawing room.

And so Mrs. Bennet's plans for the day failed. Bingley was everything that was charming, except for being Jane's fiancé. His cheerfulness made him a wonderful addition to their evening gathering. He tolerated Mrs. Bennet's silly remarks in a way that her daughters greatly appreciated. Before he went away, he had accepted an invitation to come the next morning to shoot birds with Mr. Bennet.

After this visit, Jane did not say anything about having no special feeling for Bingley. Not a word passed between the sisters, but Elizabeth went to bed with the happy thought that everything would turn out well, unless Mr. Darcy returned early.

Bingley arrived early the next morning, and he and Mr. Bennet went out shooting. Mr. Bennet had a far more enjoyable time than he had expected. Bingley was neither proud nor foolish. There was nothing about him that could invite Mr. Bennet's ridicule or disgust him into silence. In return, Mr. Bennet was more talkative and less peculiar than the younger man had ever seen him. Bingley, of course, stayed for dinner, and in the evening Mrs. Bennet worked hard again to get everybody away from Bingley and Jane. Elizabeth, who had a letter to write, went into the breakfast room for that purpose soon after tea. When she returned to the drawing room, when her letter was finished, she found her sister and Bingley standing together before the fire, as if they were engaged in serious conversation. Their faces, as they hastily turned around and moved away from each other, told her everything.

Elizabeth had turned to go away again, but Bingley whispered a few words to Jane and ran out of the room. Jane turned to Elizabeth, her face shining with joy, and hugged her warmly.

"It's too much!" she said, half-laughing and half-crying. "It is by far too much. I do not deserve it. Oh, why isn't everybody this happy?"

Elizabeth's delighted congratulations poured forth until Jane interrupted her. "I must go tell our mother," she said. "I must not let her hear it from anyone but me. He has gone to talk to Father already. Oh! Lizzy, to know that this will give such pleasure to all my dear family! How can I bear so much happiness!" She then hurried away to her mother, who was upstairs with Kitty.

Elizabeth, who was left by herself, now smiled at the ease with which the affair was finally settled, after so many months of suspense and trouble. In a few minutes she was joined by Bingley.

"Where is your sister?" he said hastily, as he opened the door.

"With my mother upstairs. She will be down in a moment, I think." He then shut the door, and, coming up to her, claimed the good wishes and affection of a sister. Elizabeth most honestly and heartily expressed her delight. Until her sister came down, she had the pleasure of listening to him describe his own joy, and all of Jane's perfections.

It was an evening of great happiness all around. Jane's delight gave her sweet face a glow that made it handsomer than ever. Kitty giggled and smiled, and hoped her turn was coming soon. Mrs. Bennet could not get over expressing her satisfaction, and when Mr. Bennet joined them at supper, his voice and manner plainly showed how really happy he was.

When their visitor left for the night, he turned to his daughter and said, "Jane, I congratulate you.

You will be a very happy woman." Jane went to him, kissed him, and thanked him for his goodness.

"You are a good girl," he replied, "and I am very pleased to think of you so happily settled. I am convinced that you and Bingley will do well together. Your personalities are very similar. You are both so easy-going and agreeable that every servant will cheat you, and so generous, that you will always exceed your income."

"Exceed their income! My dear Mr. Bennet," cried his wife, "what are you talking about? Why, he has at least four or five thousand pounds a year." Turning to her daughter, she continued. "Oh, my dear, dear Jane, I am so happy! I am sure I won't get a wink of sleep all night. I knew this would happen, I did! I was sure you could not be so beautiful for nothing! I remember, as soon as I saw him, I thought how likely it was that you should be together. Oh, he is the handsomest young man that ever was seen!"

Wickham and Lydia were entirely forgotten. Jane was without question the favorite child. Her younger sisters began to realize the advantages that she could now give them. Mary asked to use the library at Netherfield. Kitty begged very hard for a few balls there every winter.

After this, Bingley was a daily visitor at Longbourn. He frequently arrived before breakfast and stayed well into the evening, unless some horrible neighbor, who could not be hated enough, had given him an invitation to dinner than he felt he had to accept. Elizabeth and Jane had little time together anymore, for when Bingley was there, all Jane's attention was on him. But when Jane was absent, Bingley was always with Elizabeth, whom he loved as a sister, and when Bingley was gone, Jane preferred Elizabeth's company more than anyone else's.

One evening, Jane told her sister, "He has made me so happy by telling me that he did not know I was in London last spring! I wouldn't have believed it possible."

"That is what I suspected," replied Elizabeth.

"It must have been his sisters' doing," Jane said. "They did not want him to see me. I can't entirely blame them for that, since he might have chosen a wife who had more advantages. But I hope that when they see that Bingley is happy with me, we can be on good terms again. But we can never be truly intimate friends."

Elizabeth applauded her. "That is the most unforgiving speech that I ever heard from you. Good girl! It would annoy me greatly to see you tricked again by Miss Bingley's pretended friendship."

"Can you believe it, Lizzy—when he went away last November, he really loved me. It was only because he believed that I didn't care that he stayed away!"

"He made a little mistake, to be sure," answered Elizabeth, "but that is a credit to his modesty." Elizabeth was pleased to find that Bingley had not told Jane about Darcy's interference, for although Jane had the most forgiving heart in the world, Elizabeth knew the facts would color Jane's opinion of Darcy.

"I am certainly the most fortunate woman that ever existed!" said Jane. "Oh, Lizzy, if only I could see you as happy! If there were another such man for you!"

Elizabeth shook her head, laughing. "If you gave me forty such men, I never could be as happy as you. Until I have your sweet nature and goodness, I can never have your happiness. Let me worry about myself. Perhaps, if I am very lucky, I will someday meet another Mr. Collins."

The news of the engagement was not a secret for long. Mrs. Bennet was permitted to whisper it to Mrs. Philips, and Mrs. Philips, without any permission, told all her neighbors in Meryton. It was instantly decided that the Bennets were the luckiest family in the world. Only a few weeks before, when Lydia had first run away, they had been labeled the least fortunate.

CHAPTER
56

One morning, about a week after Bingley and Jane had become engaged, Mrs. Bennet, Elizabeth, and Kitty were sitting in the drawing room when the sound of a carriage reached their ears. They looked out and saw a very fine carriage, drawn by four matched horses, quite unlike anything their neighbors might use. The ladies' curiosity grew until the door was thrown open and their visitor entered. It was Lady Catherine de Bourgh.

Her ladyship entered the room looking even less gracious than usual. She responded to Elizabeth's surprised greeting with only a silent nod, and sat down without saying a word. Mrs. Bennet, quite overcome by the importance of her visitor, received her most politely.

After sitting for a moment in silence, Lady Catherine said very stiffly to Elizabeth, "I hope you are well, Miss Bennet. That lady, I suppose, is your mother."

Elizabeth replied that she was.

"And that, I suppose, is one of your sisters."

"Yes, madam," said Mrs. Bennet, delighted to

have a chance to speak. "She is my second youngest girl. My youngest was recently married, and my eldest is outside, walking with the young man who will soon become a part of our family."

"You have a very small park here," said Lady Catherine after a short silence.

"It is nothing compared to Rosings, I am sure, but it is much larger than our neighbor Sir William Lucas's," Mrs. Bennet said.

"This must be a most inconvenient room to sit in during summer evenings, as the windows face west," Lady Catherine said.

Mrs. Bennet assured her that they never sat there in the evening, then added, "May I ask your ladyship whether Mr. and Mrs. Collins were well when you left them?"

"Yes, very well. I saw them the night before last."

Elizabeth now expected that she would produce a letter for her from Charlotte, as that seemed the only possible reason for her visit. But no letter appeared, and she was completely puzzled.

Mrs. Bennet offered her ladyship some refreshment, but Lady Catherine refused, not very politely. Standing up, she said to Elizabeth, "Miss Bennet, there seemed to be a prettyish stand of trees on one side of your lawn. I would be glad to walk here, if you will favor me your company."

"Go, my dear," cried her mother, "and show her ladyship the different walks."

Elizabeth obeyed, accompanying her noble

guest downstairs. As they passed through the hall, Lady Catherine opened the doors to look into the dining room and drawing room, and pronounced them "decent looking."

They walked in silence along the gravel path that led to the stand of trees. Elizabeth was determined to make no effort to talk with a woman who was being so rude and disagreeable.

As soon as they entered the stand of trees, Lady Catherine began. "I am sure you know, Miss Bennet, the reason for my journey here. Your own heart, your own conscience, must tell you why I have come."

Elizabeth looked with honest astonishment. "You are mistaken, madam. I am completely puzzled by the honor of seeing you here."

"Miss Bennet," replied her ladyship angrily, "you ought to know that I am not someone to be treated lightly. But however insincere you may choose to be, you shall not find me so. I am famous for my sincerity and frankness. Two days ago I heard most alarming news. I was told not only that your sister was on the point of being most fortunately married, but that you, Miss Elizabeth Bennet, would soon be marrying my nephew, my own nephew, Mr. Darcy. Though I know this must be a lie, I instantly decided to come here, to make my feelings known to you."

"If you know such news to be impossible, why did you trouble yourself by coming?" asked

Elizabeth, with anger and amazement in her voice.

"To insist that you totally deny such a report!" her ladyship answered.

"If people are really saying such things, your coming to Longbourn to see me will encourage them to believe it, rather than the opposite," Elizabeth said coolly.

"If!" Lady Catherine spat out. "Do you pretend to be ignorant of it? Haven't you and your family been spreading such a rumor?"

"Indeed we have not," Elizabeth retorted.

"And can you tell me that there is absolutely no truth to such a story?"

"I do not pretend to be as frank as your ladyship. I do not choose to answer your questions."

"I will not put up with this, Miss Bennet. I insist on being satisfied. Has my nephew made you an offer of marriage?"

"Your ladyship has declared that it is impossible."

"It ought to be impossible! It is impossible, if he is in his right mind! But you may have used your feminine arts to charm him so that he forgot what he owes to himself and to all his family. You may have wickedly drawn him in."

"If I had, I would certainly not confess it to you."

"Miss Bennet, do you know who I am? I am not accustomed to being spoken to like this. I am almost the nearest relation Mr. Darcy has in the world, and I am entitled to know the details of his life."

"But you are not entitled to know mine. And behavior like this will never persuade me to tell them."

"Let me make sure you understand me. This marriage, which you have dared to hope for, can never take place. Mr. Darcy is engaged to my daughter. Now what have you to say?"

"If Mr. Darcy and your daughter are engaged, you surely cannot think he would make an offer to me."

Lady Catherine hesitated for a moment, and then replied, "Their engagement is of an unusual kind. From the time they were born, they have been intended for each other. It was his mother's wish as well as mine. While they were in their cradles, we planned the union. And now, at the moment when our wishes are to be satisfied, I will not be frustrated by a young woman of inferior birth and of no importance in the world! Do you care nothing for the wishes of his friends? For his engagement to Miss de Bourgh? Haven't you heard me say that from his earliest hours he was intended for his cousin?"

"Yes, and I had heard that before. But what does that matter to me? You and your sister did as much as you could in planning the marriage. For it to actually occur depends on Mr. Darcy and Miss de Bourgh. If Mr. Darcy has not proposed to his cousin, why shouldn't he make another choice? And if I am that choice, why should I not accept him?"

"Because honor, decency, and even self-interest forbids it. Yes, Miss Bennet, self-interest! For if you act against our wishes, do not expect to be noticed by his family or friends. You will be ignored and despised by everyone connected with him. Your marriage will be a disgrace. Your name will never even be mentioned by any of us."

"That would be terrible indeed," agreed Elizabeth. "But surely being the wife of Mr. Darcy would make up for such misfortune."

"You stubborn, headstrong girl! Is this how you thank me for my kindness to you last spring? Now listen to me carefully. My daughter and my nephew were made for each other. They are descended from the same noble ancestors. They have a splendid fortune on both sides. They have been intended for each other by their families, and what is to divide them? A young woman without family, connections, or fortune. This is madness. For your own good, you should stay with people of your own kind."

"In marrying your nephew, I would not consider myself leaving 'my own kind.' He is a gentleman; I am a gentleman's daughter. So far we are equal."

"True. You are a gentleman's daughter. But who was your mother? Who are your uncles and aunts? I know all about them."

"Whoever my relations are," said Elizabeth, "if your nephew does not object to them, that is all that matters."

"Tell me once and for all, are you engaged to him?"

"I am not."

Lady Catherine seemed pleased. "And will you promise me never to enter into such an engagement?"

"Certainly not."

"Miss Bennet, I am shocked and astonished. I expected you to be reasonable. But do not fool yourself. I will not go away until you give me the promise I must receive."

"And I shall never give it. I will not be bullied into anything so unreasonable. Your ladyship wants Mr. Darcy to marry your daughter. But would my promise make their marriage happen? Suppose that he did care for me. Would my refusal to accept him make him wish to marry his cousin? Lady Catherine, you are very mistaken if you think you can order me around like this. I do not know what Mr. Darcy would think of your interference in his affairs, but you certainly have no right to interfere with mine."

"Not so fast, if you please," retorted Lady Catherine. "I am not finished. To all the objections I have already mentioned, I have another to add. I am familiar with your younger sister's elopement. I know it all, and how the young man's marrying her was a patched-up business, paid for by your father and uncles. Is such a girl to be my nephew's sister-in-law? Is her husband, the son of his late father's steward, to be his brother? What are you thinking? Do you think I would allow Pemberley to be polluted like this?"

Elizabeth stood up. "You can now have nothing more to say," she said. "You have insulted me in every possible way. I am returning to the house."

Her ladyship was furious. "You have no regard, then, for the honor of my nephew! Selfish girl! Does it mean nothing to you that a marriage with you would disgrace him in the eyes of everybody?"

"Lady Catherine, I have nothing more to say. You know my thoughts."

"You are determined to have him, then?"

"I said no such thing. I am only saying that I will act as I please, without concern for you or anyone else who is so unconnected with me."

"Very well. Now I know how to act. Do not imagine, Miss Bennet, that your hope will ever come true. I came to try to reason with you, but I see it is useless. I will act as I think best." She continued talking in this manner until they reached her carriage. Then she turned and spat out, "I do not say goodbye, Miss Bennet. I send no regards to your mother. You do not deserve such attention. I am seriously displeased."

Elizabeth did not answer, but walked quietly into the house. Her mother met her there, impatiently asking why Lady Catherine had not come in again for some refreshments.

"She did not wish to," said her daughter. "She

preferred to go."

"She is a very fine-looking woman! And her calling here was extremely kind. I suppose she only stopped by to tell us that the Collinses were well. I imagine she was on her way somewhere, and thought she might as well call on you. She had nothing special to say to you, did she, Lizzy?" Elizabeth was forced to tell a little lie here, for she could not tell her mother the subject of their discussion.

CHAPTER
57

Thoughts of the visit obsessed Elizabeth for many hours after her ladyship left. As much as Elizabeth would have liked to only laugh at the ridiculousness of Lady Catherine's behavior, she could not help but feel uneasy about what she would do next. From what she had said, it seemed very likely that she would have a similar discussion with her nephew, and Elizabeth could only guess what the results of such a talk would be. She did not know how Darcy really felt about his aunt, or how much he trusted her judgment, but it was likely that he thought more highly of her than Elizabeth did. If he had been undecided before about what he should do, the advice of his relative might make up his mind, and persuade him to settle for having his dignity left intact. In that case, he would not return to Longbourn.

"And so, if he sends Bingley an excuse for not coming again, I will know why," Elizabeth told herself. "I will then give up any hope."

The next morning, as she was going downstairs, she was met by her father. He was coming out of his library with a letter in his hand.

"Lizzy," he said, "I was going to look for you. Come into my room." She followed him, worried that the letter might be from Lady Catherine, and she dreaded the explanation that she would have to give. They both sat down by the fireplace, and he said, "I have received a letter this morning that has astonished me. As it is primarily about you, you ought to know what it says. I did not know that I had two daughters on the brink of marriage! Let me congratulate you."

The color rushed into Elizabeth's cheeks as it occurred to her that this might be a letter from the nephew, rather than the aunt. But her father surprised her again when he continued. "Young ladies usually understand more than their fathers in such matters, but I think even you will be surprised to learn the name of your admirer. This letter is from Mr. Collins."

"From Mr. Collins! What can he have to say?"

"Something memorable, of course. He begins by congratulating me on the approaching marriage of Jane, which he has learned of from the good-natured, gossiping Lucases. I will not try your patience by reading all of that. What relates to you is next." Mr. Collins writes:

> Having offered you Mrs. Collins's and my sincere congratulations on this happy event, let me now add a short hint on another subject. Your daughter Elizabeth, we understand, will not long bear the name of Bennet, and the cho-

sen partner of her fate may be reasonably regarded as one of the most illustrious men in this land.

Mr. Bennet looked up over the letter, chuck-
ling. "Can you possibly guess, Lizzy, who Mr.
Collins is referring to?" He read on:

> This young gentleman is blessed with a great
> fortune, splendid properties, and a noble fami-
> ly—everything the mortal heart might desire. Yet
> in spite of all these temptations, let me warn my
> cousin Elizabeth and yourself of the hazards of
> accepting this gentleman's proposal.

"You cannot imagine, Lizzy, who this gentleman is!" Mr. Bennet chortled. "But now it comes
out":

> My reason for cautioning you is this. We
> have reason to believe that his aunt, Lady
> Catherine de Bourgh, does not approve of the
> match.

"Mr. Darcy, you see, is the man!" Mr. Bennet
announced, actually slapping his knee in hilarity.
"Now, Lizzy, I think I have surprised you. Could he
have chosen anyone less likely? Mr. Darcy, who
never looks at any woman except to criticize her,
and who has probably never looked at you in his
entire life!"

Elizabeth tried to join in her father's laughter,
but she could only force a reluctant smile. His wit
had never pleased her less.

"Isn't this amusing, Lizzy?"

"Oh, yes indeed," she answered. "Please go on."

After we mentioned the likelihood of this marriage to her ladyship last night, she expressed her feelings. It became apparent that she would never give her consent to what she termed so disgraceful a match. I thought it my duty to pass this news on to my cousin, so that she and her noble admirer will not rush hastily into a marriage of which his family disapproves.

"Ah, and there is something more," Mr. Bennet added.

I am rejoiced that my cousin Lydia's sad business has been so well hushed up. I must add, however, that I was amazed to hear that you had received the young couple into your house as soon as they were married. By doing so you have encouraged their vice, and if I had been consulted I would have advised you strongly against it. As a Christian, you should of course forgive them, but never allow them in your sight, or allow their names to be mentioned in your hearing.

"So that is Mr. Collins's notion of Christian forgiveness! The rest of his letter is only about his dear Charlotte's situation, and his expectation of a Collins Junior. But, Lizzy, you look as if you did not enjoy it. You are not going to be insulted by such idle gossip, I hope. For why else do we live but to provide fun for our neighbors, and to laugh at them in turn?"

"Oh yes," agreed Elizabeth, "I am greatly amused. But it is so strange!"

"Yes, that is what makes it ridiculous. If they

had named any other man it would have been nothing. But Mr. Darcy's complete indifference toward you, and your dislike of him, make it so wonderfully absurd! As much as I hate letter writing, I would not give up Mr. Collins's correspondence for anything. When I read a letter of his, I cannot help preferring him even over Wickham, as much as I value the immorality and hypocrisy of my son-in-law. And tell me, Lizzy, what did Lady Catherine say about this? Did she visit you in order to refuse her consent?"

To this question his daughter replied only with a laugh. As he has asked it as a joke, he let the matter drop.

Elizabeth had never tried harder to hide her feelings. Her father had cruelly hurt her when he referred to Mr. Darcy's indifference toward her. She had needed to laugh when she would rather have cried. She wondered at her father's lack of insight. But then, she worried that the problem was not that he saw too little, but that she imagined too much.

CHAPTER 58

Bingley did not receive a letter from Darcy canceling his visit. Instead, the two gentlemen came to Longbourn not many days after Lady Catherine's visit. Fortunately, before Mrs. Bennet had time to blurt out the news of her ladyship's call, Bingley suggested that they all go for a walk. Mrs. Bennet was not fond of walking, and Mary could never spare time, but the other five set off together.

Bingley and Jane, who wanted to be alone, lagged behind, while Elizabeth, Kitty, and Darcy walked on together. It was a silent group. Kitty was too much afraid of Darcy to talk. Elizabeth was secretly forming a desperate plan. Perhaps he was doing the same.

They walked toward the Lucases, because Kitty wanted to visit Maria. Leaving Kitty there, Elizabeth went boldly on with him alone. Now was the moment.

Seizing all her courage, she turned to him and said, "Mr. Darcy, I am a very selfish creature, and for the sake of satisfying my feelings, I will risk offending you. I must thank you for your kindness to my poor sister Lydia. Ever since I learned of it, I have wanted to tell you how grateful I am. If the rest of my family knew the truth, you would receive their warmest thanks as well."

Darcy replied with surprise and emotion in his voice. "I am very sorry that you have ever been told of this matter," he said. "I believed I could trust Mrs. Gardiner to remain silent."

"You must not blame my aunt. It was Lydia who thoughtlessly let me know that you had been present at her wedding, and after that, I could not rest until I learned the whole story. Let me thank you again, in the name of all my family, for your generosity and for going to such a great deal of trouble. I can only guess how unpleasant it was for you."

"If you want to thank me," he replied, "let it be for yourself alone. My only wish was to give happiness to you. As much as I respect your family, they owe me nothing."

Elizabeth was too embarrassed and confused to say a word.

After a short pause, Darcy went on. "You are too kind to tease me. If you still feel the way you did last April, please tell me so at once. My feelings and my wishes are what they were then. But one word from you will silence me on this subject forever."

Elizabeth forced herself to speak, although brokenly and with many stumbles. But she somehow managed to make him understand that her feelings for him had changed very greatly indeed. Her words brought such happiness to his face as to completely transform him, and the words that poured forth from him proved that he was a man very deeply and warmly in love.

They walked on, without knowing where they were going. There was too much to be thought, and felt, and said, to pay attention to anything outside of themselves. She learned that, strangely enough, they owed their present happiness to Lady Catherine. She had indeed gone directly to visit him to describe her conversation with Elizabeth. Unfortunately for her ladyship, her description of Elizabeth's spirited refusal to promise not to marry Mr. Darcy had had exactly the opposite effect she intended.

"What she told me allowed me to hope again," he said. "I knew you well enough to be sure that if you had absolutely decided against me, you would have told her, frankly and openly."

Elizabeth blushed and laughed as she replied, "Yes, you know I would be capable of that. After criticizing you so horribly to your face, I could have no problem criticizing you to your relatives."

"What did you ever say about me that I didn't deserve? It may be that your accusations were based on false information, but my behavior to you was unforgiveable. I can't think of it without shame."

"Let's not quarrel about who deserved more blame that evening," said Elizabeth. "Neither of us conducted ourselves particularly well, but since then I think we have both improved greatly."

Darcy mentioned his letter. "Did it make you think better of me?" he asked. "When you read it, did you believe what I said?" She explained how she had responded to it, and that it had taken her time to admit the truth that was in it.

"I knew that what I wrote would hurt you, but I believed it was necessary," he said. "I hope you have destroyed the letter."

"I will burn it if you wish, but I promise you that I have quite gotten over any pain I ever felt about it."

"When I wrote it," said Darcy, "I believed that I was perfectly calm and cool, but I know now that it was written in a very bitter spirit."

"Perhaps the letter began bitterly, but it did not end that way. The closing was sweet and charitable. But don't think about it any more. The feelings of the person who wrote it, and the person who received it, are now so different from what they were then, that we should forget any unpleasantness of the past."

Darcy shook his head. "But my past includes many events that I should remember, and with shame. As a child I was taught what was right, but I was not taught to control my temper. As an only son (for many years an only child), I was spoiled by my parents. Although they were kind and good themselves, they allowed me to be selfish and overbearing, and to critically compare others' worth with my own. That is how I was until I was twenty-eight, and I might still be that way except for you, dearest, loveliest Elizabeth! How much I owe you! You taught me a lesson. You humbled me. I came to you without any doubt that you would accept me. You showed me that I knew nothing about pleasing a woman who was worth pleasing."

Eventually their conversation turned to Bingley and Jane. Darcy made it clear that he was delighted with their engagement.

"Were you surprised by it?" asked Elizabeth.

"Not at all. When I went away, I felt sure that it would happen."

"That is to say, you had given your permission. I guessed as much."

He objected to the word "permission," but she found that it had been pretty much the case.

"On the evening before I went to London," he told her, "I made a confession to him, which I should have made long ago. I told him of everything that had happened to convince me that I was wrong to have interfered in his affairs. He was greatly surprised; he had not had the slightest suspicion. I told him, in addition, that I thought I had been wrong in believing that your sister did not care for him."

"And did your words immediately convince him?"

"I think so. Bingley is truly very modest. He is

not one to value himself highly, so it took the judgment of another to convince him that your sister did indeed return his affection. I did have to confess one thing which, understandably, offended him. That was concealing from him that your sister had been in London all last winter. He was angry. But his anger dissolved once he had settled things with your sister. He has heartily forgiven me now."

They walked on talking joyously, looking forward to the happiness of Jane and Bingley, which they imagined (of course) would be only slightly less than their own. They reached the house, and in the hall they parted.

CHAPTER
59

"**M**y dear Lizzy, where did you vanish to?" was the question which Jane asked Elizabeth as soon as she entered their room. But she made some offhand answer, and the evening passed quietly. The publicly known lovers talked and laughed; the unknown ones were quiet. Darcy was not the sort of person to display his happiness in shouting and laughing, and Elizabeth was worried and confused. She tried to imagine her family's response when the truth was known. She knew that no one liked him but Jane.

That night, she confessed everything to her sister. Although Jane was far from being a suspicious person, she had a great deal of trouble believing what she heard. "You are joking, Lizzy. This cannot be! Engaged to Mr. Darcy! No, no, you cannot fool me."

"Oh, this is a very bad beginning," sighed Elizabeth. "I am sure nobody else will believe me, if you do not. Yet, it is true. He still loves me, and we are engaged."

Jane looked at her doubtingly. "Lizzy, this cannot be. I know how much you dislike him."

"You know nothing of the sort. You must forget all that. Perhaps I did not always love him as well as I do now. But at times like this, a good memory is unpardonable. This is the last time I will ever remember it myself."

Miss Bennet still looked amazed. Elizabeth again, and more seriously, assured her it was the truth. "Good heavens, can it really be so? Yet I see that I must believe you," cried Jane. "My dear, dear Lizzy, I would—no, I *do* congratulate you—but are you certain? Forgive me—but are you sure that you can be happy with him?"

"There is no doubt of that," Elizabeth answered. "We have already decided that we will be the happiest couple in the world. But are you pleased, Jane? Will you be happy to have Darcy as a brother?"

"Very, very much," Jane said. "Nothing could give either Bingley or me more delight. But it seems so impossible. Do you really love him well enough? Lizzy, you must do anything other than marry without love. Are you quite sure that you feel what you ought to?"

"Oh, yes! In fact, I must confess that I love him better than I do Bingley. I am afraid you will be angry."

"My dearest sister, stop teasing now and be serious. I want to know everything, without delay. Will you tell me how long you have loved him?"

Elizabeth answered solemnly, "It has been

coming on so gradually, I hardly know when it began. But I believe I must date it from my first moment of seeing the beautiful grounds at Pemberley."

"Elizabeth, if you will not be serious I shall be very cross!" answered Jane, although she was unable to withhold a smile. And so Elizabeth was serious, and soon satisfied Jane that her love for Darcy was in every way sincere. When she was convinced, Jane had nothing more to wish. "Now I am entirely happy," she said, "for you will be as happy as myself. I always admired him. And now, as Bingley's friend and your husband, only Bingley and you will be more dear to me. But Lizzy, you have been very sly with me. How little you told me about what happened at Pemberley!"

Elizabeth told her the reasons for her secrecy. Before, she had been unwilling to mention Bingley, and the confused state of her own feelings had made her equally unwilling to talk about Darcy. But now she told Jane everything, including Darcy's involvement in Lydia's marriage. The girls spent half the night in conversation.

"Good gracious!" cried Mrs. Bennet, as she stood at a window the next morning, "That disagreeable Mr. Darcy is coming here again with our dear Bingley! It is so tiresome of him to always be coming here. I thought he would spend his time shooting at Netherfield, not bothering us. What shall we do with him? Lizzy, you must go walking

with him again, and get him out of Bingley's way."
Elizabeth could hardly help laughing at such a convenient idea, but she was irritated that her mother
was so critical of him.

As the gentlemen entered, Bingley looked at
Elizabeth so happily, and shook her hand with such
warmth, that she was sure he knew the news. Soon
afterward he said, "Mrs. Bennet, aren't there any
other lanes where Lizzy may get lost again today?"

"I advise Mr. Darcy, Lizzy, and Kitty to walk to
Mount Oakham this morning," said Mrs. Bennet.
"It is a nice long walk, and Mr. Darcy has never
seen the view."

"That sounds ideal for the others," replied Mr.
Bingley, "but I am sure it is too far for Kitty. Isn't it,
Kitty?" Kitty agreed that she had rather stay at home.
Darcy claimed to be very curious to see the view
from the mount, and Elizabeth agreed. As she went
upstairs to get ready, Mrs. Bennet followed her, saying, "I am sorry, Lizzy, that you should have to
spend time with that disagreeable man. But I hope
you will not mind doing it for Jane's sake. There is
no need to talk to him, except now and then."

During their walk, Darcy and Elizabeth decided that he would ask Mr. Bennet's consent during
the evening, and that Elizabeth herself would speak
to her mother. Elizabeth could not decide how her
mother would respond. Would all of Darcy's wealth
be enough to overcome her dislike? But whether
she hated the idea of the match, or was delighted by

it, it was certain that she would overreact. Elizabeth did not want Mr. Darcy to hear either the first raptures of her joy or her first expressions of horror.

After dinner, soon after Mr. Bennet withdrew to the library, she saw Mr. Darcy rise and follow him. Her heart pounded with anxiety. She did not fear that her father would disapprove, but he was going to be unhappy. The idea that she, his favorite child, should distress him by her choice, was a very unhappy one. She sat in misery until Mr. Darcy appeared again. She was a little relieved by his smile. In a few minutes, he approached the table where she was sitting and whispered, "Go to your father. He wants you in the library."

She found her father walking about the room, looking grave and anxious. "Lizzy," he said, "what are you doing? Have you lost your mind, to accept this man? Haven't you always hated him?"

How much Elizabeth wished that she had been less outspoken and more reasonable in the past! Now it was necessary to give some painful and confusing explanations, assuring her father of her affection for Darcy.

"In other words, you are determined to have him," Mr. Bennet said. "He is rich, to be sure, and you will have more fine clothes and fine carriages than Jane. But will they make you happy?"

"Do you have any other objection to him, besides your belief that I dislike him?" asked Elizabeth.

"None at all," answered her father. "We all know him to be a proud, unpleasant sort of man, but that would not matter if you really liked him."

"I do, I do like him," she replied, with tears in her eyes, "I love him. And he is not improperly proud. He is kind and generous. You do not know what he really is. Please, do not hurt me by speaking of him in such a way."

"Lizzy," said her father, "I have given him my consent. I give it to you as well, if you are determined to have him. But let me advise you to think better of it. I know you, Lizzy. You could not be happy unless you truly respected your husband. You have a lively mind and talents that put you in danger in an unequal marriage. My child, spare me the grief of seeing you unable to respect your partner in life."

Elizabeth was deeply moved. She solemnly reassured her father, and talked with him at length about the gradual change in her feelings about Darcy. She showed him that her affection was not a sudden thing, but that it had stood the test of many months. As she described in detail Darcy's many good qualities, she finally overcame her father's disbelief.

"Well, my dear," he said, when she ceased speaking, "I have no more to say. If all this is true, he deserves you. I could not have parted with you, my Lizzy, for anyone less worthy." To complete her story, she then told him what Mr. Darcy had done for Lydia. He listened with astonishment. "This is an evening of wonders, indeed! And so, Darcy did everything—made up the match, gave the money, paid the fellow's debts, and got him his job! So much the better. This will save me a world of trouble. If it had been your uncle's doing, I must have paid him. But these passionate young lovers do everything their own way. I will offer to pay him tomorrow; he will rant and storm about his love for you, and that will be an end of the matter."

He then remembered Elizabeth's embarrassment of a few days before, when he read Mr. Collins's letter. After laughing at her for some time, he finally allowed her to go. His final words, as she left the room, were, "If any young men come for Mary or Kitty, send them in, for I am quite free to talk to them."

Elizabeth's mind was much relieved, and she joined the others for a quiet evening. When her mother went up to her room for the night, she followed her, and told her the news. Its effect was extraordinary. At first, Mrs. Bennet sat quite still, unable to utter a syllable. It was many, many minutes before she could fully understand what Elizabeth had said. Finally, she began to recover, to fidget about in her chair, get up, sit down again, wonder, and get up again.

"Good gracious! Lord bless me! Only think! Dear me! Mr. Darcy! Who would have thought it! And is it really true? Oh, my sweetest Lizzy! How rich and how great you will be! What jewels, what carriages you will have! Jane's fortune is nothing beside it. I am so pleased—so happy. Such a charming man! So handsome! So tall! Oh, my dear Lizzy! Please apologize to him for my having disliked him so much before. I hope he will overlook it. Dear, dear Lizzy. A house in London! Three daughters married! Ten thousand a year! Oh, Lord, what will become of me? I shall quite lose my senses!"

Elizabeth soon went to her own room, glad that only she had heard her mother's first reaction. But three minutes later, her mother appeared at her door. "My dearest child," she cried, "I can think of nothing else! Ten thousand a year, and very likely more! It's as good as a lord! But my dearest love, tell me what dish Mr. Darcy is particularly fond of, and I will serve it for dinner tomorrow."

The following day passed off better than Elizabeth had expected. Luckily, Mrs. Bennet was so in awe of her intended son-in-law that she hardly dared speak to him, unless it was to offer him something or ask his opinion. Elizabeth was pleased to see her father going out of his way to get acquainted with her fiancé, and Mr. Bennet later told her that his affection for Darcy was growing.

"I admire all my three sons-in-law highly," he said. "Wickham, perhaps, is my favorite, but I think I shall like your husband quite as well as Jane's."

After the ordeal of facing her parents, Elizabeth's spirits soon rose back to playfulness, and she asked Mr. Darcy to describe falling in love with her. "When and how did you begin?" she asked him. "I want to know it all."

"I cannot tell you the hour, or the spot, or the look, or the words, which laid the foundation of my love," he said. "It is too long ago, and I was in the middle before I knew that I had begun."

"You had resisted my beauty," she reminded him. "And my behavior to you bordered on rudeness. I never spoke to you without some desire to give you pain. Now, be honest—did you admire me for my rudeness?"

"For the liveliness of your mind, I did."

"You may as well call it rudeness. It was very little less. The fact is that you were sick of politeness. You were disgusted with the women who were always speaking, and looking, and thinking for your approval alone. I interested you, because I was so unlike them. There—I have saved you the trouble of explaining it! To be sure, you knew nothing good about me, but nobody thinks of that when they fall in love."

"Was there nothing good about your affectionate behavior to Jane while she was ill at Netherfield?"

"Dearest Jane! Who could have done less for her? But praise me for it, by all means. It is your job to exaggerate all my good qualities as much as possible. And now, what made you so shy of me, when you first came to Longbourn? Why were you silent, and looked as if you did not care about me?"

"Because *you* were grave and silent, and gave me no encouragement."

"But I was embarrassed."

"And so was I."

"You might have talked to me more when you came to dinner."

"A man who had felt less might have."

"But I wonder when you would have spoken, if I had not asked you! My decision to thank you for your kindness to Lydia had a wonderful effect."

"You need not worry about that. Lady Catherine's attempt to separate us had persuaded me to speak. My aunt's report had given me hope, and I was determined to know where you stood."

"That will make Lady Catherine very happy. But tell me, what did you come down to Netherfield for?"

"My purpose was to see you, and to judge whether I could ever hope to make you love me. My other purpose, the one that I admitted to myself, was to see whether your sister still cared for

Bingley. If she did, I planned to make the confession to him which I have since made."

"Will you ever have the courage to tell Lady Catherine what is to happen?"

"Ah, it must be done, and if you will give me a sheet of paper, it shall be done now."

"And if I did not have a letter to write myself, I would sit by you and admire the evenness of your handwriting, as another young lady once did. But I have an aunt, too, who has been neglected for too long."

Because she was embarrassed over what to say about Mr. Darcy earlier, Elizabeth had not yet answered Mrs. Gardiner's long letter. But now, having news to tell which she knew would be most welcome, she wrote as follows:

> I would have thanked you before, my dear aunt, for your long, kind letter, but to tell you the truth, I was too cross to write. You imagined more than really existed. But now you may imagine as much as you choose. Unless you imagine me already married, you can hardly go wrong.
>
> You must write again very soon, and praise him a great deal more than you did in your last letter. Your idea of the ponies is delightful. We will drive around the Park every day. I am the happiest creature in the world. Perhaps other people have said so before, but not one meant it as much as I do. I am happier even than Jane. She only smiles—I laugh.

Mr. Darcy sends you all the love in the world that he can spare from me. You must all come to Pemberley at Christmas.

Your affectionate niece.

Mr. Darcy's letter to Lady Catherine was in a somewhat different style. And different from either was what Mr. Bennet wrote to Mr. Collins:

Dear sir,

I must trouble you once more for congratulations. Elizabeth will soon be the wife of Mr. Darcy. Comfort Lady Catherine as well as you can. But, if I were you, I would side with the nephew. He has more to give.

When Miss Bingley wrote to her brother about his approaching marriage, her letter was everything that was affectionate and insincere. She wrote to Jane to express her delight, and repeat all her former declarations of friendship. Jane was not deceived, but she wrote her a much kinder answer than she deserved.

The joy which Miss Darcy expressed in her letter was far more honest. Four pages were not enough to express her delight and her sincere desire of being loved as a sister by Elizabeth. Before any answer could arrive from Mr. Collins, the Bennets heard that the Collinses had suddenly arrived at Lucas Lodge. Charlotte explained the reason for this change. Lady Catherine had been so enraged by her nephew's letter that Charlotte was anxious to get away until the storm blew over.

CHAPTER
61

How happy Mrs. Bennet was on the day she got rid of her two most deserving daughters! One might imagine with what delighted pride she later visited Mrs. Bingley, and talked to everyone of Mrs. Darcy. I wish I could say, for the sake of her family, that these happy events turned her into a sensible, good-natured, well-informed woman for the rest of her life. But perhaps it was best for her husband that she remained nervous and often silly. He might not have been able to stand the shock.

Mr. Bennet missed Elizabeth a great deal. His affection for her took him away from home more often than anything else he could do. He loved going to Pemberley, especially when he was least expected.

Mr. Bingley and Jane lived at Netherfield for only a year. Being so near to Mrs. Bennet was too much even for Bingley's easy nature or Jane's affectionate heart. Bingley bought an estate in the county that bordered Derbyshire. As a result, Jane and Elizabeth were within thirty miles of each other, making both sisters entirely happy.

Kitty, to her great advantage, spent most of her time living with her two older sisters. In such good company, she improved a great deal. She was not as wild as Lydia and, removed from her influence, she became less irritable, less ignorant, and less foolish. Although Lydia frequently invited her to come and stay with them, with the promise of balls and young men, her father would never let her go.

Mary was the only daughter who remained at home. Because Mrs. Bennet was quite unable to be alone, Mary was forced to mix more with the world. As she no longer had to put up with comparisons between her sisters' beauty and her own, her father suspected that she rather enjoyed the change.

As for Wickham and Lydia, her sisters' marriages did nothing to change their characters. Wickham realized Elizabeth must now know everything about his lies and deceptions, and kept his distance. Even so, the letter of congratulations Elizabeth received from Lydia made it clear that she, at least, was hopeful of benefiting from the family connection. The letter said this:

My dear Lizzy,

I wish you joy. If you love Mr. Darcy half as well as I do my dear Wickham, you will be very happy. It is wonderful to have you so rich, and when you have nothing else to do, I hope you will think of us. I am sure Wickham would like a position at the King's court, and I do not think we will have money enough to live upon without some help. Any position would do, paying about three or four hundred a year. But don't say anything to Mr. Darcy about it if you would rather not.

As it happened, Elizabeth would much rather not, and she discouraged Lydia from expecting any such assistance. But over the years, as she was able from her own money, she frequently sent them something. They were constantly moving from place to place in search of a cheaper situation, and always spending more than they should. Wickham's affection for Lydia soon became indifference. Hers lasted a little longer.

Although Darcy would never receive Wickham at Pemberley, Lydia was sometimes a visitor there, when her husband was gone to enjoy himself in London or Bath. The Wickhams visited the Bingleys so often and so long that even Bingley's good humor was exhausted, and he had to hint that it was time they leave.

Pemberley was now Georgiana's home. The affection that grew between her and Elizabeth was exactly what Darcy had hoped to see. Georgiana admired Elizabeth enormously. At first, she listened with an astonishment bordering on alarm at her sister-in-law's lively, teasing manner of talking to Darcy. But she learned much from her new sister. She began to understand that a woman may take liberties with her husband which a sister does not take with a brother who is more than ten years older than herself.

Lady Catherine was extremely angry about the marriage of her nephew. She expressed all the frankness of which she was so proud in a letter which was so abusive, especially of Elizabeth, that her relationship with Darcy ended for some time. Finally, Elizabeth persuaded him to seek a reconciliation, for the family's sake. Either due to affection for him, or curiosity to see how his wife conducted herself, she agreed to visit them at Pemberley, despite the way that great house had been polluted.

With the Gardiners, they were always on warmest and friendliest terms. Darcy, as well as Elizabeth, really loved them. They both felt great gratitude toward the couple who, by bringing Elizabeth to Pemberley, had been the cause of them coming together.

AFTERWORD

About the Author

The fact that Jane Austen is one of the best-known authors in the English-speaking world would greatly astonish the lady herself. Her own life was as sheltered and unremarkable as that of any of her novels' heroines. But within that quiet life, she found the material to create a world of characters that is as real to her adoring readers as any of their own friends and neighbors. Elizabeth Bennet, Mr. Darcy, Lady Catherine de Bourgh, and Mr. Collins are just a few of the characters whose names will bring a fond smile or an amused chuckle to Austen's devoted fans. Despite her lack of fame in her own lifetime, her creations ensure that Austen is remembered long after most writers of her day are forgotten.

Jane Austen was born in 1775, one year before the American Revolution, in Hampshire, England, to a clergyman and his wife. Jane was the seventh of a total of eight Austen children—six boys and two girls. The two girls, Jane and Cassandra, were extremely close friends throughout their lives. When Cassandra briefly went away to boarding school at the age of twelve, Jane insisted on going too, although her parents thought that at age ten she was too young. At the time her mother reportedly said, "If Cassandra's head was going to be cut off, Jane would have hers cut off too." That year at boarding school was the extent of Jane's formal education. But like the Bennet girls in *Pride and Prejudice,* Jane and her sister were free to learn as much as they liked at home. Their father had a large library, and the girls were enthusiastic readers. Visiting "masters" helped the girls learn to draw and play the piano. (The Austen brothers received far more formal education, and several of them attended Oxford University.)

Much like the Bennets, the Austen family lived comfortably but without any sense of long-term security. Mr. Austen had been given a modest living as a clergyman, and he made extra money by tutoring students. But he had eight children to support, and the income from his living would cease when he died. Therefore, the boys prepared themselves for careers—several became clergymen like their father, others went into business, and the youngest two entered the Navy, both eventually becoming admirals. Cassandra and Jane, of course, were supposed to find husbands.

Cassandra did fall in love and become engaged to a young man named Thomas Fowler, a military chaplain. Unfortunately, while he was posted in the Caribbean, Thomas caught yellow fever and died. It is unclear if Jane ever really lost her heart to anyone. What does seem true is that she was a lively young lady who enjoyed going to dances, plays, and parties. In fact, one neighbor was reported as saying that Jane was "the prettiest, silliest, most affected, husband-hunting butterfly" she had ever met. It is hard to match this description with the author of *Pride and Prejudice,* though, so perhaps the neighbor was just jealous of Jane's literary talents!

As far as Jane's own romantic life goes, we have only two stories handed down to us. The first occurred during the summer of 1800, when the Austen family was vacationing at a seaside town. According to family sources, a young man there fell in love with Jane, and he was someone who Cassandra thoroughly approved of. At the summer's end the young man promised that he would contact Jane again soon. Instead, the family soon learned of his accidental death. What is missing from this story is any hint of how Jane felt about the young man, or how affected she was by his death.

The second story may tell us more about Jane. In the winter of 1802, the Austen sisters were staying with a family whose daughters were their close friends. The son of the family proposed to Jane, and she accepted him. But by the next day she had thought better of it, and she told the young man that she had changed her mind. This must have been a difficult decision for Jane, as well as an embarrassing one. Although the man was six years younger than she, and was reportedly "big and awkward," he was also a wealthy gentleman who could have given her a lovely home. But like Elizabeth

Bennet herself, Jane chose not to marry for financial benefit alone. Ultimately, neither Jane nor Cassandra ever married, and they (along with their mother) were supported in their later lives by their brothers.

Jane began her writing career at a very early age. Between the ages of twelve and eighteen, she wrote enough humorous poems and parodies of popular literature to fill three large notebooks. Most of them were dedicated to her family members and friends, such as the one called (and misspelled) "The Beautifull Cassandra." Between 1795 and 1799, (when she was twenty to twenty-four), she began working on three novels: *Sense and Sensibility, Pride and Prejudice,* and *Northanger Abbey.* In 1803 she sold the rights to *Northanger Abbey* for the sum of ten pounds, but the publisher did not release the book until after Austen's death in 1817. But in 1811, *Sense and Sensibility* was published. As it was not usual in those days to see a woman's name on a book cover, the novel was published anonymously—"By a Lady" was all that identified the author. The book attracted some praise, and earned its author 140 pounds. Encouraged by this success, she began revising *Pride and Prejudice,* and the book was published in January 1813. Another novel, *Mansfield Park,* came out in 1814, followed by *Emma* in 1815. By then, Jane had already begun work on her final novel, *Persuasion,* although her health was beginning to fail. In April of 1817 she made out her will, leaving almost everything to Cassandra. On July 18 she died at the age of forty-one.

By the time of Jane's death, her novels were becoming modestly popular, but their author's name was still known only to her family and friends. At the end of 1817, a combined edition of *Northanger Abbey* and *Persuasion* was published. On its cover it said only, "By the author of *Pride and Prejudice* and *Mansfield Park*," but it included a "biographical note" written by her brother Henry that finally identified Jane Austen as the author.

Today, the novels of Jane Austen have been through countless editions and translated into dozens of languages. At least six movie versions of *Pride and Prejudice* have been filmed, and it has been the basis of a five-episode television miniseries. Author Helen Fielding borrowed heavily from the story to write her 1996 best-seller *Bridget Jones's Diary.* There are Jane Austen societies devoted to studying the life and works of the author. The name "Jane Austen," unknown in the writer's own lifetime, has become one of the literary world's most famous.

About the Book

"Everyone knows that a rich single man needs a wife."

The first line of *Pride and Prejudice* alerts us instantly as to one of the major themes of this novel: Marriage. Sometimes seriously, often comically, Jane Austen makes us think about marriage: good marriages, bad marriages, marriages whose partners go into them foolishly or wisely, greedily or with generous hearts.

In order to explore her theme, Austen focuses on five marriages. She begins with Mr. and Mrs. Bennet, parents of the five Bennet sisters. Their marriage is a disastrous one, but in a quiet, odd, even amusing way. Mrs. Bennet is a foolish, flighty woman who talks too much and thinks too little. She embarrasses her oldest daughters horribly, and encourages the worst behavior in her younger ones. By contrast, Mr. Bennet is intelligent, sensible, and witty. He had apparently been swept away by Mrs. Bennet's one-time youth and beauty, and now regrets his choice. But Mrs. Bennet is not the only one to blame for their empty marriage. Her husband is also at fault. Instead of encouraging Mrs. Bennet to act more sensibly, thereby protecting their daughters from her foolish influence, Mr. Bennet hides in his library and makes jokes about how silly she is. In the Bennets' marriage, we see what happens when an ignorant, foolish woman marries a passive, lazy man. There is no love or respect between them, and their children suffer the consequences.

A second marriage that is observed in *Pride and Prejudice* is that of Mr. and Mrs. Gardiner, the girls' aunt and uncle. From the way that both Elizabeth and Jane welcome the chance to spend time with them, it is clear that the Gardiners have a marriage that is pleasant to be around. In contrast with the Bennets, the couple appears to be not only kind and generous, but practical and levelheaded. Mrs. Gardiner gives Elizabeth firm but loving advice about her flirtation with Wickham—the kind of sensible advice Elizabeth never would have gotten from her own mother. And after Lydia disappears to London, Mr. Gardiner springs into action, responding to the crisis as a responsible father would. Once Lydia is found, the Gardiners take her into their home, doing everything possible to protect the foolish girl's reputation. And unlike the Bennets, the Gardiners are the kind of courteous, well-mannered people that Elizabeth can be proud to introduce to Mr. Darcy as her relatives. It is significant that the novel ends with a reference to the warm relationship existing between Darcy and Elizabeth and the Gardiners. It is the Gardiners' marriage, more than any other, that serves as a model for their own.

The third marriage that Austen studies is that of Charlotte Lucas and Mr. Collins. This marriage represents one of the more heart-tugging situations in the novel. Charlotte is a very likeable character. She is a devoted friend to Elizabeth, intelligent and insightful. Her warning that Jane should not hide her feelings about Bingley turns out to be exactly on target. As readers, we want good things to happen to Charlotte. Instead, she marries Mr. Collins —one of the silliest, most puffed-up characters in English literature. Worse, Charlotte marries him knowing exactly how foolish he is. It is through the Charlotte-Mr. Collins marriage that Jane Austen demonstrates the difficult situation a young lady of her time faced, unless that young lady was wealthy. There were very few options open to unmarried women. Going out and getting a job was unheard of for a lady of Charlotte's social class. It is possible that she could have been hired by a rich family as a governess (a live-in teacher) or as a companion to an elderly lady, but she would then have lived a lonely life as a kind of upper-class servant, without a home of her own. No longer very young, and not pretty, Charlotte could not expect to receive many, if any, other offers of marriage. So she put away any dreams she might have had of a loving marriage and accepted Mr. Collins. We have to comfort ourselves that Mr. Collins is not a bad man, just a silly one. He will be kind to Charlotte, and she will live comfortably. But her marriage is one that is based only on material gain, not love or respect or even liking.

And then there is the marriage of Lydia and Wickham. Lydia is very much like her mother— empty-headed and only interested in having a good time. Wickham can be charming but as we slowly learn, he is completely lacking in morals. They are sexually attracted to one another, but it becomes clear that their relationship, at least on Wickham's side, goes no deeper than that. The novel makes it evident that their marriage will be a meaningless one, with Lydia becoming ever more cheap, loud, and brassy, and Wickham pursuing affairs on the side whenever possible. A marriage based only on animal attraction, Austen implies, is not desirable.

Finally, there is the marriage of Elizabeth and Darcy themselves. Although we do not get a chance to observe the couple closely after their marriage, by the time they wed we have a very good idea of their relationship. Their marriage will be one of equals: two intelligent, strong-willed people who not only love but respect each other greatly. Elizabeth will teach Darcy to unbend, perhaps even become a little playful. Darcy will influence Elizabeth to be more thoughtful, a little less hasty with her opinions. They will not always agree, but they will love and honor one another sincerely. Their marriage, Austen suggests, will be as nearly ideal as two imperfect humans' marriage can be.